THE NAMELESS CITY

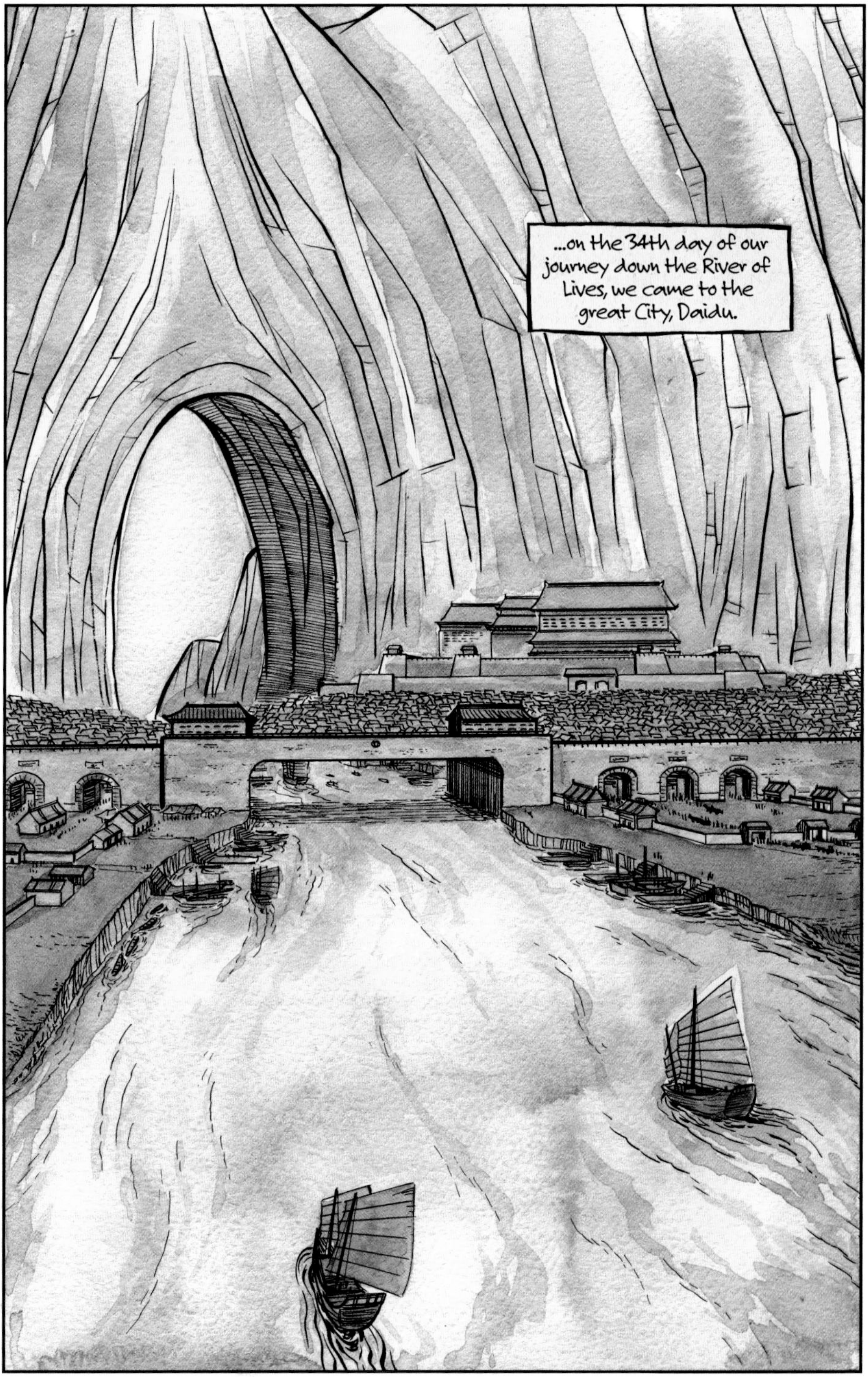
...on the 34th day of our journey down the River of Lives, we came to the great City, Daidu.

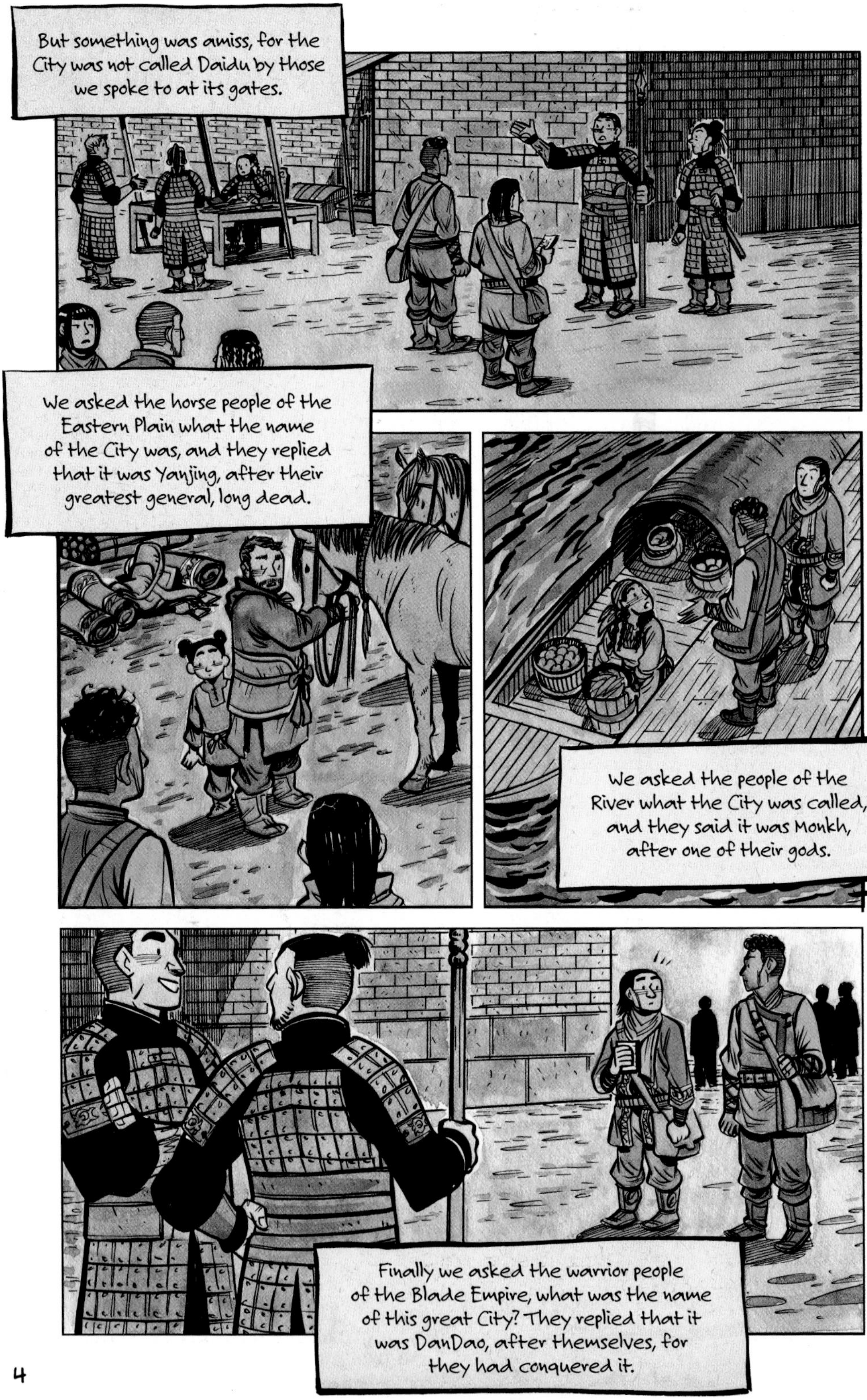
But something was amiss, for the City was not called Daidu by those we spoke to at its gates.
We asked the horse people of the Eastern Plain what the name of the City was, and they replied that it was Yanjing, after their greatest general, long dead.
We asked the people of the River what the City was called, and they said it was Monkh, after one of their gods.
Finally we asked the warrior people of the Blade Empire, what was the name of this great City? They replied that it was DanDao, after themselves, for they had conquered it.

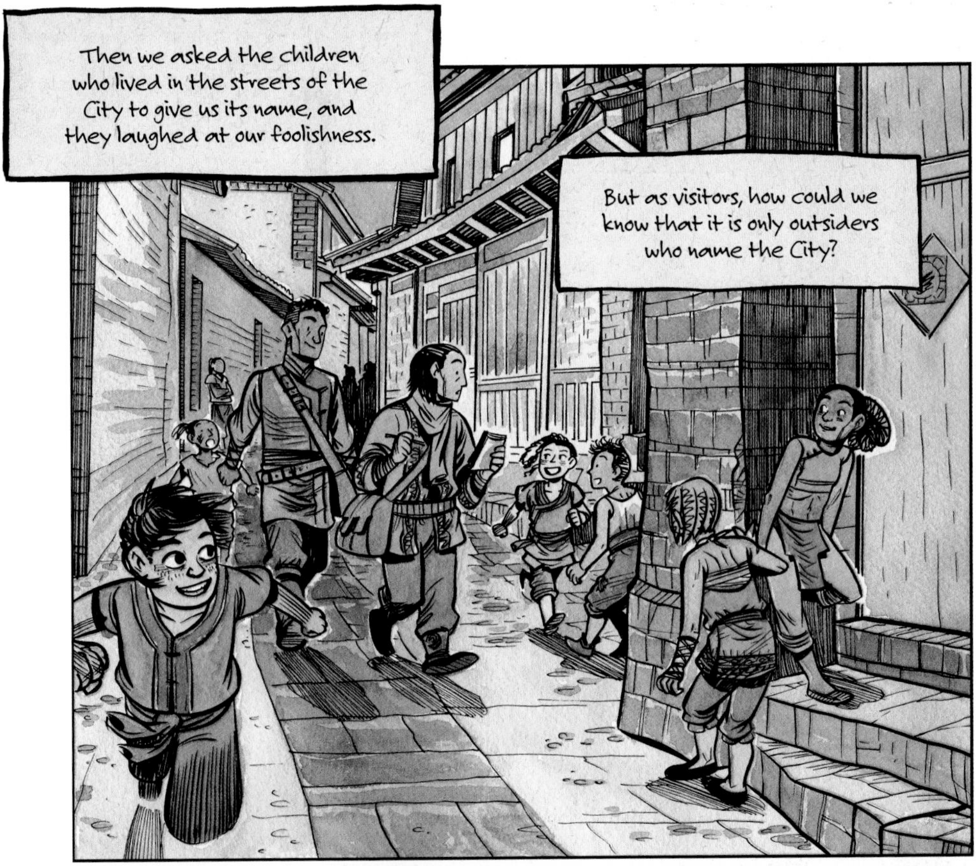
Then we asked the children who lived in the streets of the City to give us its name, and they laughed at our foolishness.
But as visitors, how could we know that it is only outsiders who name the City?

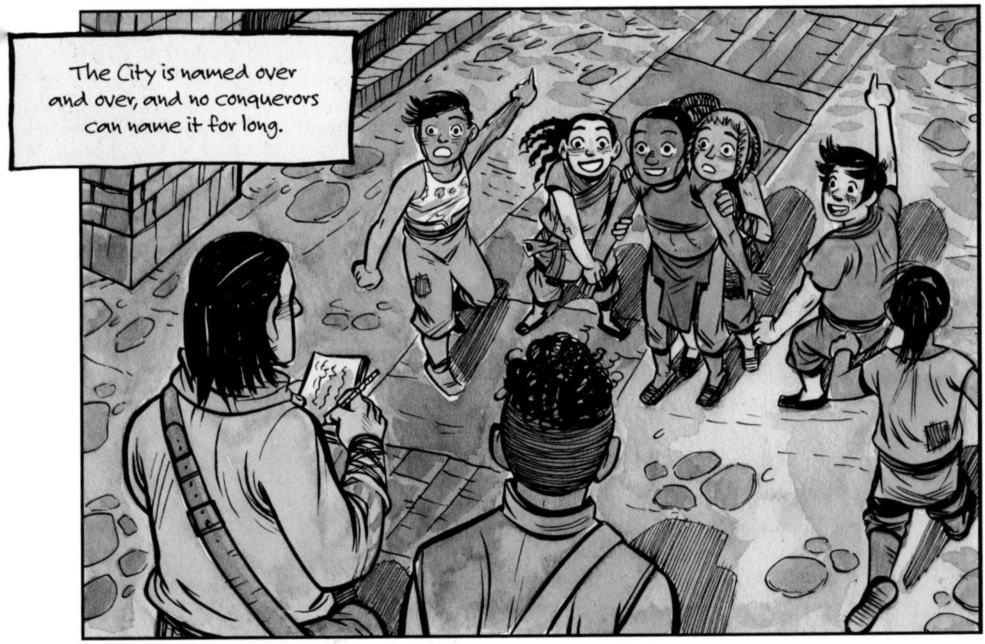
The City is named over and over, and no conquerors can name it for long.

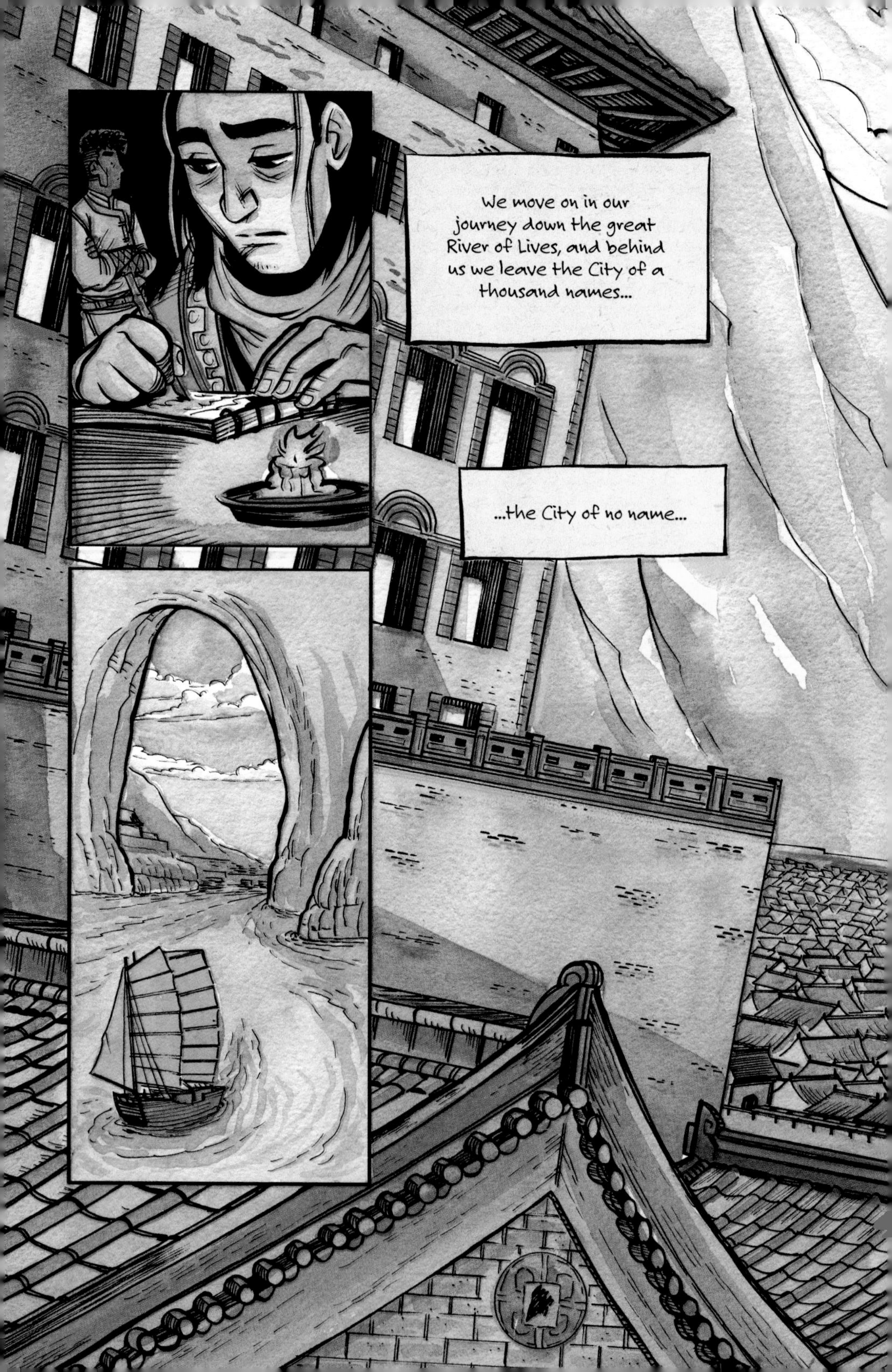
We move on in our journey down the great River of Lives, and behind us we leave the City of a thousand names...
...the City of no name...

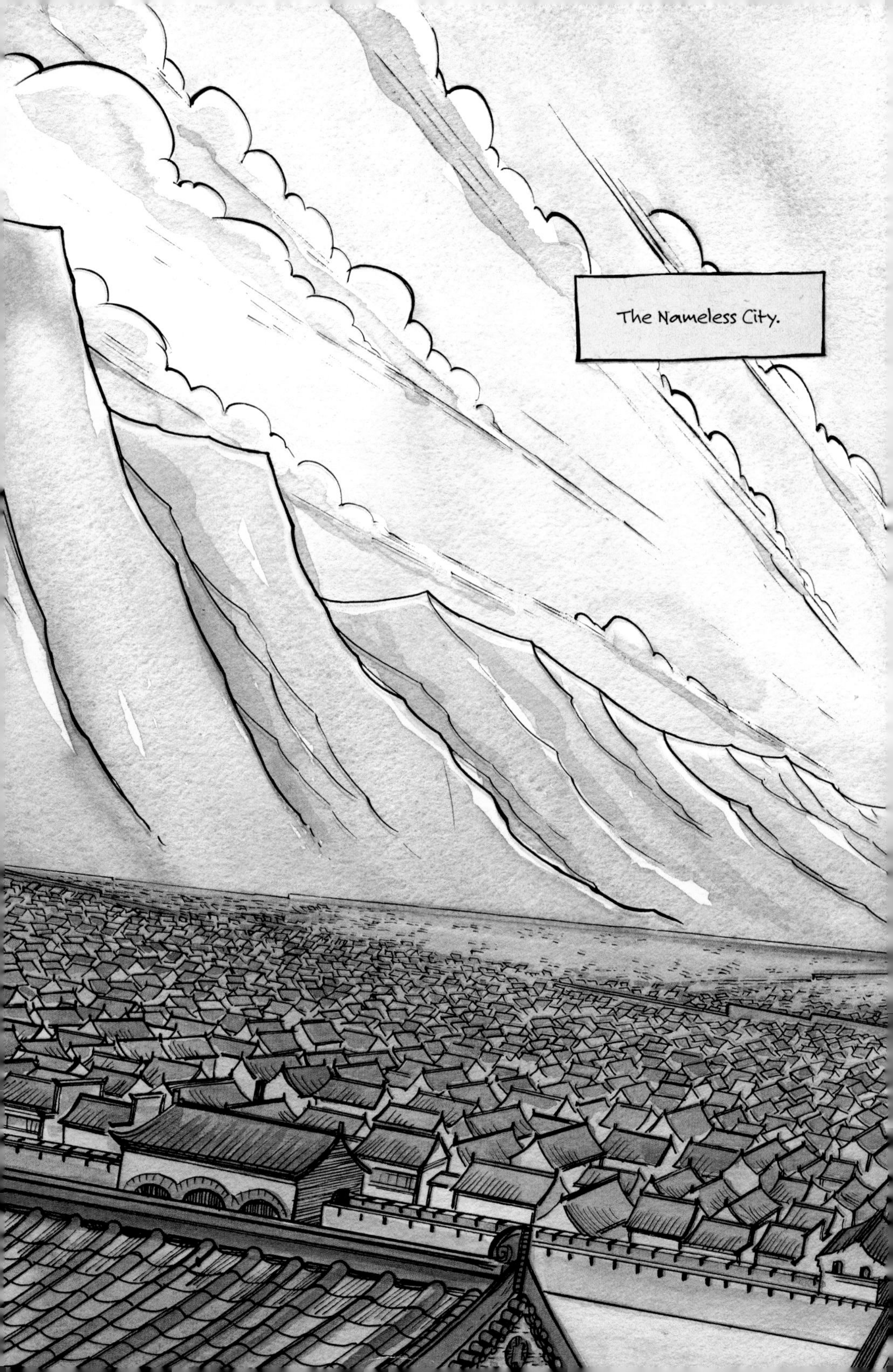
The Nameless City.

THE NAMELESS CITY

FAITH ERIN HICKS
COLOR BY JORDIE BELLAIRE

:01

First Second
NEW YORK

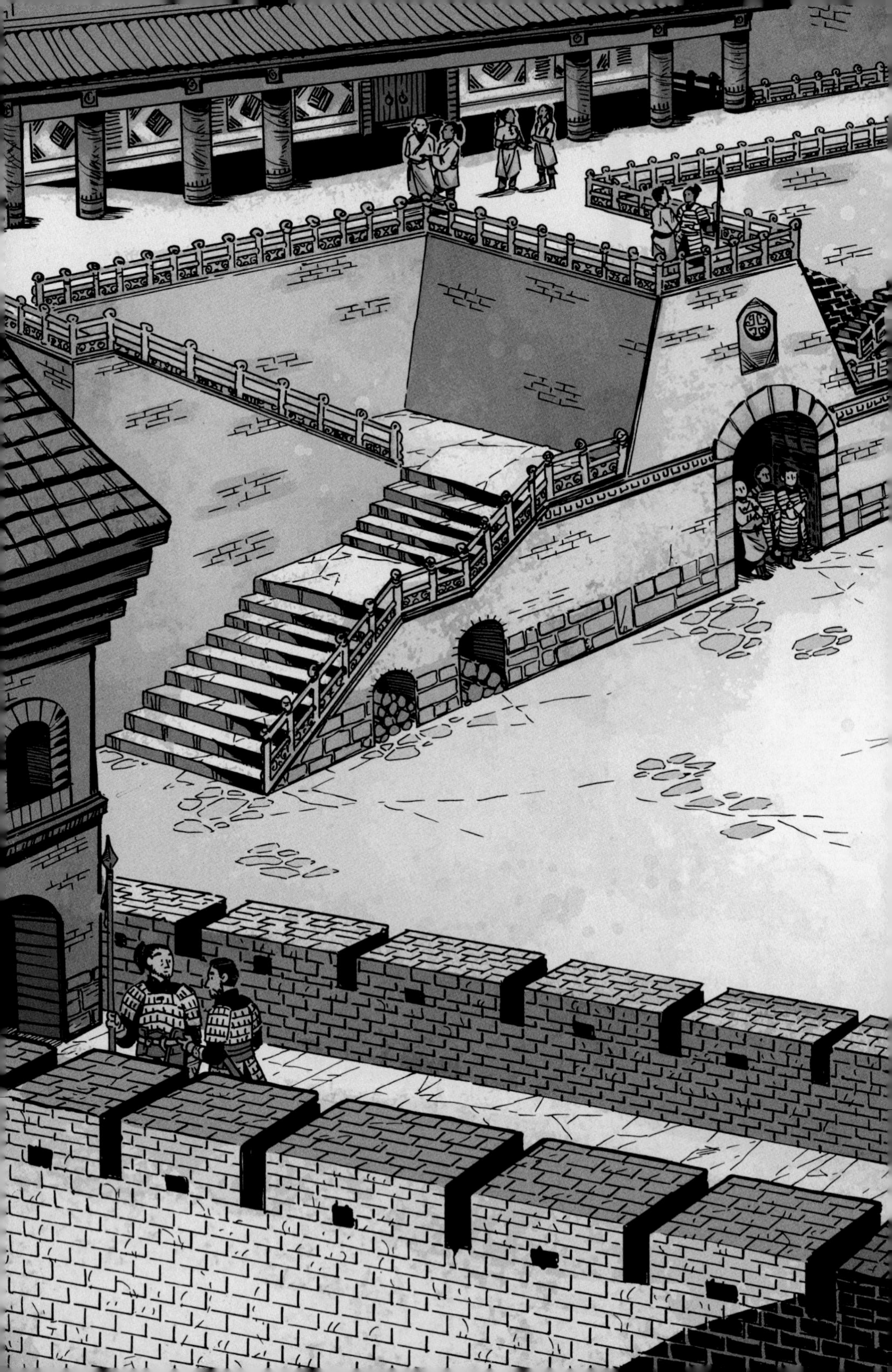

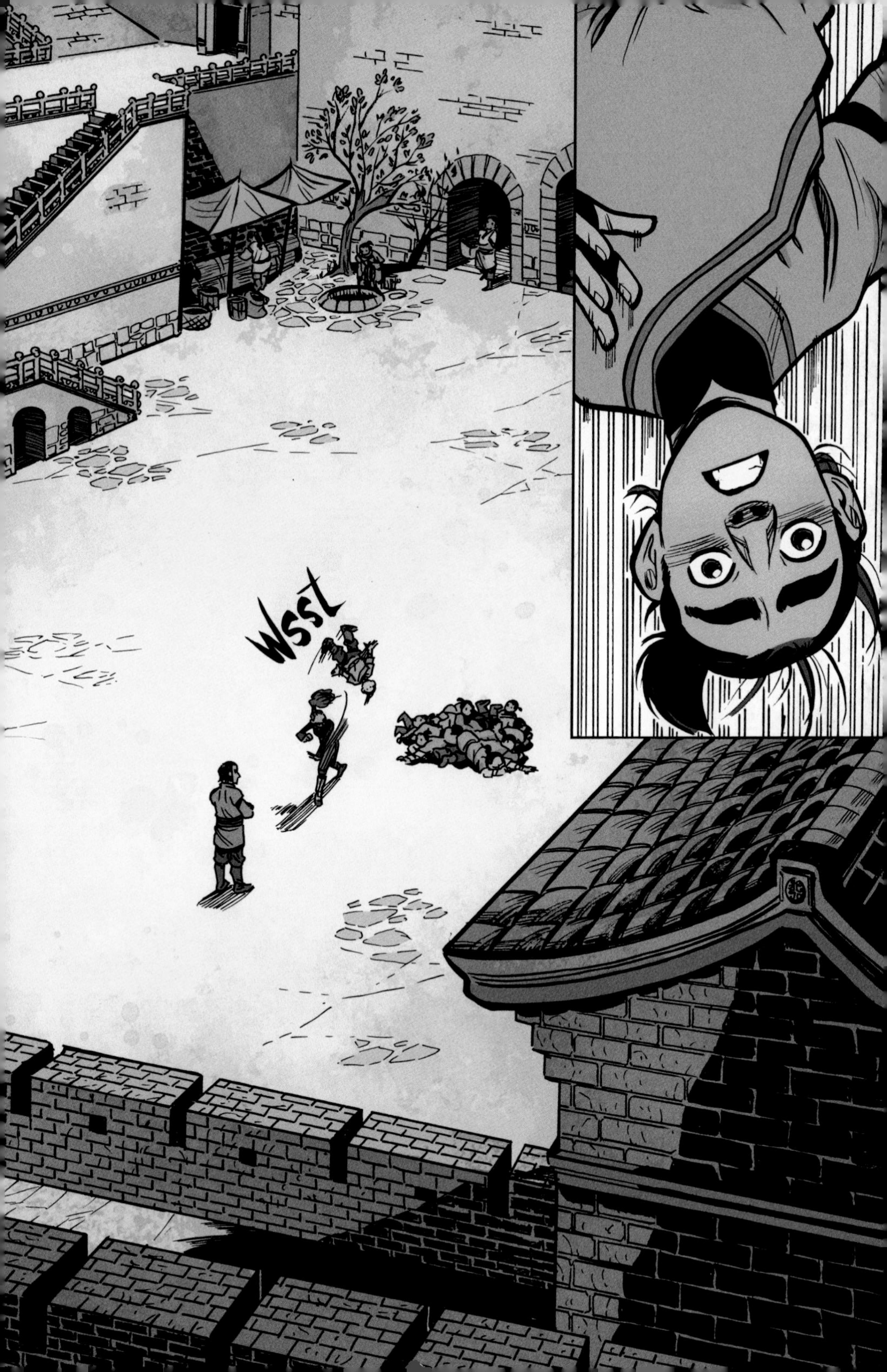
Wsst

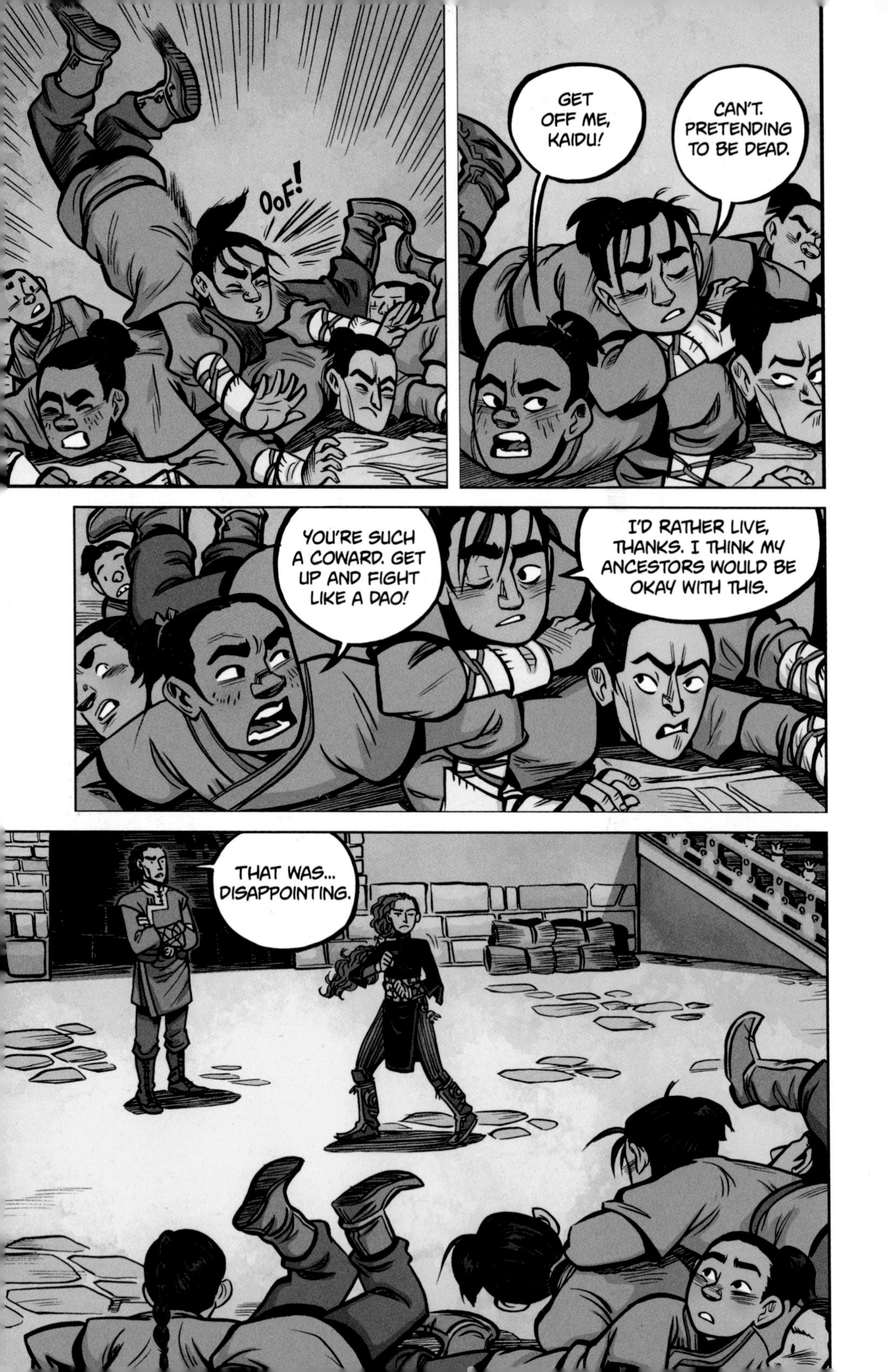
OOF!
GET OFF ME, KAIDU!
CAN'T. PRETENDING TO BE DEAD.
YOU'RE SUCH A COWARD. GET UP AND FIGHT LIKE A DAO!
I'D RATHER LIVE, THANKS. I THINK MY ANCESTORS WOULD BE OKAY WITH THIS.
THAT WAS... DISAPPOINTING.

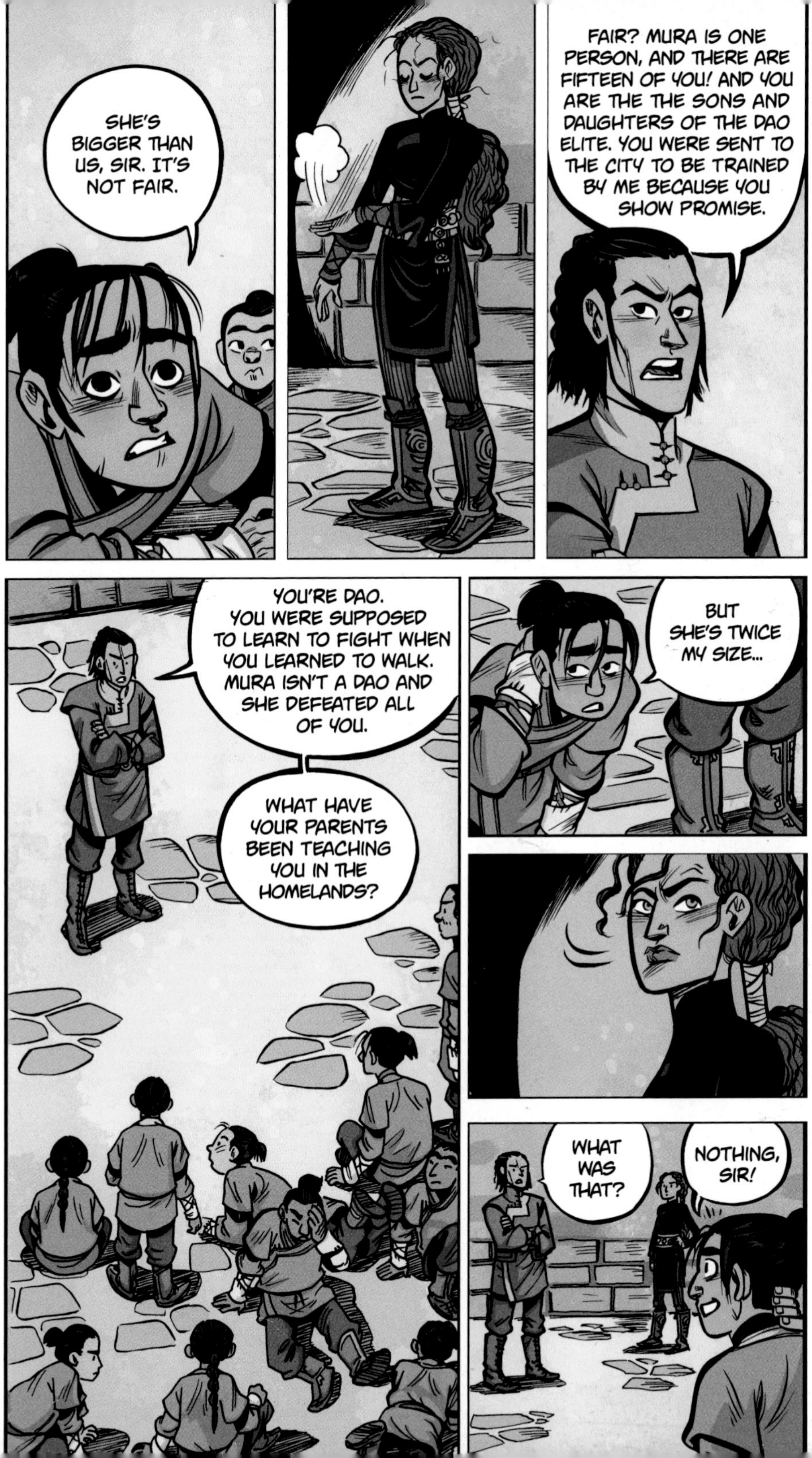
SHE'S BIGGER THAN US, SIR. IT'S NOT FAIR.
FAIR? MURA IS ONE PERSON, AND THERE ARE FIFTEEN OF YOU! AND YOU ARE THE THE SONS AND DAUGHTERS OF THE DAO ELITE. YOU WERE SENT TO THE CITY TO BE TRAINED BY ME BECAUSE YOU SHOW PROMISE.
YOU'RE DAO. YOU WERE SUPPOSED TO LEARN TO FIGHT WHEN YOU LEARNED TO WALK. MURA ISN'T A DAO AND SHE DEFEATED ALL OF YOU.
WHAT HAVE YOUR PARENTS BEEN TEACHING YOU IN THE HOMELANDS?
BUT SHE'S TWICE MY SIZE...
WHAT WAS THAT?
NOTHING, SIR!

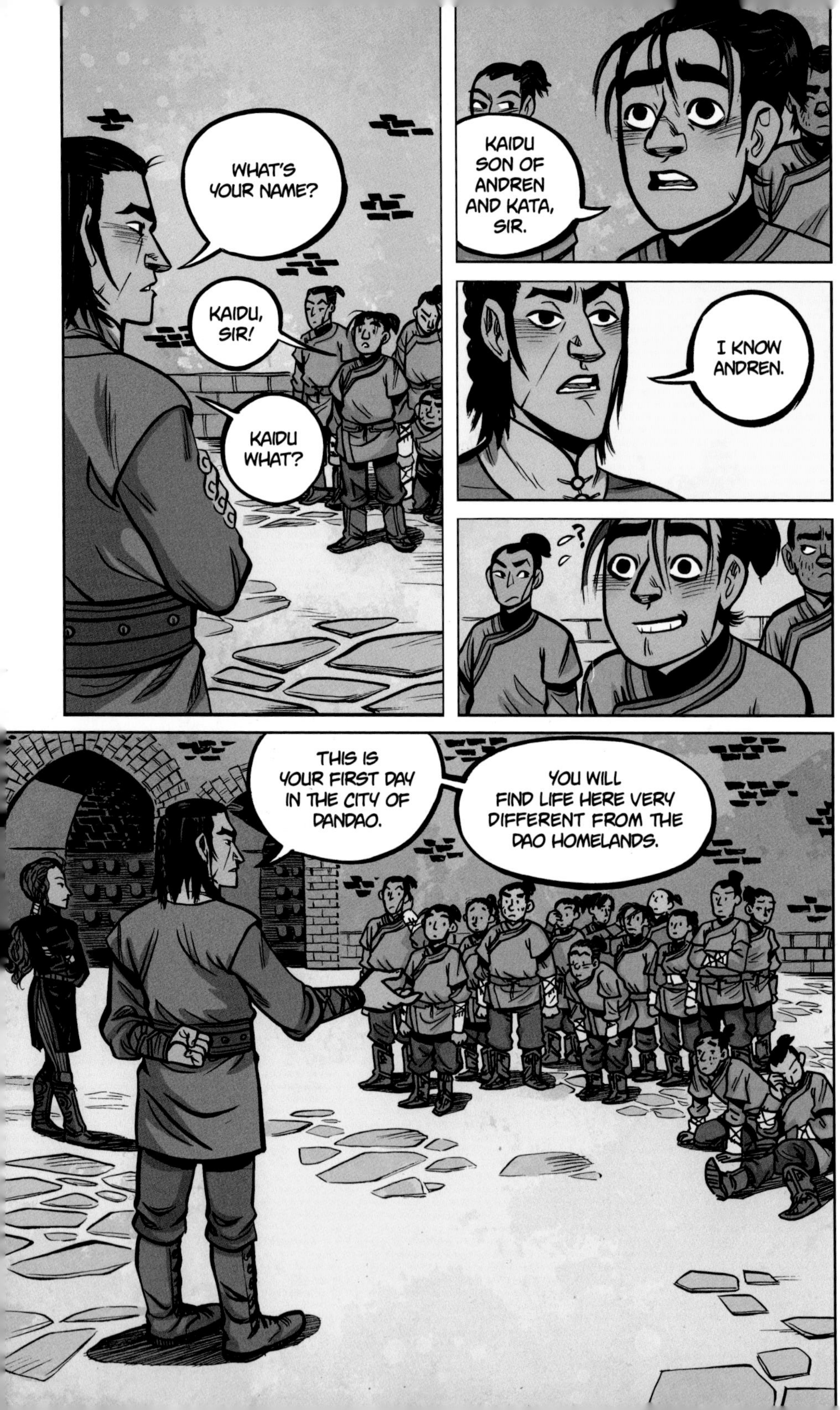
WHAT'S YOUR NAME?
KAIDU, SIR!
KAIDU WHAT?
KAIDU SON OF ANDREN AND KATA, SIR.
I KNOW ANDREN.
?
THIS IS YOUR FIRST DAY IN THE CITY OF DANDAO.
YOU WILL FIND LIFE HERE VERY DIFFERENT FROM THE DAO HOMELANDS.

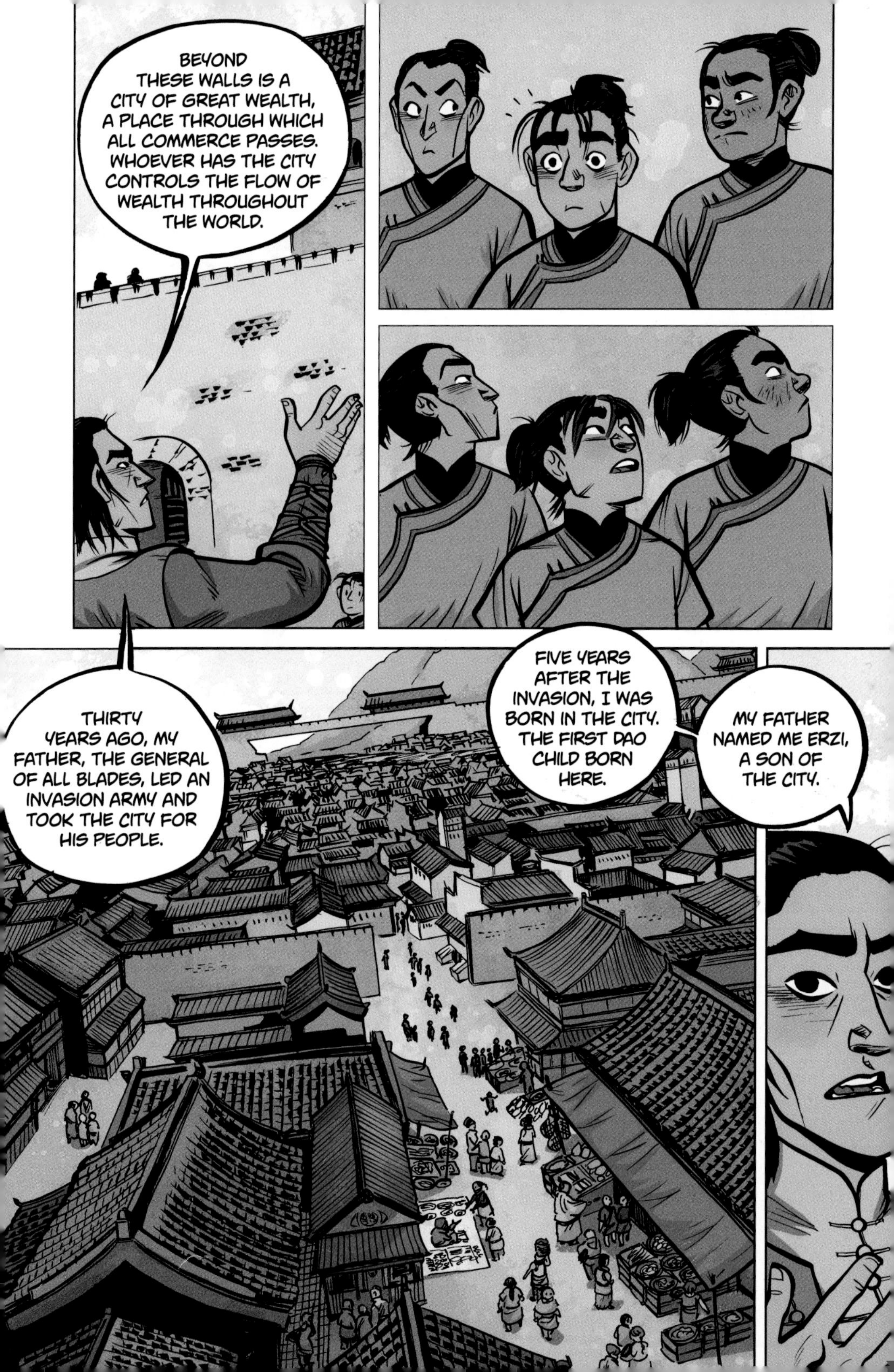
BEYOND THESE WALLS IS A CITY OF GREAT WEALTH, A PLACE THROUGH WHICH ALL COMMERCE PASSES. WHOEVER HAS THE CITY CONTROLS THE FLOW OF WEALTH THROUGHOUT THE WORLD.
THIRTY YEARS AGO, MY FATHER, THE GENERAL OF ALL BLADES, LED AN INVASION ARMY AND TOOK THE CITY FOR HIS PEOPLE.
FIVE YEARS AFTER THE INVASION, I WAS BORN IN THE CITY. THE FIRST DAO CHILD BORN HERE.
MY FATHER NAMED ME ERZI, A SON OF THE CITY.

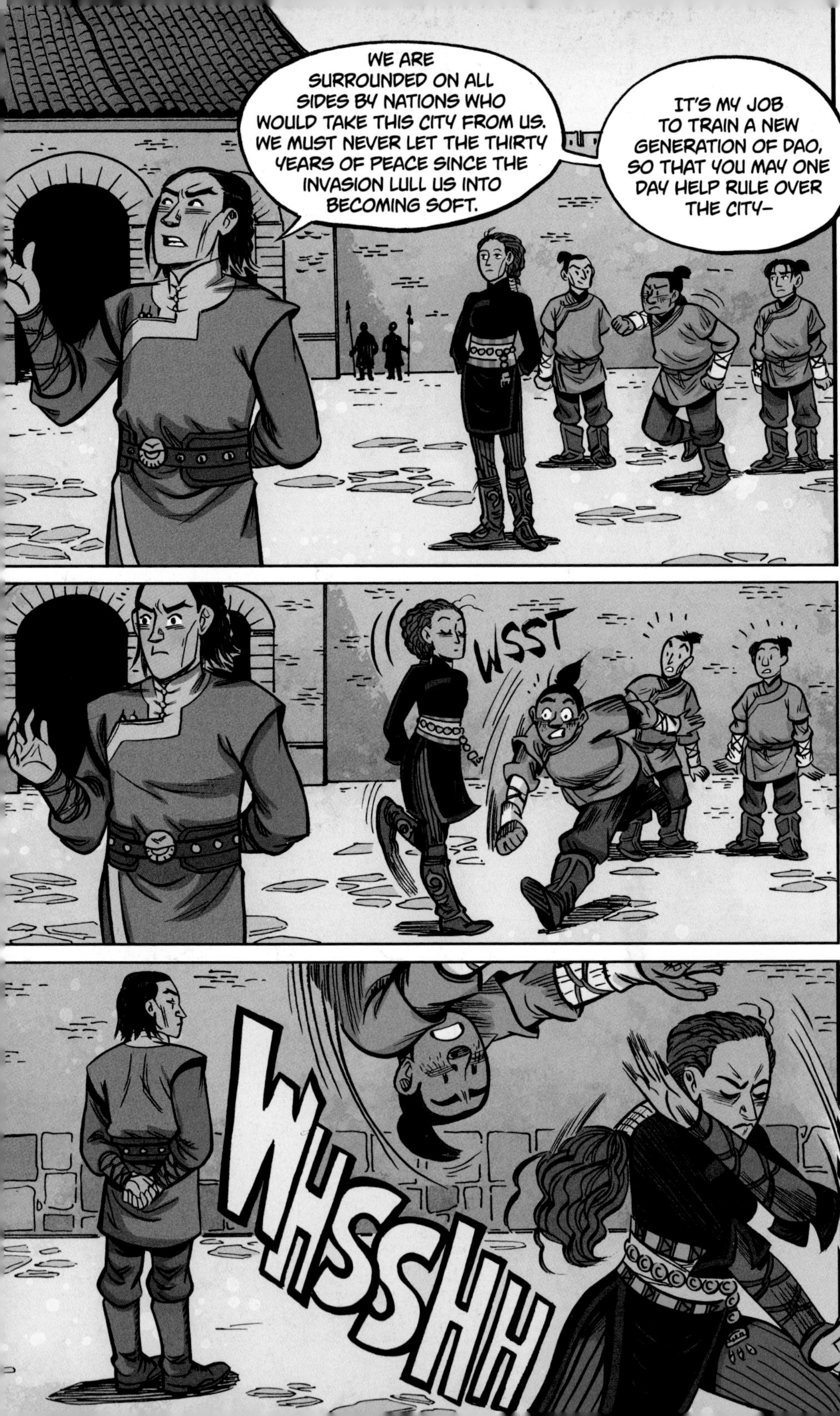
WE ARE SURROUNDED ON ALL SIDES BY NATIONS WHO WOULD TAKE THIS CITY FROM US. WE MUST NEVER LET THE THIRTY YEARS OF PEACE SINCE THE INVASION LULL US INTO BECOMING SOFT.
IT'S MY JOB TO TRAIN A NEW GENERATION OF DAO, SO THAT YOU MAY ONE DAY HELP RULE OVER THE CITY–
WSST
WHSSHH

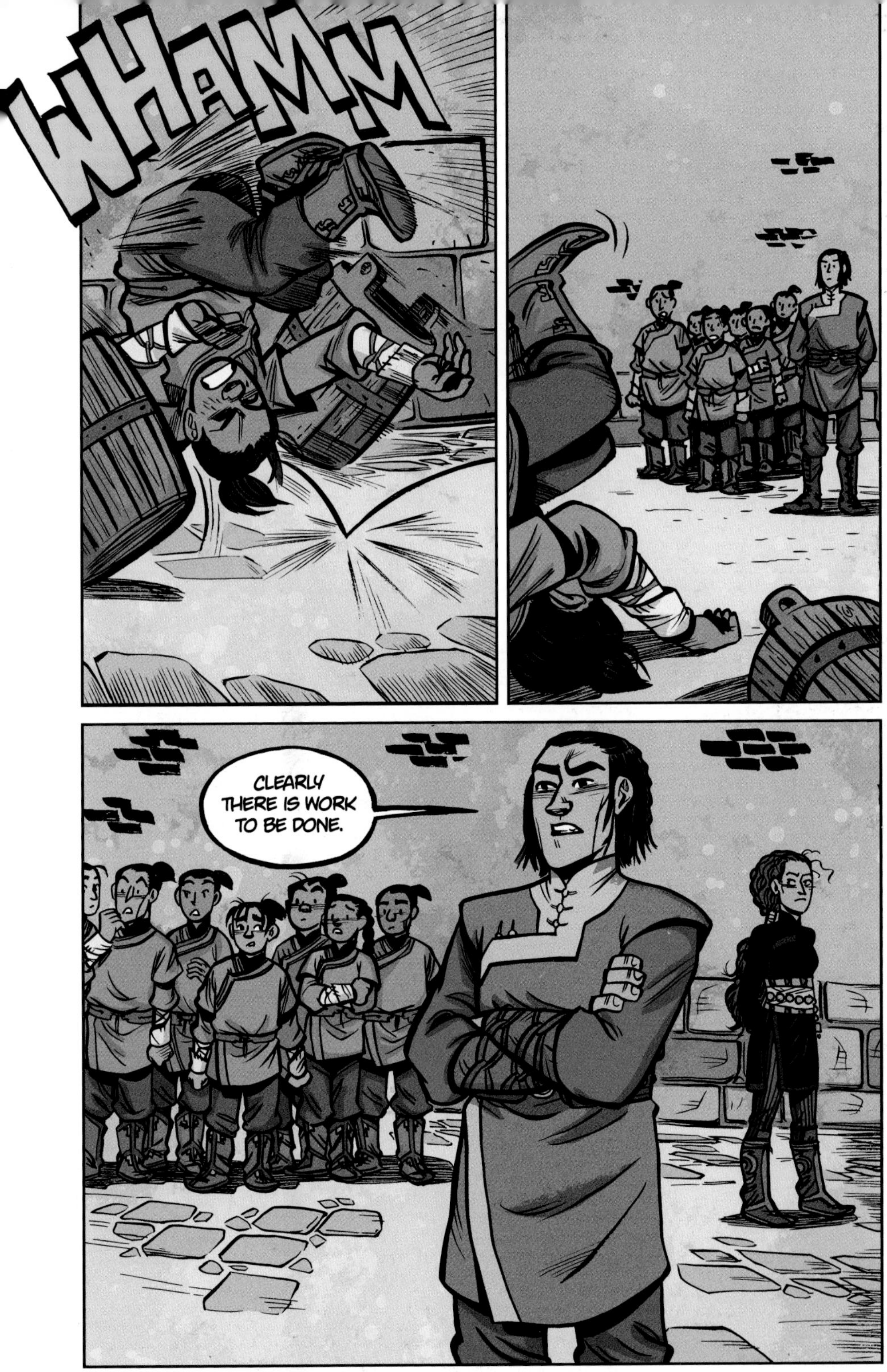
WHAMM
CLEARLY THERE IS WORK TO BE DONE.

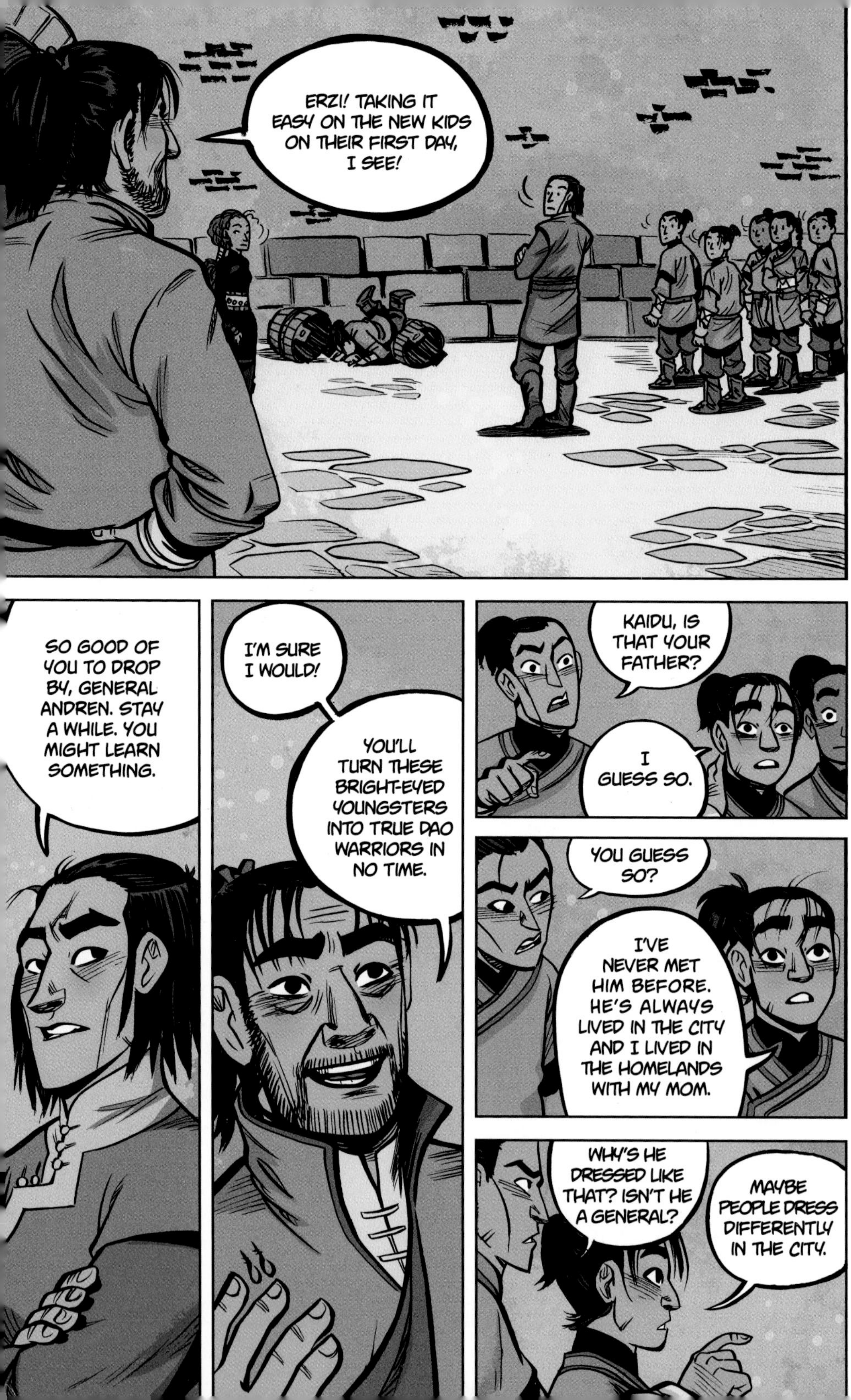
ERZI! TAKING IT EASY ON THE NEW KIDS ON THEIR FIRST DAY, I SEE!
SO GOOD OF YOU TO DROP BY, GENERAL ANDREN. STAY A WHILE. YOU MIGHT LEARN SOMETHING.
I'M SURE I WOULD!
YOU'LL TURN THESE BRIGHT-EYED YOUNGSTERS INTO TRUE DAO WARRIORS IN NO TIME.
KAIDU, IS THAT YOUR FATHER?
I GUESS SO.
YOU GUESS SO?
I'VE NEVER MET HIM BEFORE. HE'S ALWAYS LIVED IN THE CITY AND I LIVED IN THE HOMELANDS WITH MY MOM.
WHY'S HE DRESSED LIKE THAT? ISN'T HE A GENERAL?
MAYBE PEOPLE DRESS DIFFERENTLY IN THE CITY.

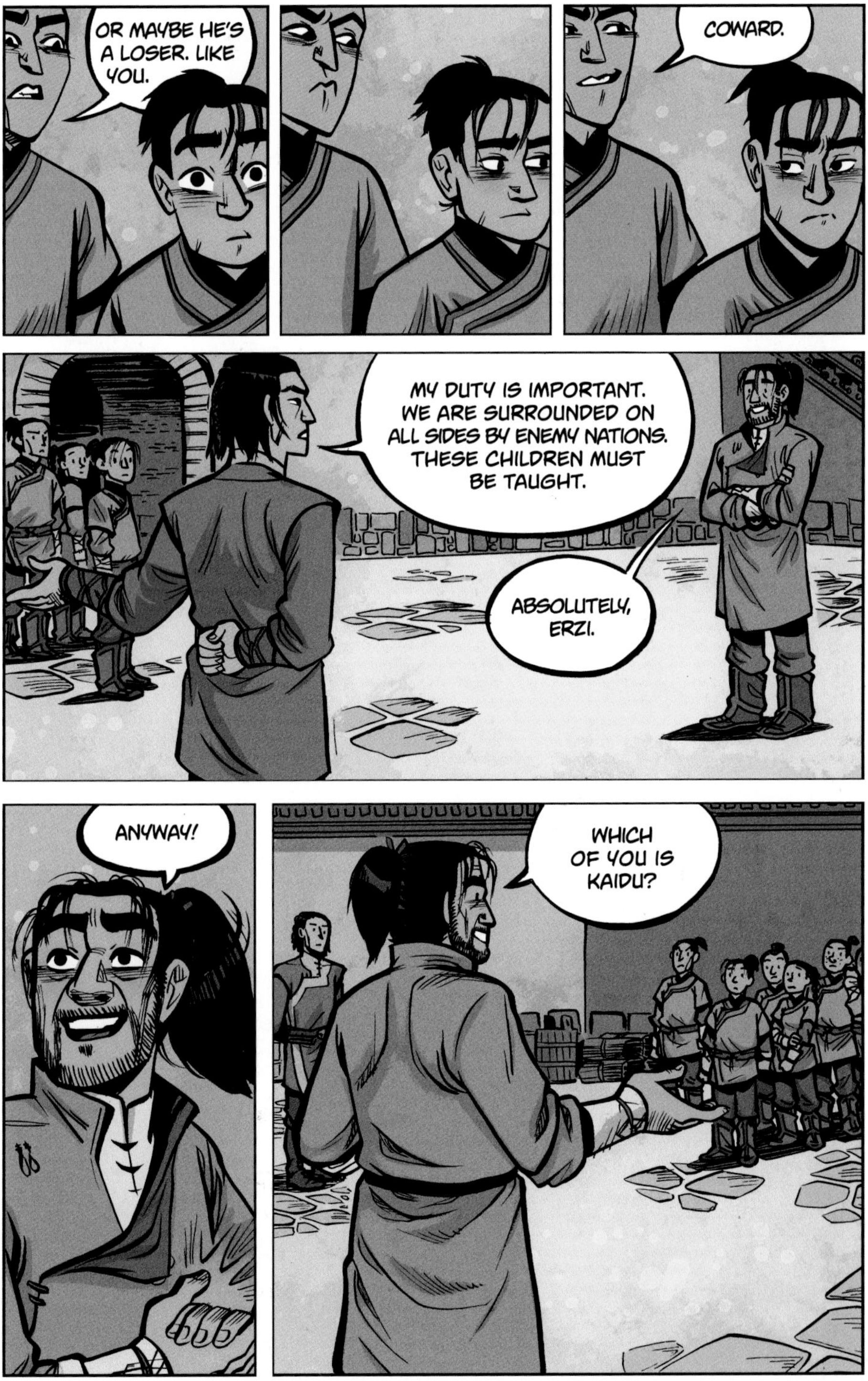
OR MAYBE HE'S A LOSER. LIKE YOU.
COWARD.
MY DUTY IS IMPORTANT. WE ARE SURROUNDED ON ALL SIDES BY ENEMY NATIONS. THESE CHILDREN MUST BE TAUGHT.
ABSOLUTELY, ERZI.
ANYWAY!
WHICH OF YOU IS KAIDU?

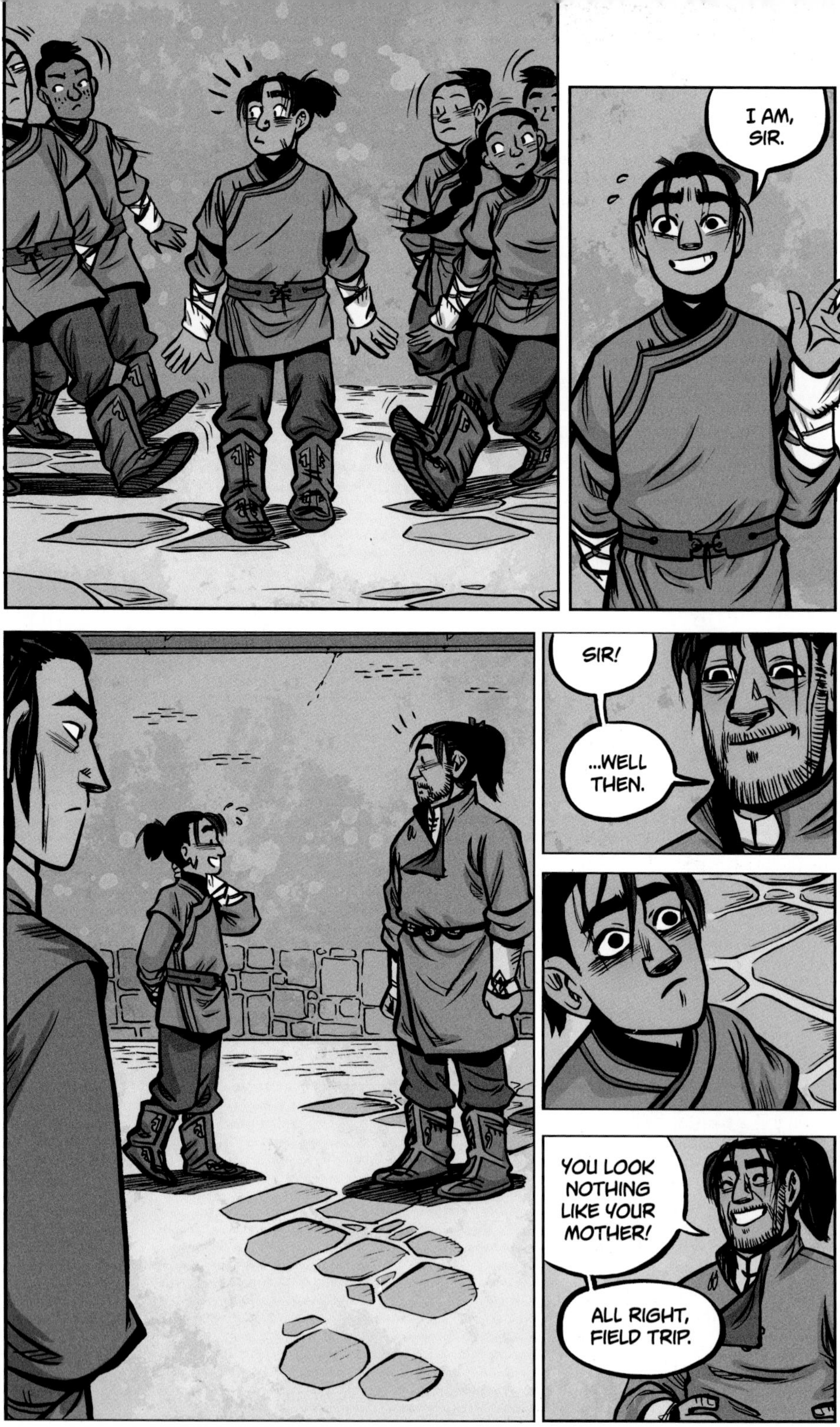
I AM, SIR.
SIR!
...WELL THEN.
YOU LOOK NOTHING LIKE YOUR MOTHER!
ALL RIGHT, FIELD TRIP.

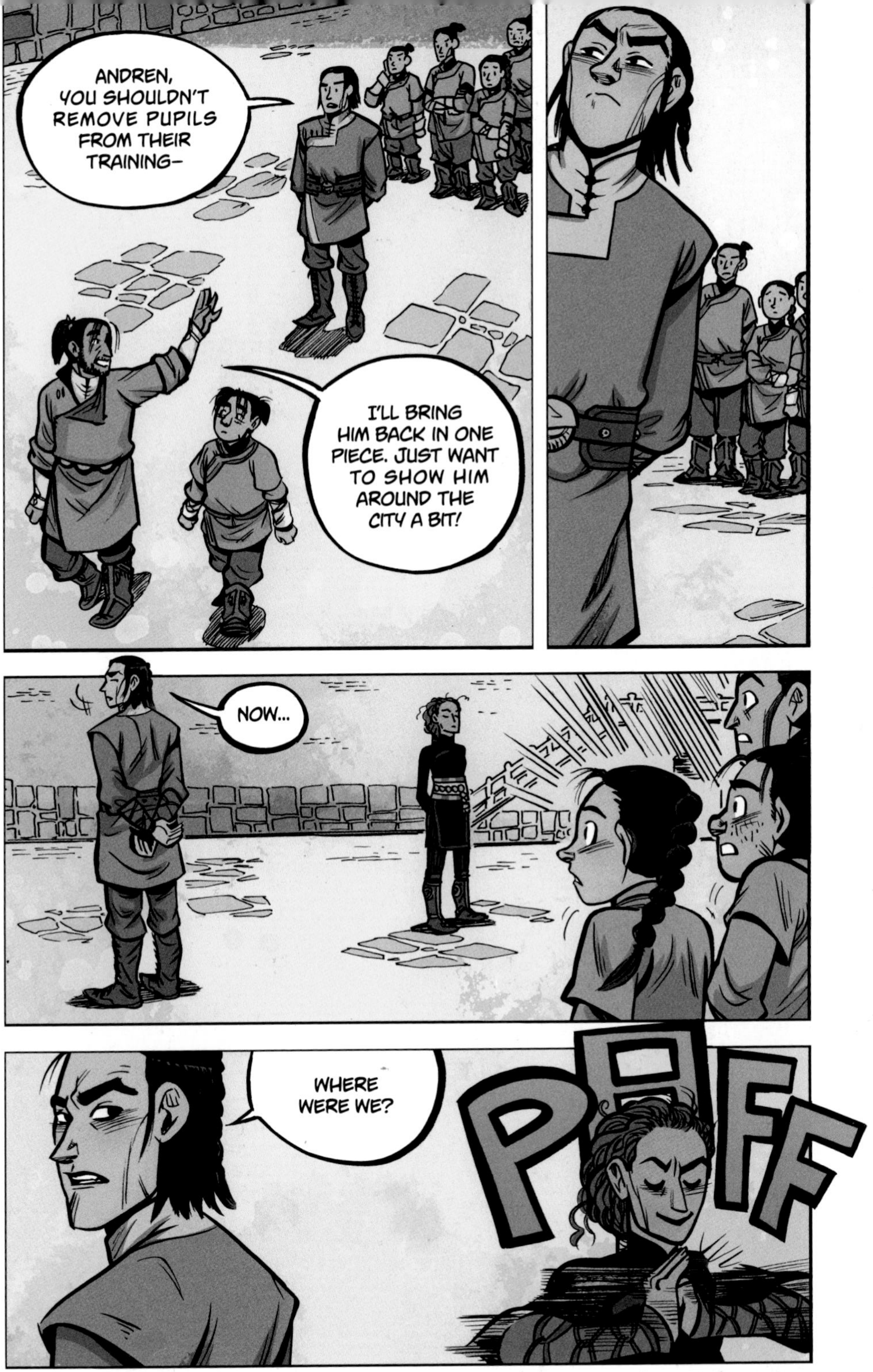
ANDREN, YOU SHOULDN'T REMOVE PUPILS FROM THEIR TRAINING–
I'LL BRING HIM BACK IN ONE PIECE. JUST WANT TO SHOW HIM AROUND THE CITY A BIT!
NOW...
WHERE WERE WE?
POFF

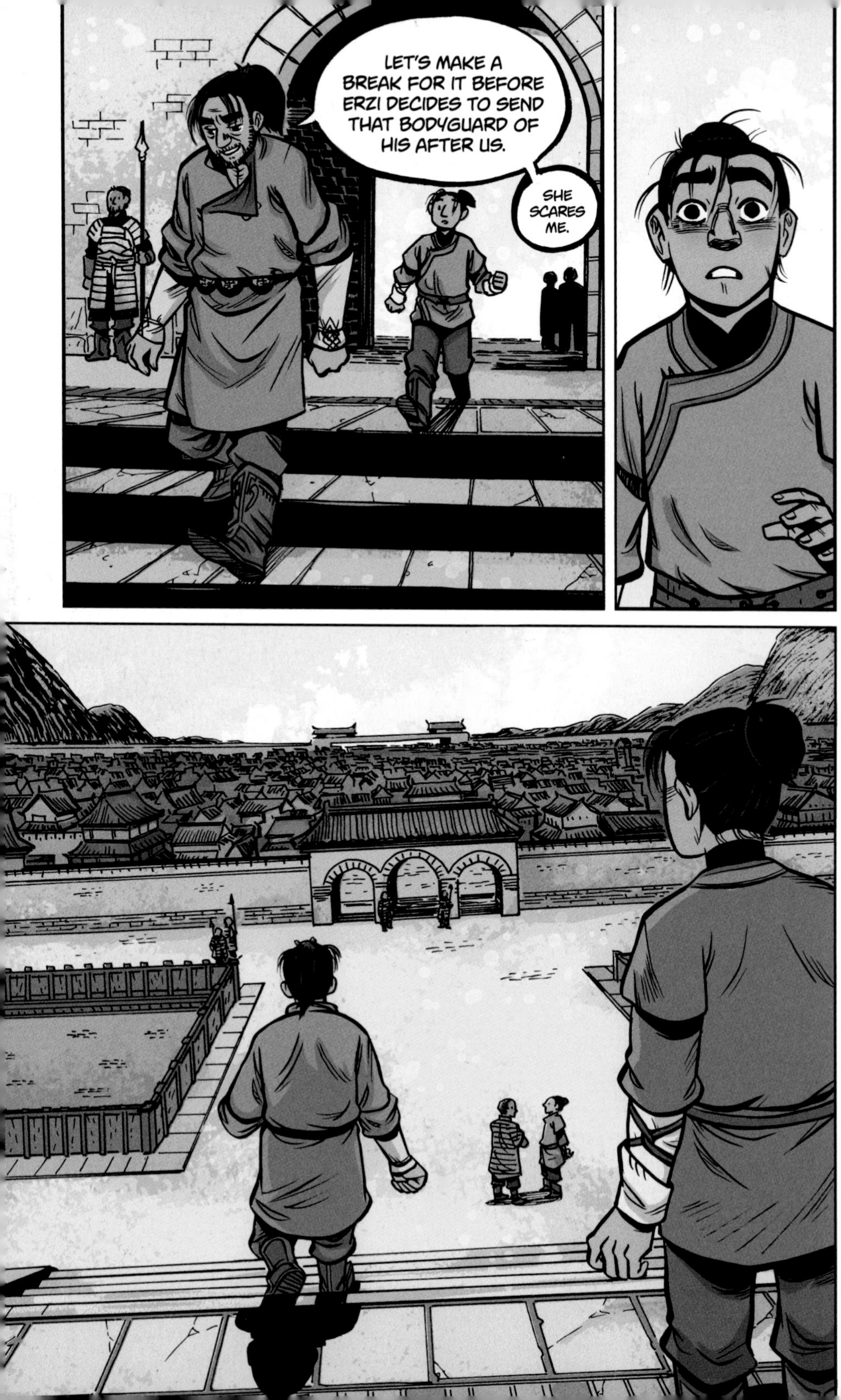
LET'S MAKE A BREAK FOR IT BEFORE ERZI DECIDES TO SEND THAT BODYGUARD OF HIS AFTER US.
SHE SCARES ME.

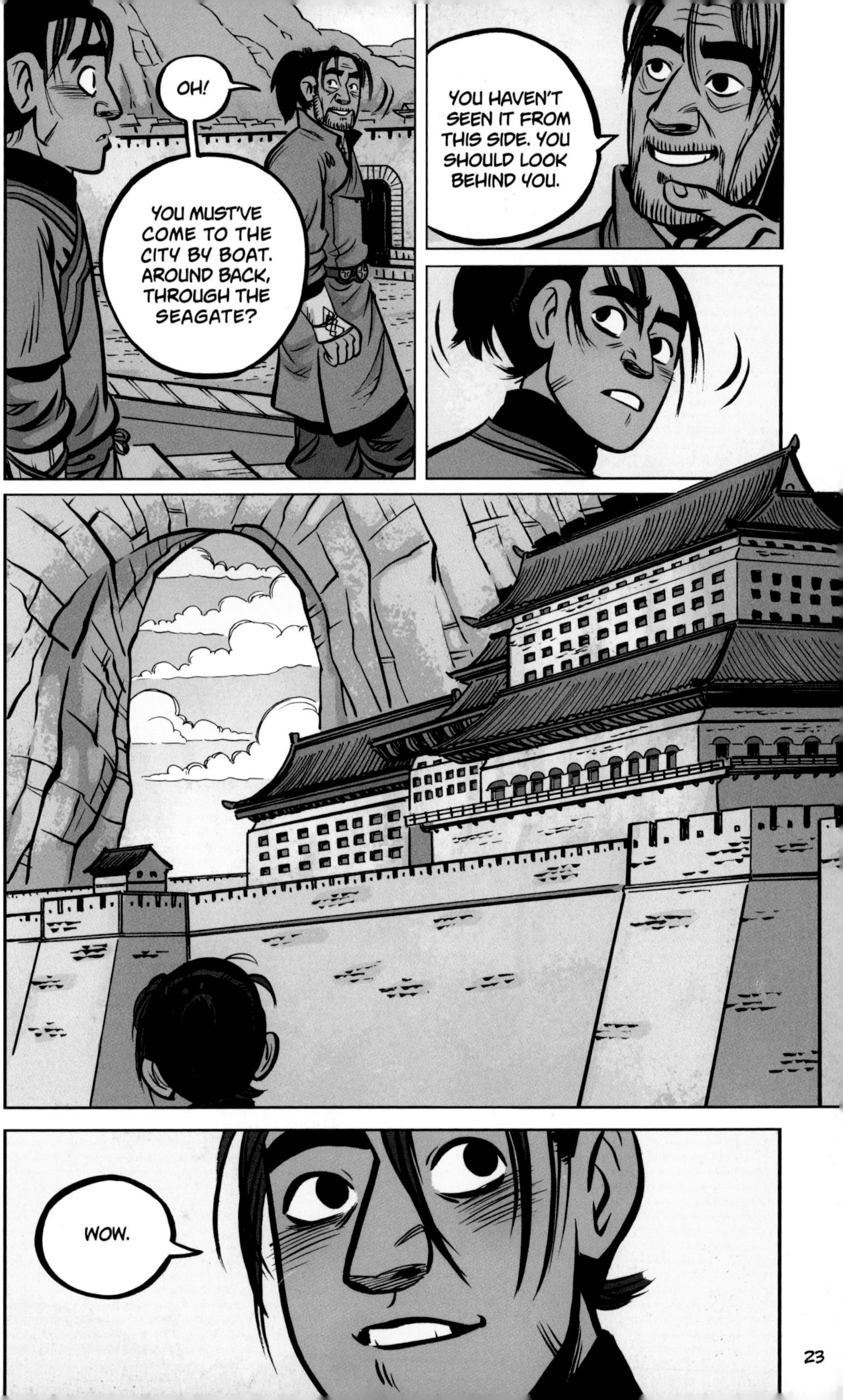
OH!
YOU MUST'VE COME TO THE CITY BY BOAT. AROUND BACK, THROUGH THE SEAGATE?
YOU HAVEN'T SEEN IT FROM THIS SIDE. YOU SHOULD LOOK BEHIND YOU.
WOW.

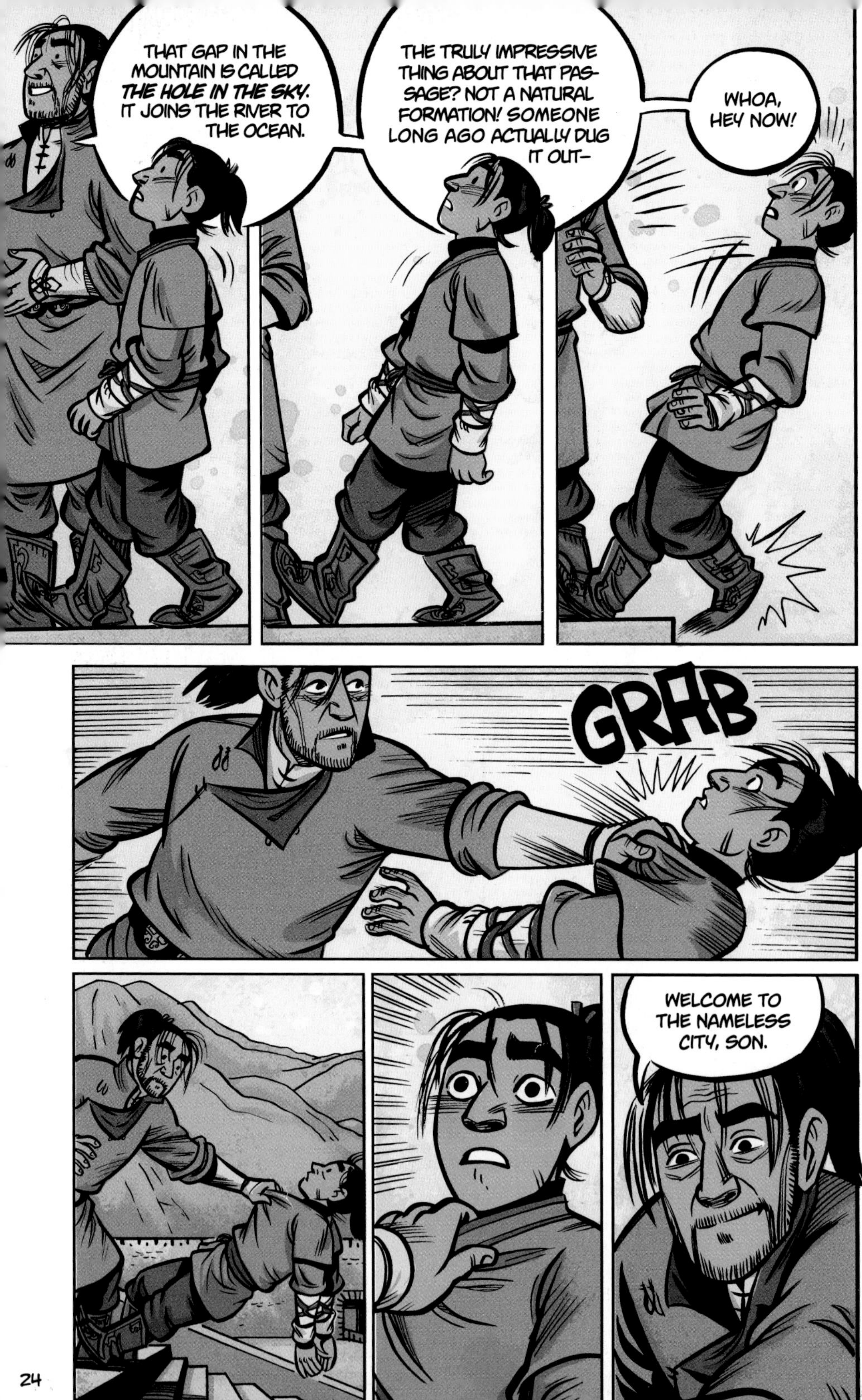
THAT GAP IN THE MOUNTAIN IS CALLED *THE HOLE IN THE SKY*. IT JOINS THE RIVER TO THE OCEAN.
THE TRULY IMPRESSIVE THING ABOUT THAT PAS-SAGE? NOT A NATURAL FORMATION! SOMEONE LONG AGO ACTUALLY DUG IT OUT–
WHOA, HEY NOW!
GRAB
WELCOME TO THE NAMELESS CITY, SON.

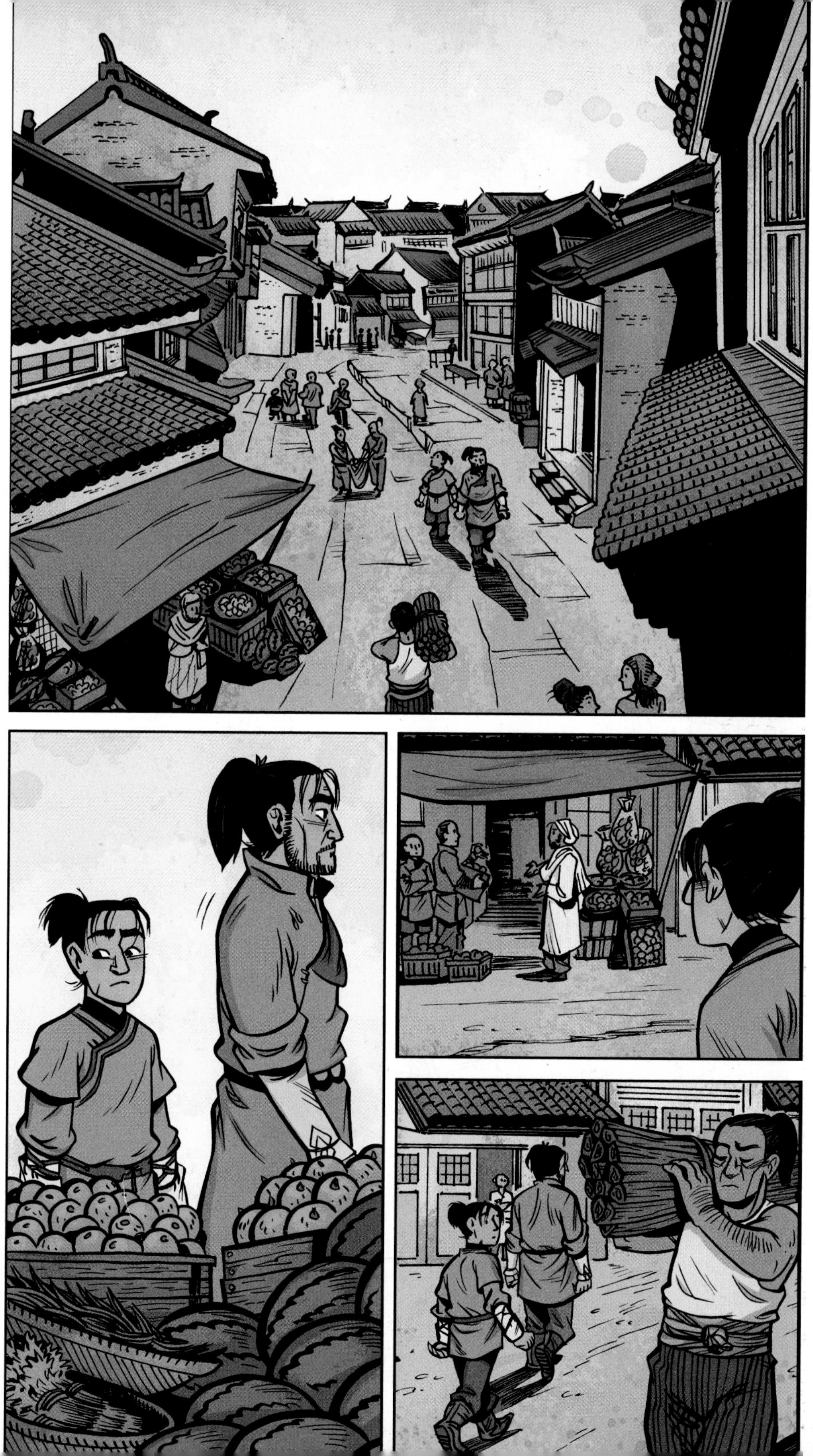

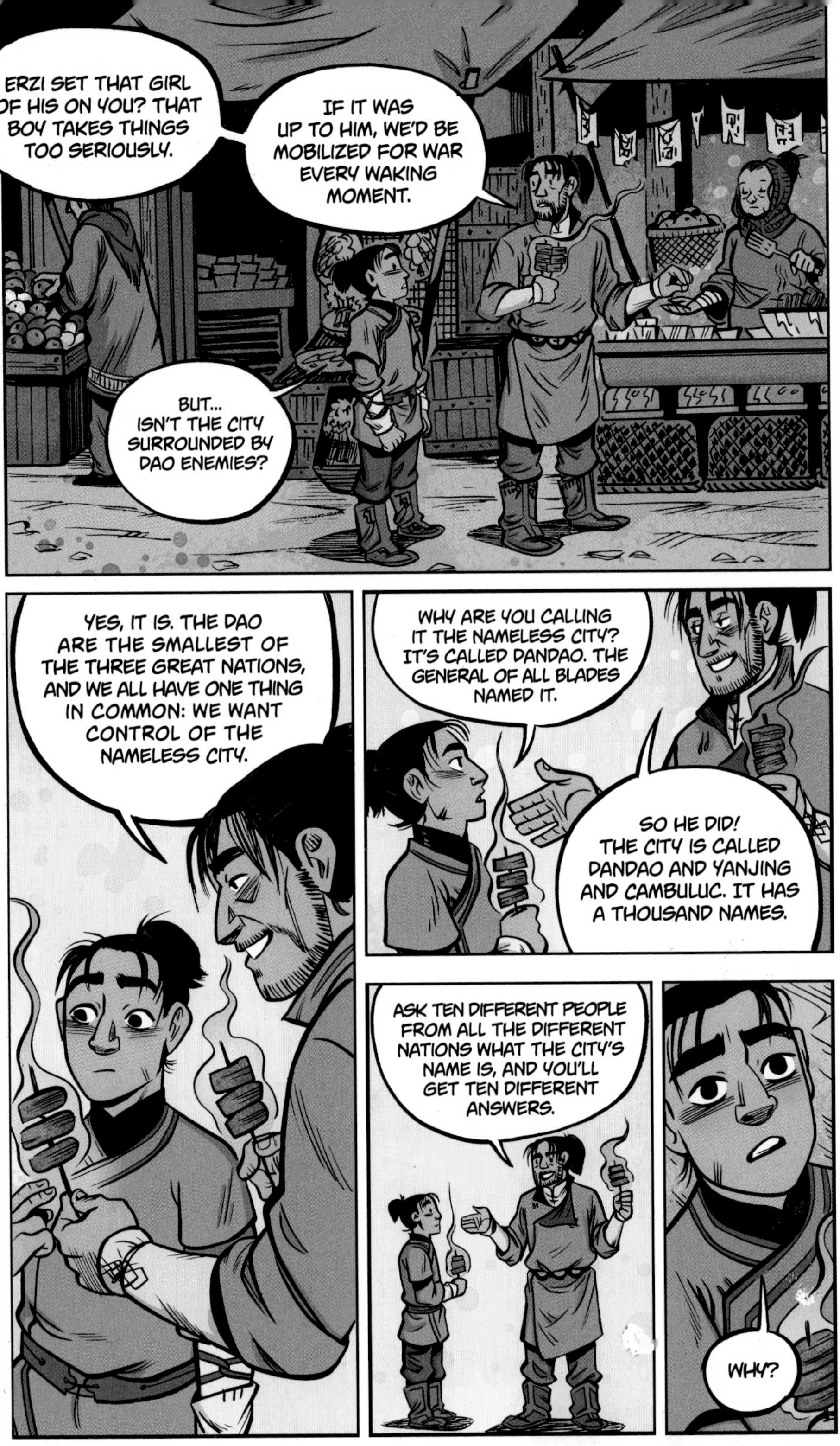
ERZI SET THAT GIRL OF HIS ON YOU? THAT BOY TAKES THINGS TOO SERIOUSLY.
IF IT WAS UP TO HIM, WE'D BE MOBILIZED FOR WAR EVERY WAKING MOMENT.
BUT... ISN'T THE CITY SURROUNDED BY DAO ENEMIES?
YES, IT IS. THE DAO ARE THE SMALLEST OF THE THREE GREAT NATIONS, AND WE ALL HAVE ONE THING IN COMMON: WE WANT CONTROL OF THE NAMELESS CITY.
WHY ARE YOU CALLING IT THE NAMELESS CITY? IT'S CALLED DANDAO. THE GENERAL OF ALL BLADES NAMED IT.
SO HE DID! THE CITY IS CALLED DANDAO AND YANJING AND CAMBULUC. IT HAS A THOUSAND NAMES.
ASK TEN DIFFERENT PEOPLE FROM ALL THE DIFFERENT NATIONS WHAT THE CITY'S NAME IS, AND YOU'LL GET TEN DIFFERENT ANSWERS.
WHY?

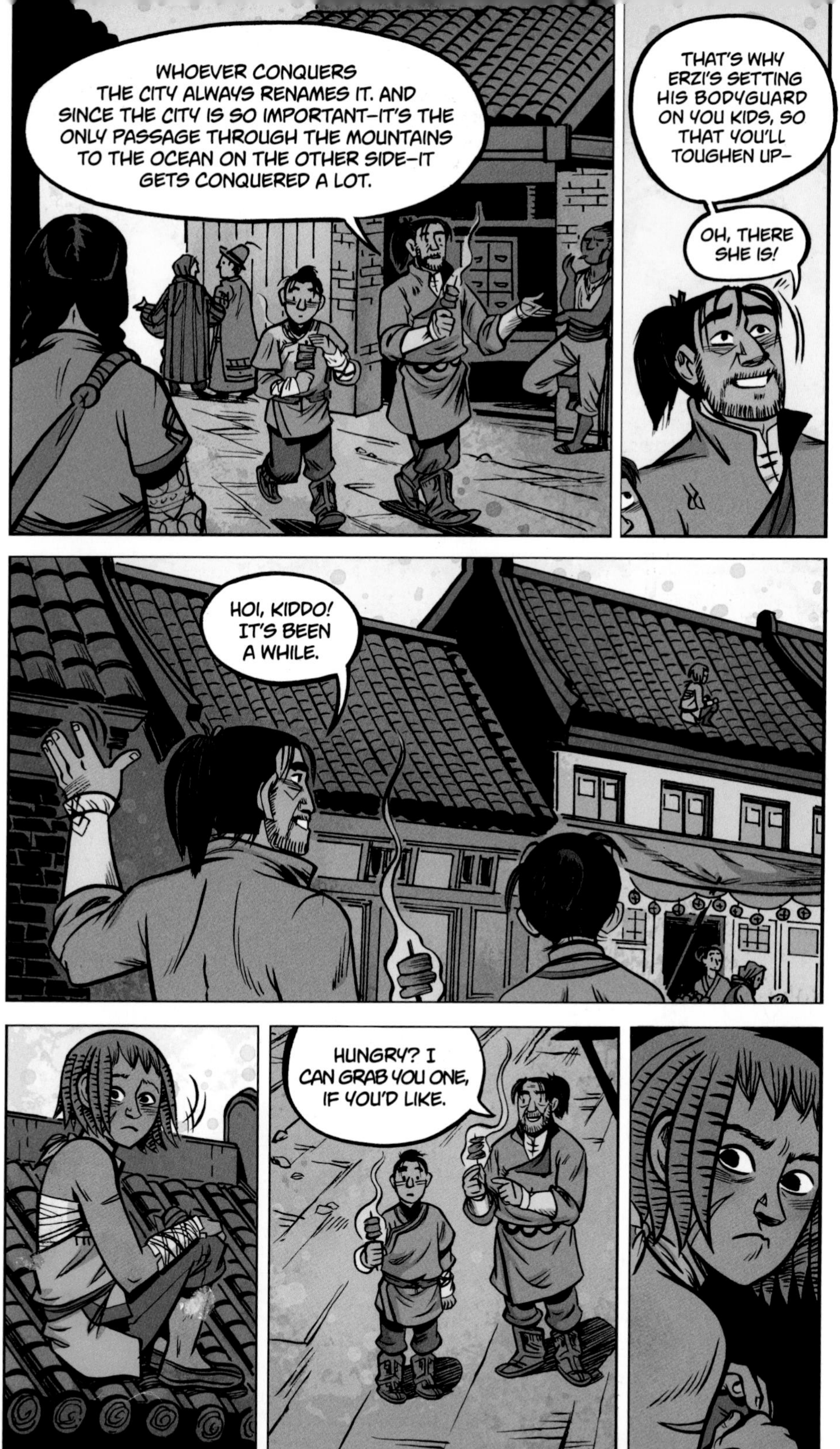
WHOEVER CONQUERS THE CITY ALWAYS RENAMES IT. AND SINCE THE CITY IS SO IMPORTANT–IT'S THE ONLY PASSAGE THROUGH THE MOUNTAINS TO THE OCEAN ON THE OTHER SIDE–IT GETS CONQUERED A LOT.
THAT'S WHY ERZI'S SETTING HIS BODYGUARD ON YOU KIDS, SO THAT YOU'LL TOUGHEN UP–
OH, THERE SHE IS!
HOI, KIDDO! IT'S BEEN A WHILE.
HUNGRY? I CAN GRAB YOU ONE, IF YOU'D LIKE.

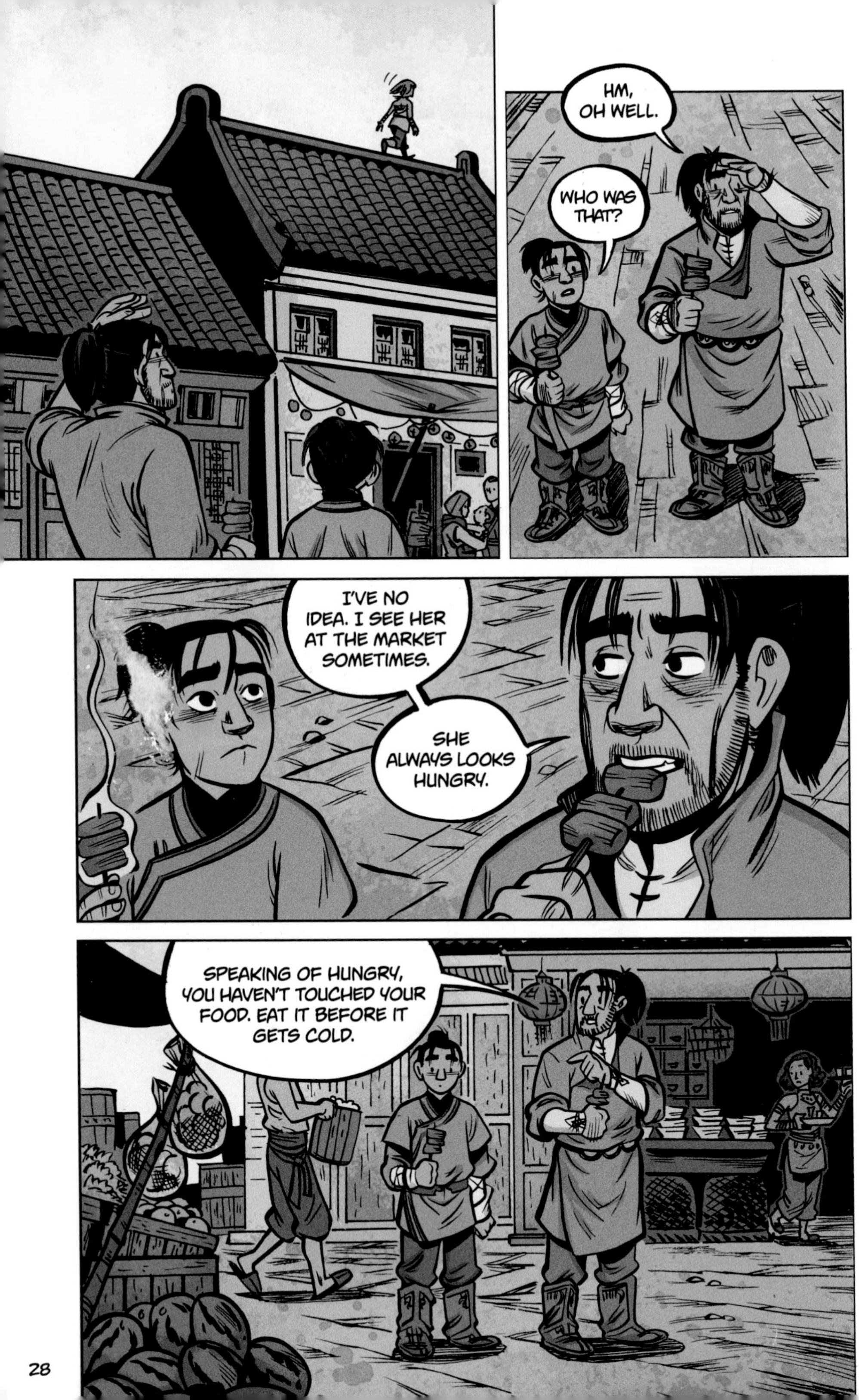

HM, OH WELL.
WHO WAS THAT?
I'VE NO IDEA. I SEE HER AT THE MARKET SOMETIMES.
SHE ALWAYS LOOKS HUNGRY.
SPEAKING OF HUNGRY, YOU HAVEN'T TOUCHED YOUR FOOD. EAT IT BEFORE IT GETS COLD.

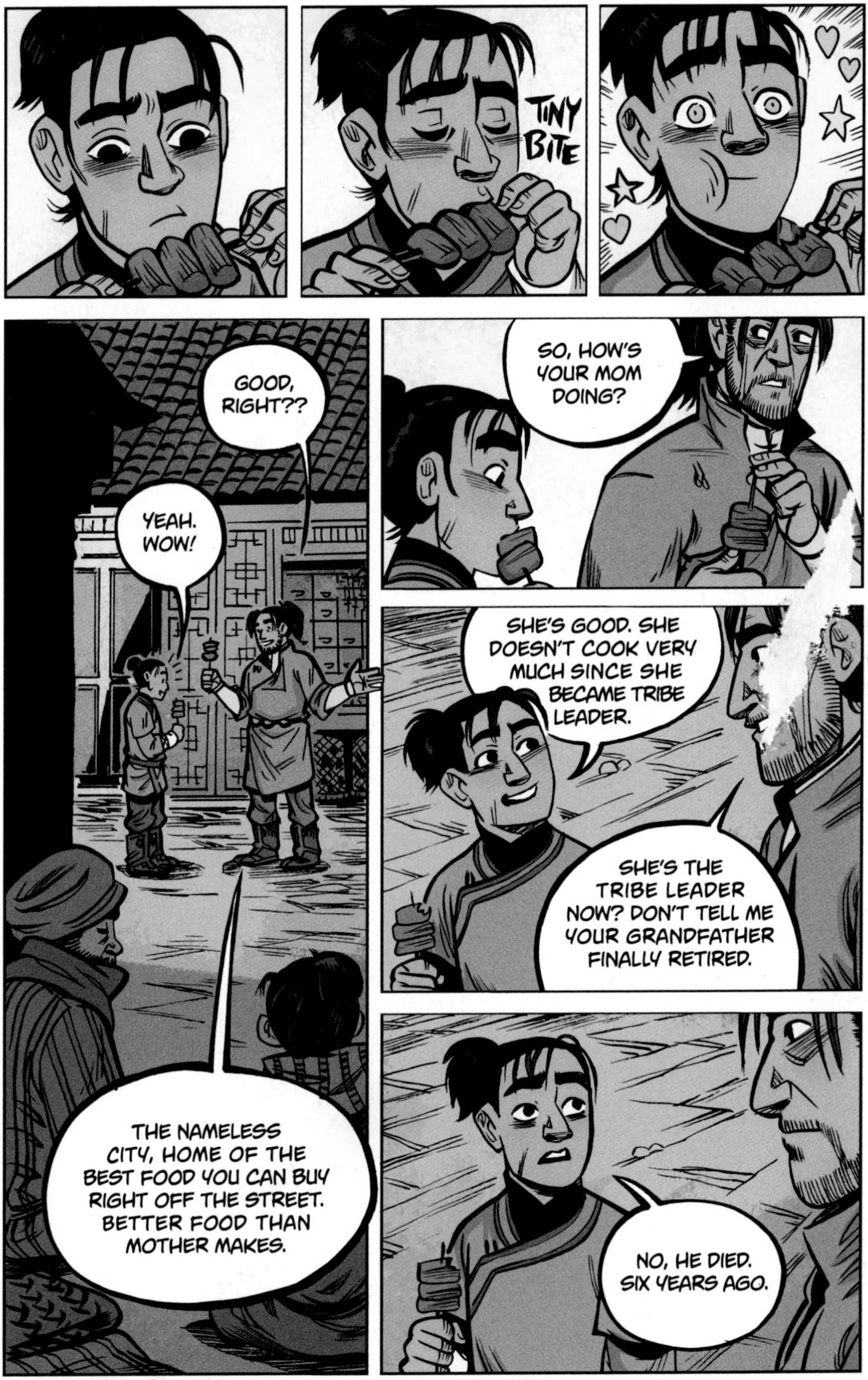
TINY BITE
GOOD, RIGHT??
YEAH. WOW!
THE NAMELESS CITY, HOME OF THE BEST FOOD YOU CAN BUY RIGHT OFF THE STREET. BETTER FOOD THAN MOTHER MAKES.
SO, HOW'S YOUR MOM DOING?
SHE'S GOOD. SHE DOESN'T COOK VERY MUCH SINCE SHE BECAME TRIBE LEADER.
SHE'S THE TRIBE LEADER NOW? DON'T TELL ME YOUR GRANDFATHER FINALLY RETIRED.
NO, HE DIED. SIX YEARS AGO.

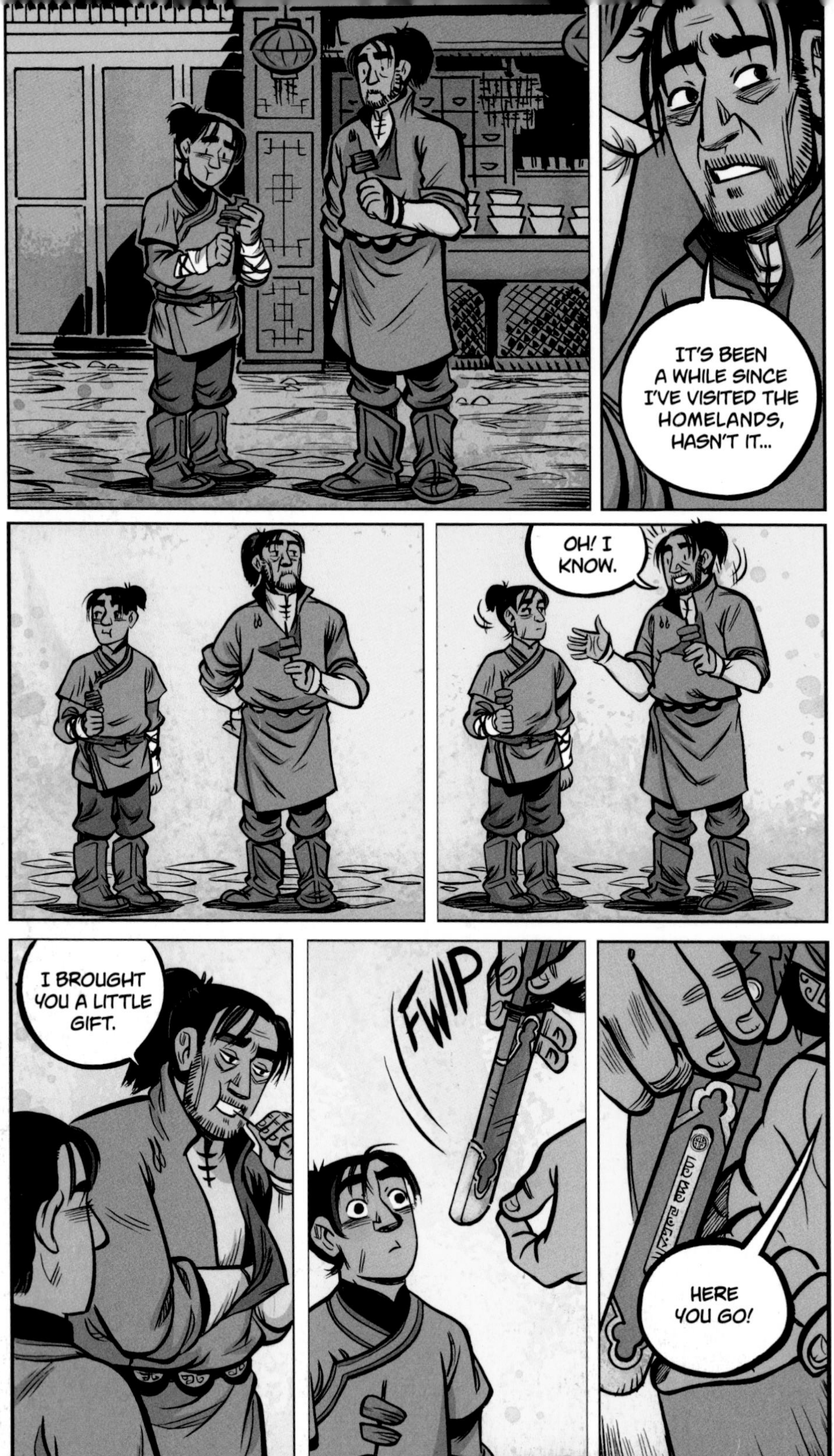
IT'S BEEN A WHILE SINCE I'VE VISITED THE HOMELANDS, HASN'T IT...
OH! I KNOW.
I BROUGHT YOU A LITTLE GIFT.
FWIP
HERE YOU GO!

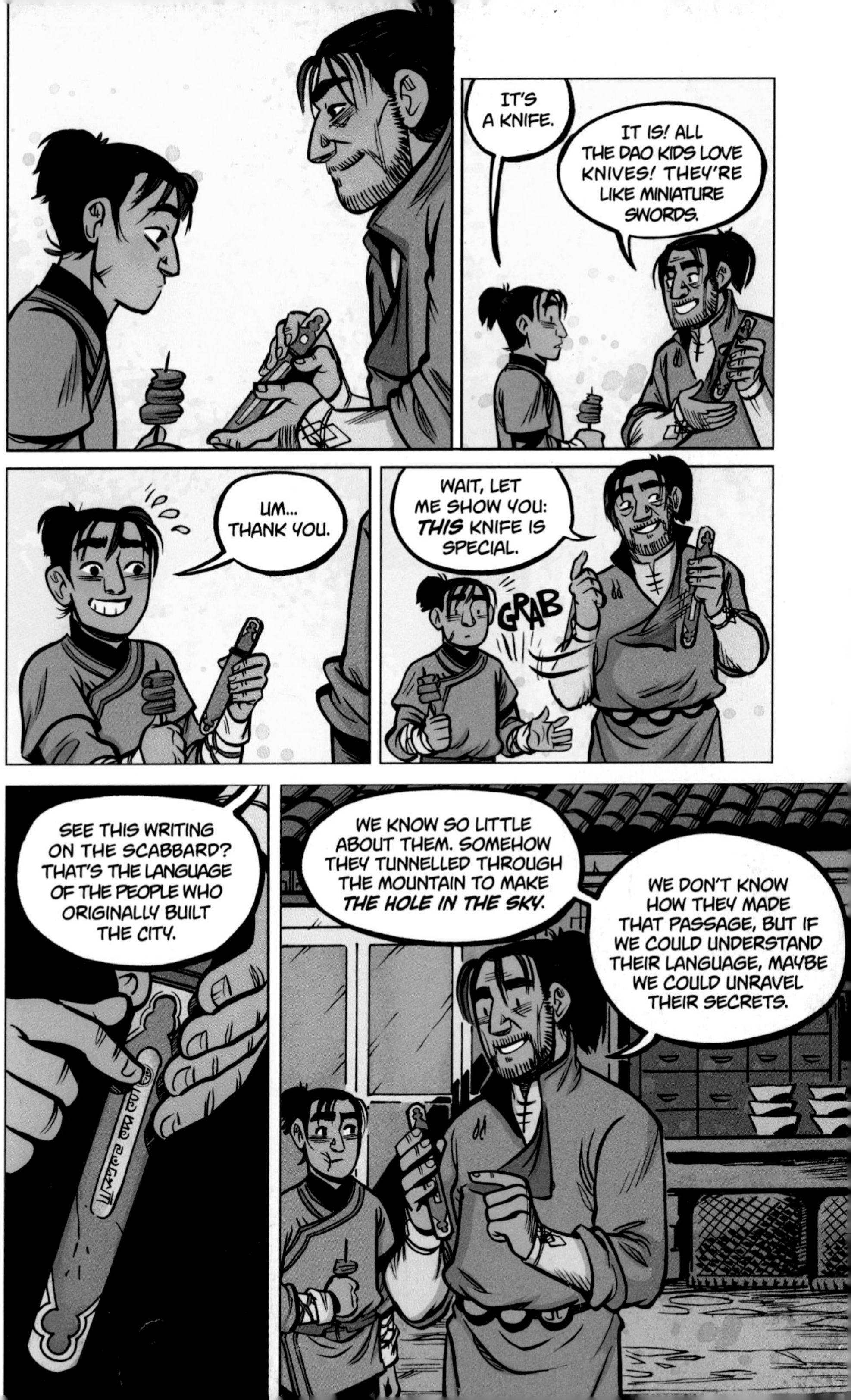
IT'S A KNIFE.
IT IS! ALL THE DAO KIDS LOVE KNIVES! THEY'RE LIKE MINIATURE SWORDS.
UM... THANK YOU.
WAIT, LET ME SHOW YOU: THIS KNIFE IS SPECIAL.
GRAB
SEE THIS WRITING ON THE SCABBARD? THAT'S THE LANGUAGE OF THE PEOPLE WHO ORIGINALLY BUILT THE CITY.
WE KNOW SO LITTLE ABOUT THEM. SOMEHOW THEY TUNNELLED THROUGH THE MOUNTAIN TO MAKE THE HOLE IN THE SKY.
WE DON'T KNOW HOW THEY MADE THAT PASSAGE, BUT IF WE COULD UNDERSTAND THEIR LANGUAGE, MAYBE WE COULD UNRAVEL THEIR SECRETS.

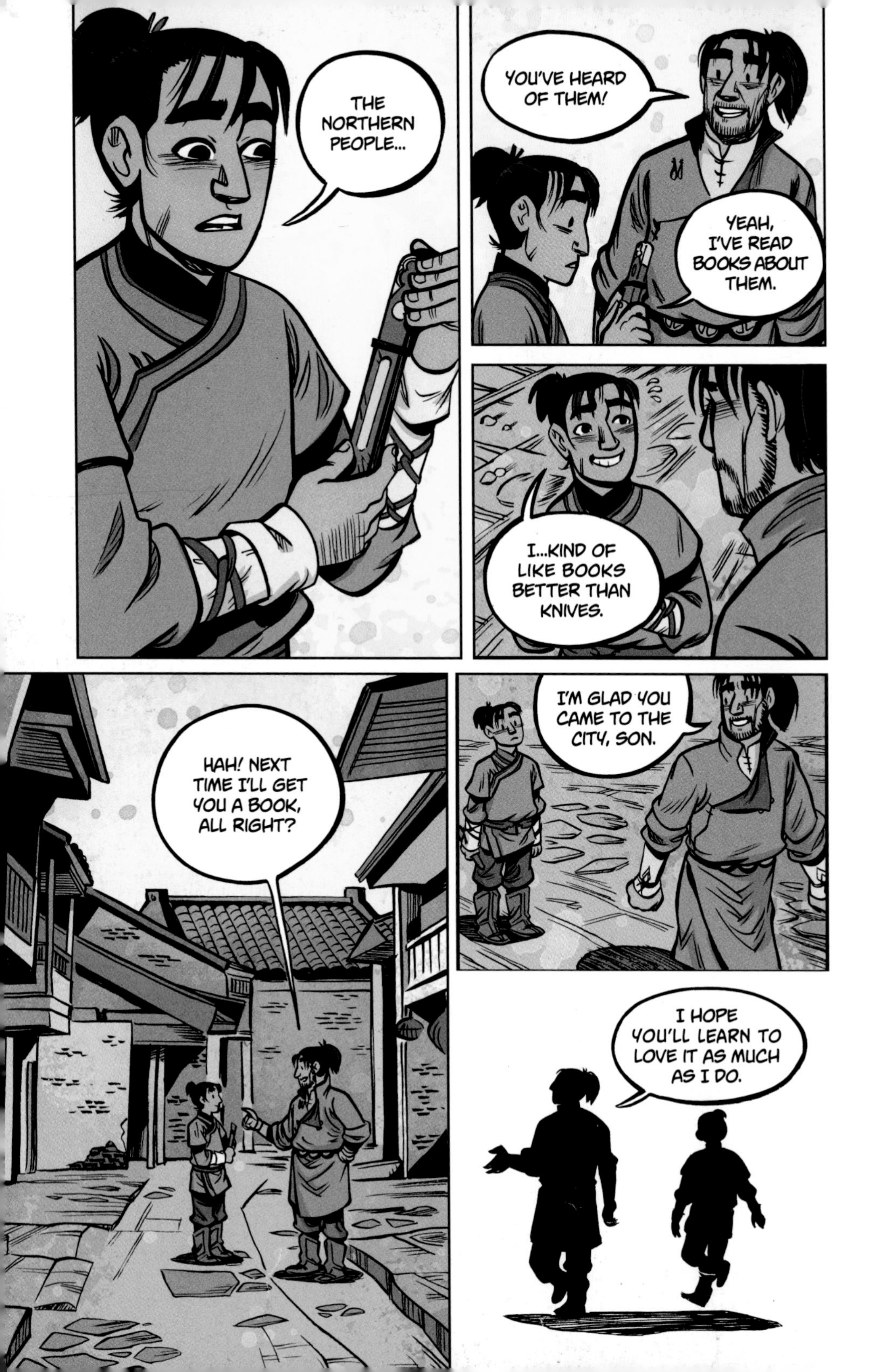
THE NORTHERN PEOPLE...
YOU'VE HEARD OF THEM!
YEAH, I'VE READ BOOKS ABOUT THEM.
I...KIND OF LIKE BOOKS BETTER THAN KNIVES.
HAH! NEXT TIME I'LL GET YOU A BOOK, ALL RIGHT?
I'M GLAD YOU CAME TO THE CITY, SON.
I HOPE YOU'LL LEARN TO LOVE IT AS MUCH AS I DO.

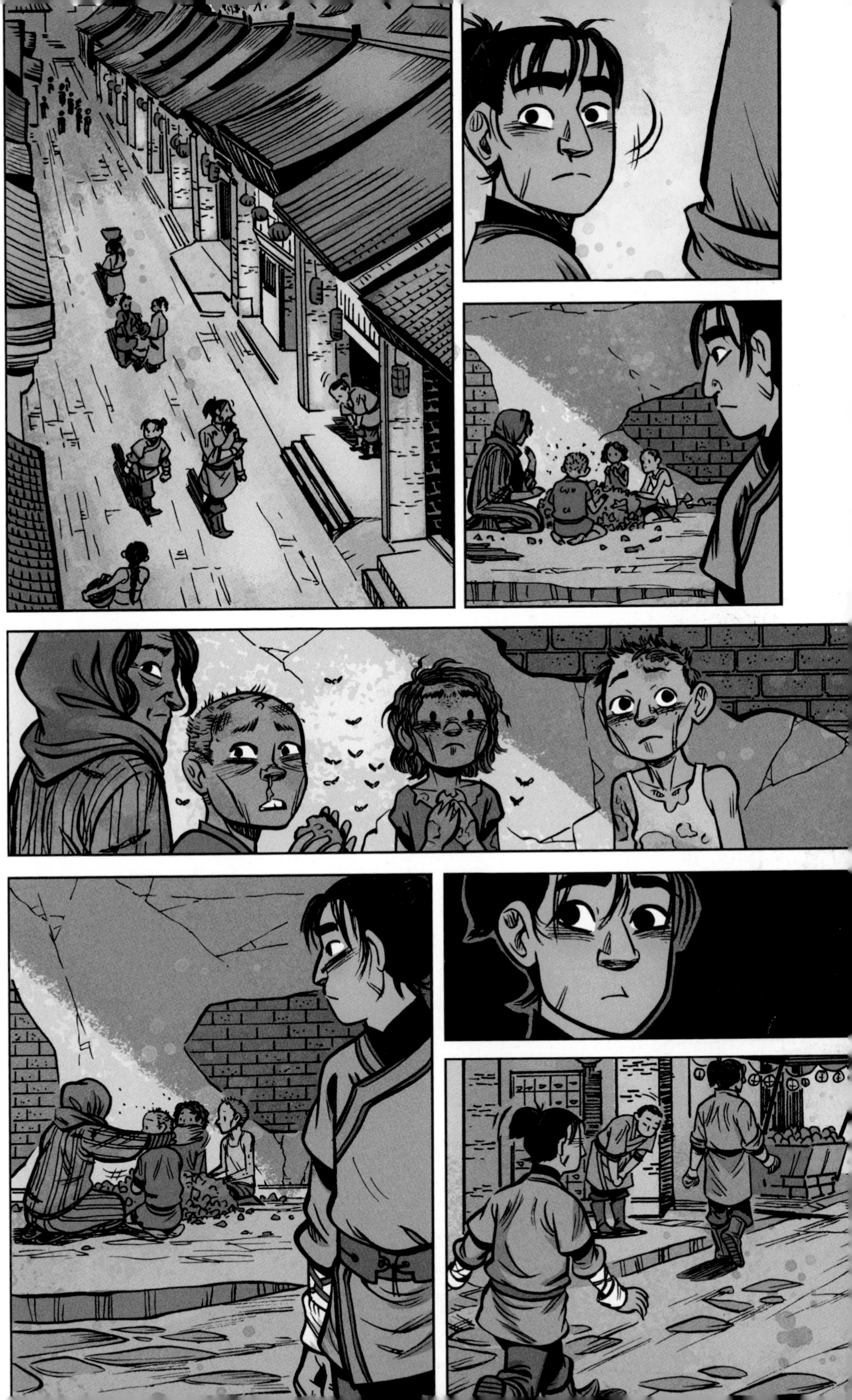

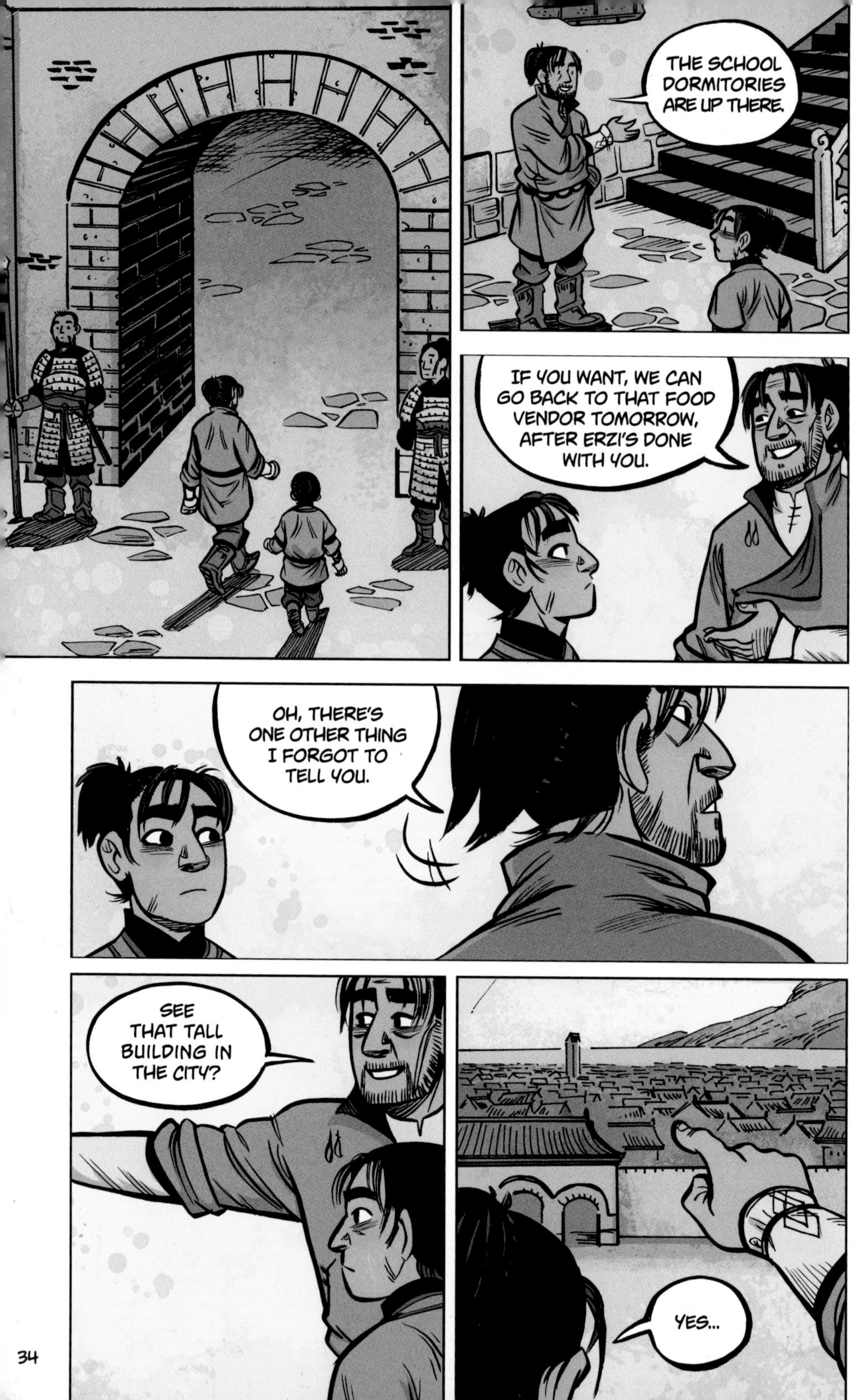
THE SCHOOL DORMITORIES ARE UP THERE.
IF YOU WANT, WE CAN GO BACK TO THAT FOOD VENDOR TOMORROW, AFTER ERZI'S DONE WITH YOU.
OH, THERE'S ONE OTHER THING I FORGOT TO TELL YOU.
SEE THAT TALL BUILDING IN THE CITY?
YES...

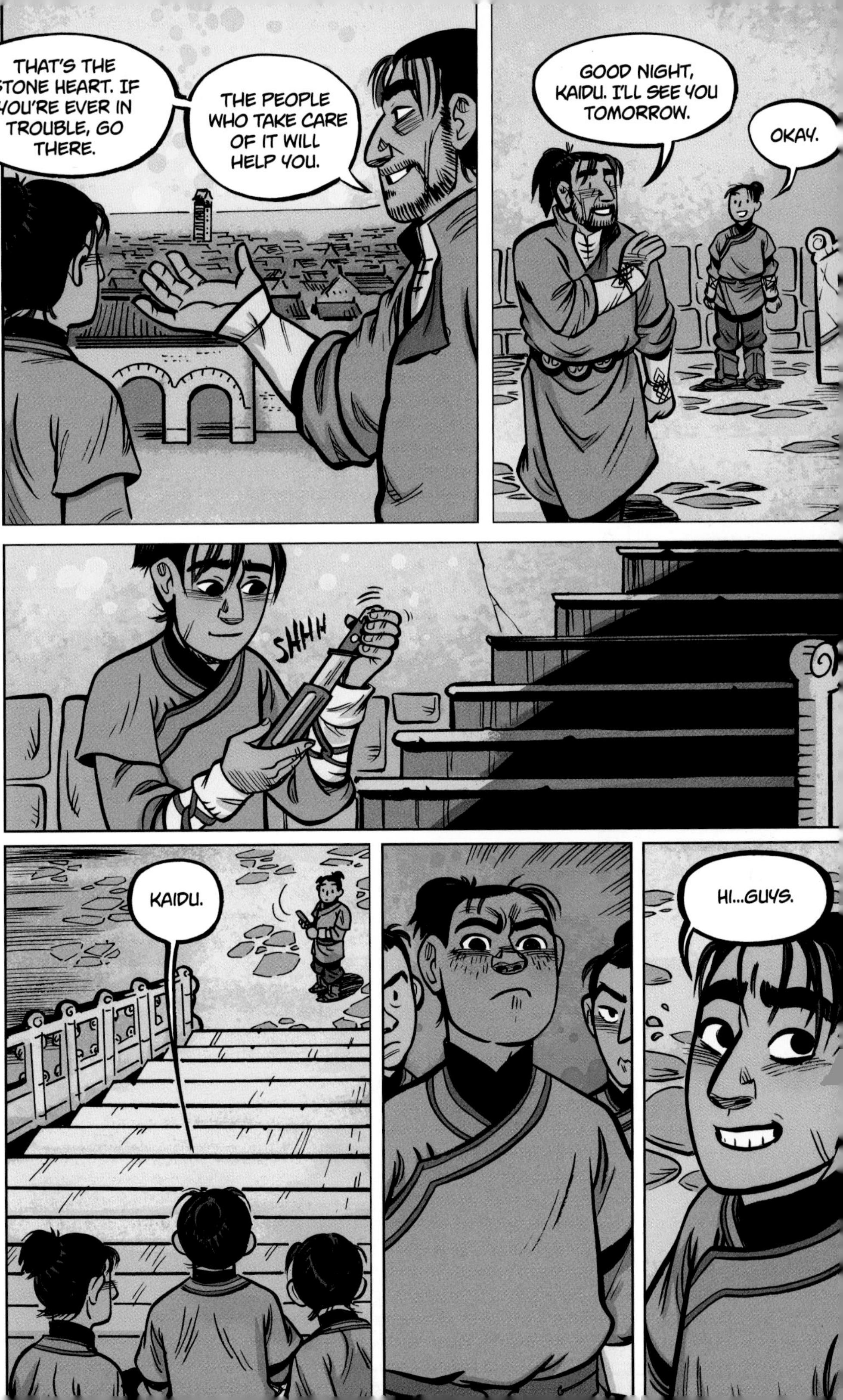
THAT'S THE STONE HEART. IF YOU'RE EVER IN TROUBLE, GO THERE.
THE PEOPLE WHO TAKE CARE OF IT WILL HELP YOU.
GOOD NIGHT, KAIDU. I'LL SEE YOU TOMORROW.
OKAY.
SHHH
KAIDU.
HI...GUYS.

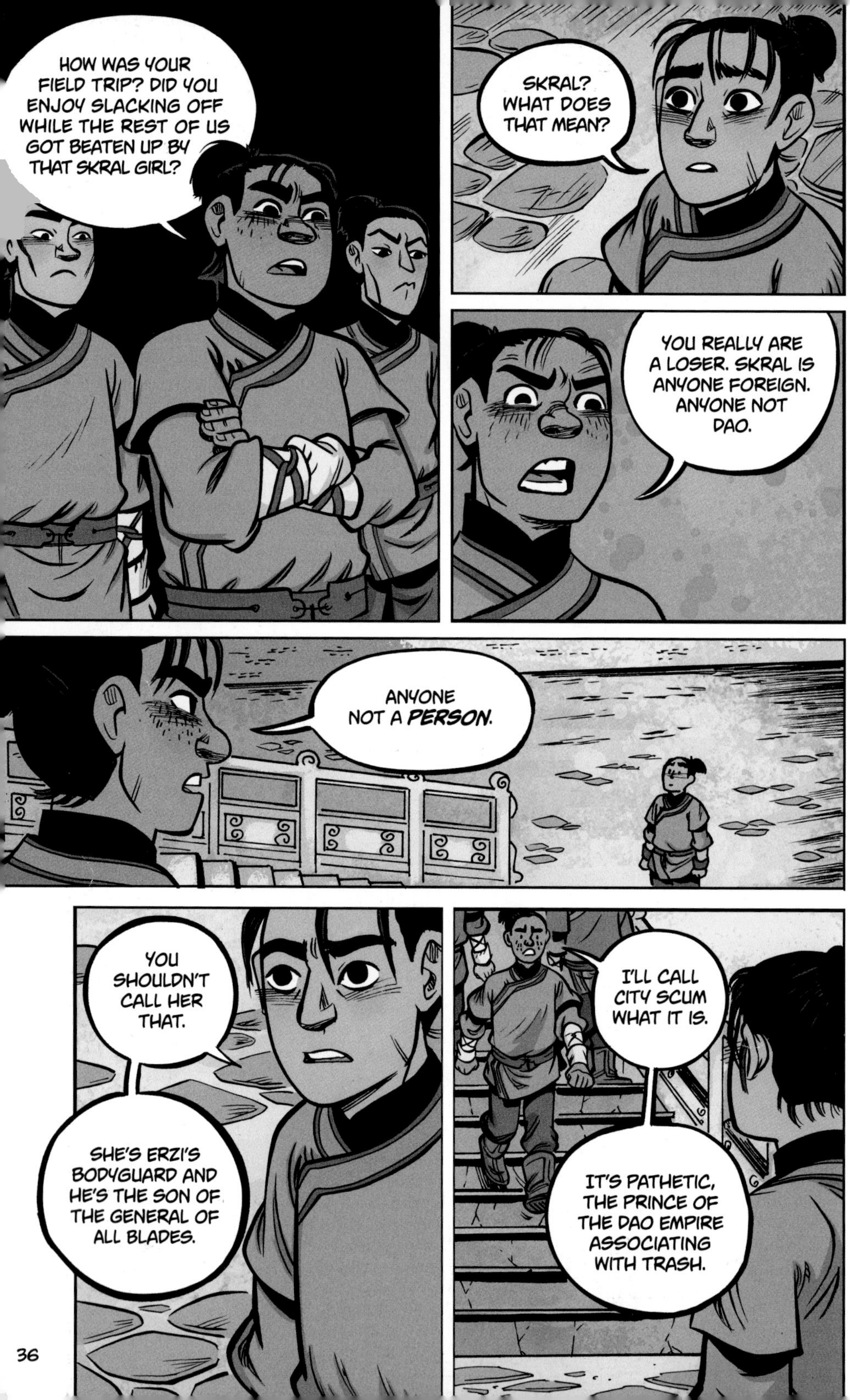

HOW WAS YOUR FIELD TRIP? DID YOU ENJOY SLACKING OFF WHILE THE REST OF US GOT BEATEN UP BY THAT SKRAL GIRL?
SKRAL? WHAT DOES THAT MEAN?
YOU REALLY ARE A LOSER. SKRAL IS ANYONE FOREIGN. ANYONE NOT DAO.
ANYONE NOT A *PERSON*.
YOU SHOULDN'T CALL HER THAT.
SHE'S ERZI'S BODYGUARD AND HE'S THE SON OF THE GENERAL OF ALL BLADES.
I'LL CALL CITY SCUM WHAT IT IS.
IT'S PATHETIC, THE PRINCE OF THE DAO EMPIRE ASSOCIATING WITH TRASH.

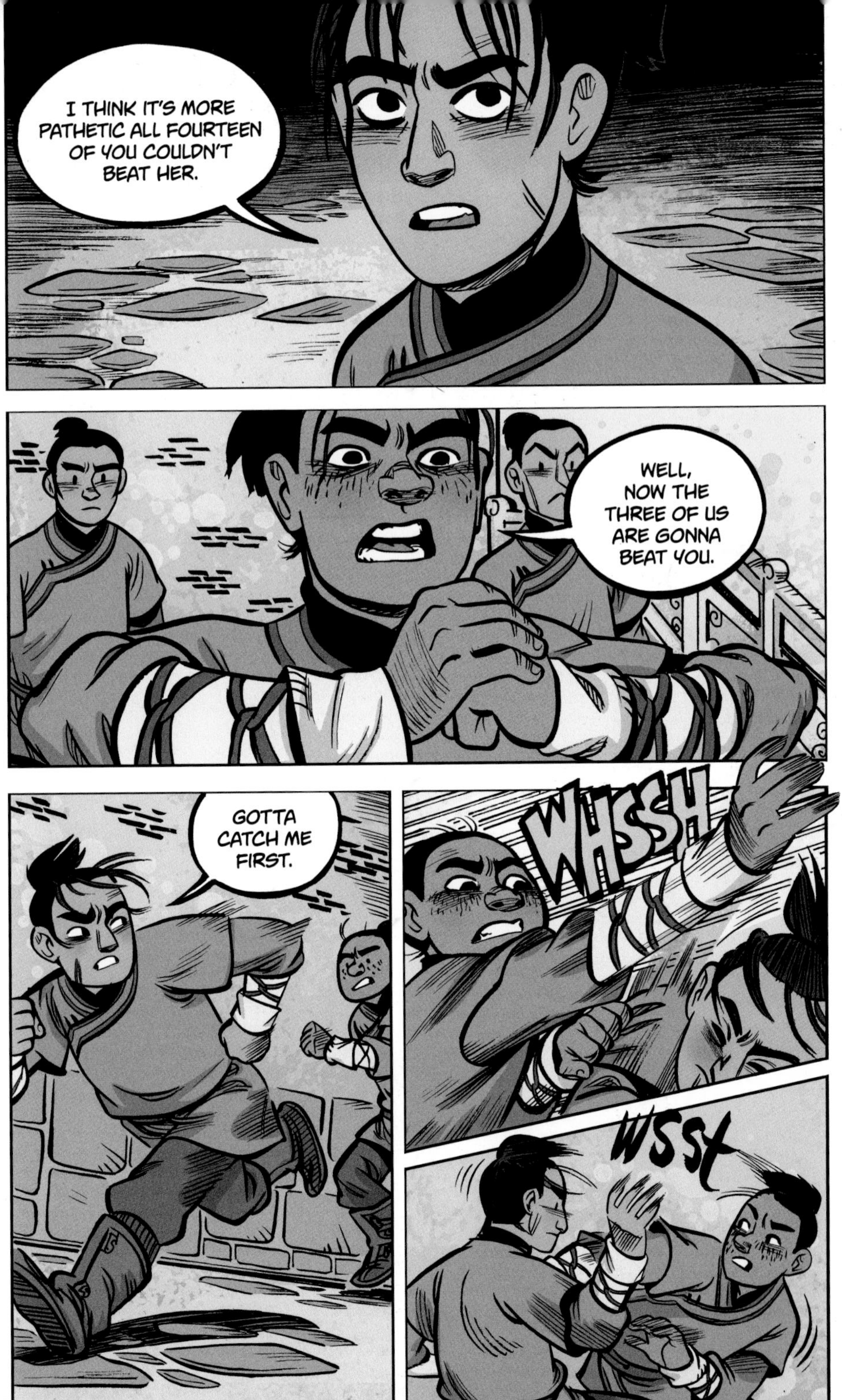
I THINK IT'S MORE PATHETIC ALL FOURTEEN OF YOU COULDN'T BEAT HER.
WELL, NOW THE THREE OF US ARE GONNA BEAT YOU.
GOTTA CATCH ME FIRST.
WHSSH
WSST

WHAMM

STOP.

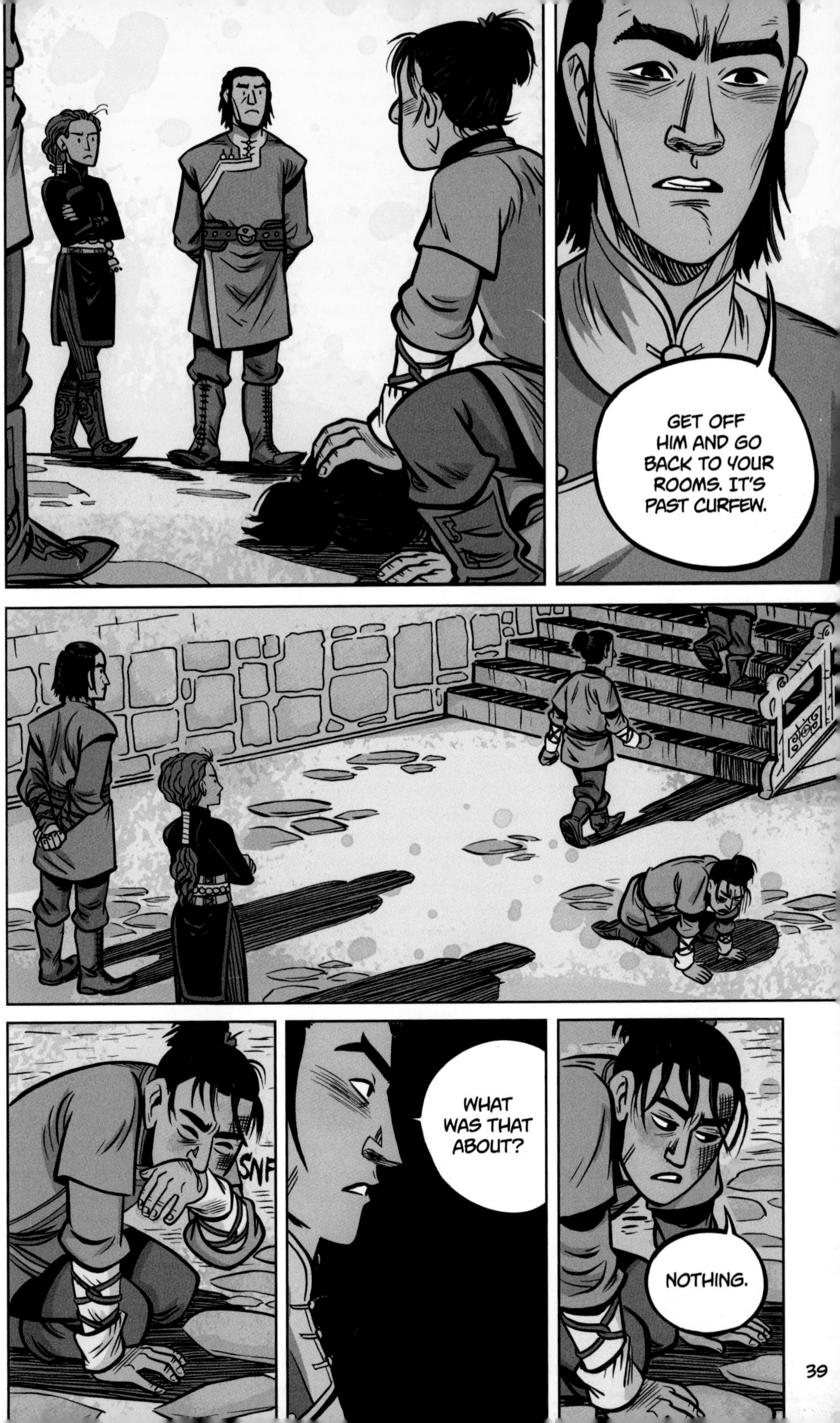
GET OFF HIM AND GO BACK TO YOUR ROOMS. IT'S PAST CURFEW.
SNF
WHAT WAS THAT ABOUT?
NOTHING.

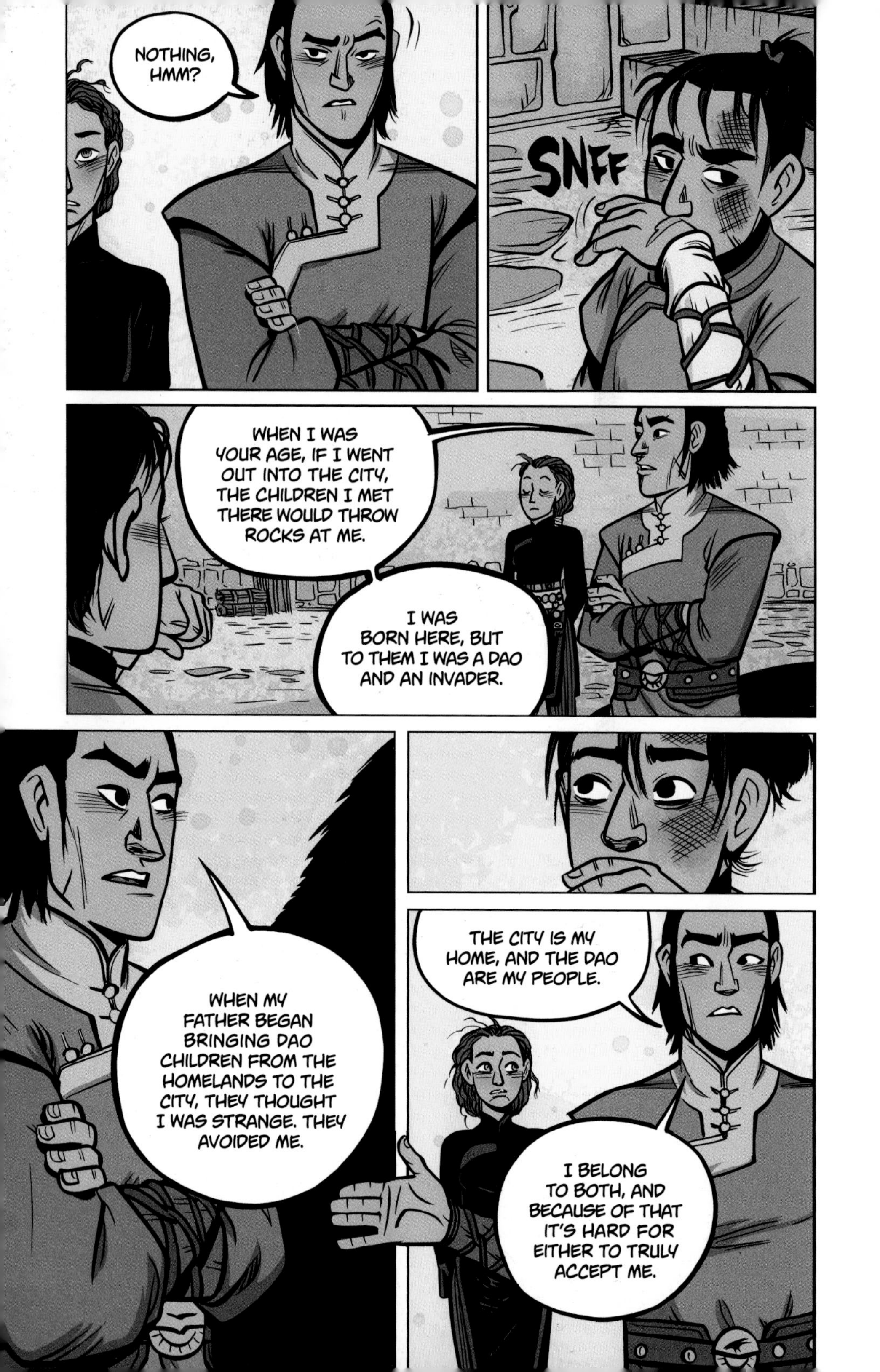
NOTHING, HMM?
SNFF
WHEN I WAS YOUR AGE, IF I WENT OUT INTO THE CITY, THE CHILDREN I MET THERE WOULD THROW ROCKS AT ME.
I WAS BORN HERE, BUT TO THEM I WAS A DAO AND AN INVADER.
WHEN MY FATHER BEGAN BRINGING DAO CHILDREN FROM THE HOMELANDS TO THE CITY, THEY THOUGHT I WAS STRANGE. THEY AVOIDED ME.
THE CITY IS MY HOME, AND THE DAO ARE MY PEOPLE.
I BELONG TO BOTH, AND BECAUSE OF THAT IT'S HARD FOR EITHER TO TRULY ACCEPT ME.

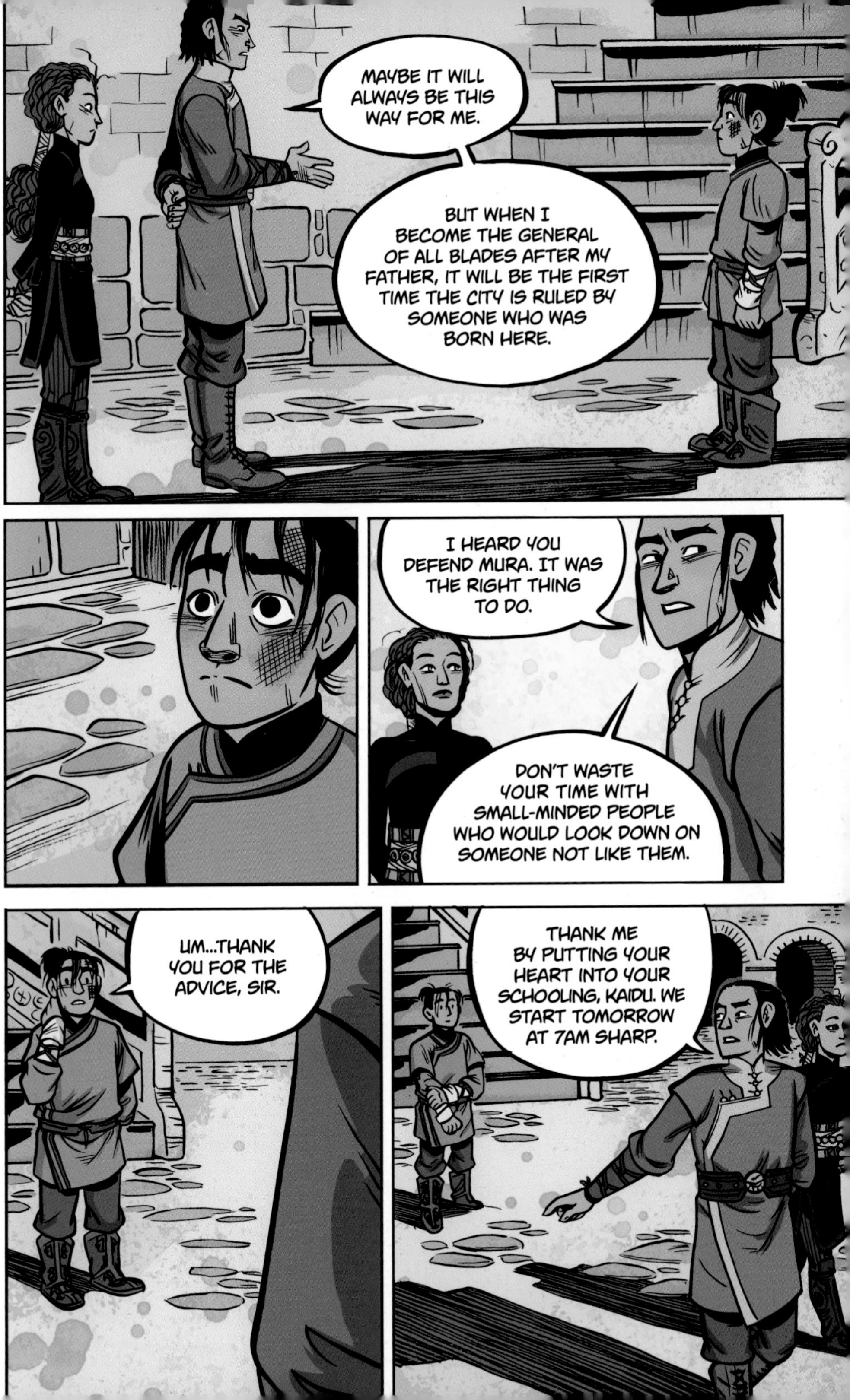
MAYBE IT WILL ALWAYS BE THIS WAY FOR ME.
BUT WHEN I BECOME THE GENERAL OF ALL BLADES AFTER MY FATHER, IT WILL BE THE FIRST TIME THE CITY IS RULED BY SOMEONE WHO WAS BORN HERE.
I HEARD YOU DEFEND MURA. IT WAS THE RIGHT THING TO DO.
DON'T WASTE YOUR TIME WITH SMALL-MINDED PEOPLE WHO WOULD LOOK DOWN ON SOMEONE NOT LIKE THEM.
UM...THANK YOU FOR THE ADVICE, SIR.
THANK ME BY PUTTING YOUR HEART INTO YOUR SCHOOLING, KAIDU. WE START TOMORROW AT 7AM SHARP.

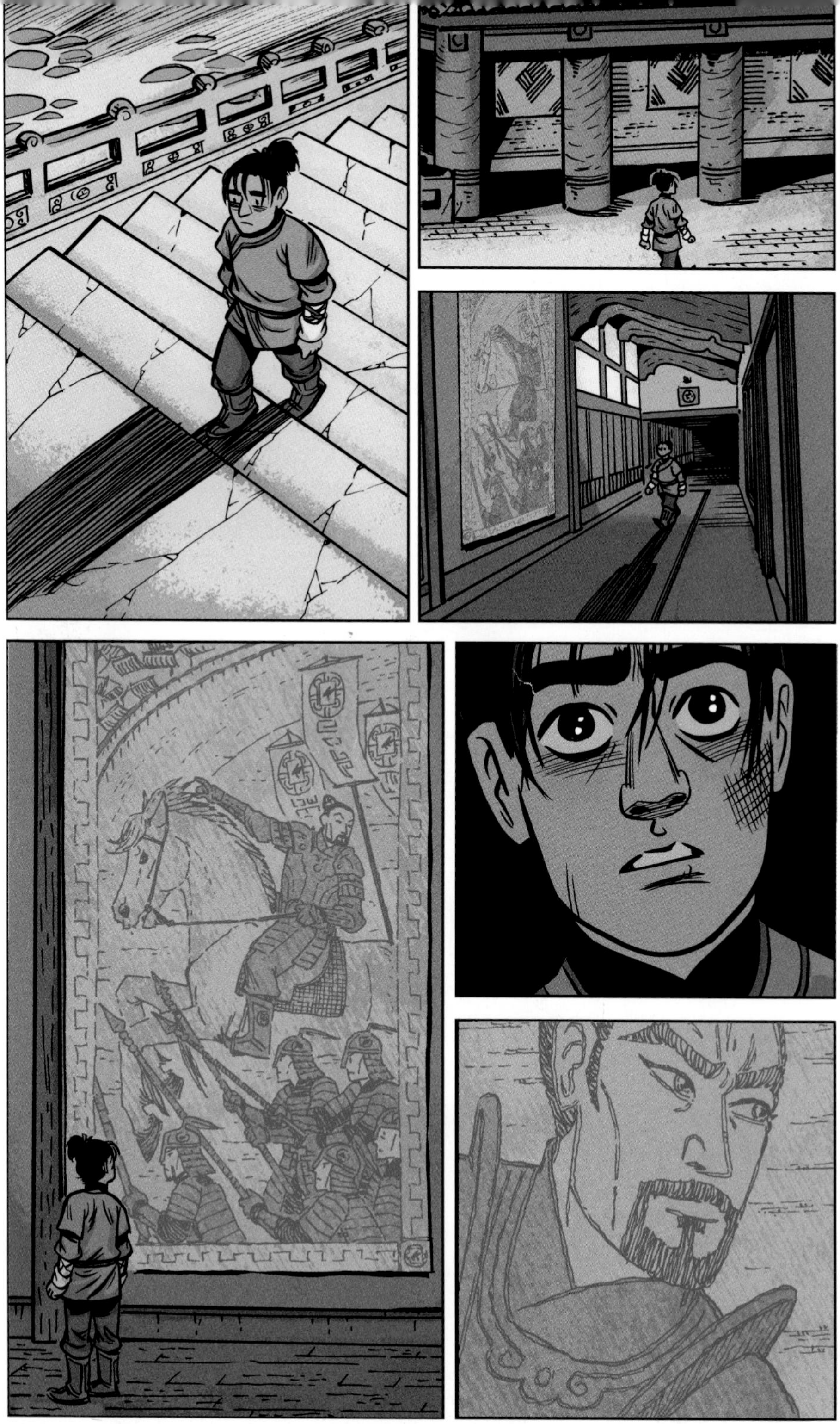

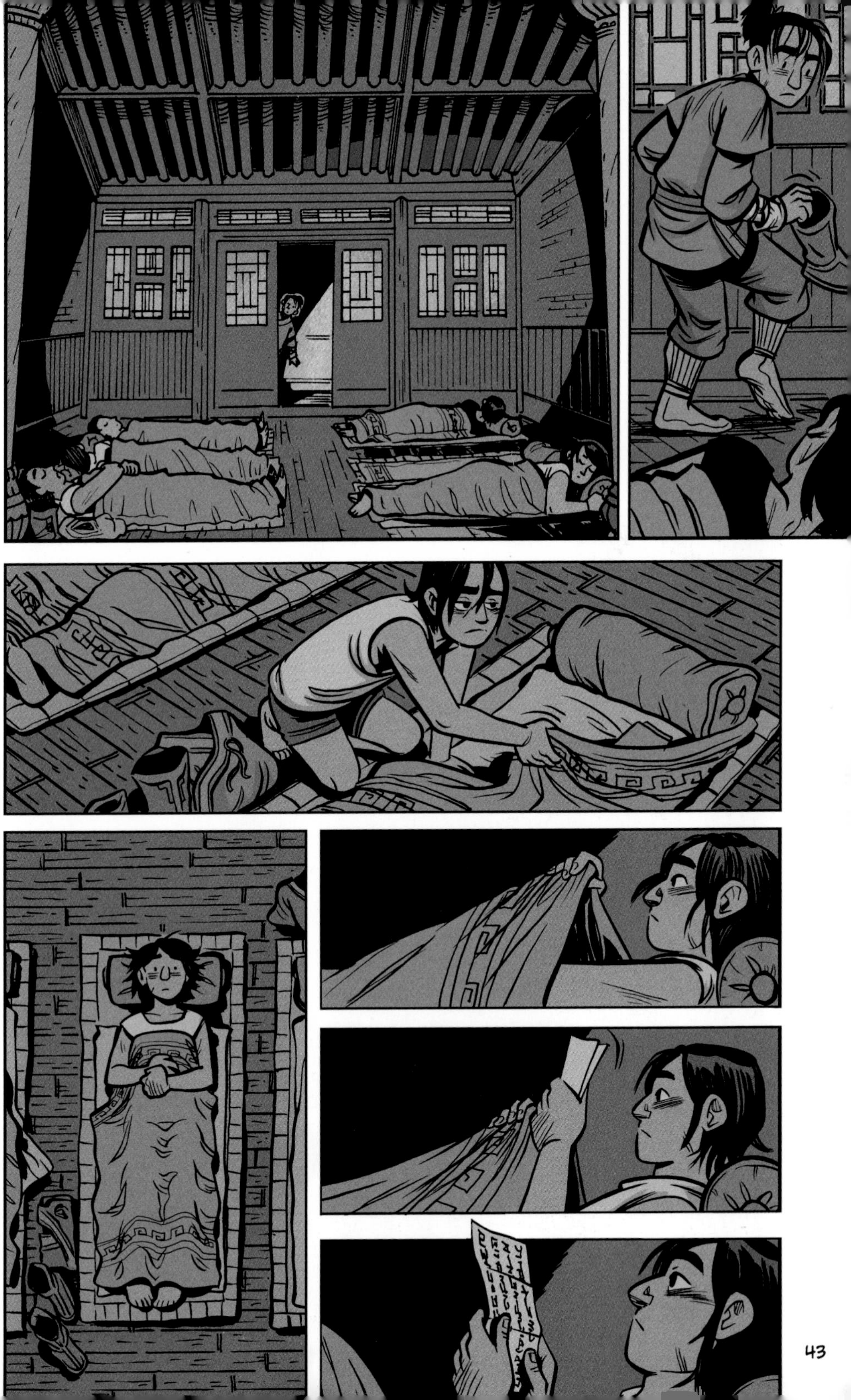

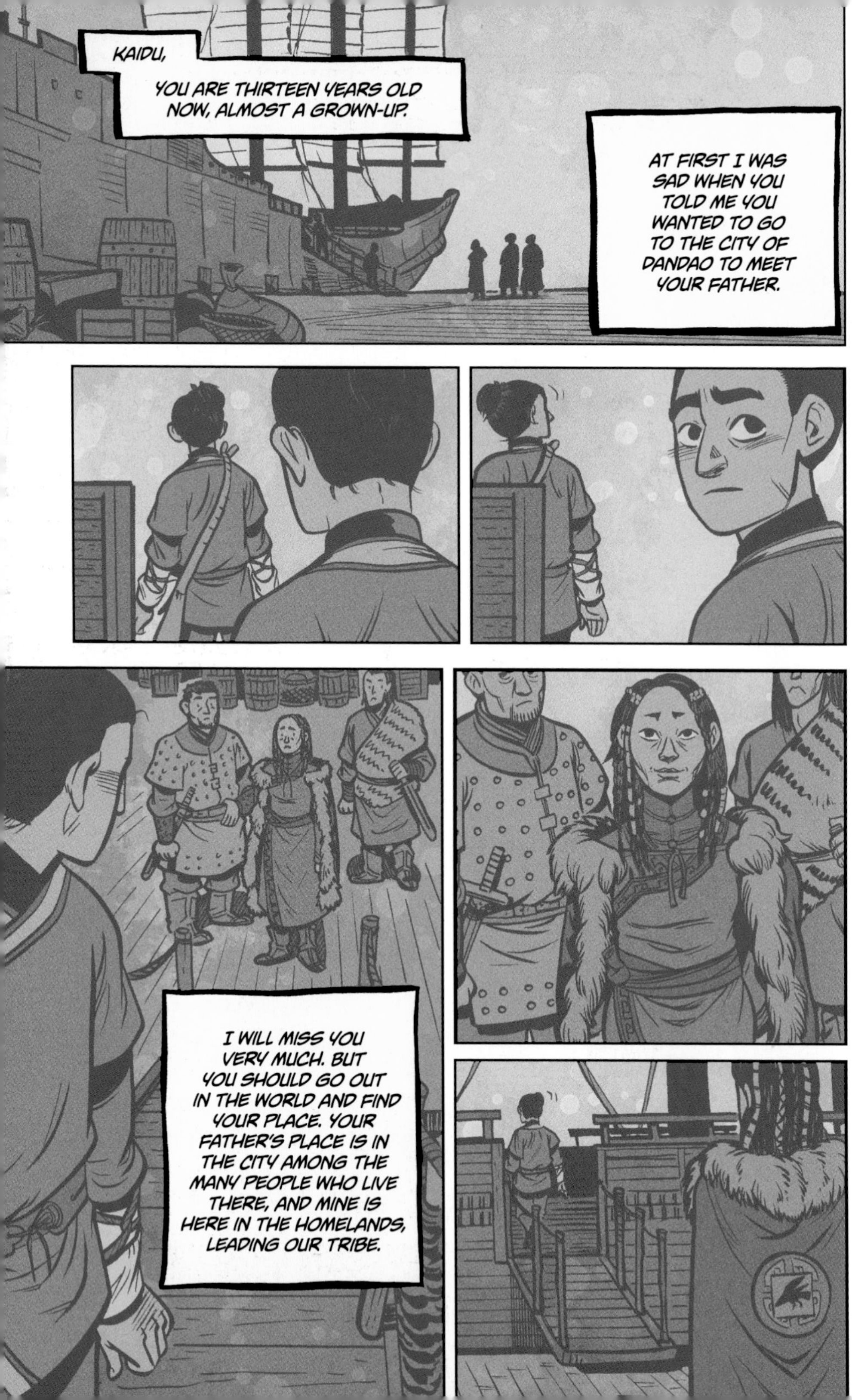
KAIDU,
YOU ARE THIRTEEN YEARS OLD NOW, ALMOST A GROWN-UP.
AT FIRST I WAS SAD WHEN YOU TOLD ME YOU WANTED TO GO TO THE CITY OF DANDAO TO MEET YOUR FATHER.
I WILL MISS YOU VERY MUCH. BUT YOU SHOULD GO OUT IN THE WORLD AND FIND YOUR PLACE. YOUR FATHER'S PLACE IS IN THE CITY AMONG THE MANY PEOPLE WHO LIVE THERE, AND MINE IS HERE IN THE HOMELANDS, LEADING OUR TRIBE.

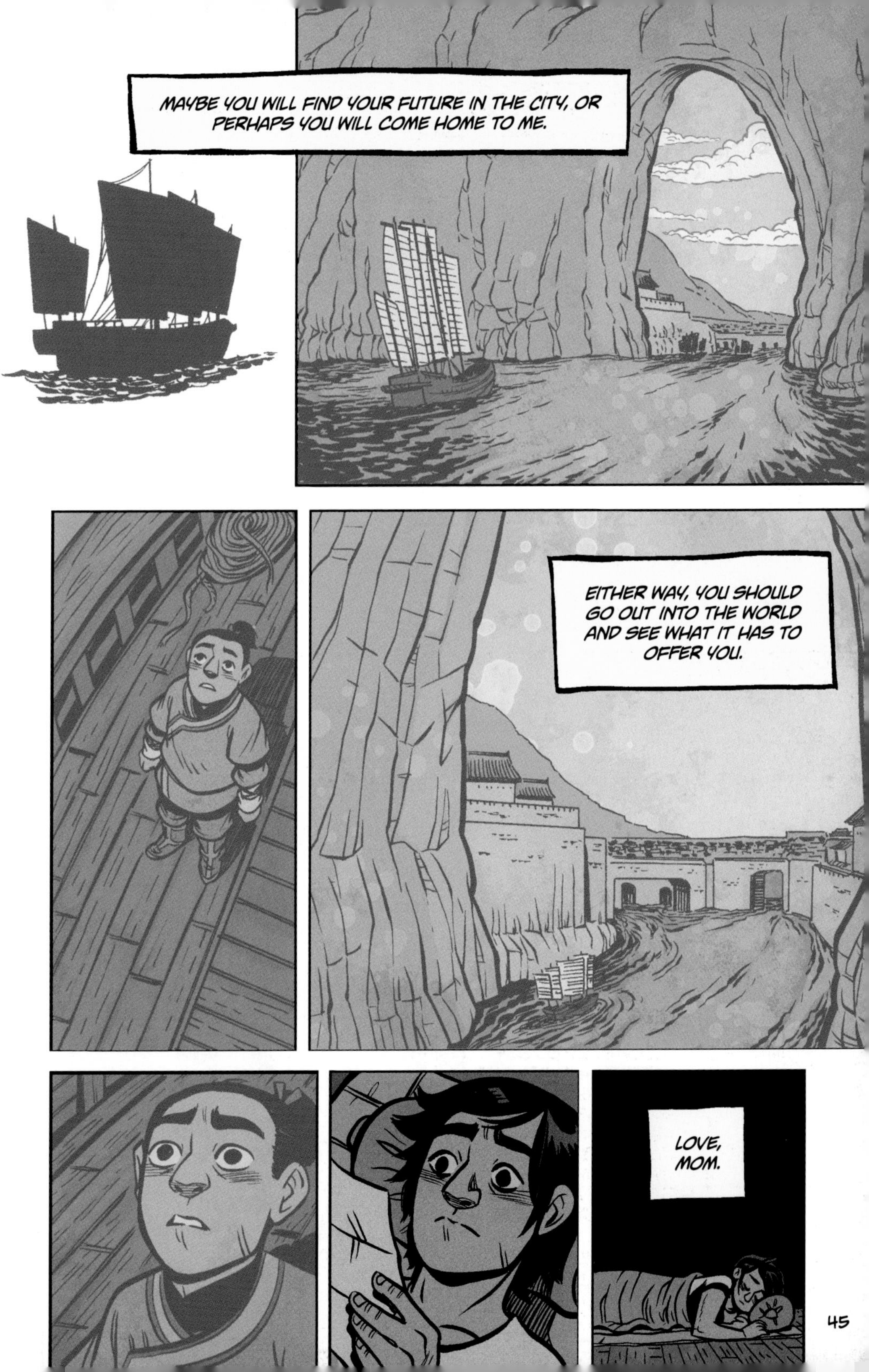
MAYBE YOU WILL FIND YOUR FUTURE IN THE CITY, OR PERHAPS YOU WILL COME HOME TO ME.
EITHER WAY, YOU SHOULD GO OUT INTO THE WORLD AND SEE WHAT IT HAS TO OFFER YOU.
LOVE, MOM.

DAY 2

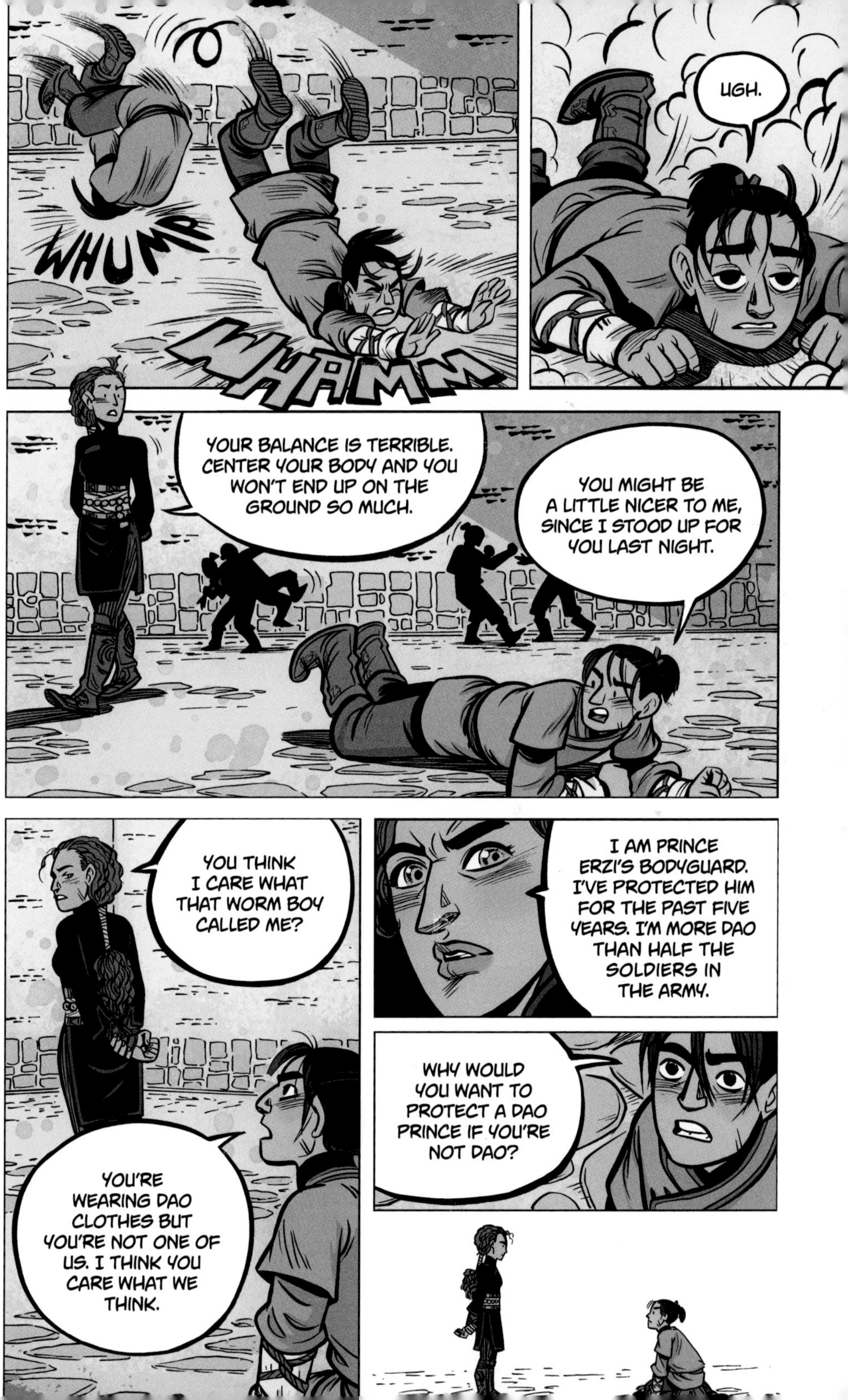
WHUMP
WHAMM
UGH.
YOUR BALANCE IS TERRIBLE. CENTER YOUR BODY AND YOU WON'T END UP ON THE GROUND SO MUCH.
YOU MIGHT BE A LITTLE NICER TO ME, SINCE I STOOD UP FOR YOU LAST NIGHT.
YOU THINK I CARE WHAT THAT WORM BOY CALLED ME?
YOU'RE WEARING DAO CLOTHES BUT YOU'RE NOT ONE OF US. I THINK YOU CARE WHAT WE THINK.
I AM PRINCE ERZI'S BODYGUARD. I'VE PROTECTED HIM FOR THE PAST FIVE YEARS. I'M MORE DAO THAN HALF THE SOLDIERS IN THE ARMY.
WHY WOULD YOU WANT TO PROTECT A DAO PRINCE IF YOU'RE NOT DAO?

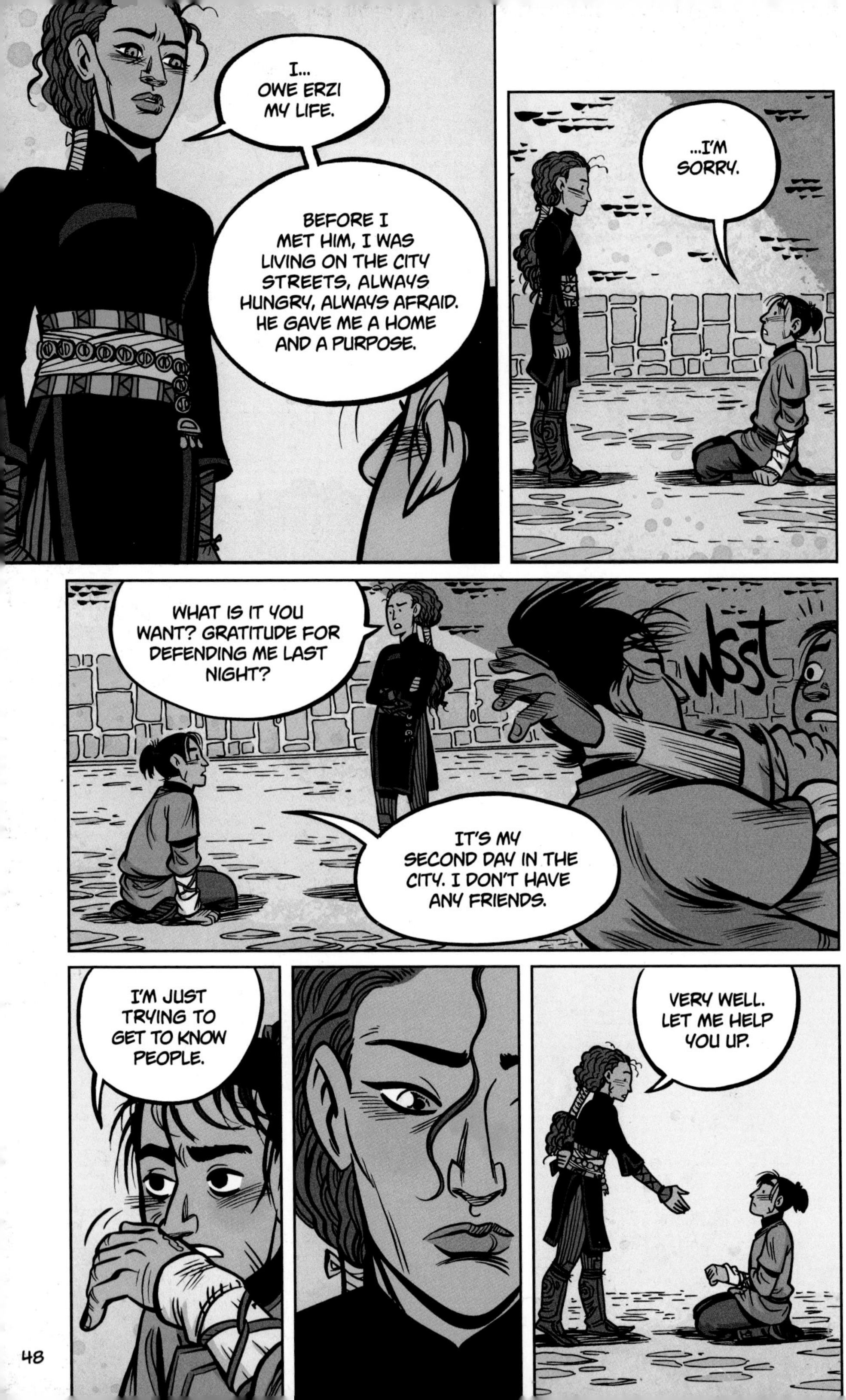
I... OWE ERZI MY LIFE.
BEFORE I MET HIM, I WAS LIVING ON THE CITY STREETS, ALWAYS HUNGRY, ALWAYS AFRAID. HE GAVE ME A HOME AND A PURPOSE.
...I'M SORRY.
WHAT IS IT YOU WANT? GRATITUDE FOR DEFENDING ME LAST NIGHT?
WOSt
IT'S MY SECOND DAY IN THE CITY. I DON'T HAVE ANY FRIENDS.
I'M JUST TRYING TO GET TO KNOW PEOPLE.
VERY WELL. LET ME HELP YOU UP.

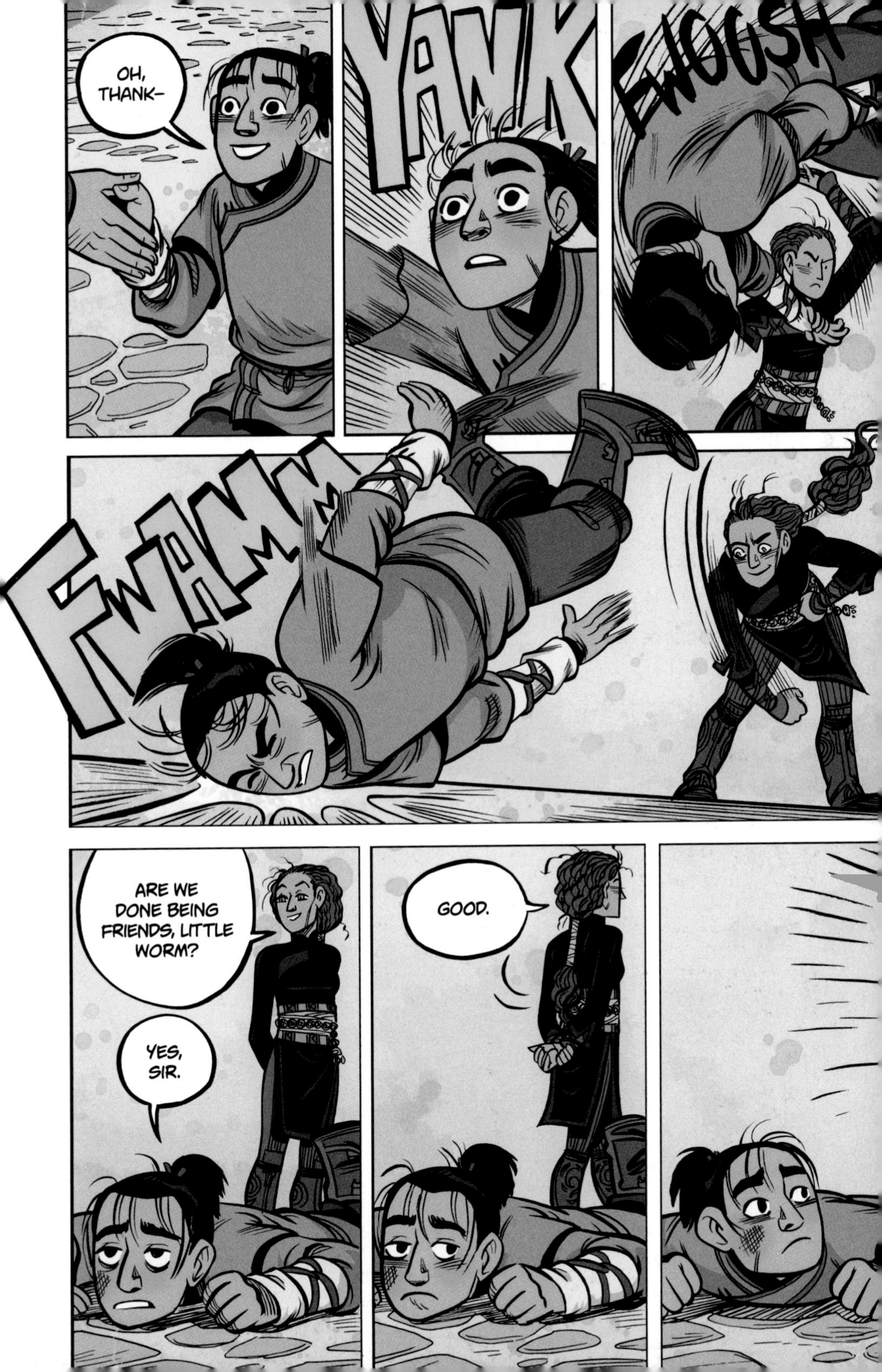
OH, THANK–
YANK
FWOOSH
FWAMM
ARE WE DONE BEING FRIENDS, LITTLE WORM?
YES, SIR.
GOOD.

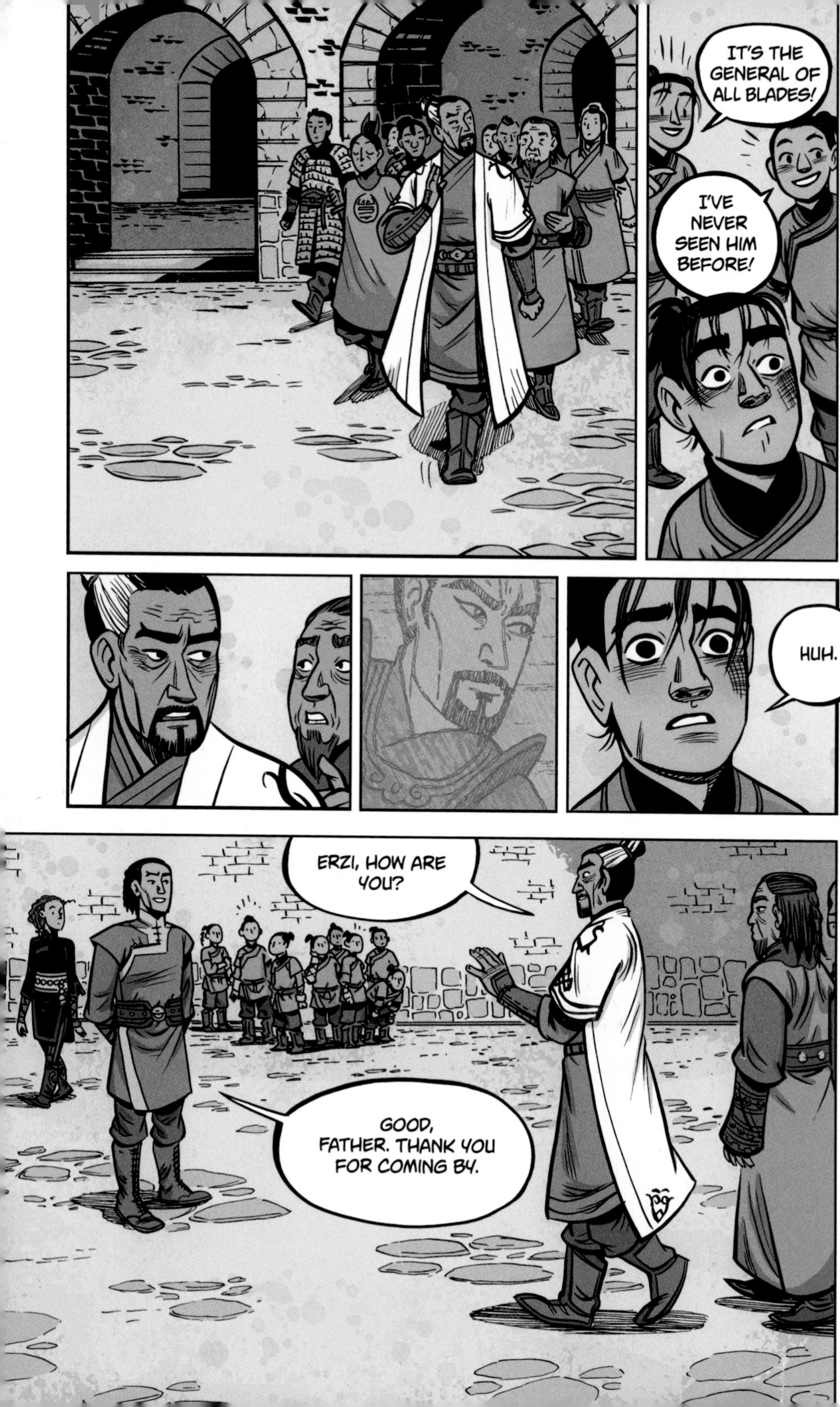
IT'S THE GENERAL OF ALL BLADES!
I'VE NEVER SEEN HIM BEFORE!
HUH.
ERZI, HOW ARE YOU?
GOOD, FATHER. THANK YOU FOR COMING BY.

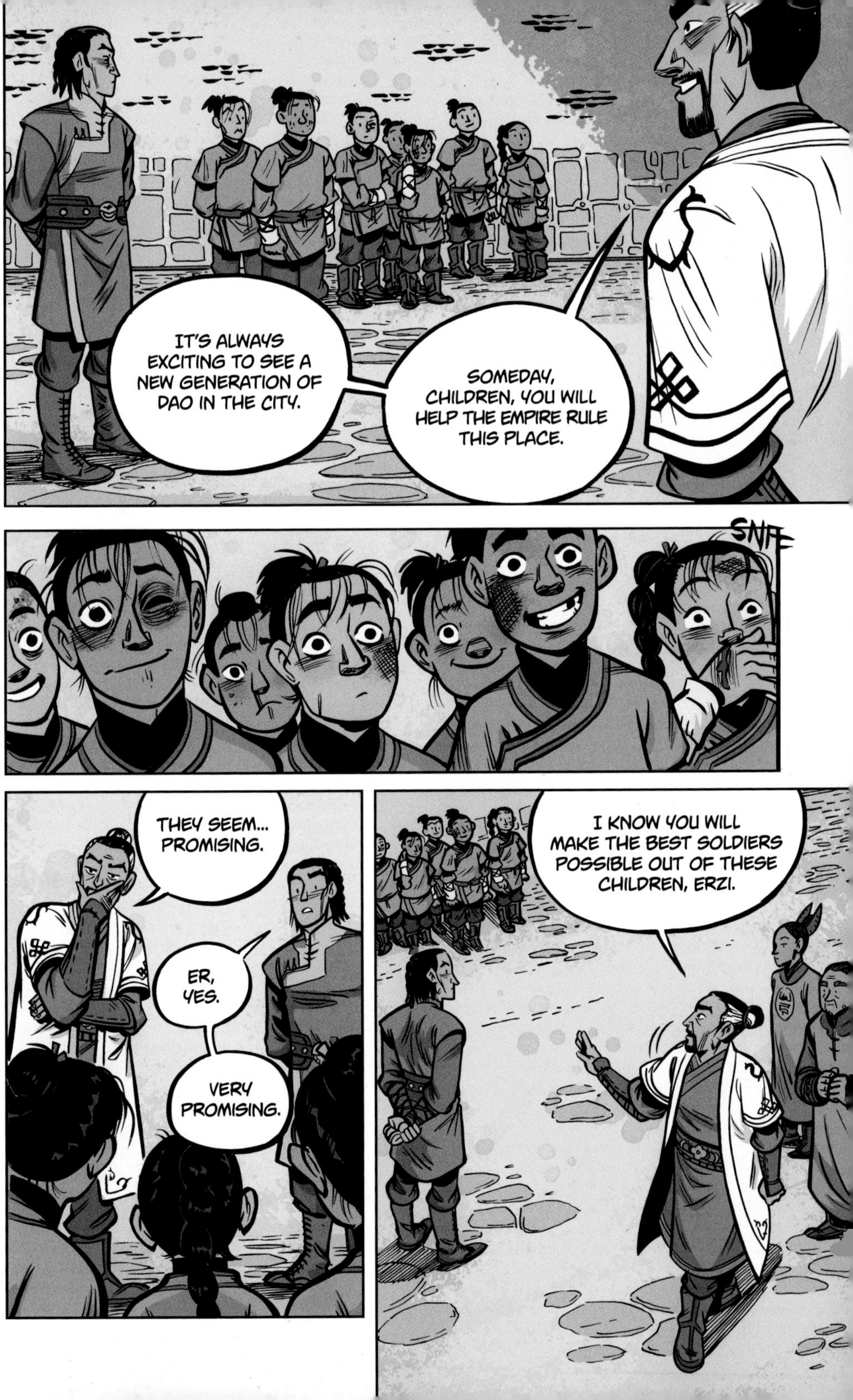
IT'S ALWAYS EXCITING TO SEE A NEW GENERATION OF DAO IN THE CITY.
SOMEDAY, CHILDREN, YOU WILL HELP THE EMPIRE RULE THIS PLACE.
SNIFF
THEY SEEM... PROMISING.
ER, YES.
VERY PROMISING.
I KNOW YOU WILL MAKE THE BEST SOLDIERS POSSIBLE OUT OF THESE CHILDREN, ERZI.

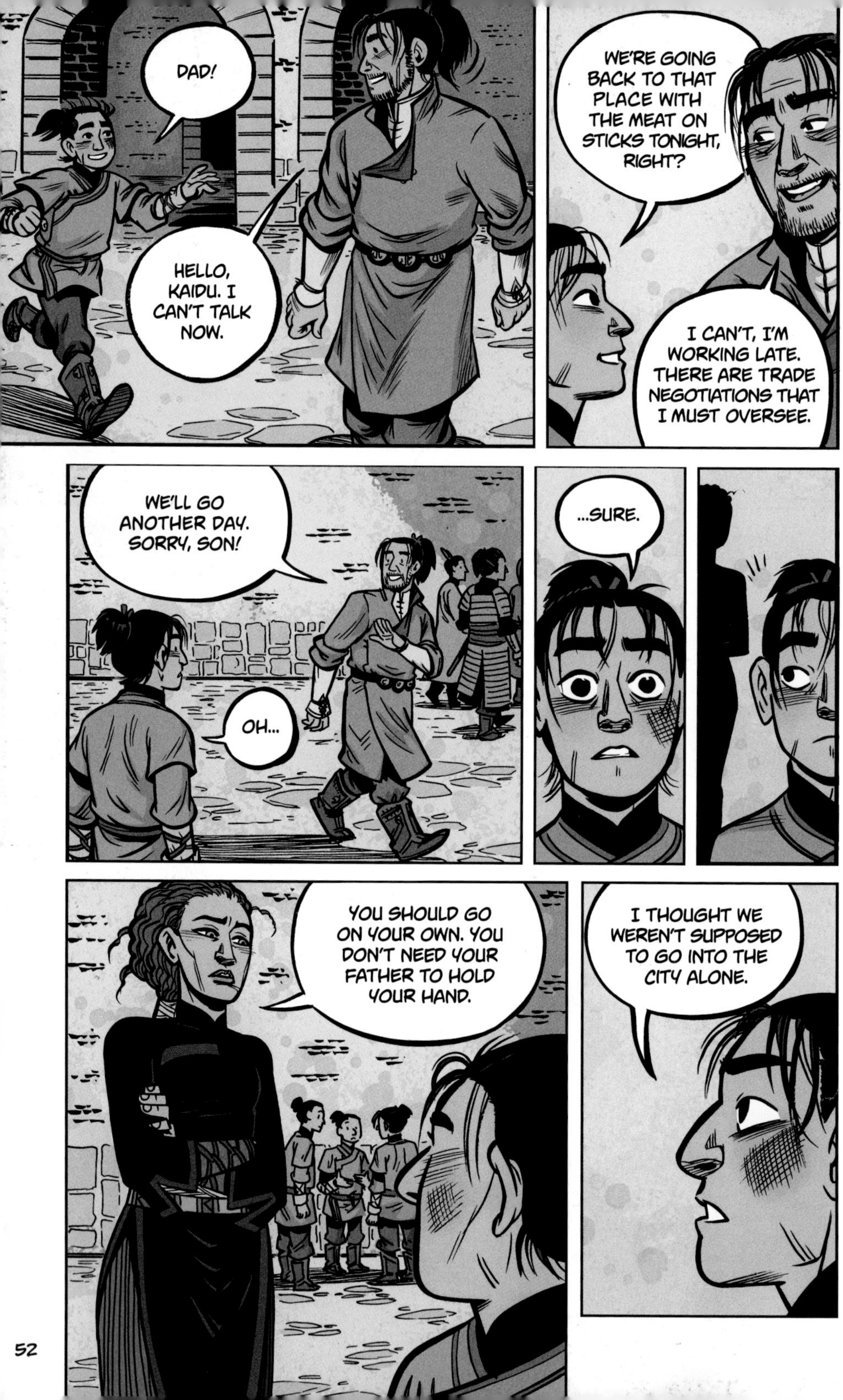
DAD!
HELLO, KAIDU. I CAN'T TALK NOW.
WE'RE GOING BACK TO THAT PLACE WITH THE MEAT ON STICKS TONIGHT, RIGHT?
I CAN'T, I'M WORKING LATE. THERE ARE TRADE NEGOTIATIONS THAT I MUST OVERSEE.
WE'LL GO ANOTHER DAY. SORRY, SON!
OH...
...SURE.
YOU SHOULD GO ON YOUR OWN. YOU DON'T NEED YOUR FATHER TO HOLD YOUR HAND.
I THOUGHT WE WEREN'T SUPPOSED TO GO INTO THE CITY ALONE.

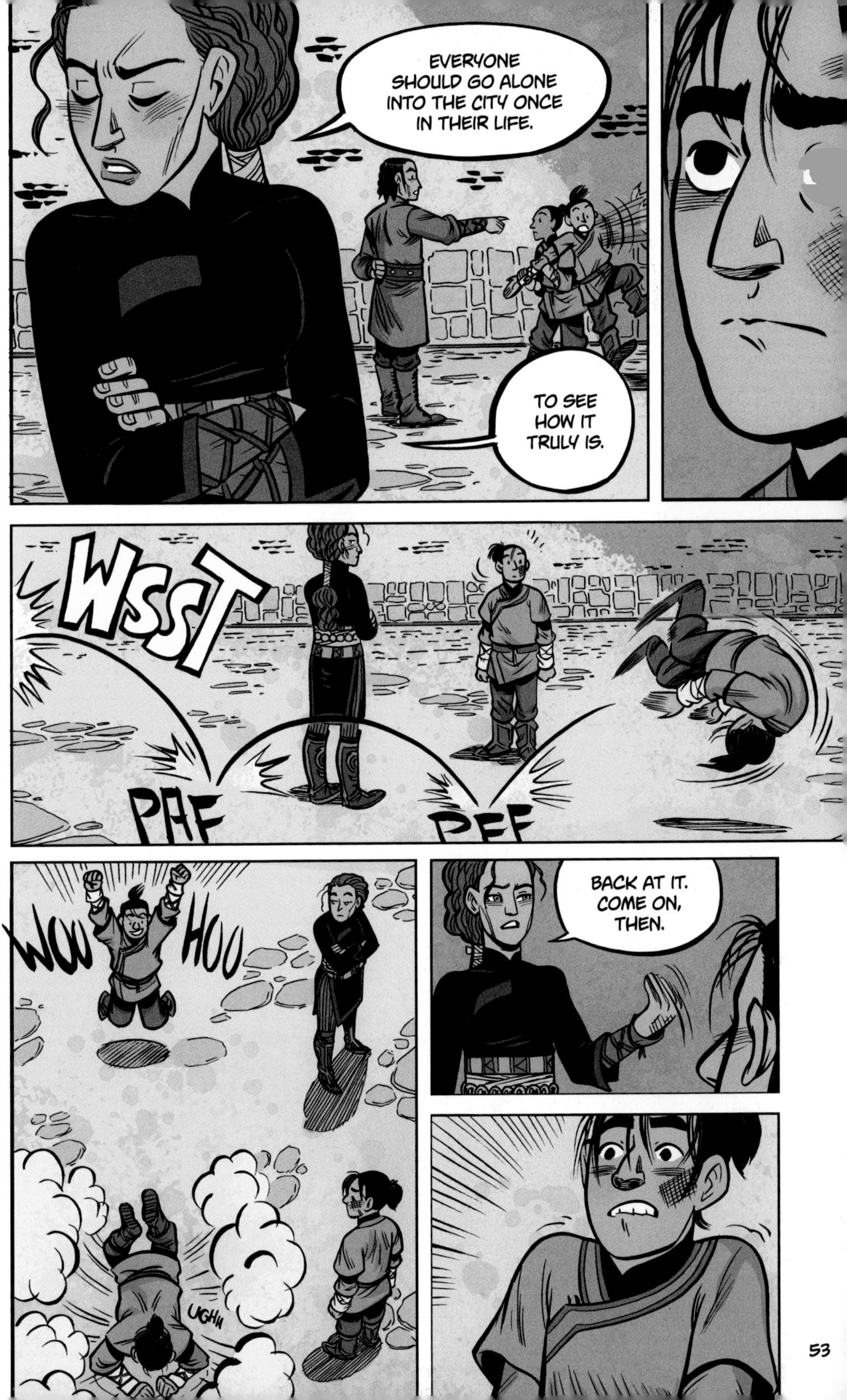
EVERYONE SHOULD GO ALONE INTO THE CITY ONCE IN THEIR LIFE.
TO SEE HOW IT TRULY IS.
WSST
PAF
PFF
WOO
HOO
BACK AT IT. COME ON, THEN.
UGH

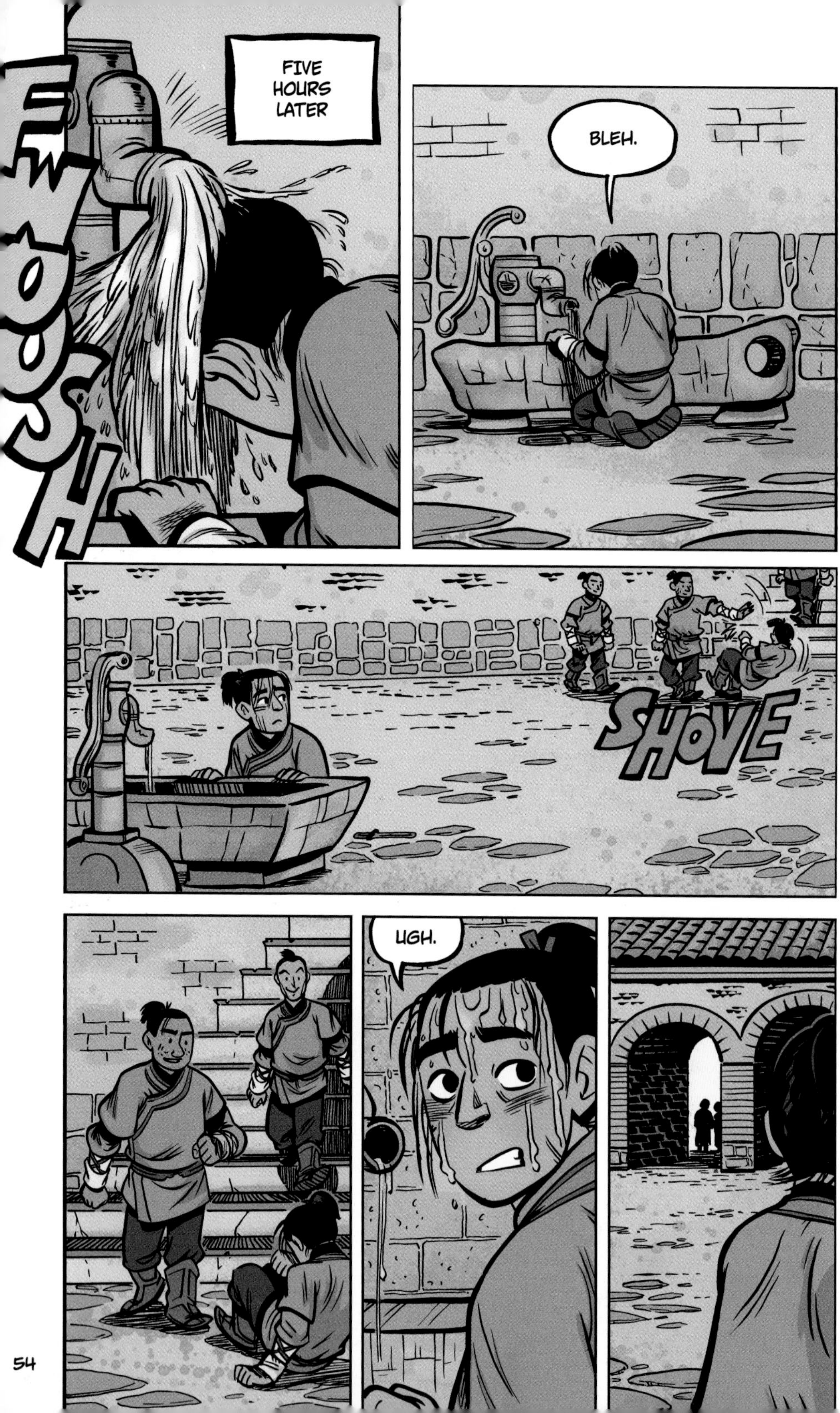
FIVE HOURS LATER
FWOOSH
BLEH.
SHOVE
UGH.

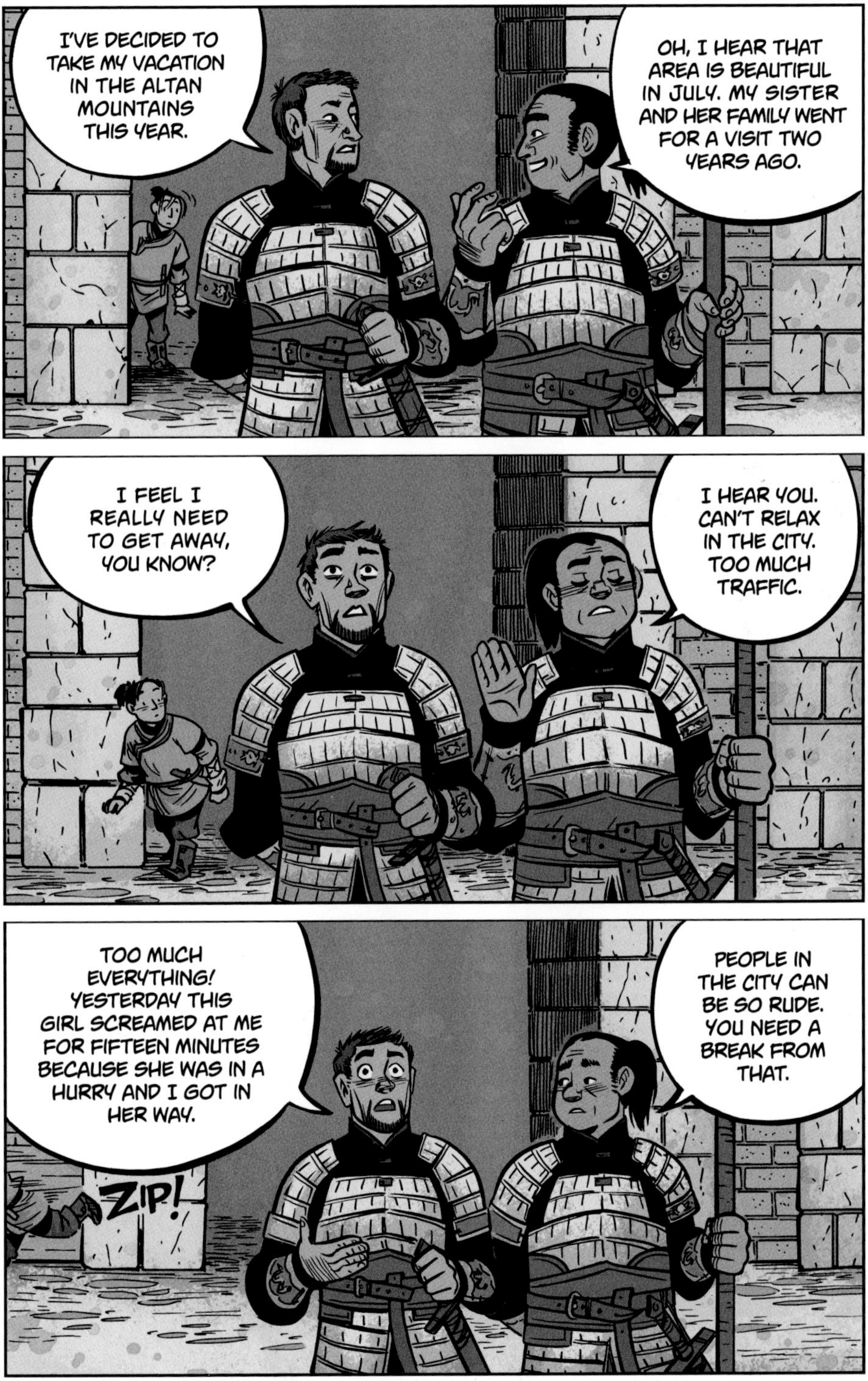
I'VE DECIDED TO TAKE MY VACATION IN THE ALTAN MOUNTAINS THIS YEAR.
OH, I HEAR THAT AREA IS BEAUTIFUL IN JULY. MY SISTER AND HER FAMILY WENT FOR A VISIT TWO YEARS AGO.
I FEEL I REALLY NEED TO GET AWAY, YOU KNOW?
I HEAR YOU. CAN'T RELAX IN THE CITY. TOO MUCH TRAFFIC.
TOO MUCH EVERYTHING! YESTERDAY THIS GIRL SCREAMED AT ME FOR FIFTEEN MINUTES BECAUSE SHE WAS IN A HURRY AND I GOT IN HER WAY.
PEOPLE IN THE CITY CAN BE SO RUDE. YOU NEED A BREAK FROM THAT.
ZIP!

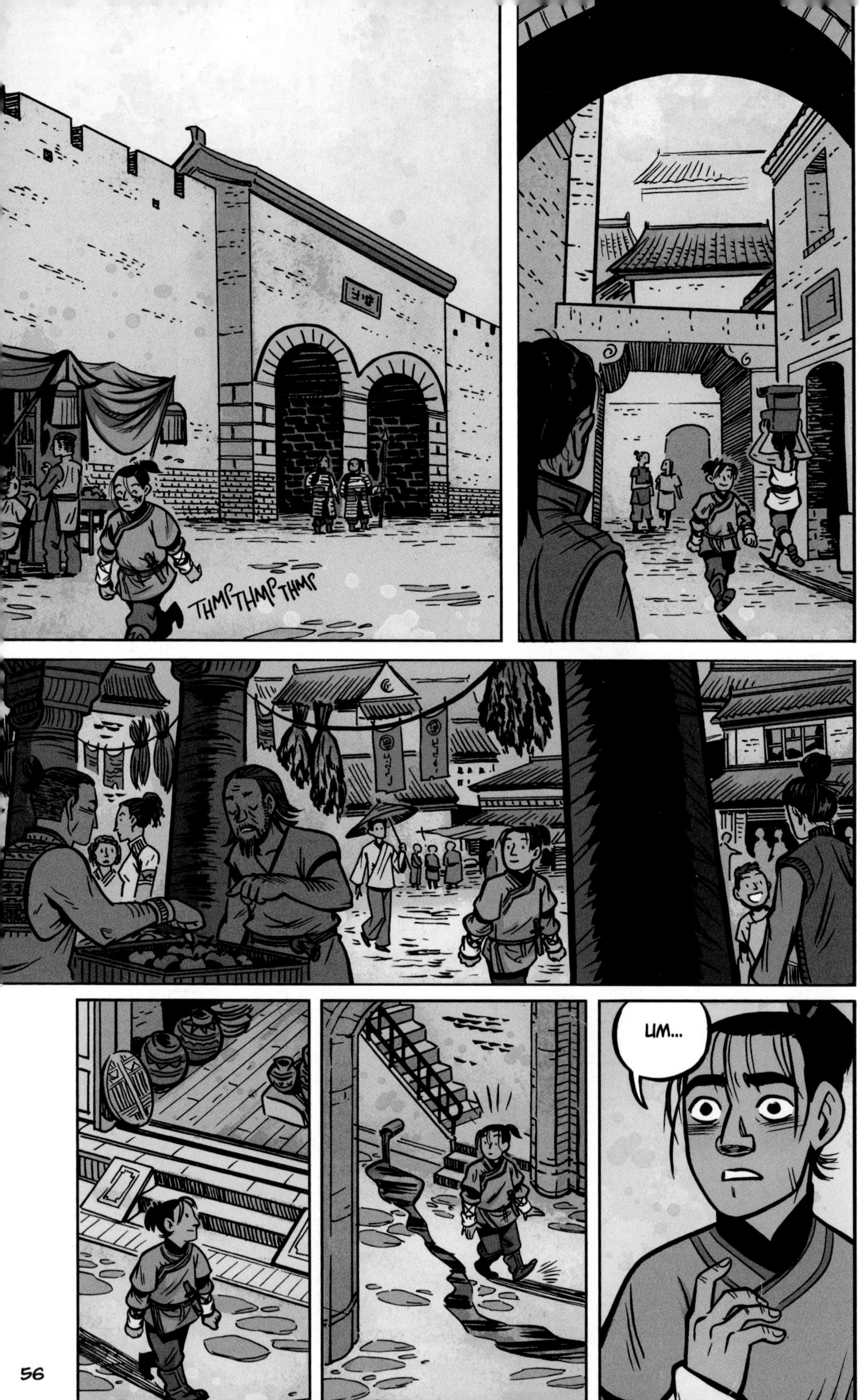
THMP THMP THMP
UM...

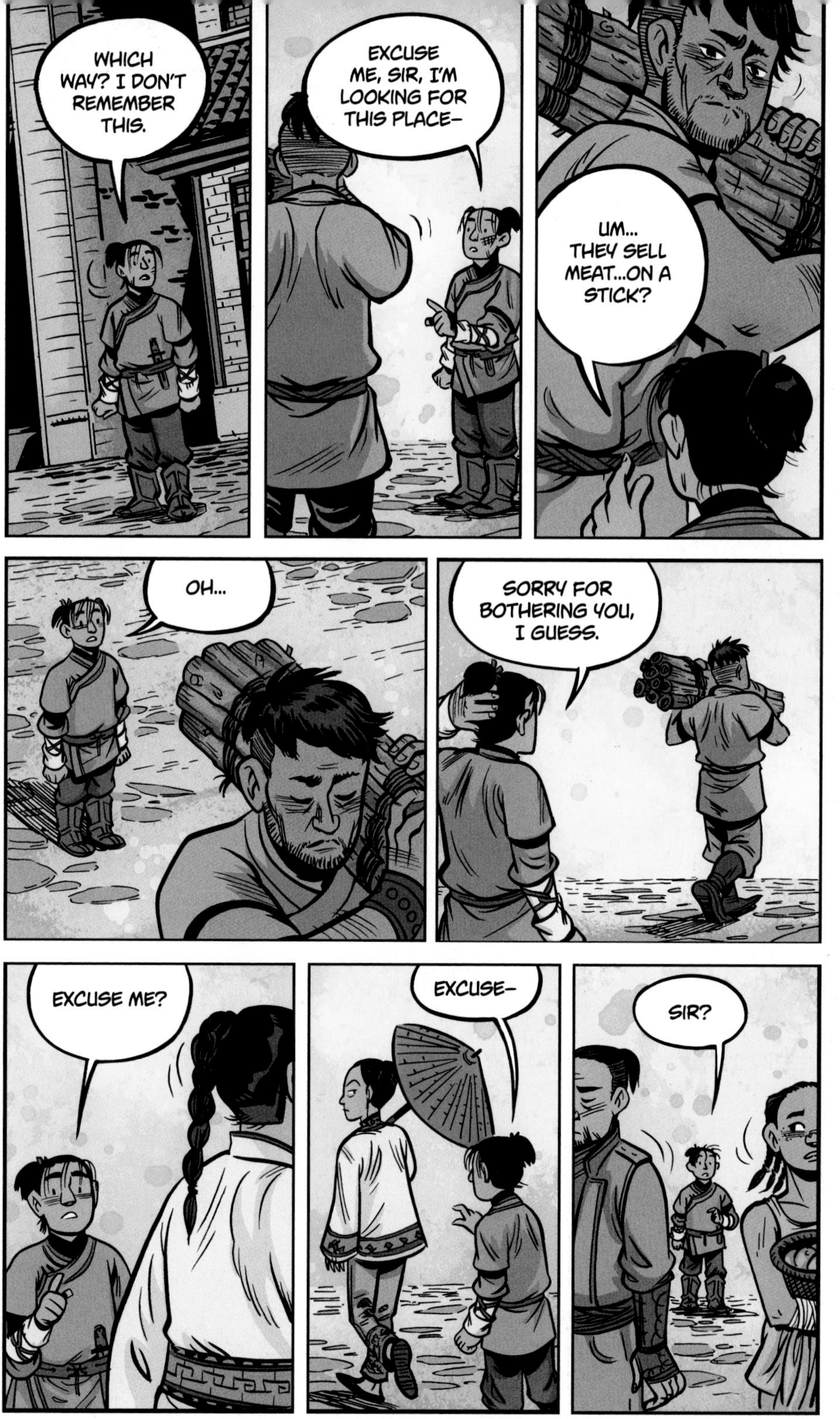

WHICH WAY? I DON'T REMEMBER THIS.
EXCUSE ME, SIR, I'M LOOKING FOR THIS PLACE–
UM... THEY SELL MEAT...ON A STICK?
OH...
SORRY FOR BOTHERING YOU, I GUESS.
EXCUSE ME?
EXCUSE–
SIR?

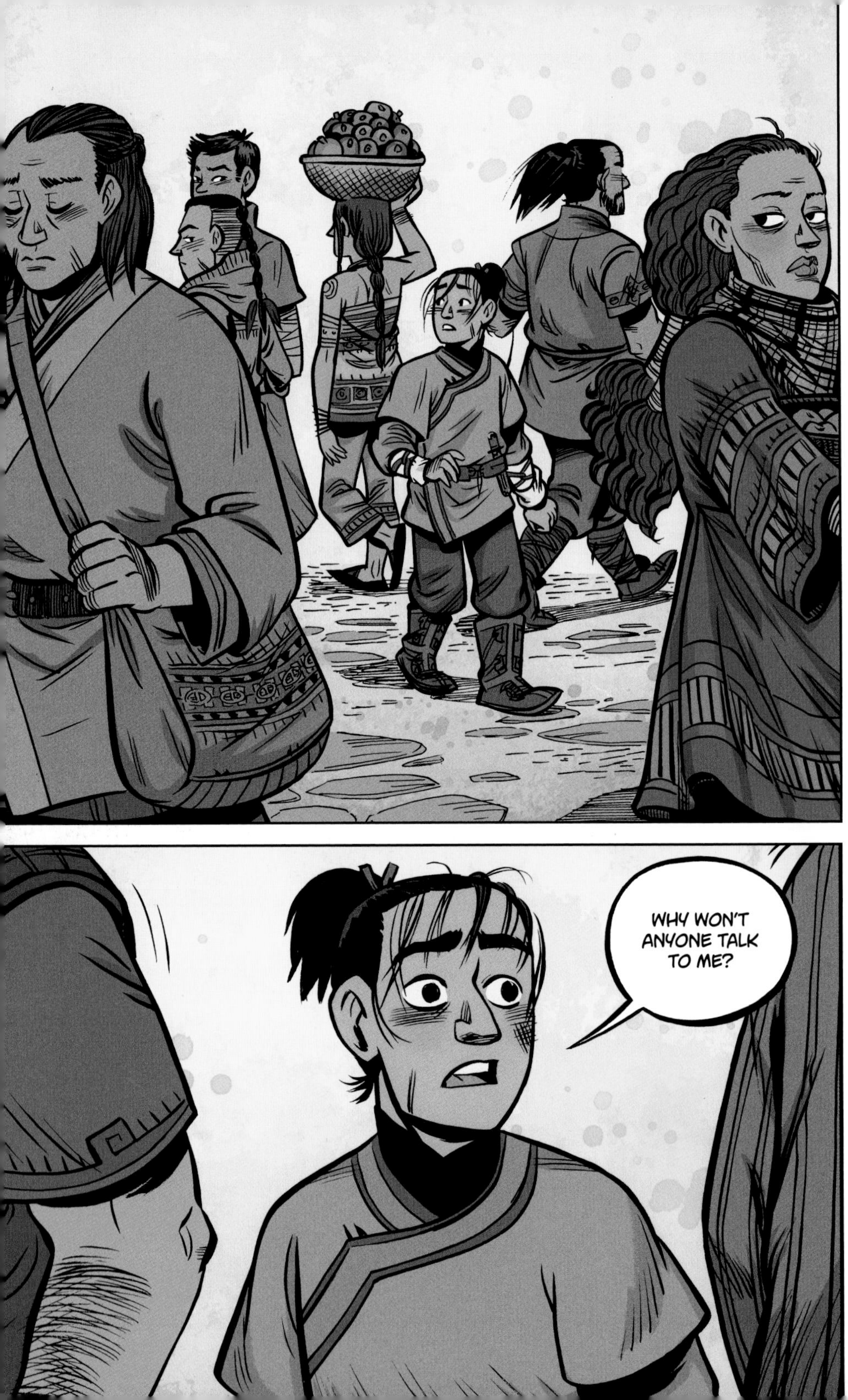
WHY WON'T ANYONE TALK TO ME?

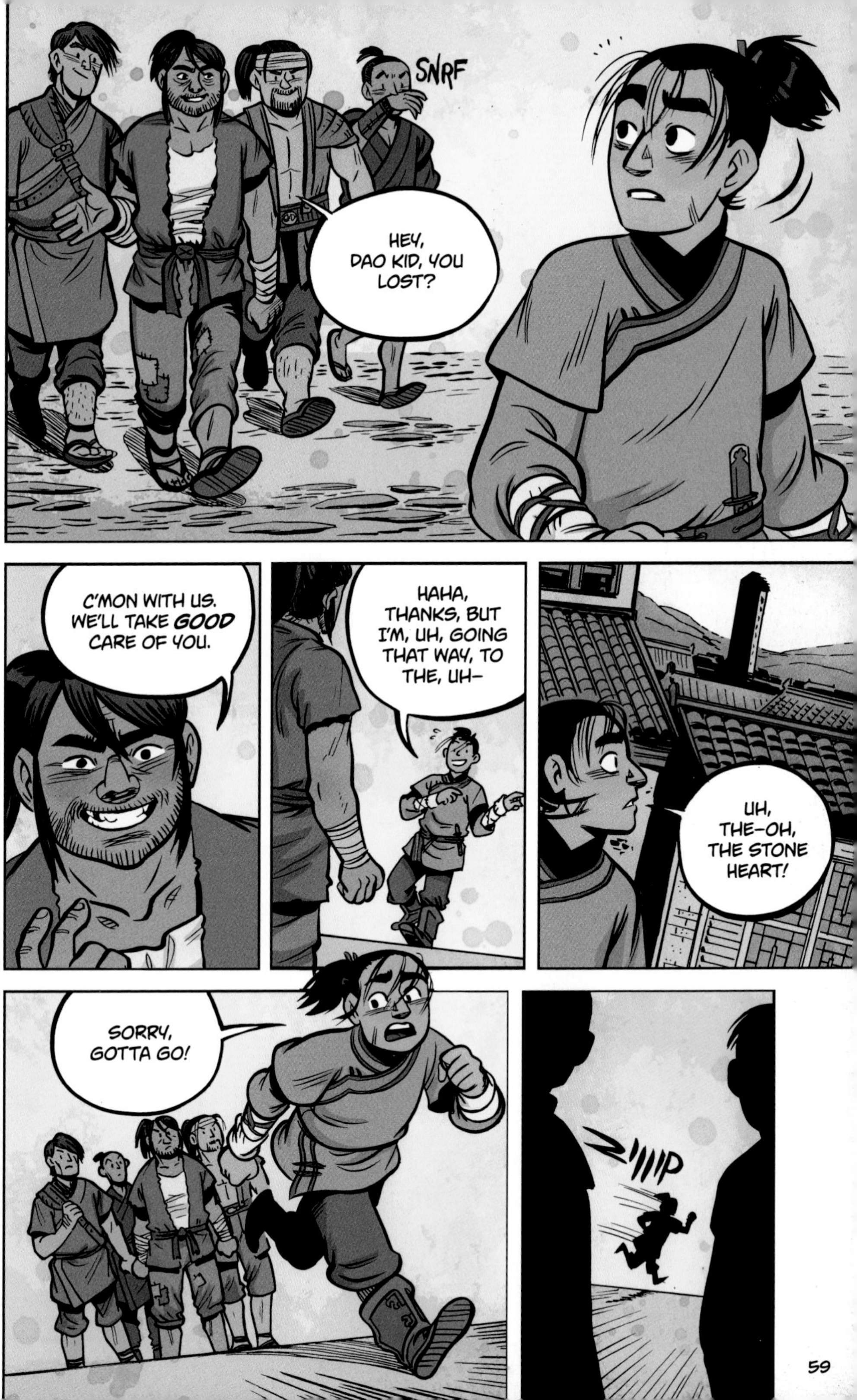
SNRF
HEY, DAO KID, YOU LOST?
C'MON WITH US. WE'LL TAKE GOOD CARE OF YOU.
HAHA, THANKS, BUT I'M, UH, GOING THAT WAY, TO THE, UH–
UH, THE–OH, THE STONE HEART!
SORRY, GOTTA GO!
ZIIIIP

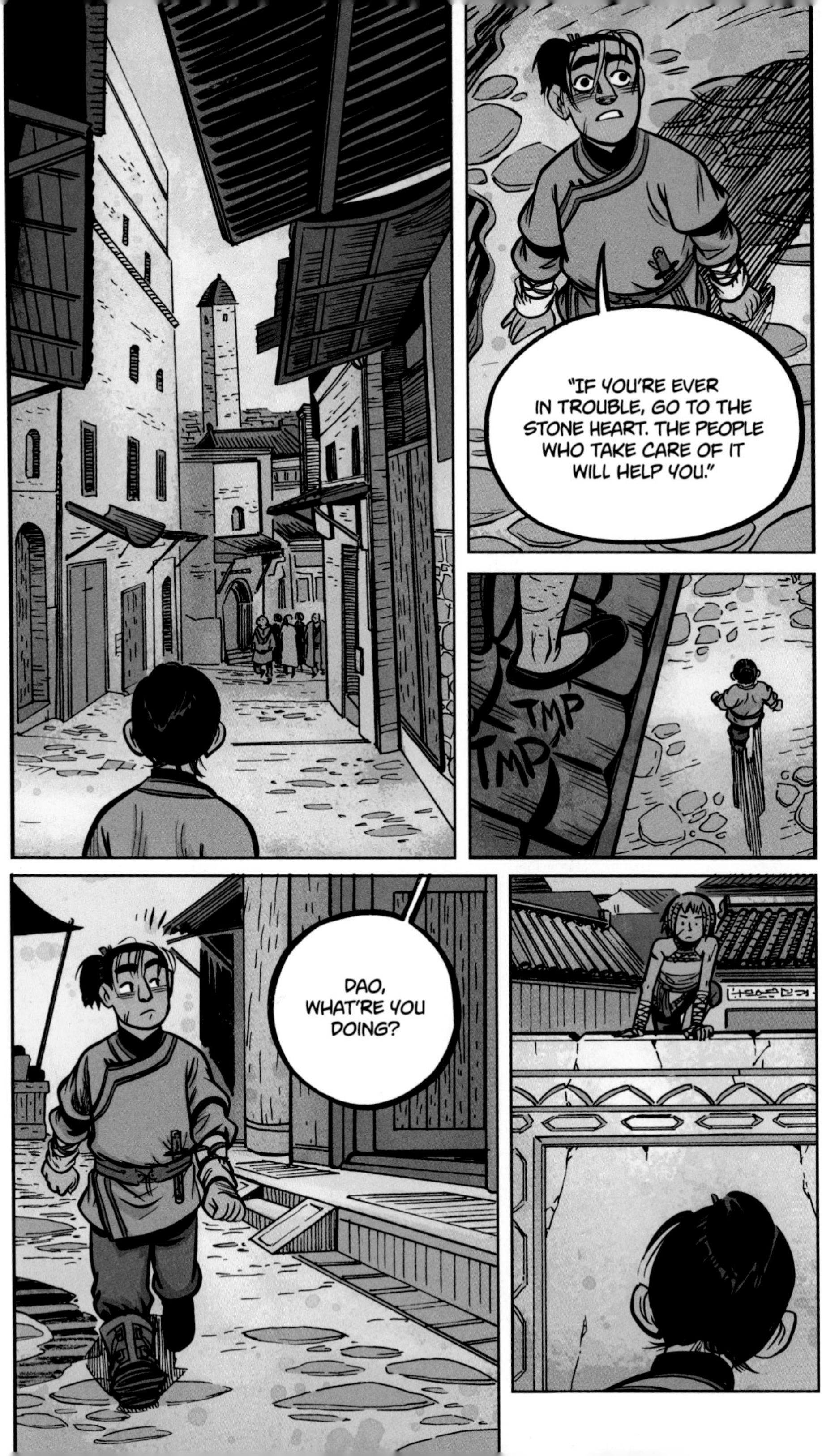

"IF YOU'RE EVER IN TROUBLE, GO TO THE STONE HEART. THE PEOPLE WHO TAKE CARE OF IT WILL HELP YOU."
TMP
TMP
DAO, WHAT'RE YOU DOING?

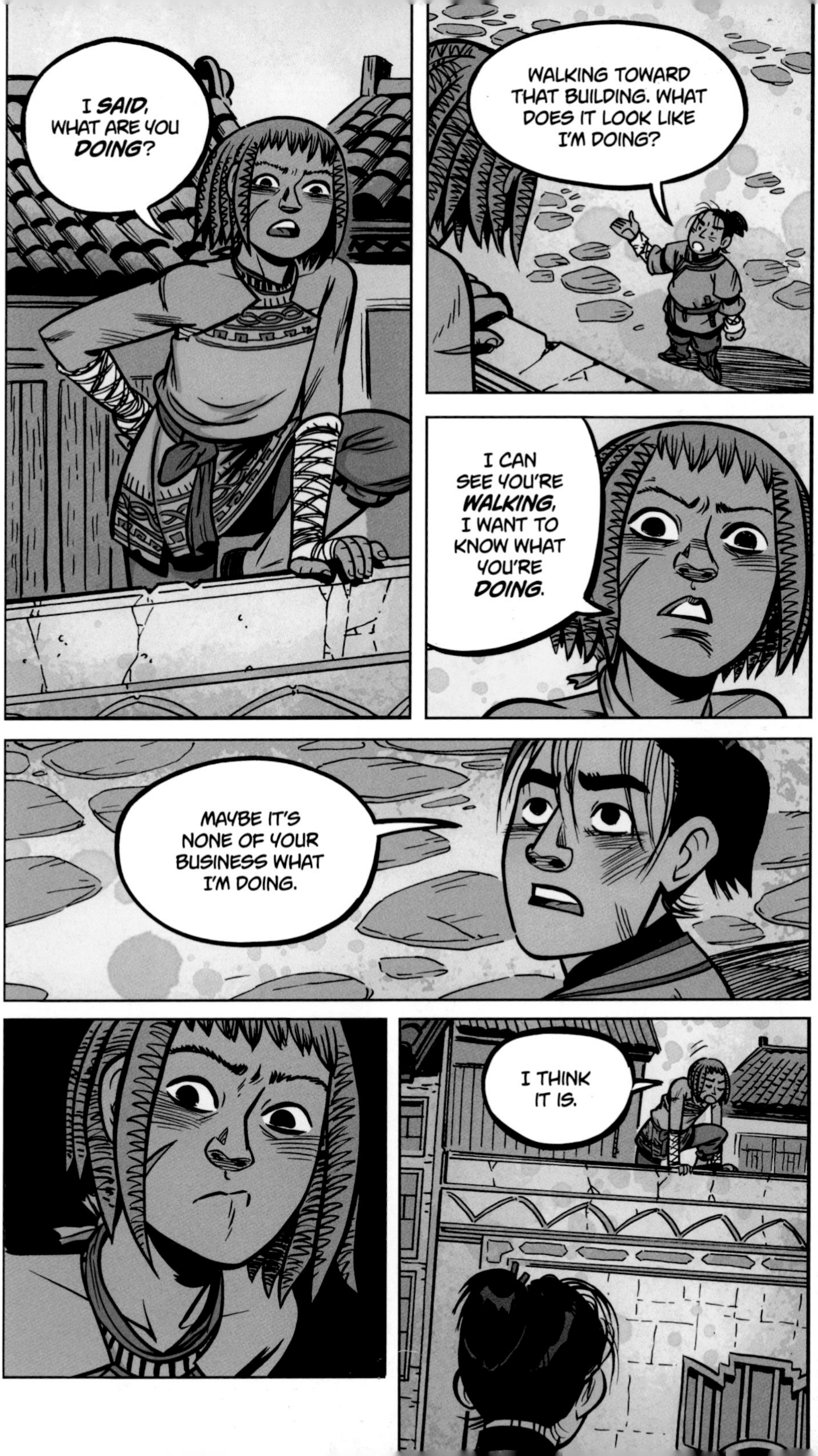

I *SAID*, WHAT ARE YOU *DOING*?
WALKING TOWARD THAT BUILDING. WHAT DOES IT LOOK LIKE I'M DOING?
I CAN SEE YOU'RE *WALKING*, I WANT TO KNOW WHAT YOU'RE *DOING*.
MAYBE IT'S NONE OF YOUR BUSINESS WHAT I'M DOING.
I THINK IT IS.

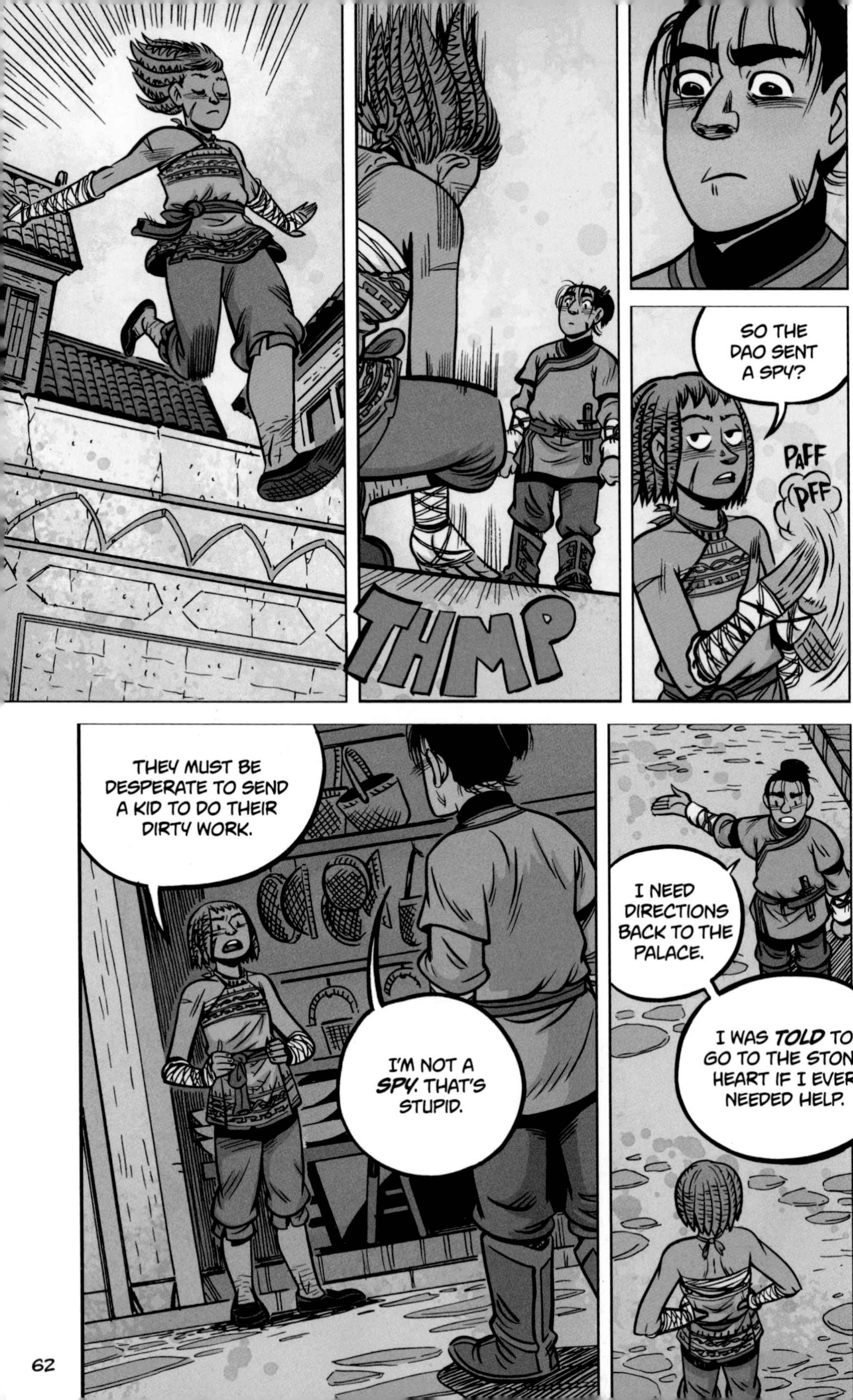
THMP
SO THE DAO SENT A SPY?
PAFF
PFF
THEY MUST BE DESPERATE TO SEND A KID TO DO THEIR DIRTY WORK.
I'M NOT A *SPY*. THAT'S STUPID.
I NEED DIRECTIONS BACK TO THE PALACE.
I WAS ***TOLD*** TO GO TO THE STONE HEART IF I EVER NEEDED HELP.

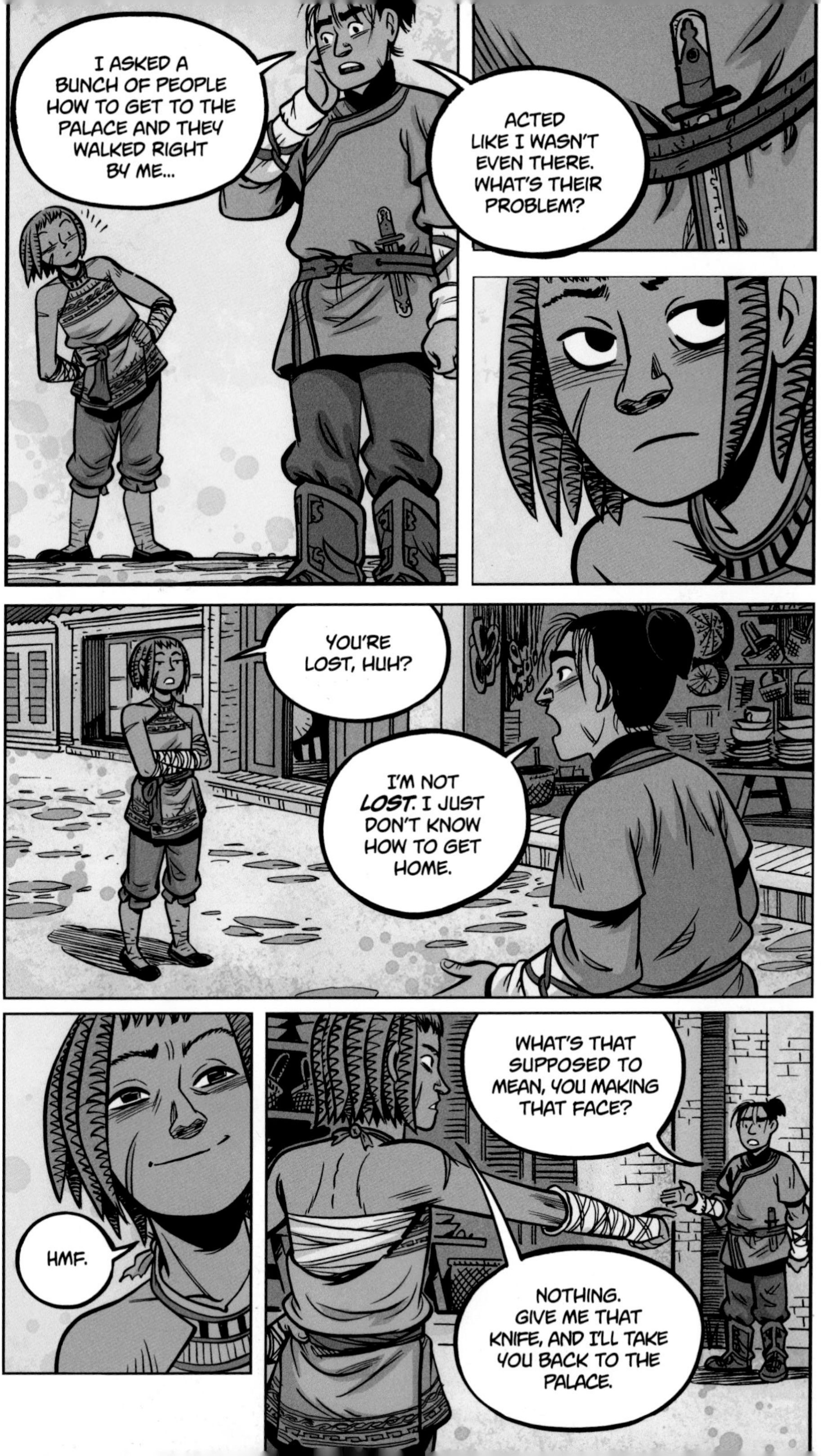
I ASKED A BUNCH OF PEOPLE HOW TO GET TO THE PALACE AND THEY WALKED RIGHT BY ME...
ACTED LIKE I WASN'T EVEN THERE. WHAT'S THEIR PROBLEM?
YOU'RE LOST, HUH?
I'M NOT *LOST*. I JUST DON'T KNOW HOW TO GET HOME.
HMF.
WHAT'S THAT SUPPOSED TO MEAN, YOU MAKING THAT FACE?
NOTHING. GIVE ME THAT KNIFE, AND I'LL TAKE YOU BACK TO THE PALACE.

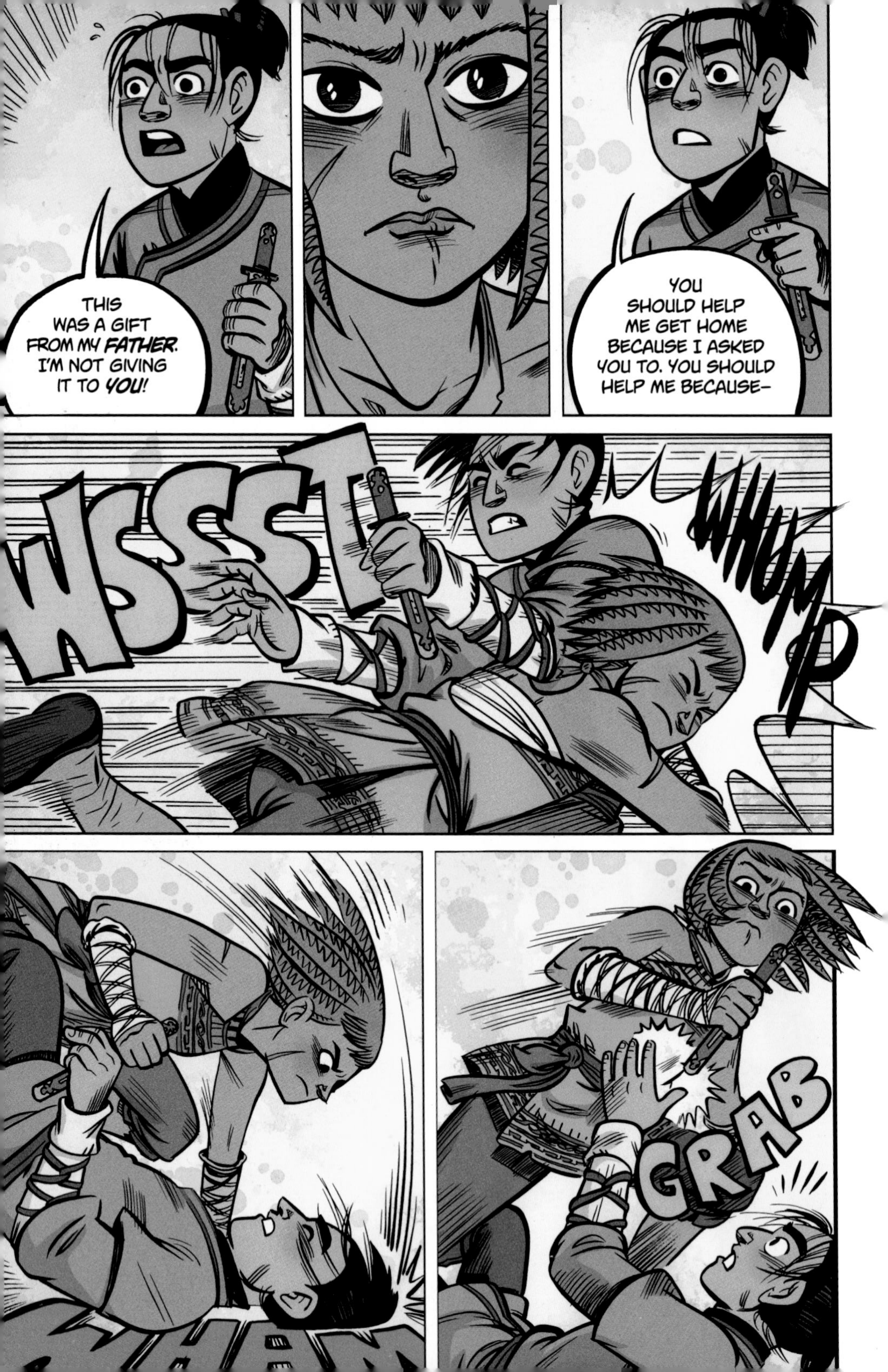
THIS WAS A GIFT FROM MY *FATHER*. I'M NOT GIVING IT TO *YOU*!
YOU SHOULD HELP ME GET HOME BECAUSE I ASKED YOU TO. YOU SHOULD HELP ME BECAUSE–
WSSST
WHUMP
GRAB

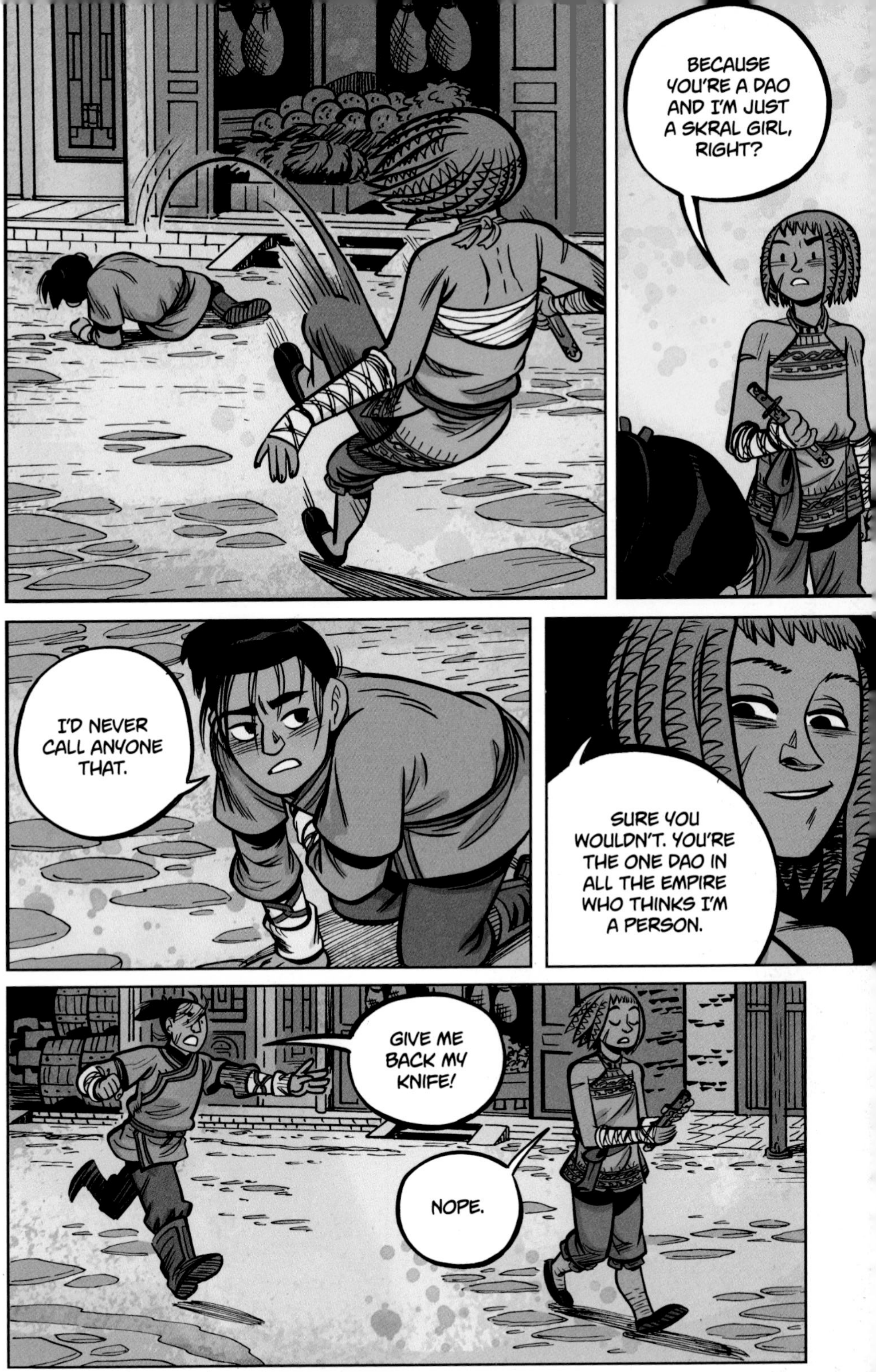
BECAUSE YOU'RE A DAO AND I'M JUST A SKRAL GIRL, RIGHT?
I'D NEVER CALL ANYONE THAT.
SURE YOU WOULDN'T. YOU'RE THE ONE DAO IN ALL THE EMPIRE WHO THINKS I'M A PERSON.
GIVE ME BACK MY KNIFE!
NOPE.

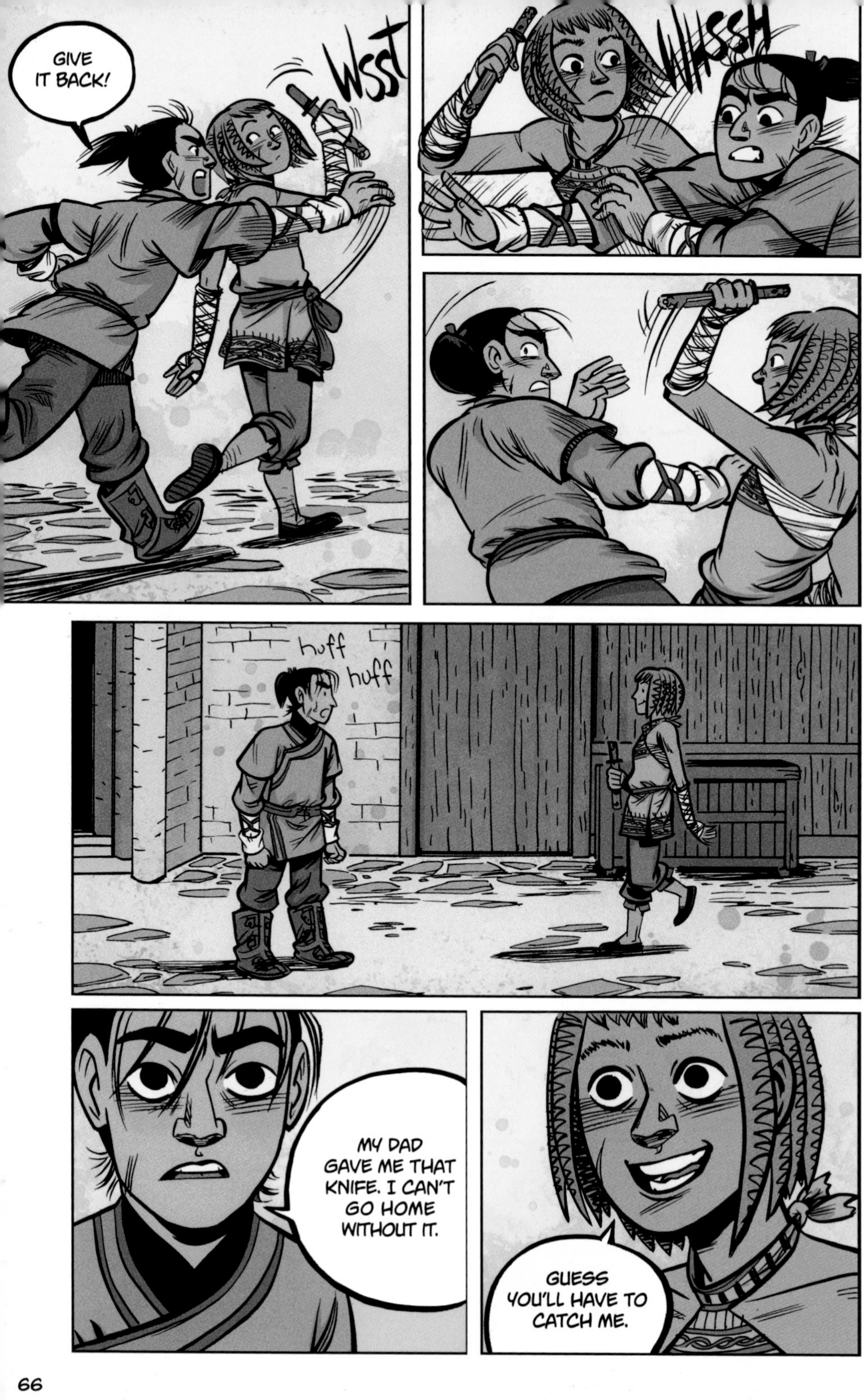
GIVE IT BACK!
WSST
WHSSH
huff
huff
MY DAD GAVE ME THAT KNIFE. I CAN'T GO HOME WITHOUT IT.
GUESS YOU'LL HAVE TO CATCH ME.

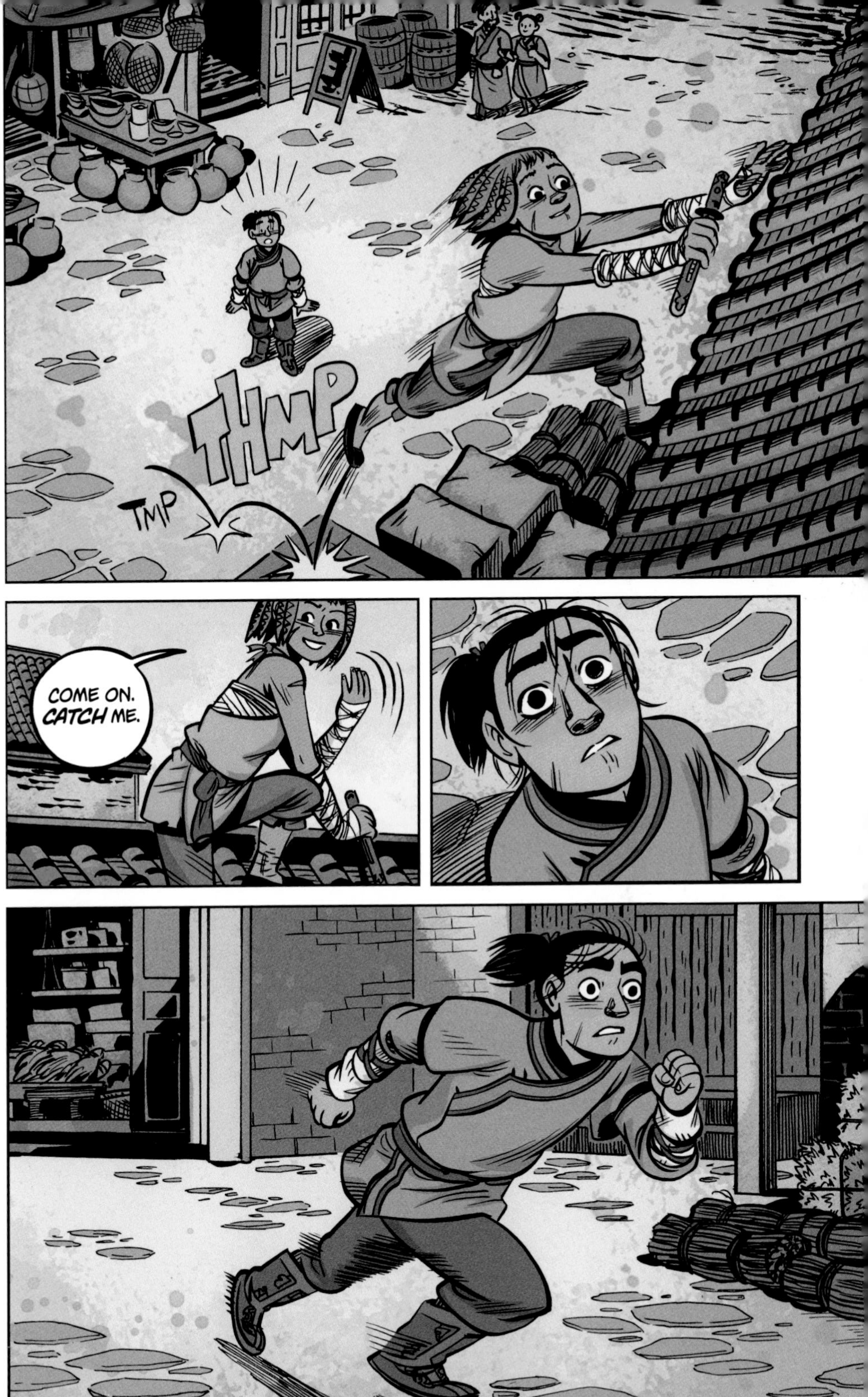
THMP
TMP
COME ON. CATCH ME.

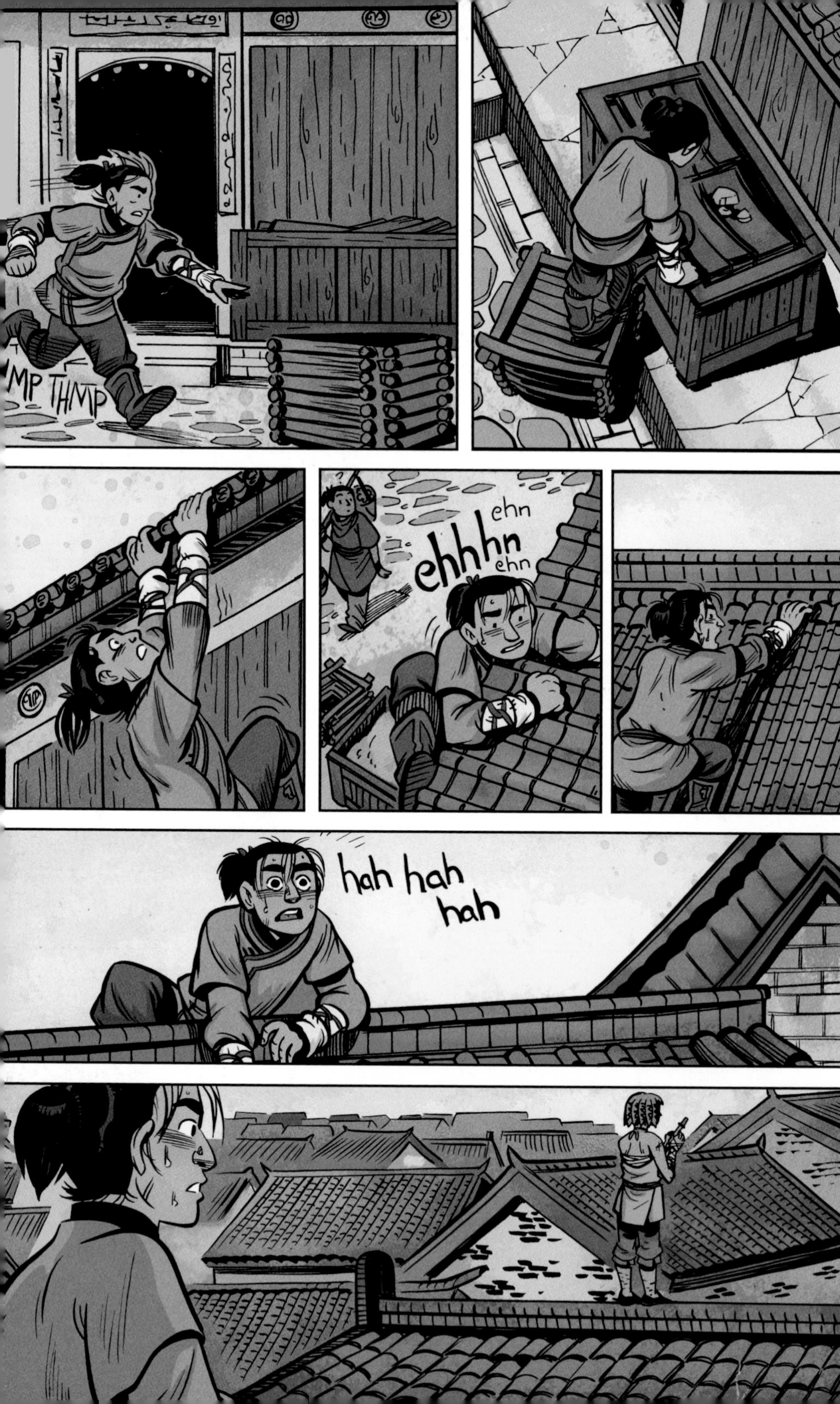
MP THMP
?
ehhhn
ehn
ehn
hah hah
hah

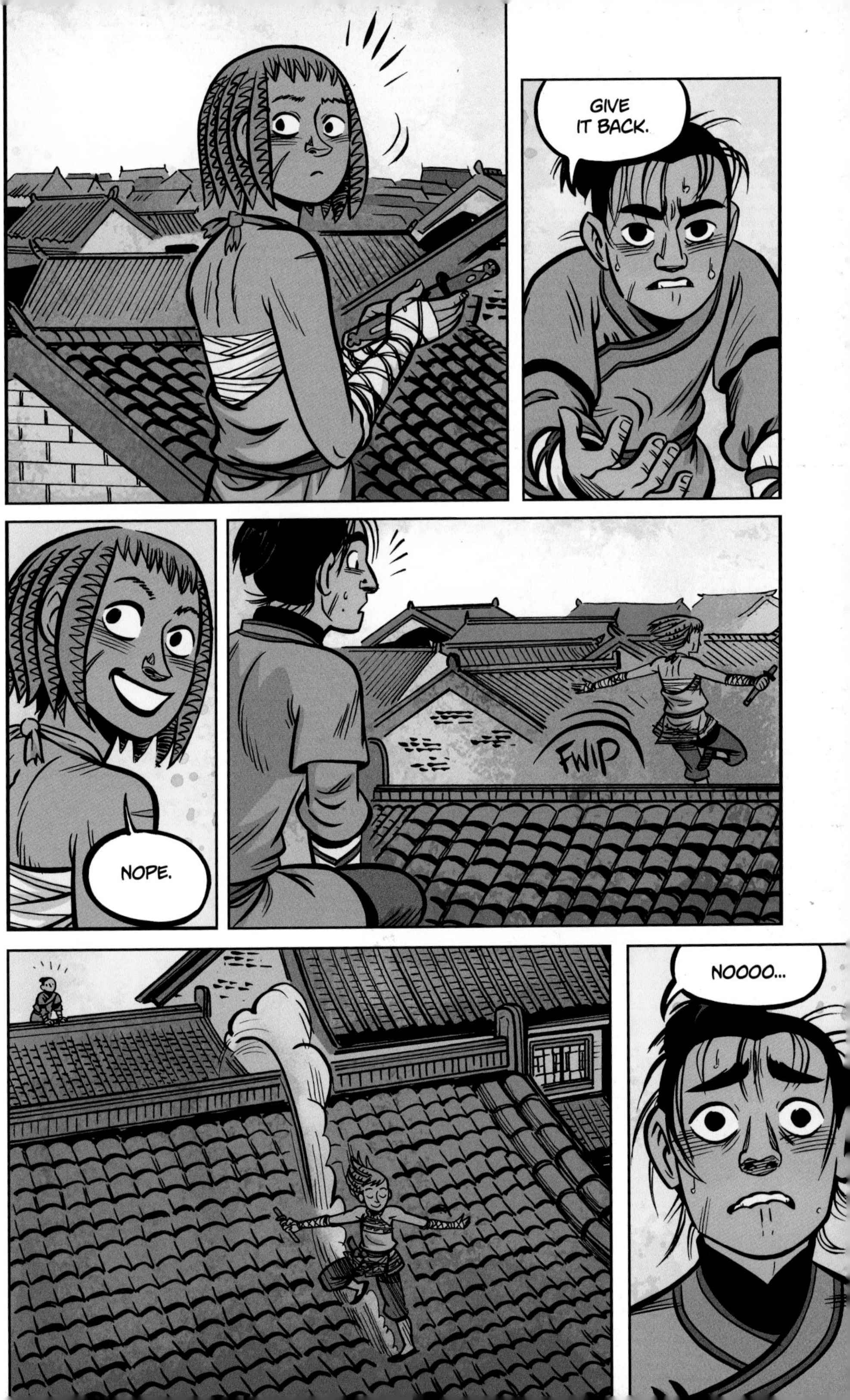
GIVE IT BACK.
NOPE.
FWIP
NOOOO...

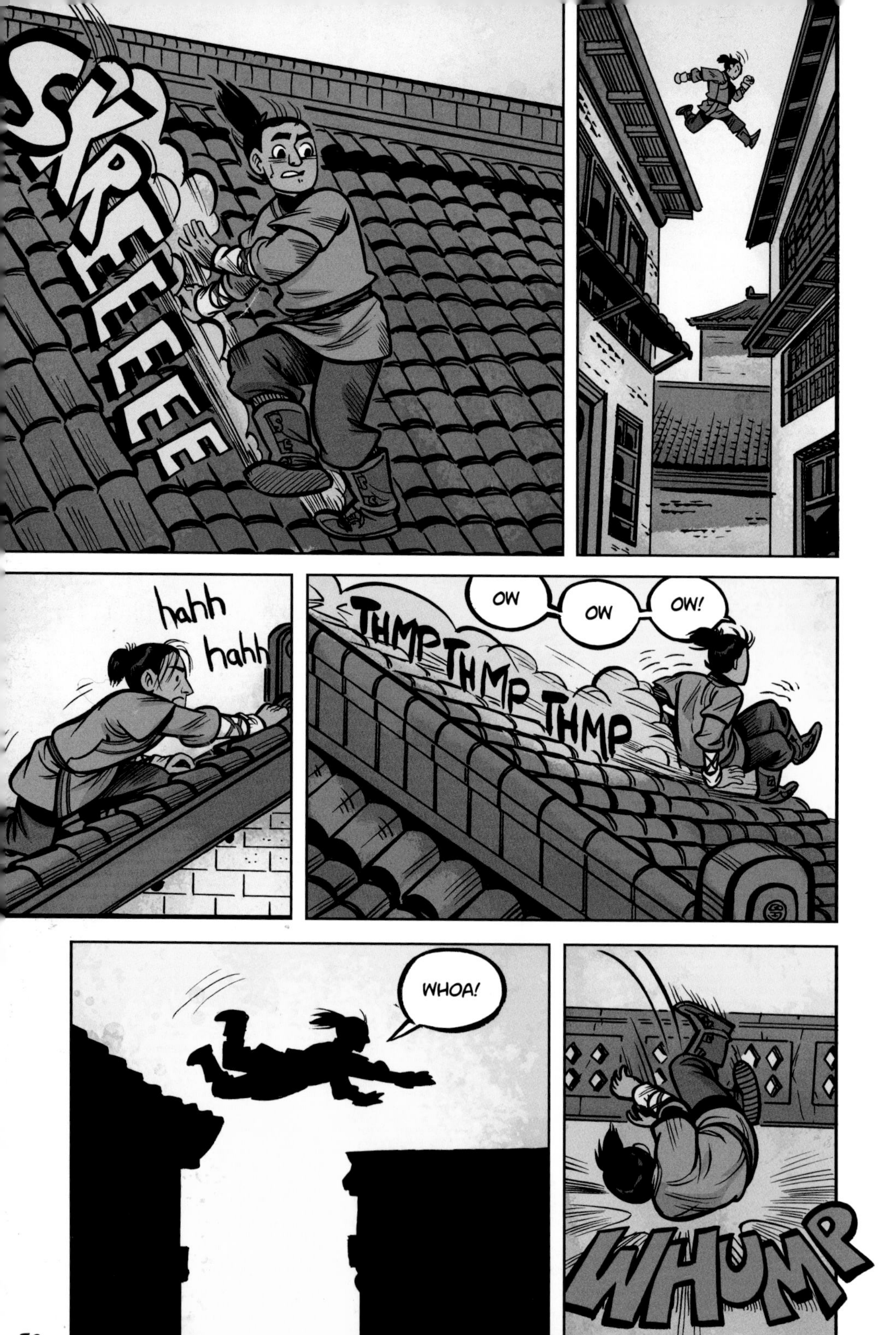
SKREEEEEE
hahh
hahh
THMP THMP THMP
OW
OW
OW!
WHOA!
WHUMP

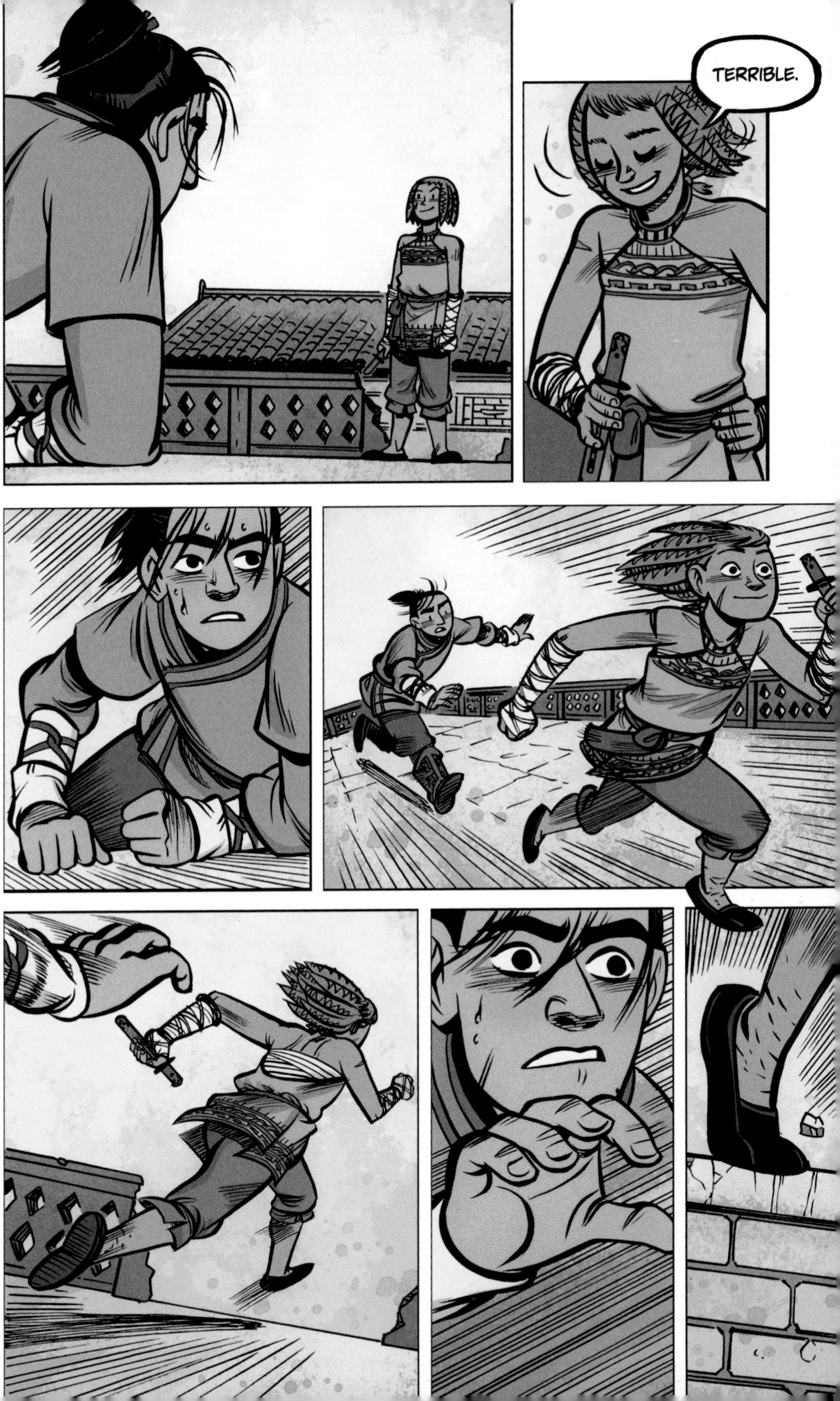
TERRIBLE.

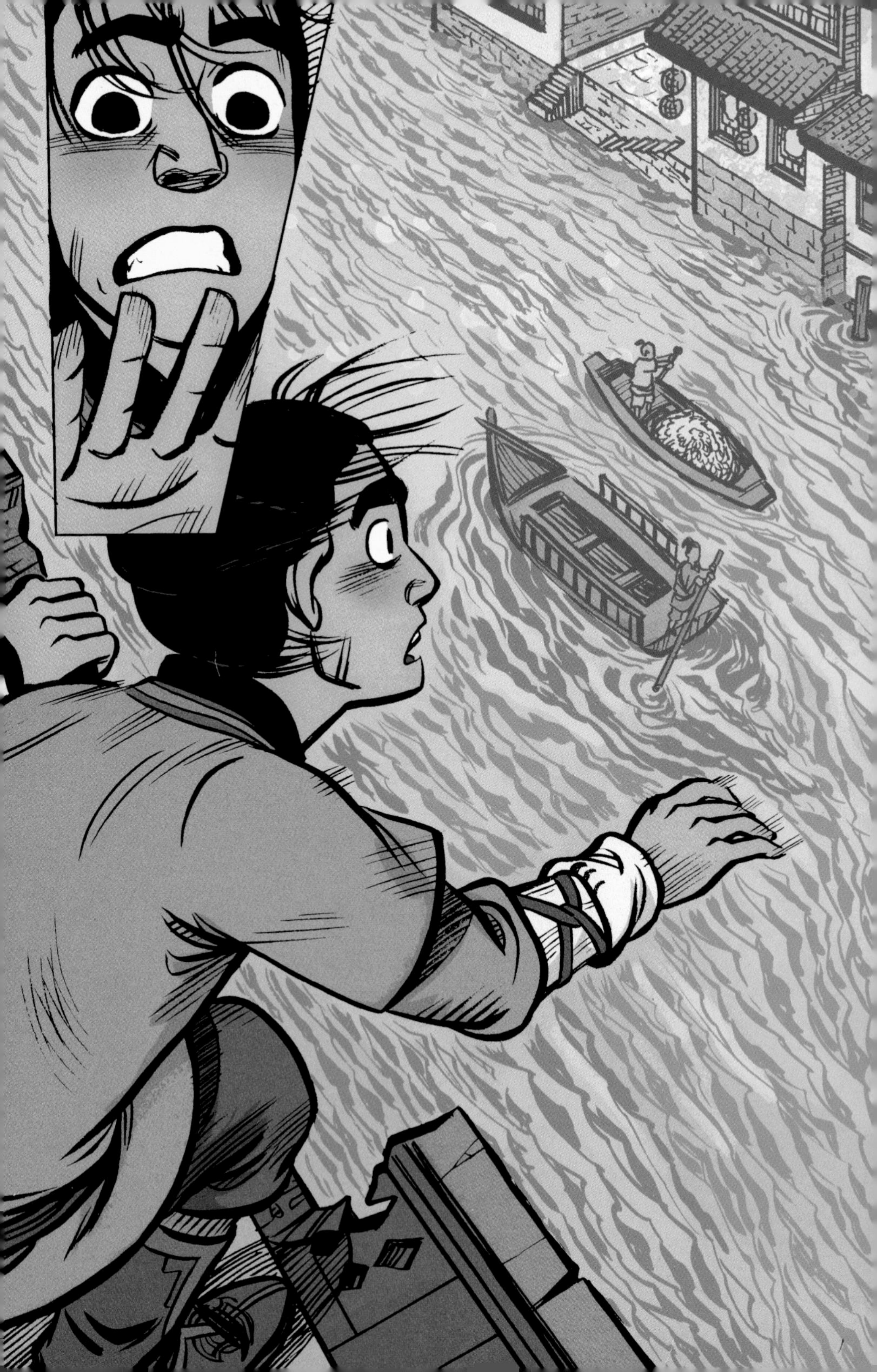

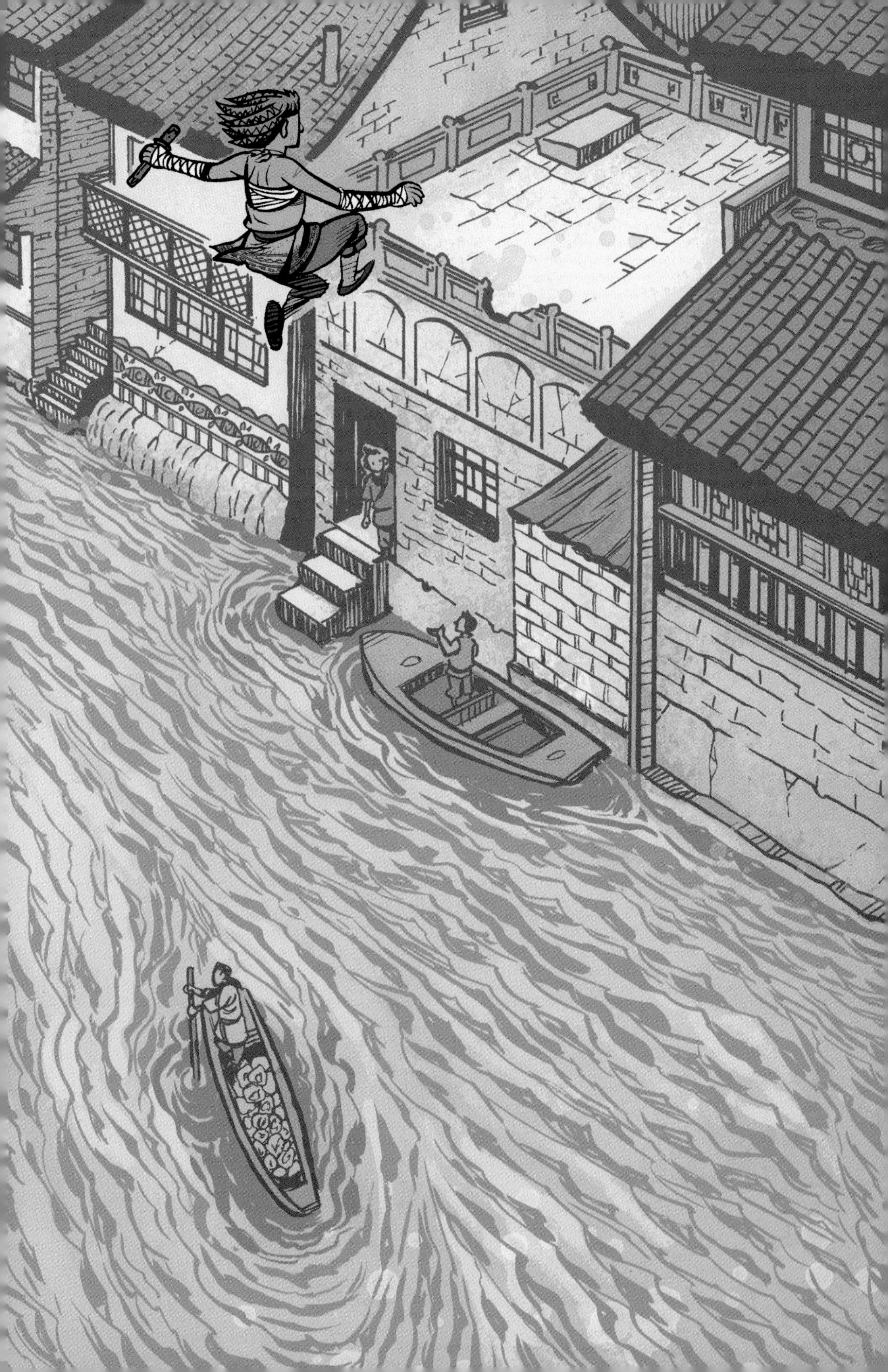

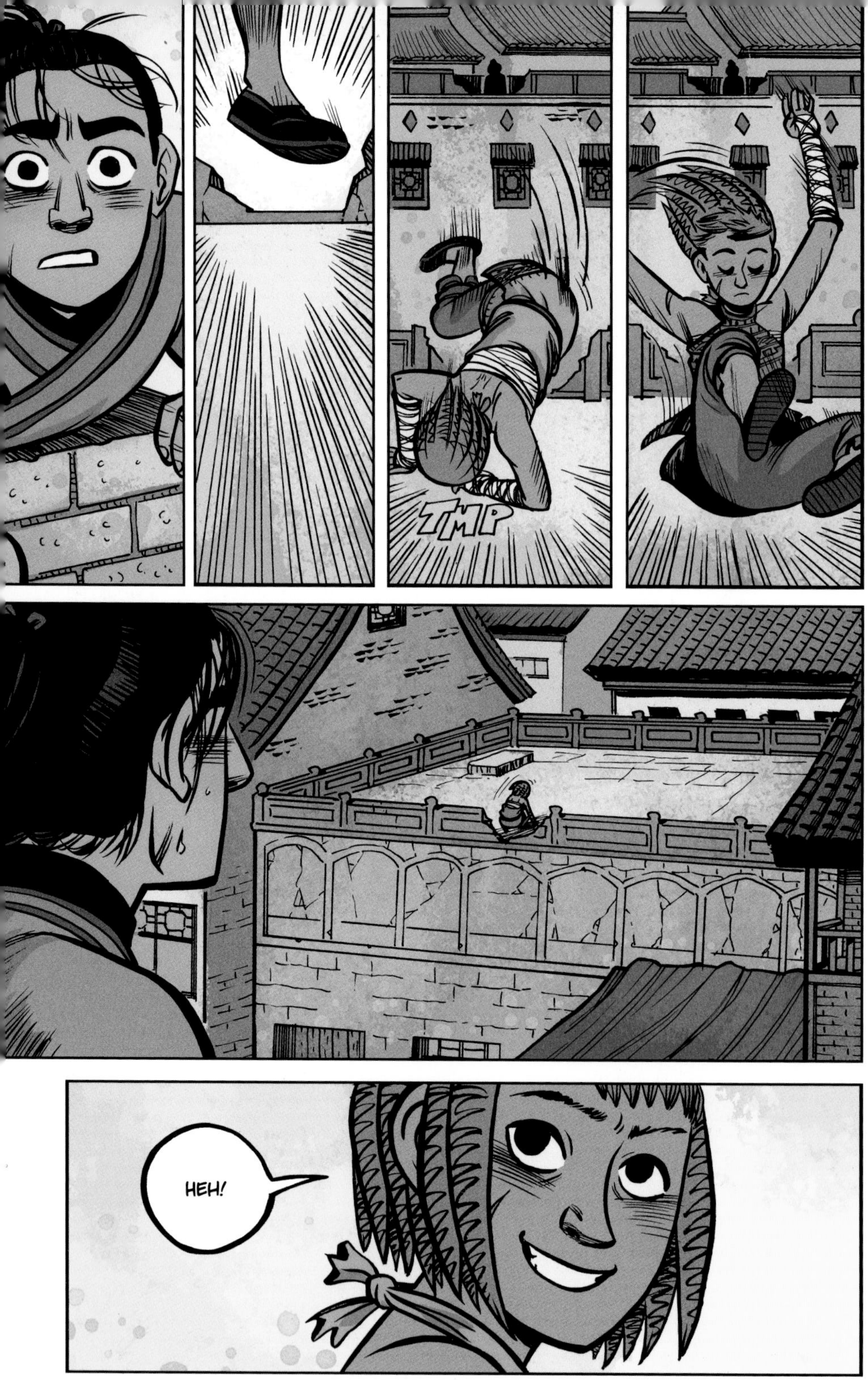
TMP
HEH!

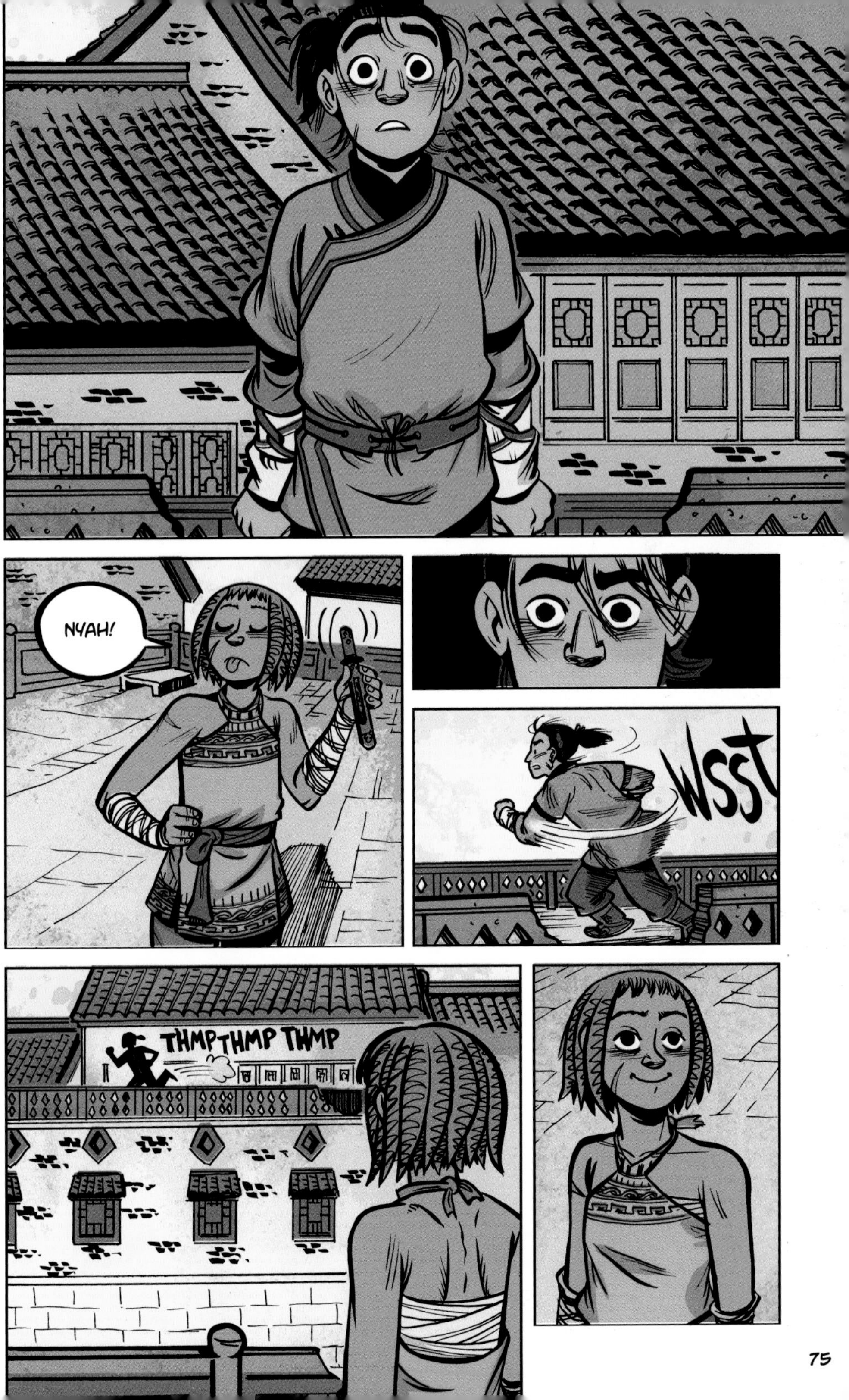
NYAH!
WSST
THMP THMP THMP

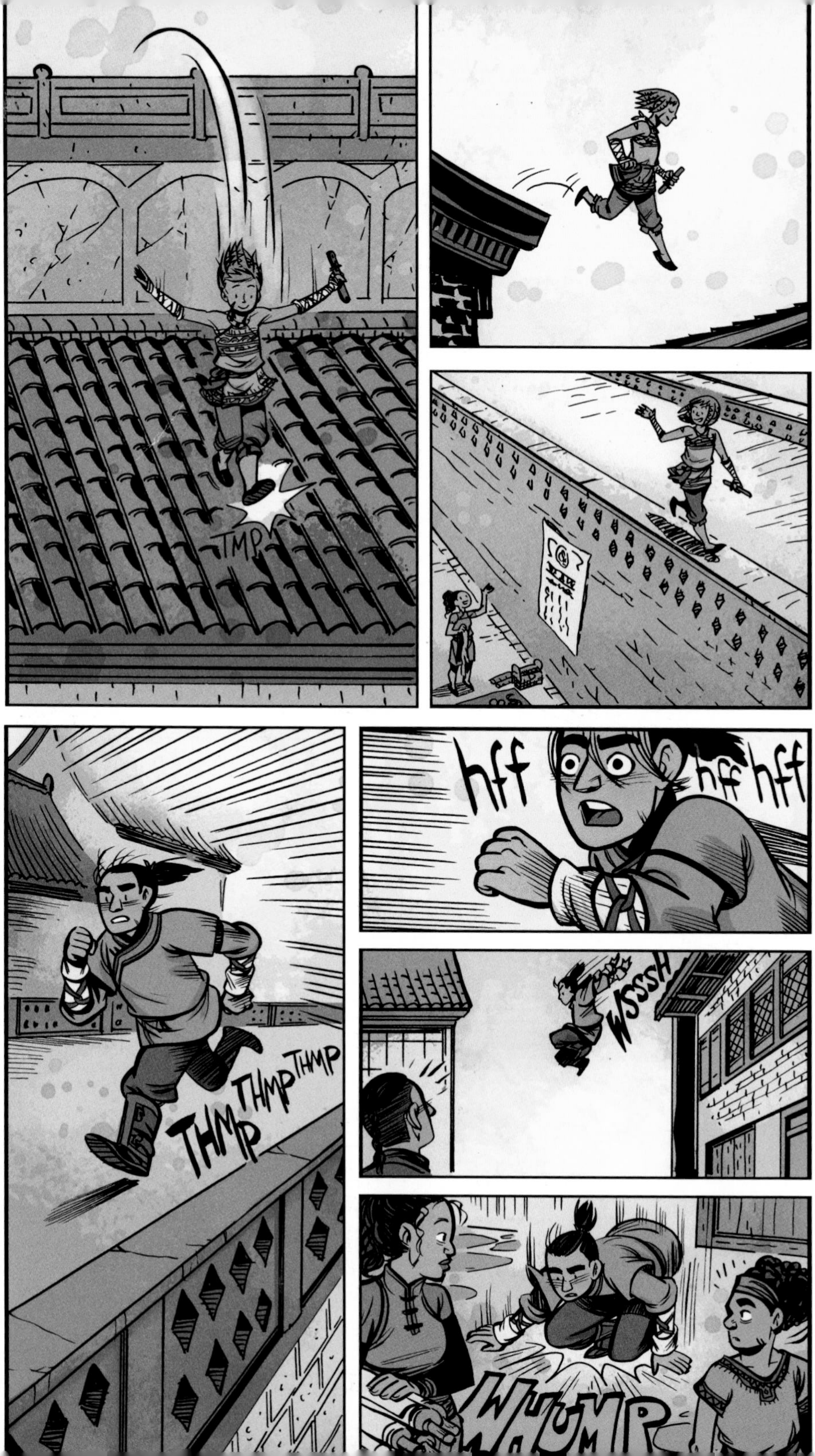
TMP
hff
hff hff
THMP THMP THMP
WSSSH
WHUMP

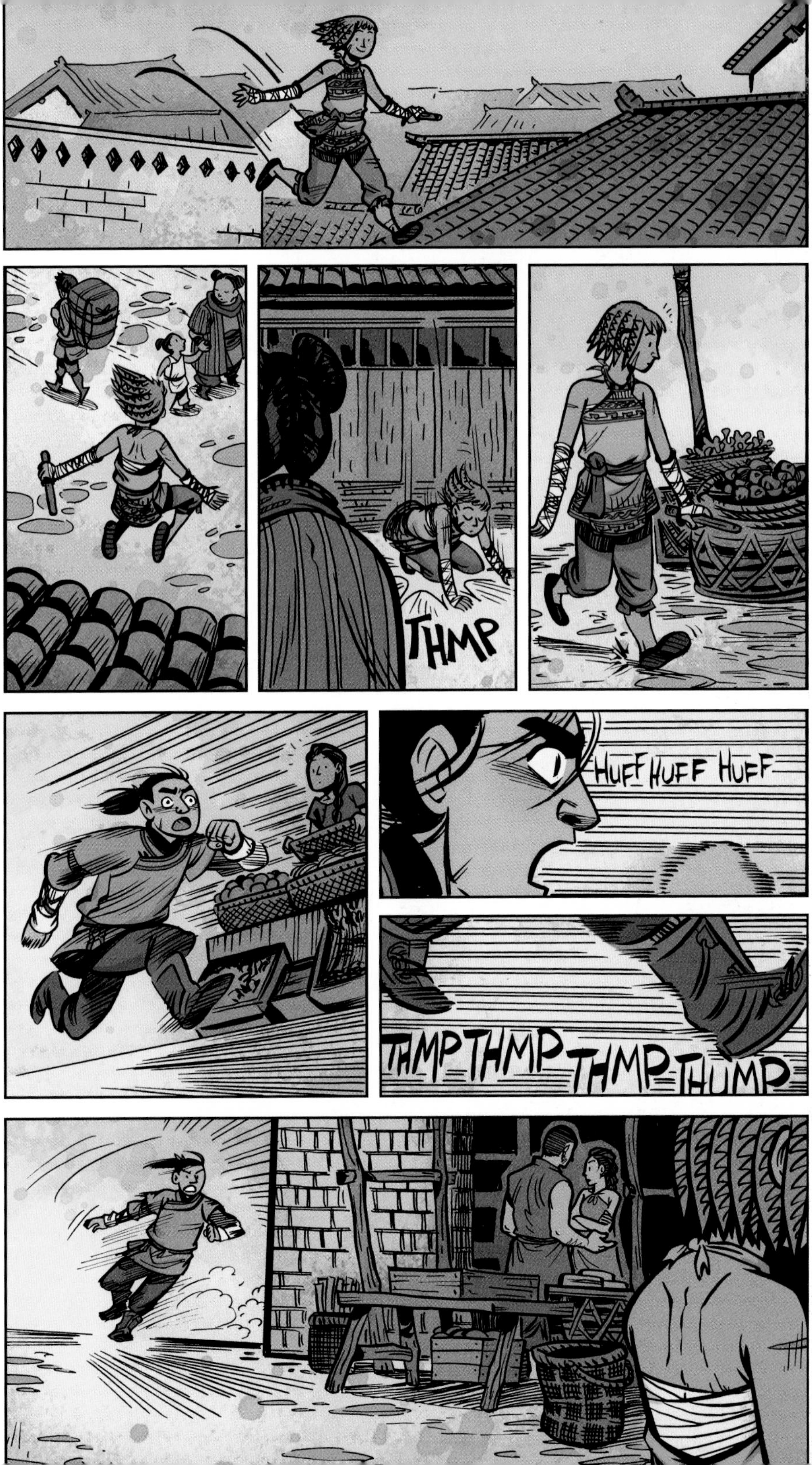
THMP
HUFF HUFF HUFF
THMP THMP THMP THUMP

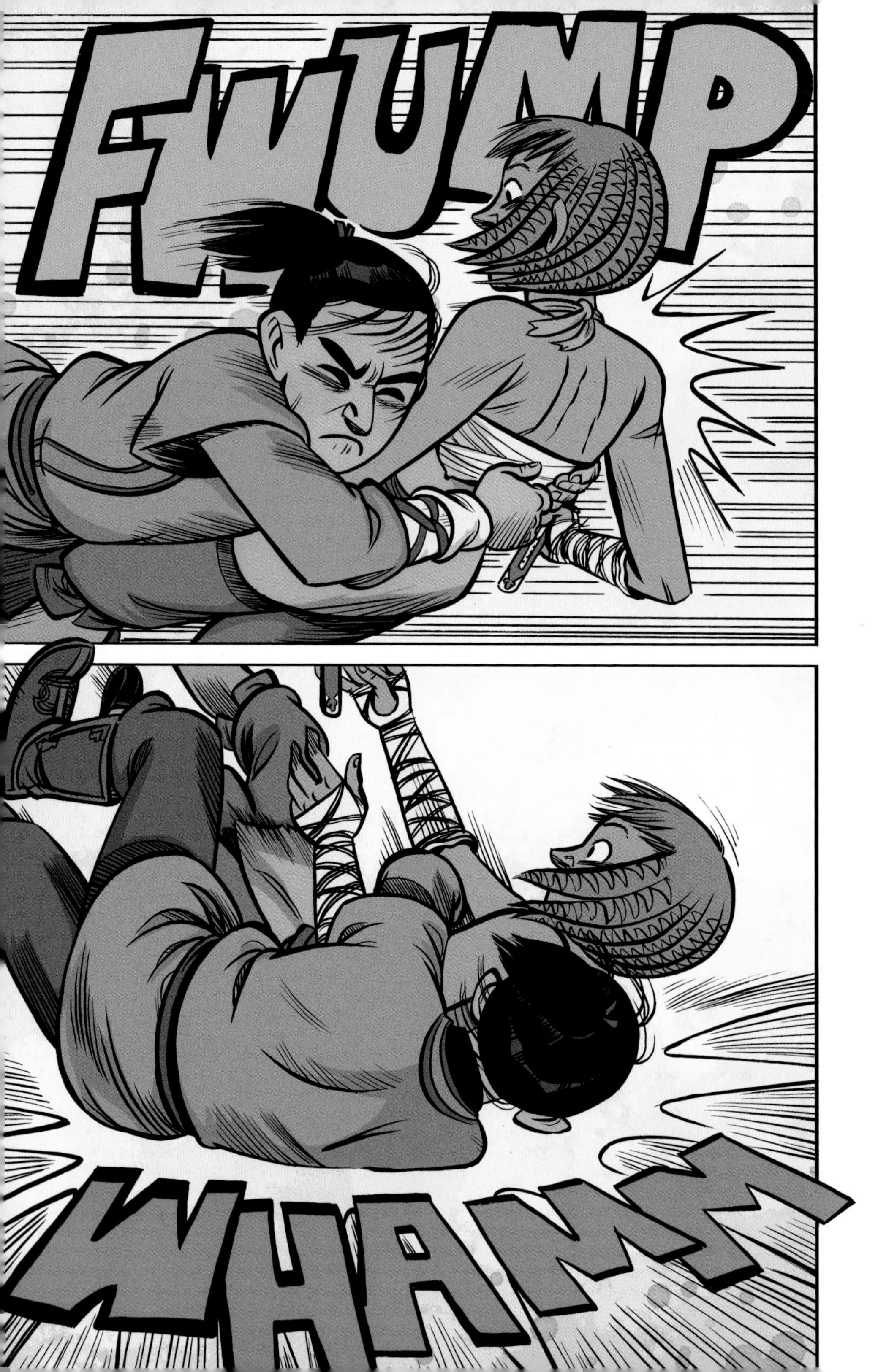
FWUMP
WHAM!

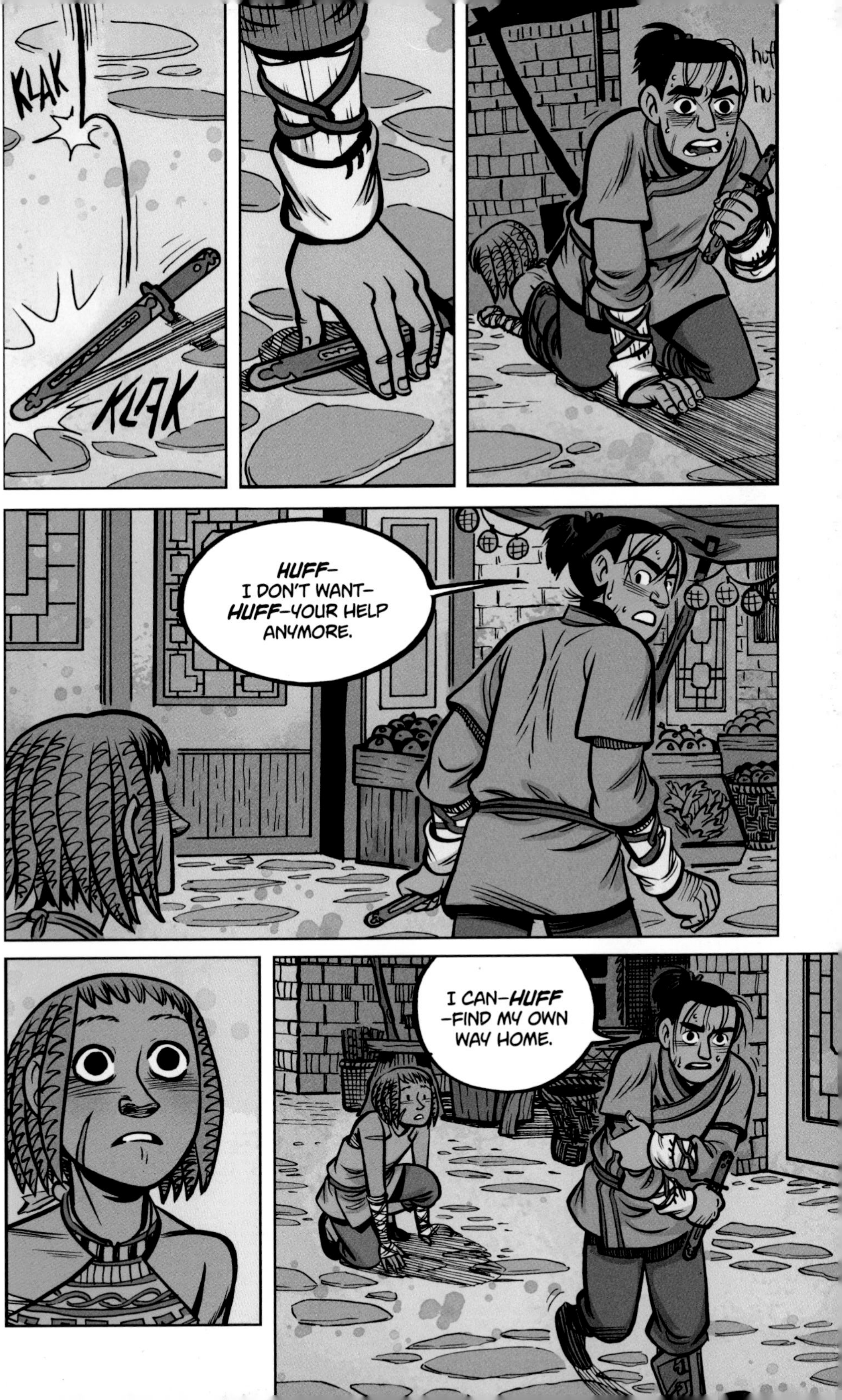
KLAK
KLAK
huff
huff
HUFF- I DON'T WANT- HUFF-YOUR HELP ANYMORE.
I CAN-HUFF -FIND MY OWN WAY HOME.

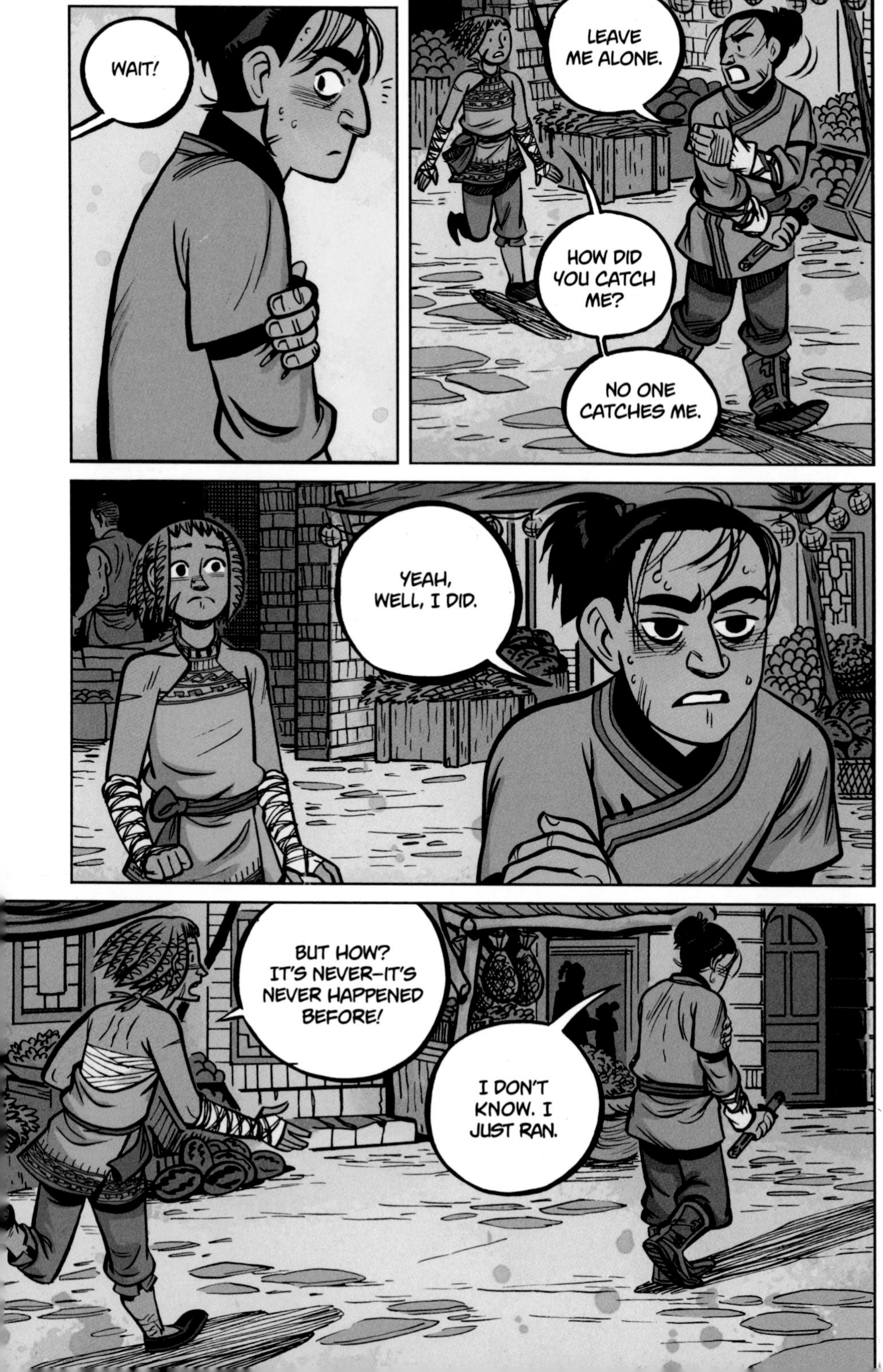
WAIT!
LEAVE ME ALONE.
HOW DID YOU CATCH ME?
NO ONE CATCHES ME.
YEAH, WELL, I DID.
BUT HOW? IT'S NEVER–IT'S NEVER HAPPENED BEFORE!
I DON'T KNOW. I JUST RAN.

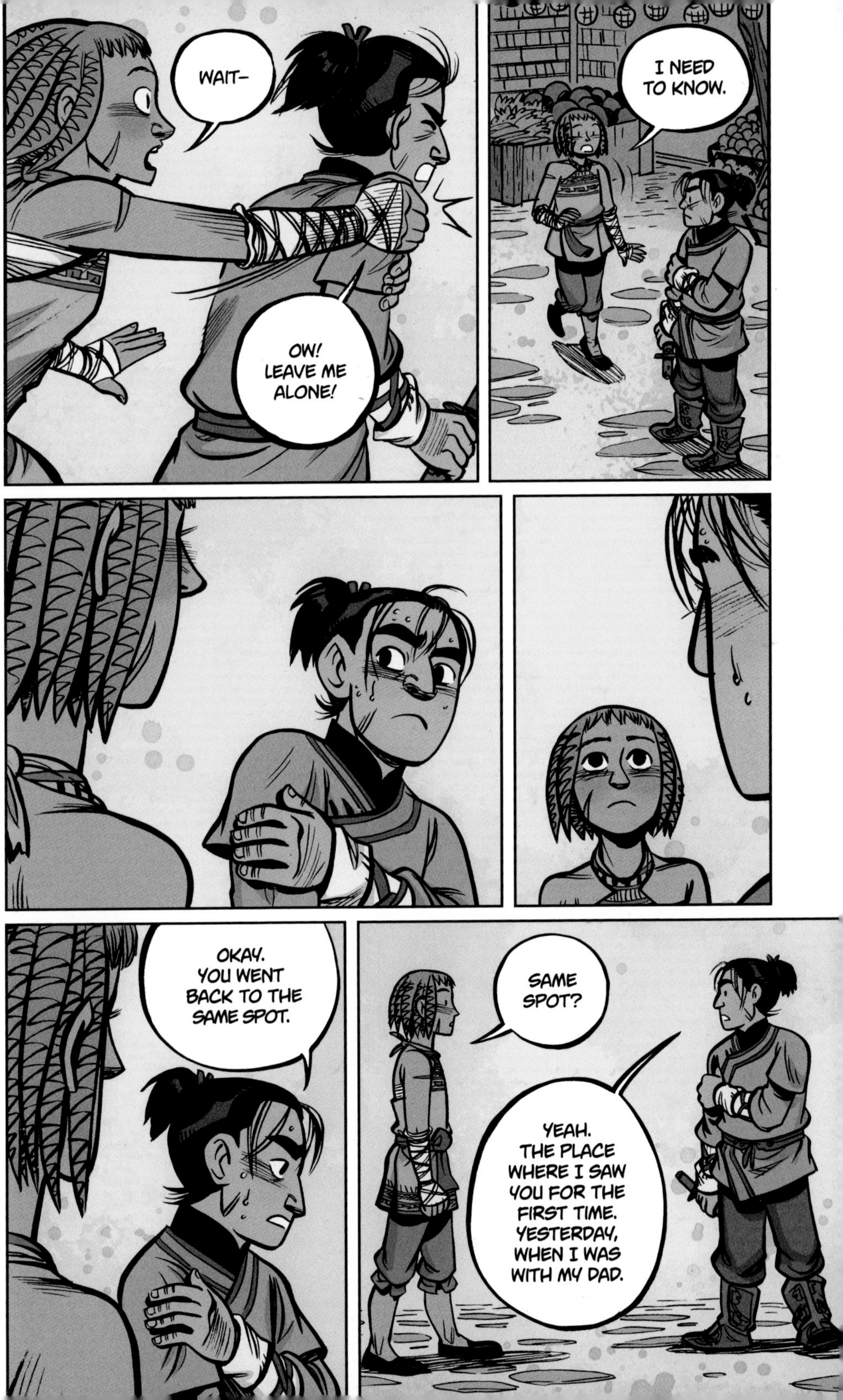
WAIT-
OW! LEAVE ME ALONE!
I NEED TO KNOW.
OKAY. YOU WENT BACK TO THE SAME SPOT.
SAME SPOT?
YEAH. THE PLACE WHERE I SAW YOU FOR THE FIRST TIME. YESTERDAY, WHEN I WAS WITH MY DAD.

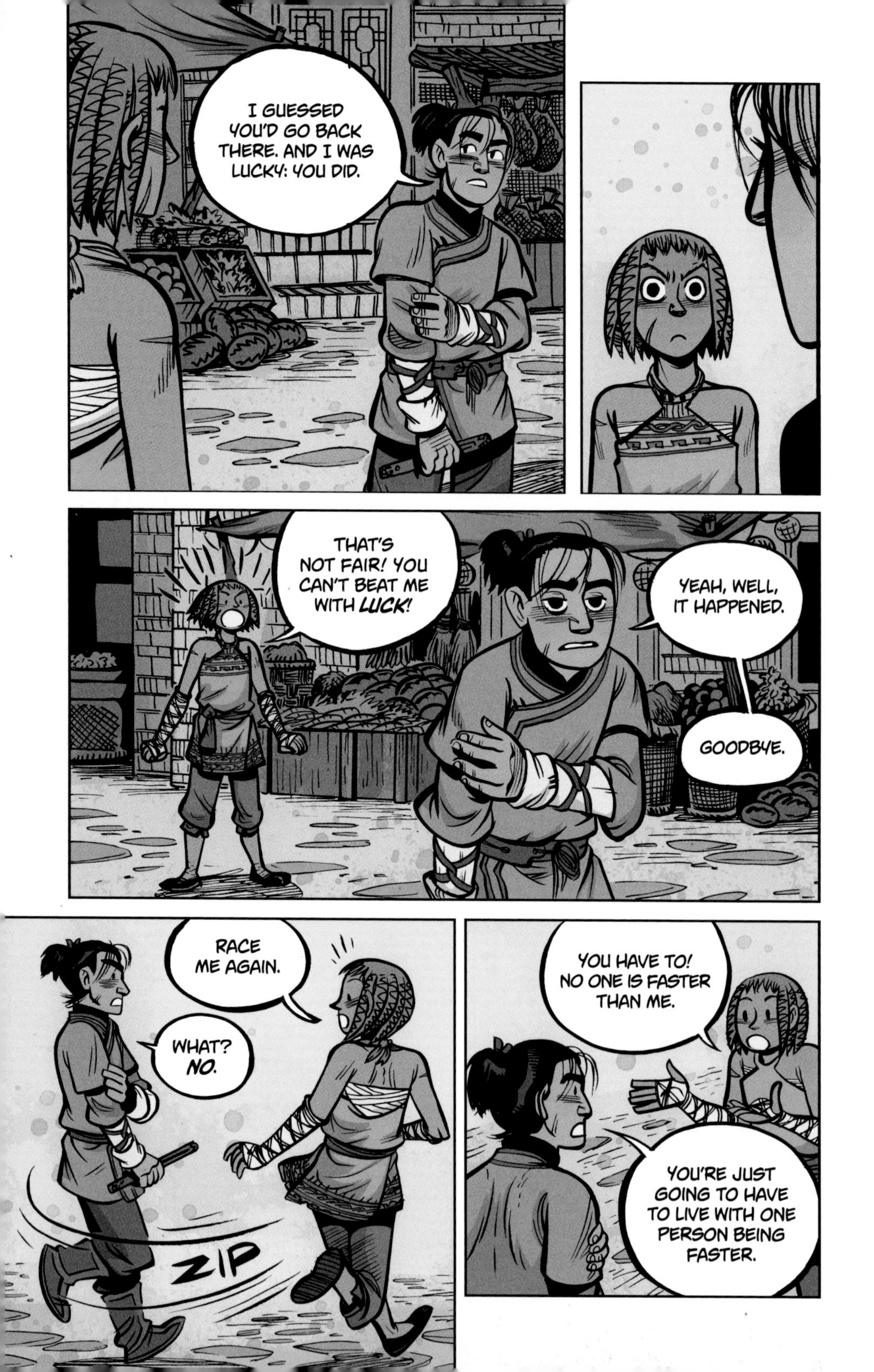
I GUESSED YOU'D GO BACK THERE. AND I WAS LUCKY: YOU DID.
THAT'S NOT FAIR! YOU CAN'T BEAT ME WITH *LUCK*!
YEAH, WELL, IT HAPPENED.
GOODBYE.
RACE ME AGAIN.
WHAT? *NO*.
ZIP
YOU HAVE TO! NO ONE IS FASTER THAN ME.
YOU'RE JUST GOING TO HAVE TO LIVE WITH ONE PERSON BEING FASTER.

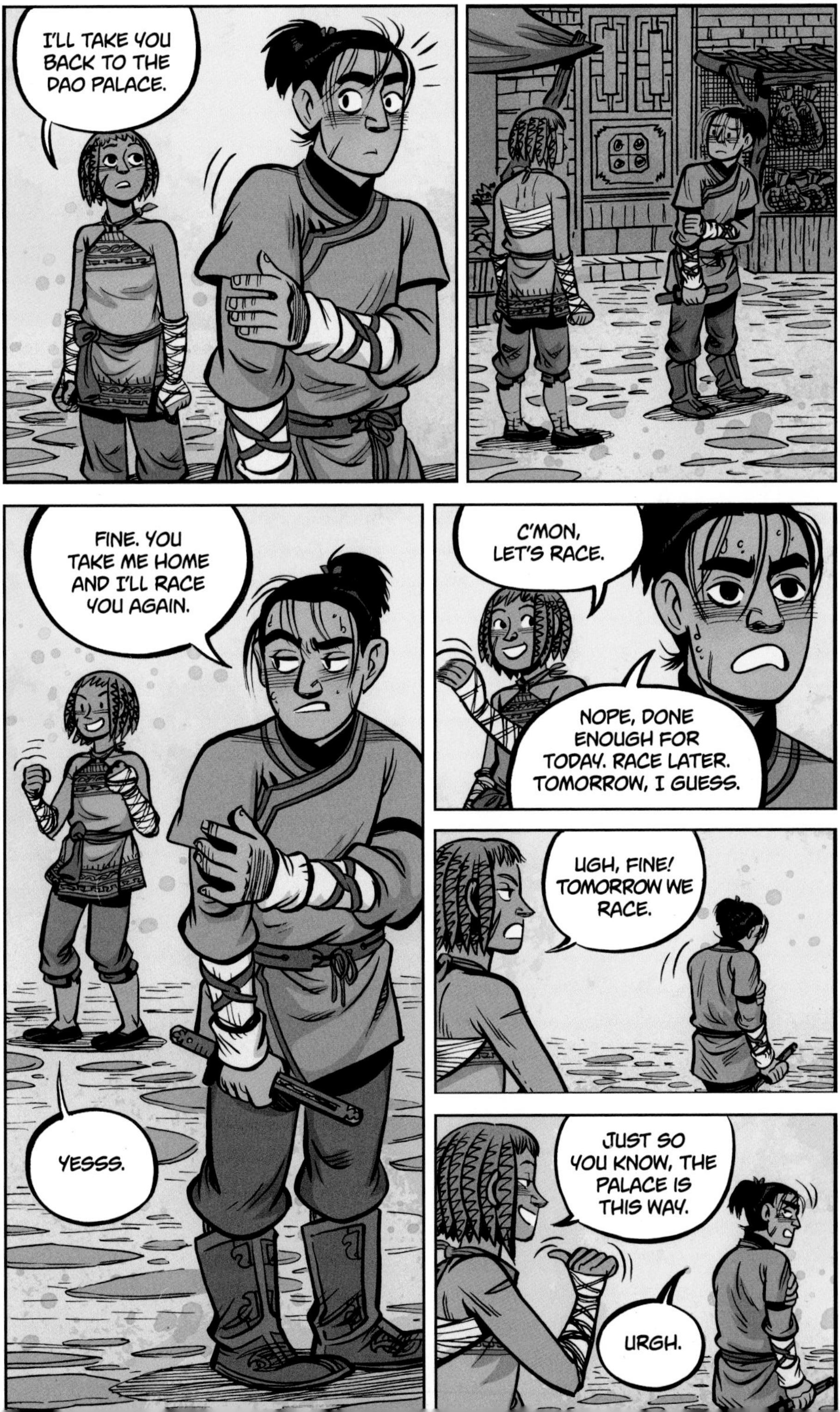
I'LL TAKE YOU BACK TO THE DAO PALACE.
FINE. YOU TAKE ME HOME AND I'LL RACE YOU AGAIN.
YESSS.
C'MON, LET'S RACE.
NOPE, DONE ENOUGH FOR TODAY. RACE LATER. TOMORROW, I GUESS.
UGH, FINE! TOMORROW WE RACE.
JUST SO YOU KNOW, THE PALACE IS THIS WAY.
URGH.

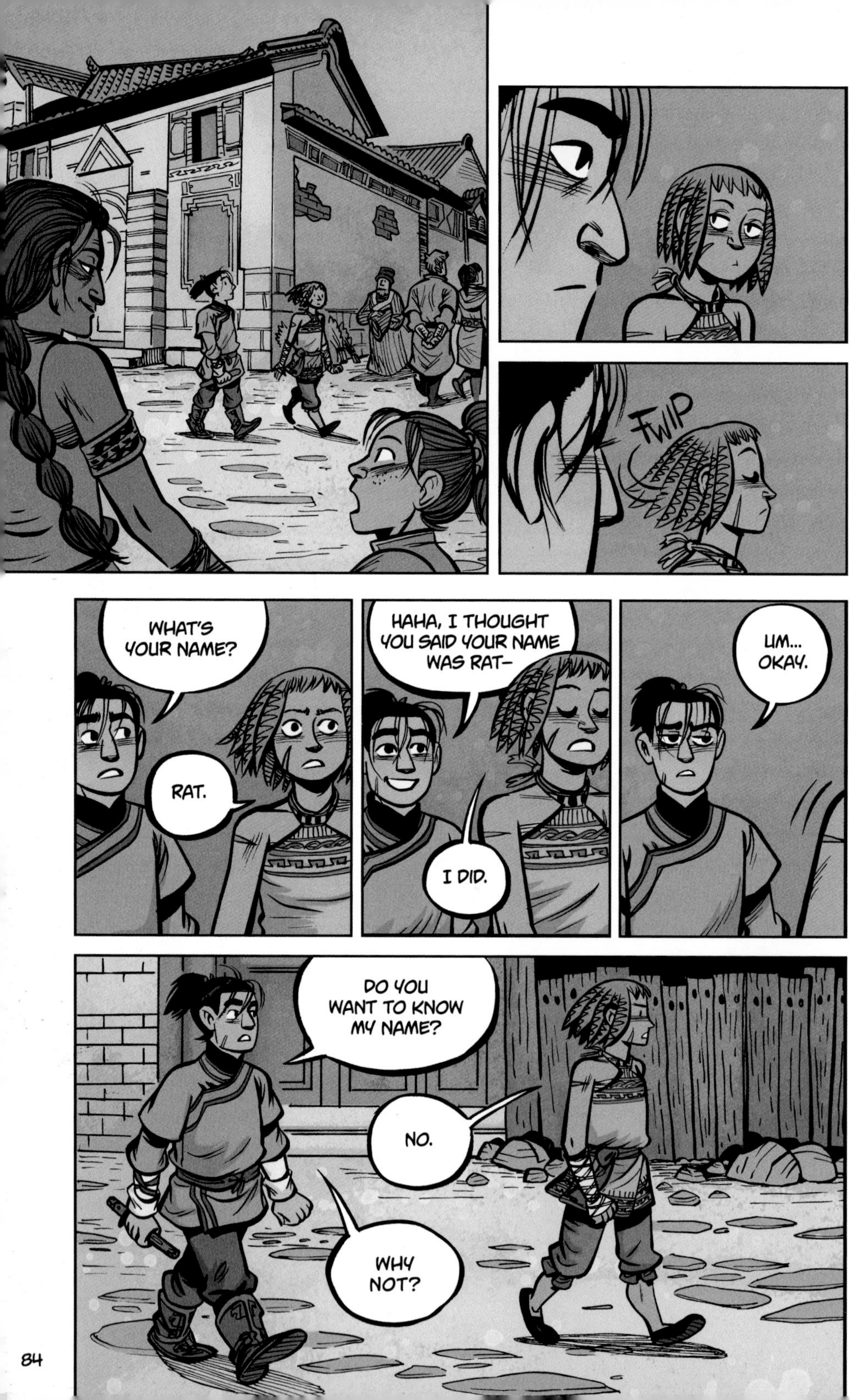
FWIP
WHAT'S YOUR NAME?
RAT.
HAHA, I THOUGHT YOU SAID YOUR NAME WAS RAT–
I DID.
UM... OKAY.
DO YOU WANT TO KNOW MY NAME?
NO.
WHY NOT?

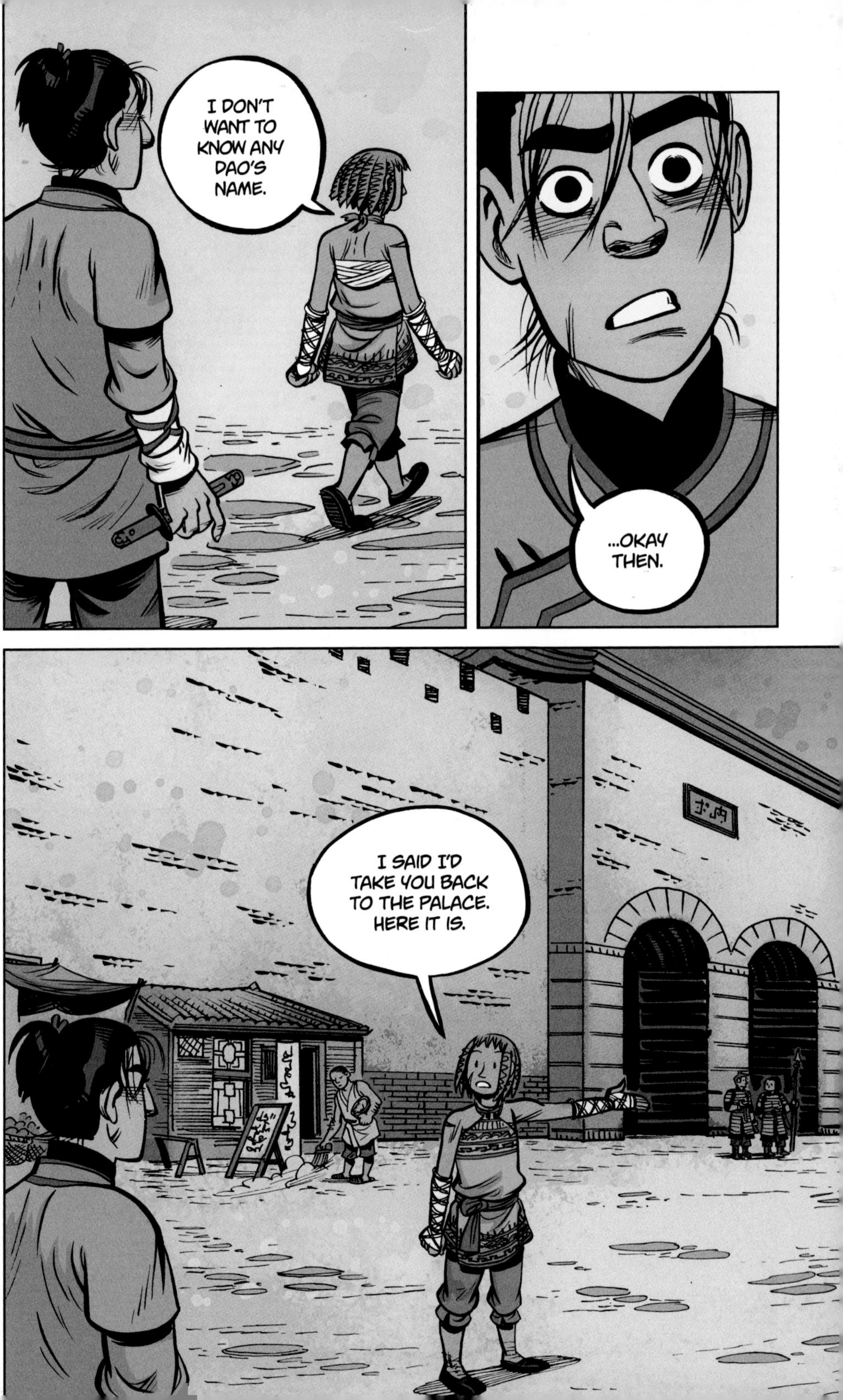
I DON'T WANT TO KNOW ANY DAO'S NAME.
...OKAY THEN.
I SAID I'D TAKE YOU BACK TO THE PALACE. HERE IT IS.

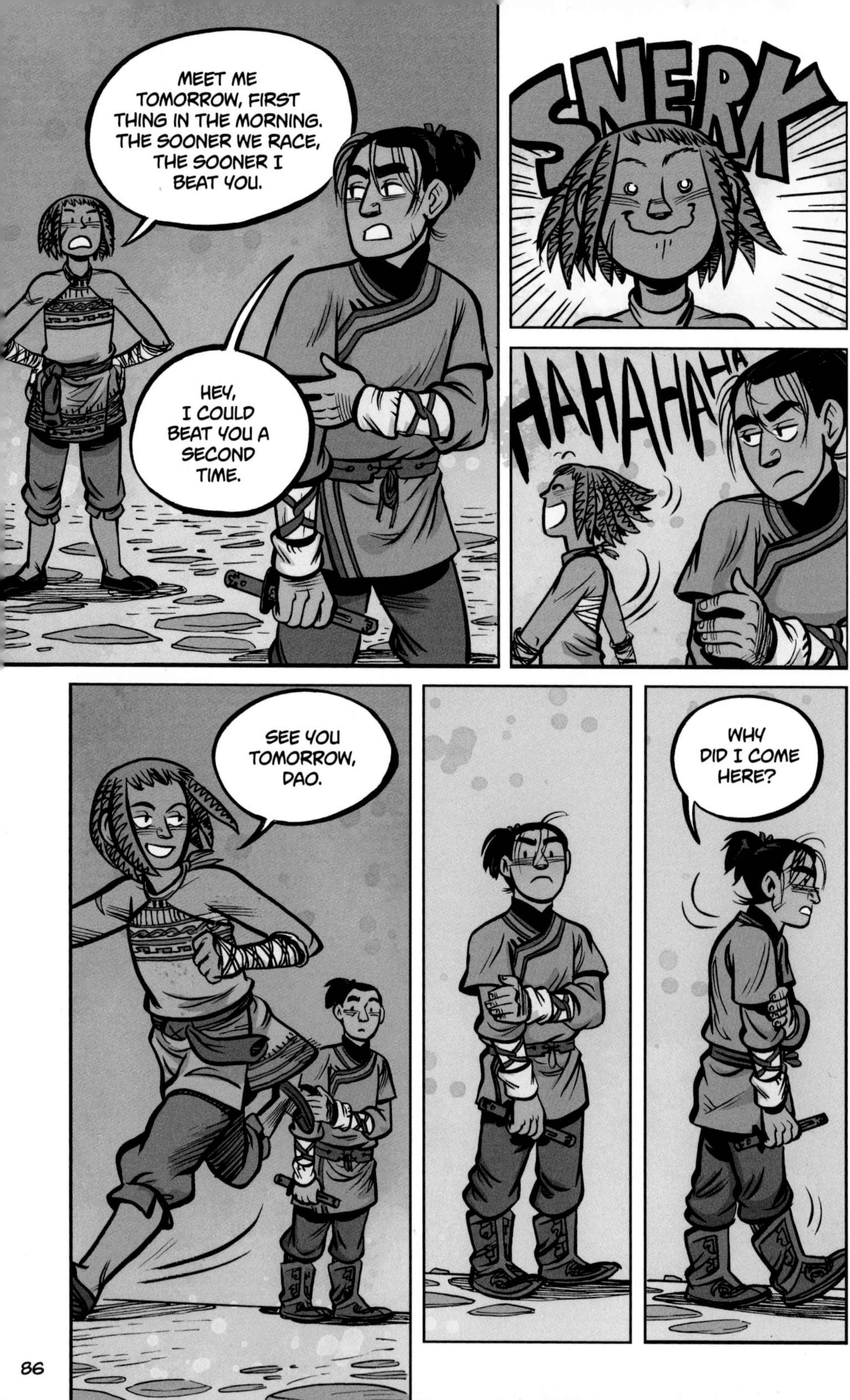
MEET ME TOMORROW, FIRST THING IN THE MORNING. THE SOONER WE RACE, THE SOONER I BEAT YOU.
HEY, I COULD BEAT YOU A SECOND TIME.
SNERK
HAHAHAHA
SEE YOU TOMORROW, DAO.
WHY DID I COME HERE?

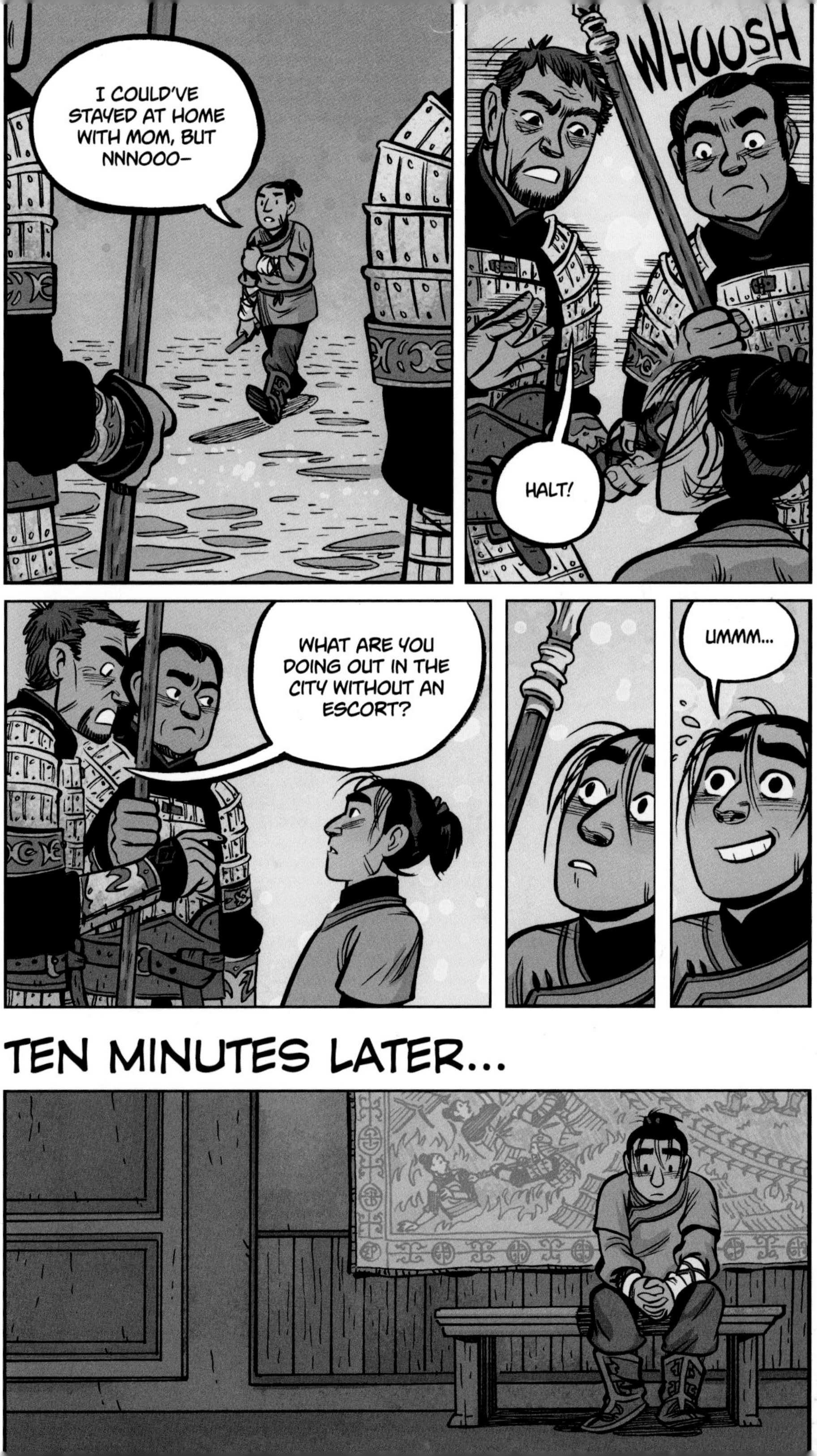
I COULD'VE STAYED AT HOME WITH MOM, BUT NNNOOO-
WHOOSH
HALT!
WHAT ARE YOU DOING OUT IN THE CITY WITHOUT AN ESCORT?
UMMM...
TEN MINUTES LATER...

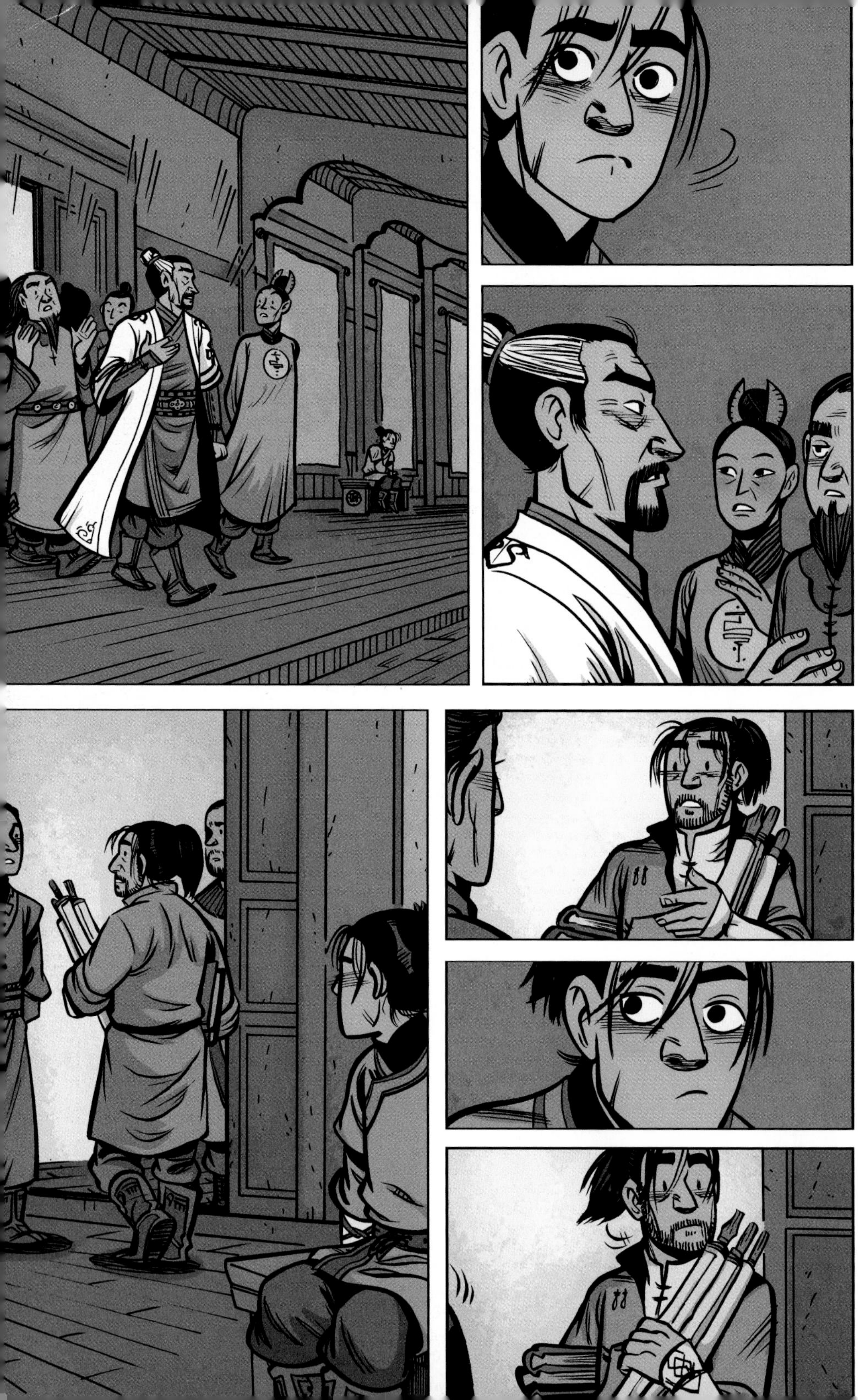

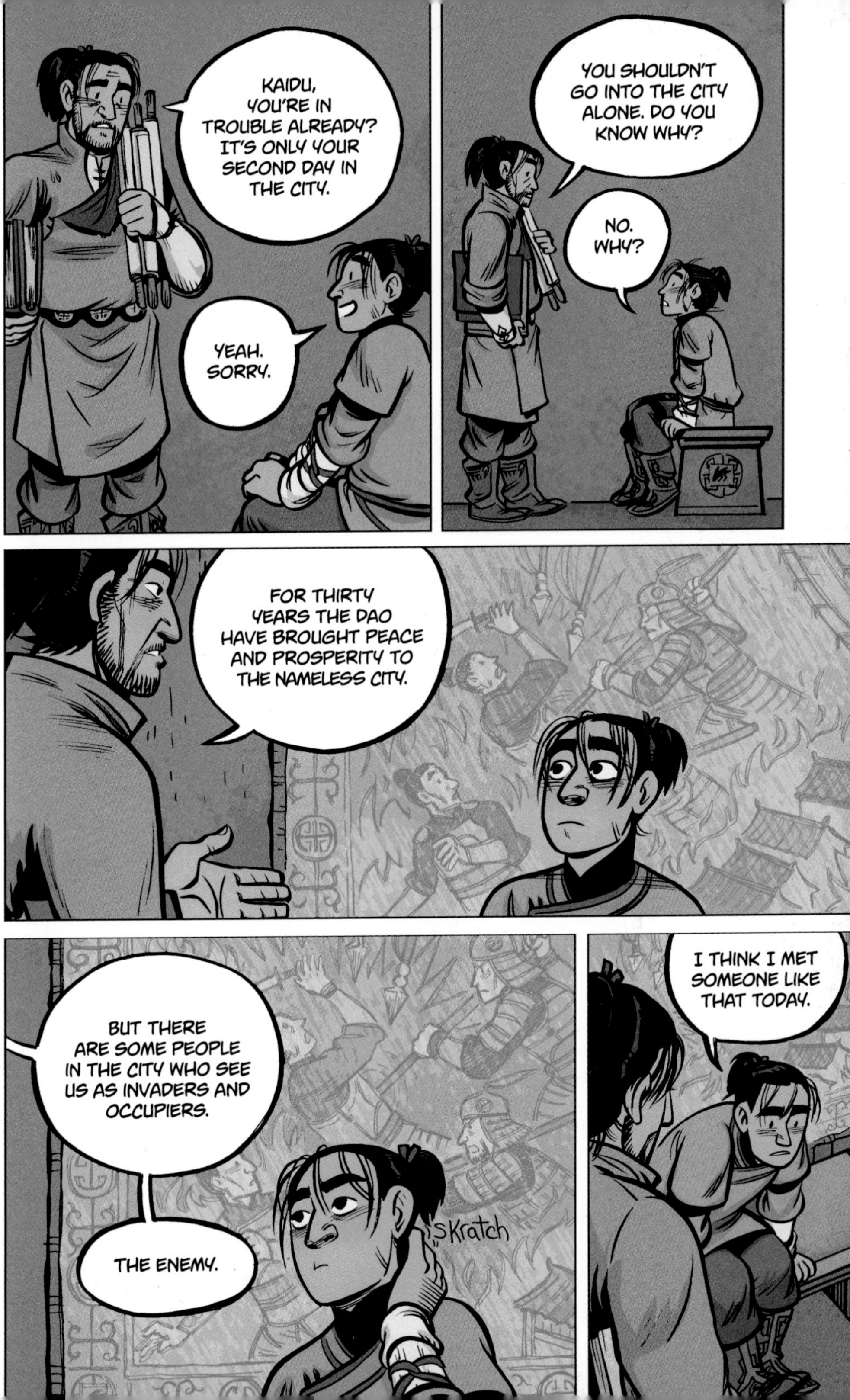
KAIDU, YOU'RE IN TROUBLE ALREADY? IT'S ONLY YOUR SECOND DAY IN THE CITY.
YEAH. SORRY.
YOU SHOULDN'T GO INTO THE CITY ALONE. DO YOU KNOW WHY?
NO. WHY?
FOR THIRTY YEARS THE DAO HAVE BROUGHT PEACE AND PROSPERITY TO THE NAMELESS CITY.
BUT THERE ARE SOME PEOPLE IN THE CITY WHO SEE US AS INVADERS AND OCCUPIERS.
THE ENEMY.
SKratch
I THINK I MET SOMEONE LIKE THAT TODAY.

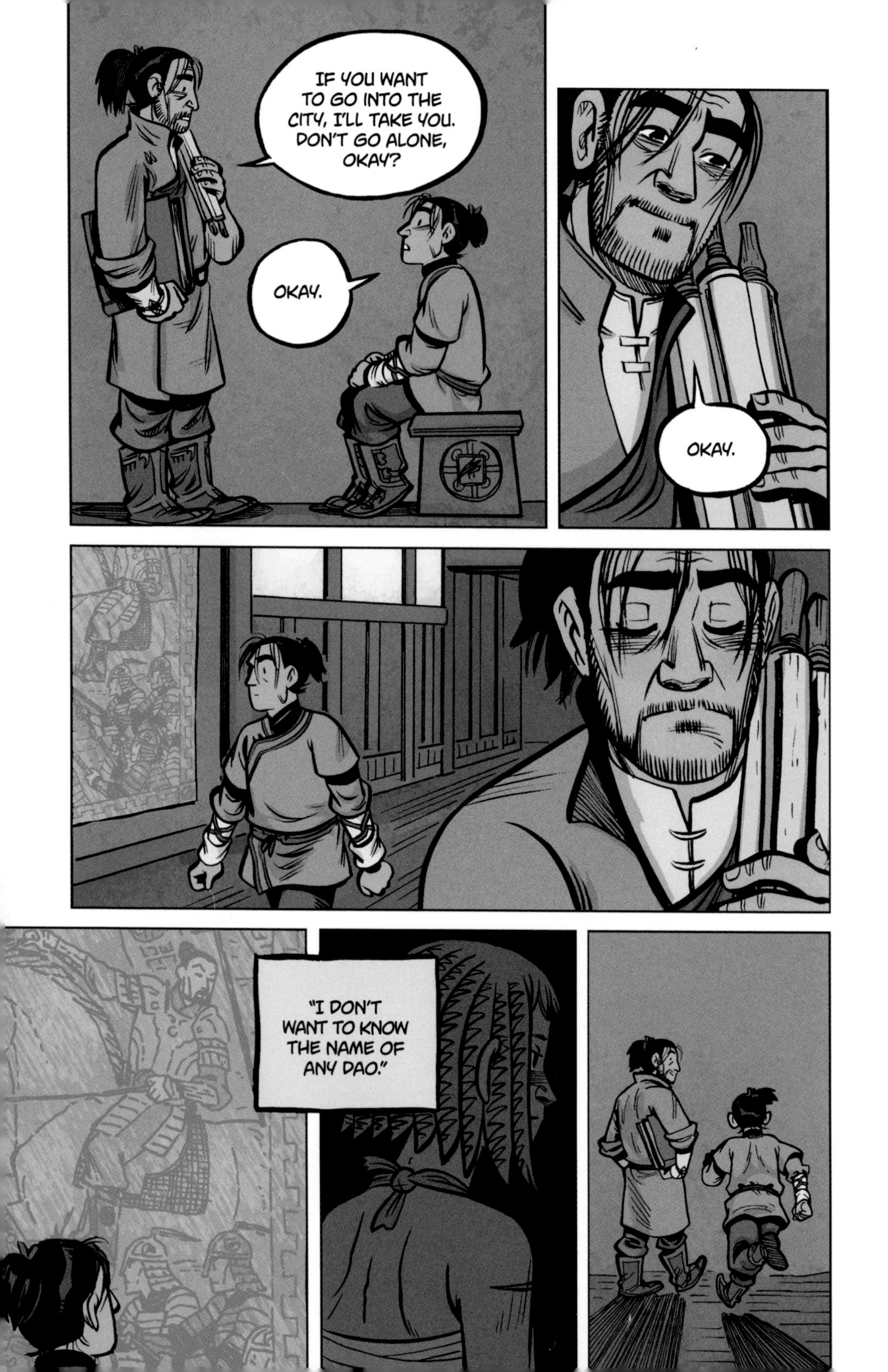
IF YOU WANT TO GO INTO THE CITY, I'LL TAKE YOU. DON'T GO ALONE, OKAY?
OKAY.
OKAY.
"I DON'T WANT TO KNOW THE NAME OF ANY DAO."

DAY 3

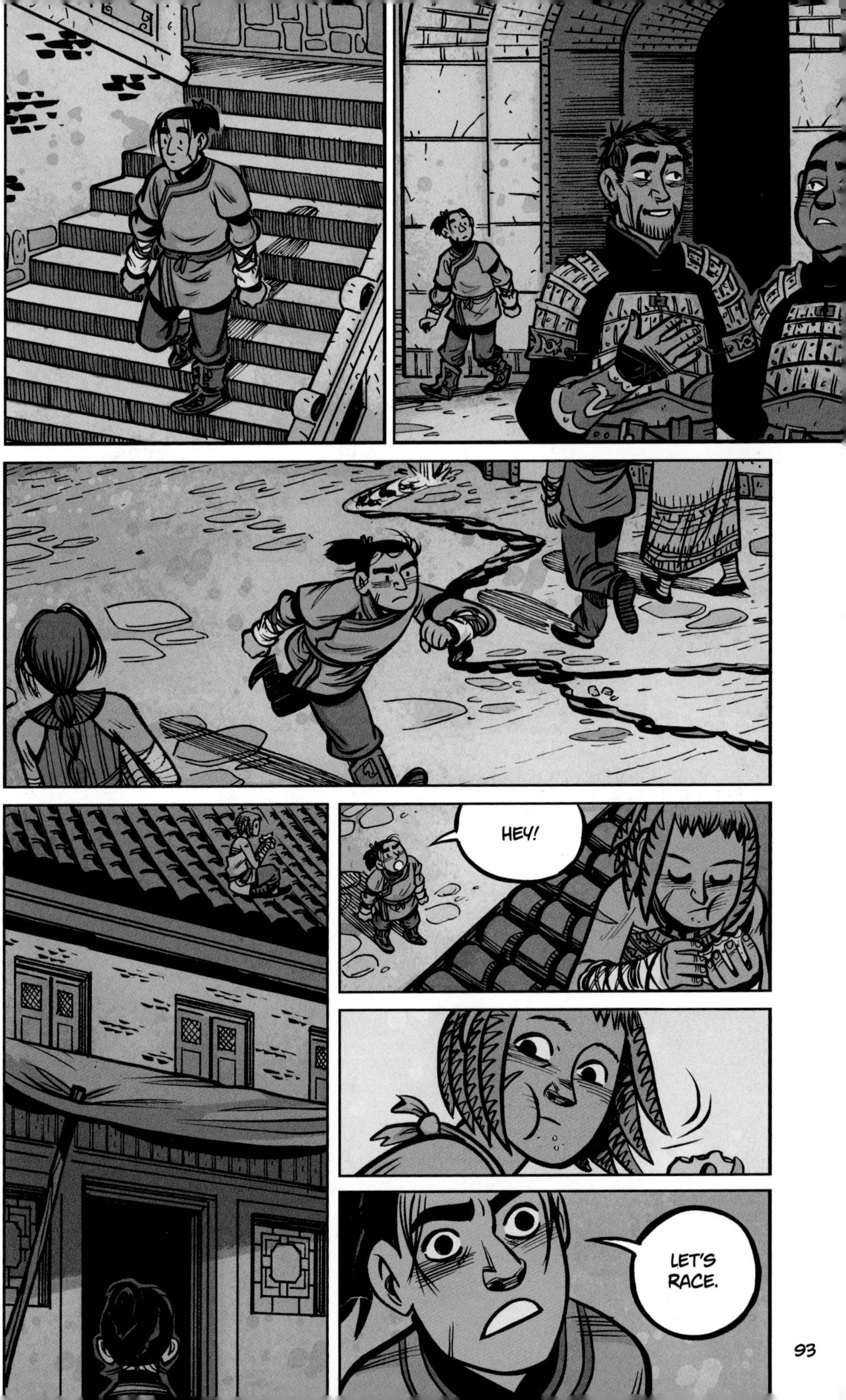
HEY!
LET'S RACE.

TEN MINUTES LATER...

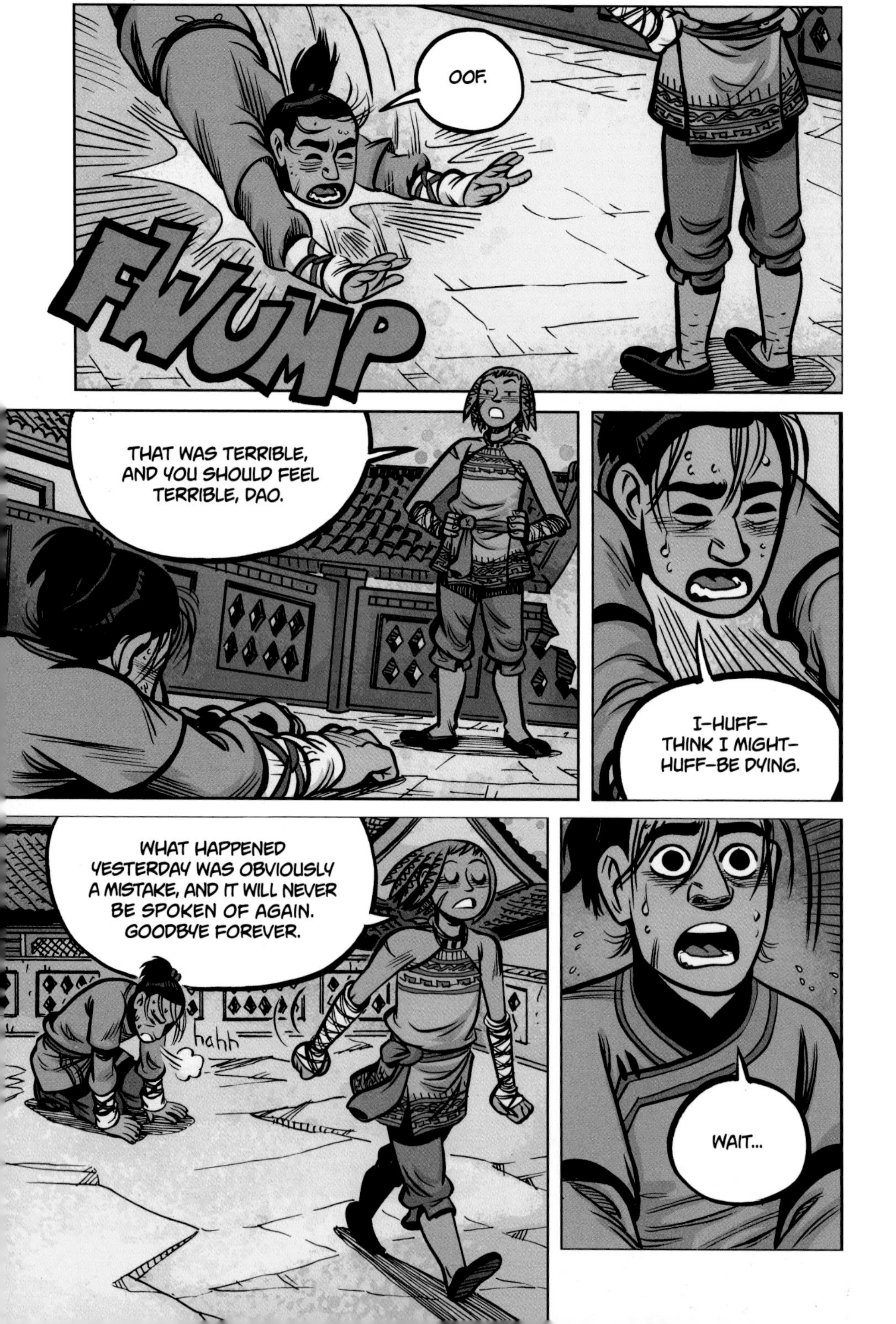
OOF.
FWUMP
THAT WAS TERRIBLE, AND YOU SHOULD FEEL TERRIBLE, DAO.
I-HUFF- THINK I MIGHT- HUFF-BE DYING.
WHAT HAPPENED YESTERDAY WAS OBVIOUSLY A MISTAKE, AND IT WILL NEVER BE SPOKEN OF AGAIN. GOODBYE FOREVER.
hahh
WAIT...

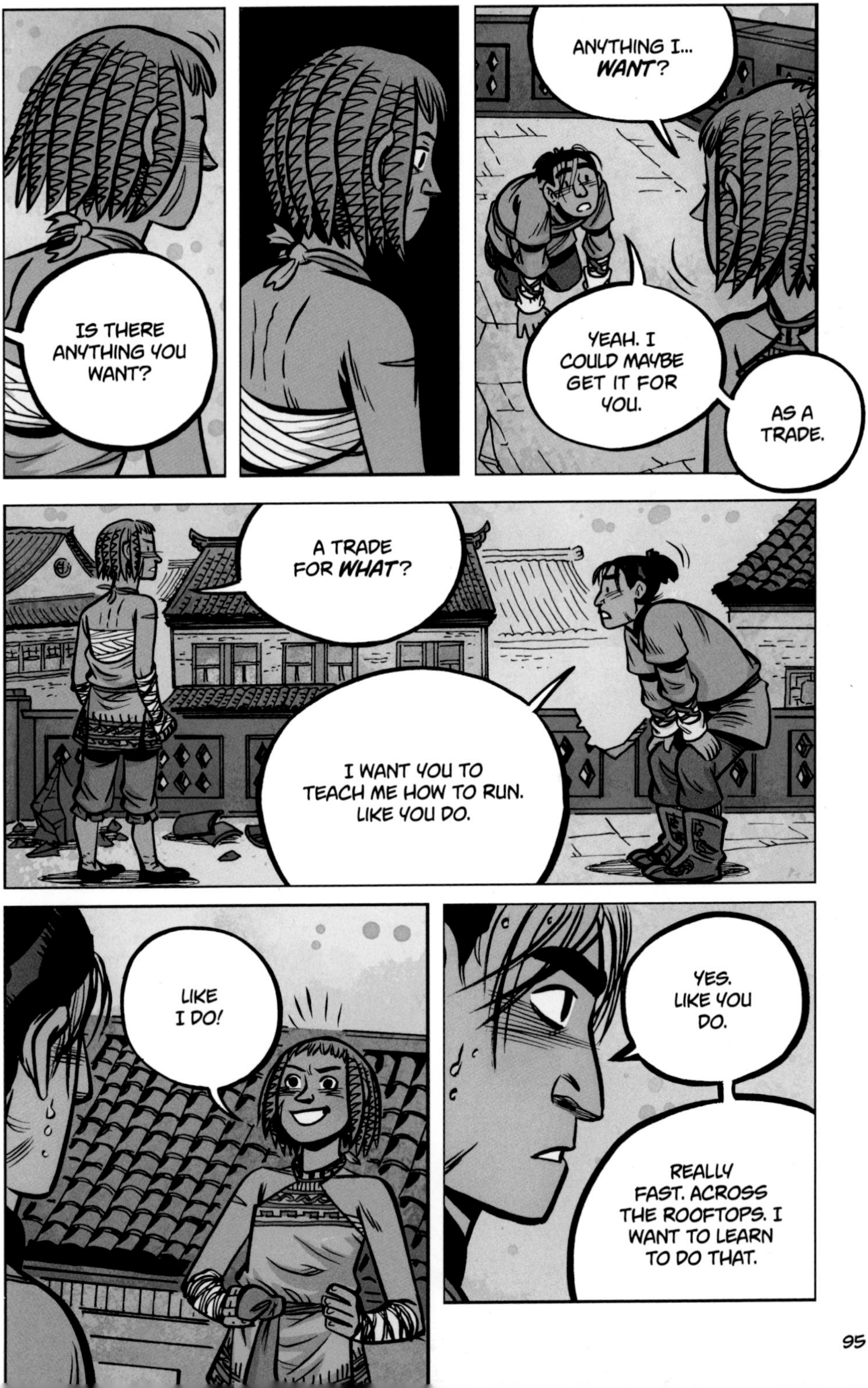
IS THERE ANYTHING YOU WANT?
ANYTHING I... *WANT*?
YEAH. I COULD MAYBE GET IT FOR YOU.
AS A TRADE.
A TRADE FOR *WHAT*?
I WANT YOU TO TEACH ME HOW TO RUN. LIKE YOU DO.
LIKE I DO!
YES. LIKE YOU DO.
REALLY FAST. ACROSS THE ROOFTOPS. I WANT TO LEARN TO DO THAT.

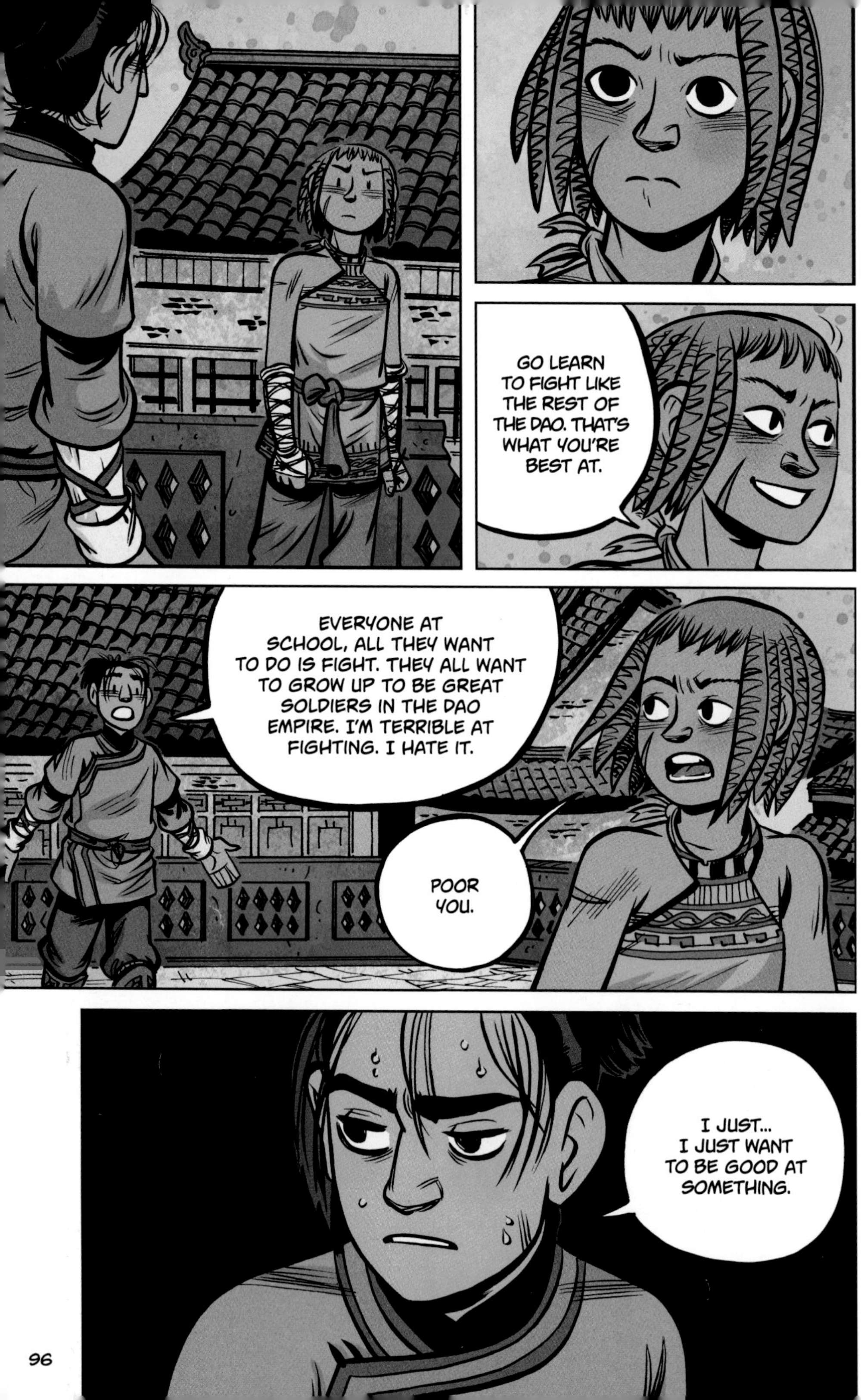
GO LEARN TO FIGHT LIKE THE REST OF THE DAO. THAT'S WHAT YOU'RE BEST AT.
EVERYONE AT SCHOOL, ALL THEY WANT TO DO IS FIGHT. THEY ALL WANT TO GROW UP TO BE GREAT SOLDIERS IN THE DAO EMPIRE. I'M TERRIBLE AT FIGHTING. I HATE IT.
POOR YOU.
I JUST... I JUST WANT TO BE GOOD AT SOMETHING.

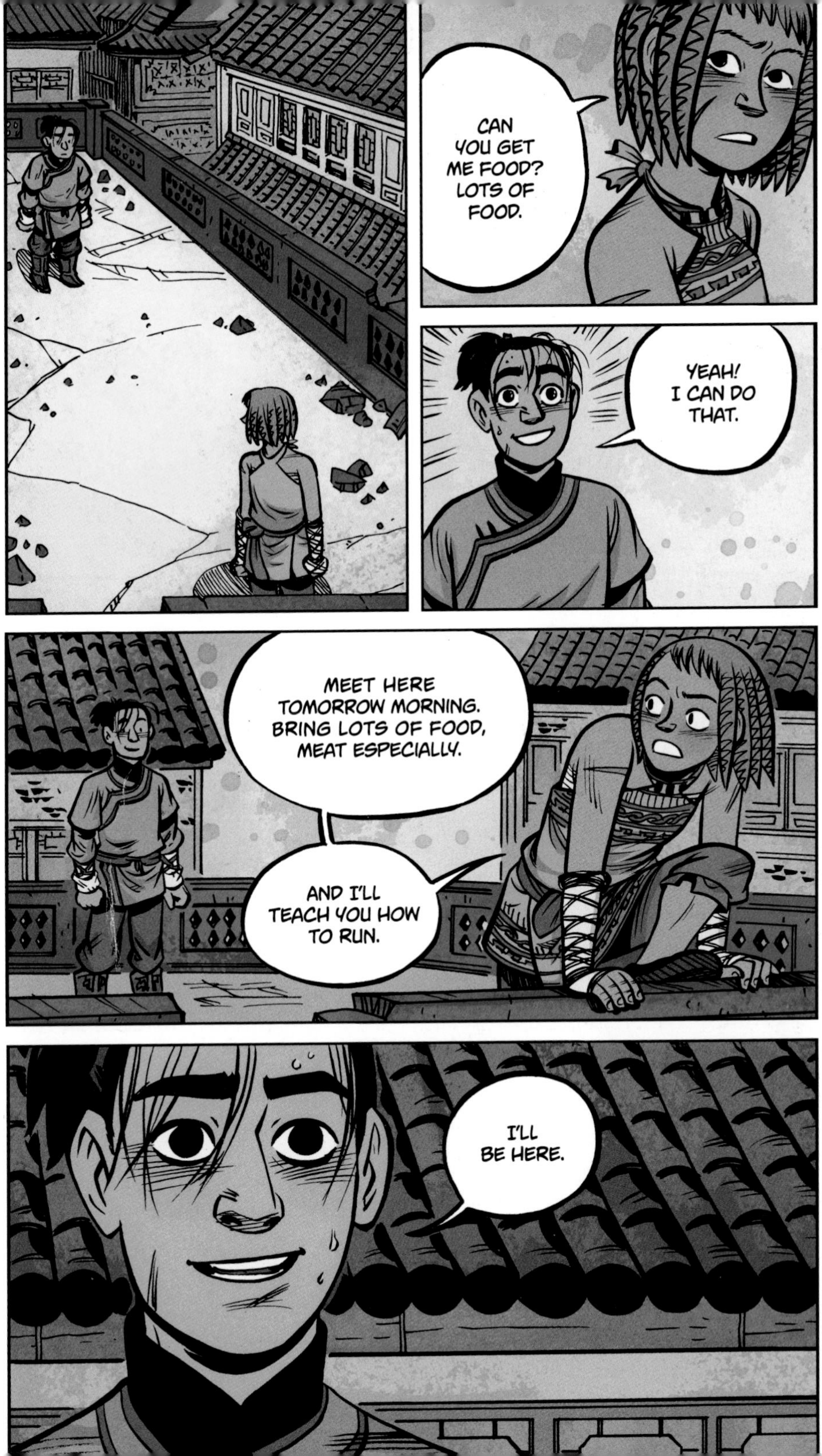
CAN YOU GET ME FOOD? LOTS OF FOOD.
YEAH! I CAN DO THAT.
MEET HERE TOMORROW MORNING. BRING LOTS OF FOOD, MEAT ESPECIALLY.
AND I'LL TEACH YOU HOW TO RUN.
I'LL BE HERE.

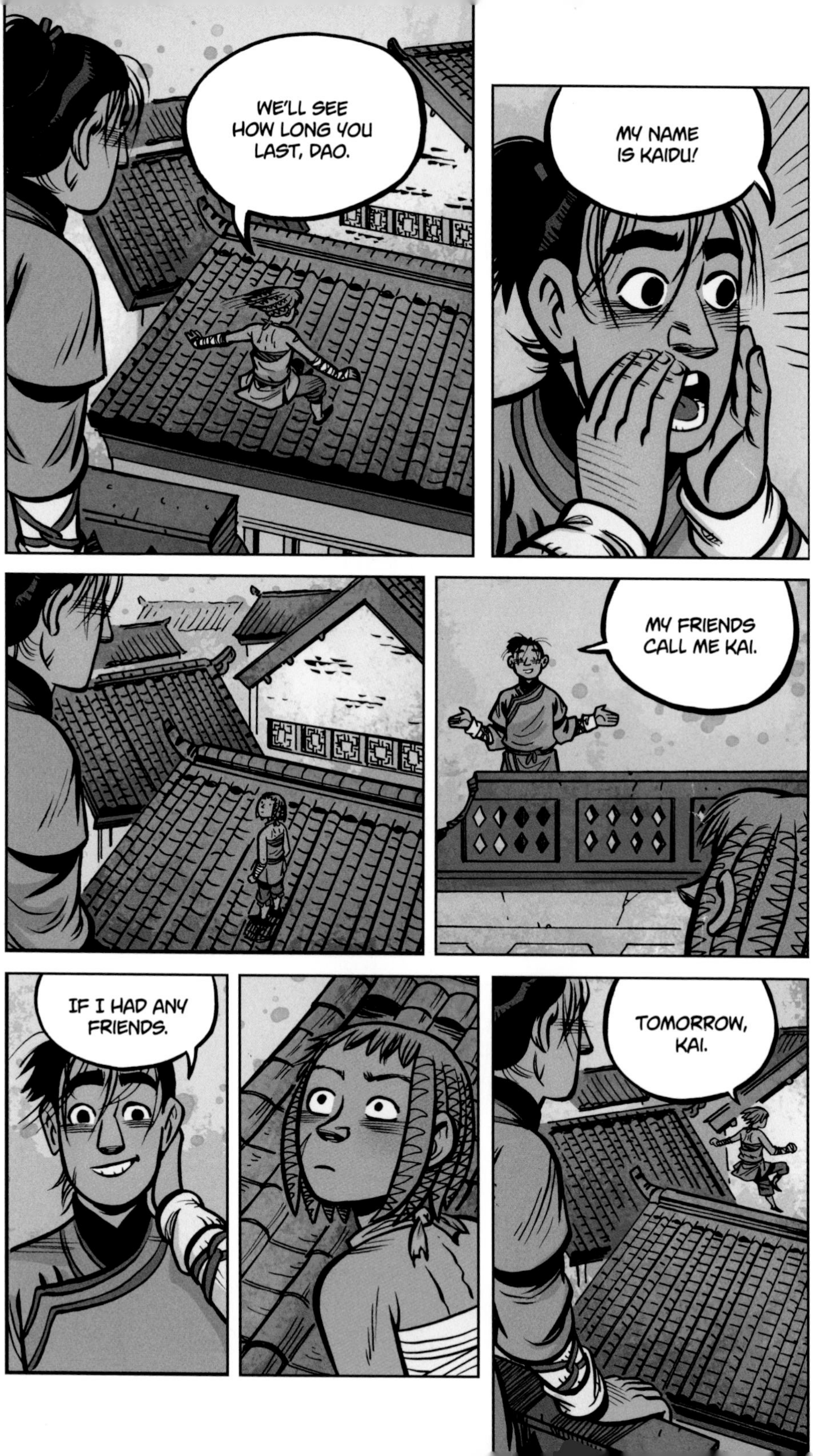
WE'LL SEE HOW LONG YOU LAST, DAO.
MY NAME IS KAIDU!
MY FRIENDS CALL ME KAI.
IF I HAD ANY FRIENDS.
TOMORROW, KAI.

DAY 4

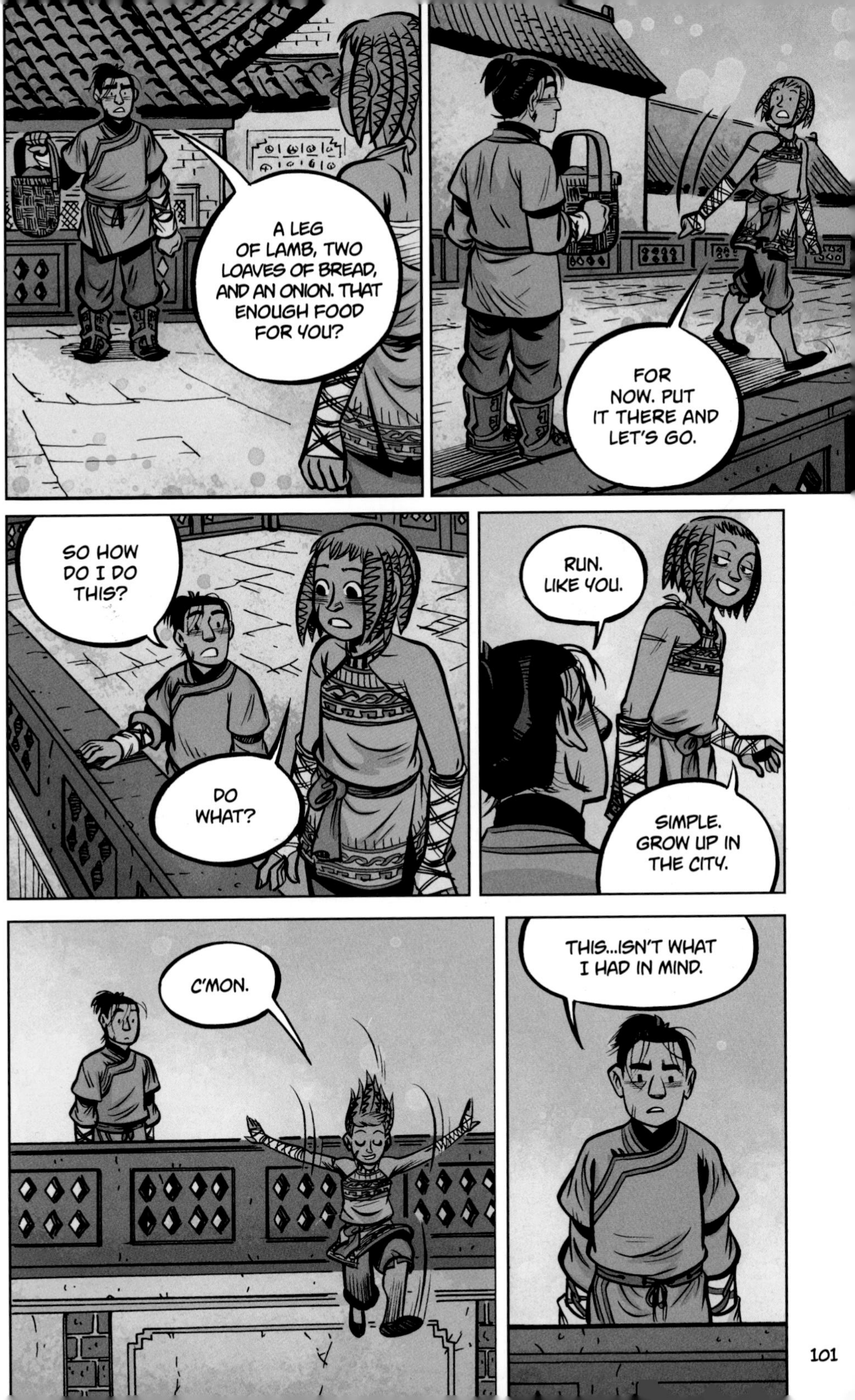
A LEG OF LAMB, TWO LOAVES OF BREAD, AND AN ONION. THAT ENOUGH FOOD FOR YOU?
FOR NOW. PUT IT THERE AND LET'S GO.
SO HOW DO I DO THIS?
DO WHAT?
RUN. LIKE YOU.
SIMPLE. GROW UP IN THE CITY.
C'MON.
THIS...ISN'T WHAT I HAD IN MIND.

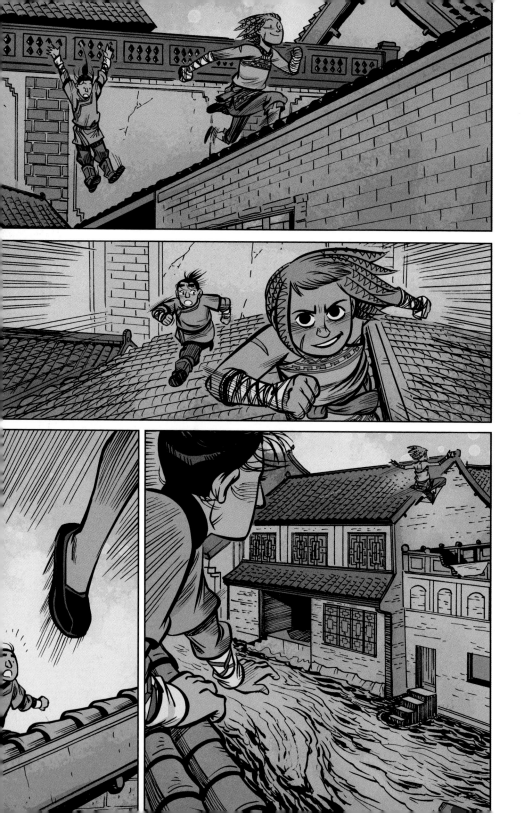

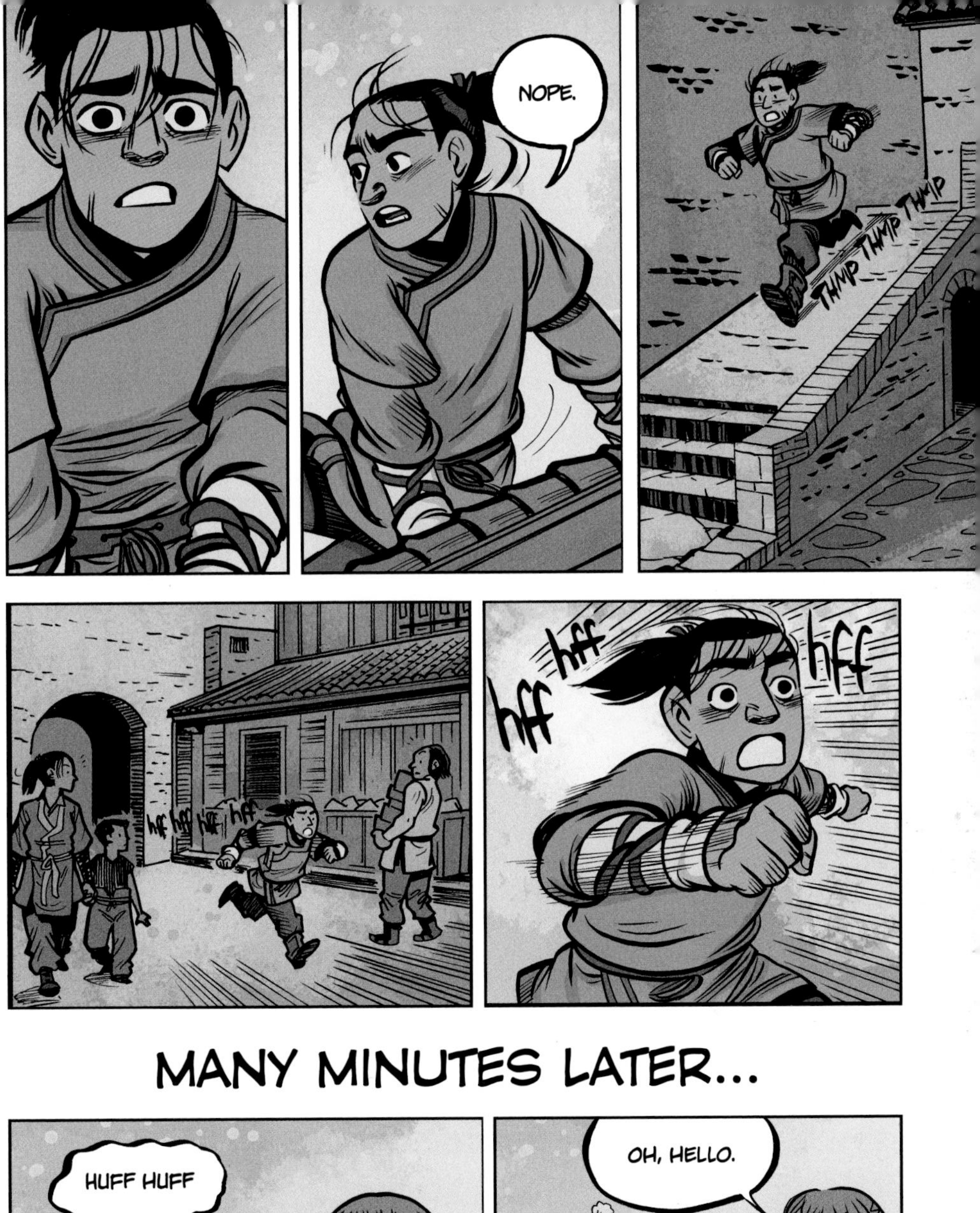
NOPE.
THMP THMP THMP
hff hff hff hff
hff
hff
hff

MANY MINUTES LATER...

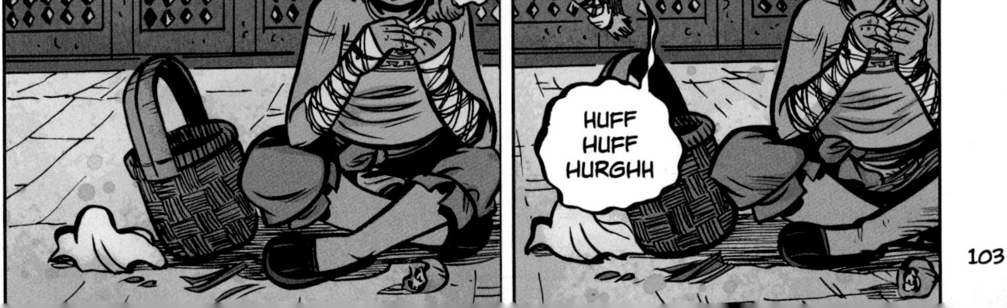
HUFF HUFF
OH, HELLO.
HUFF
HUFF
HURGHH

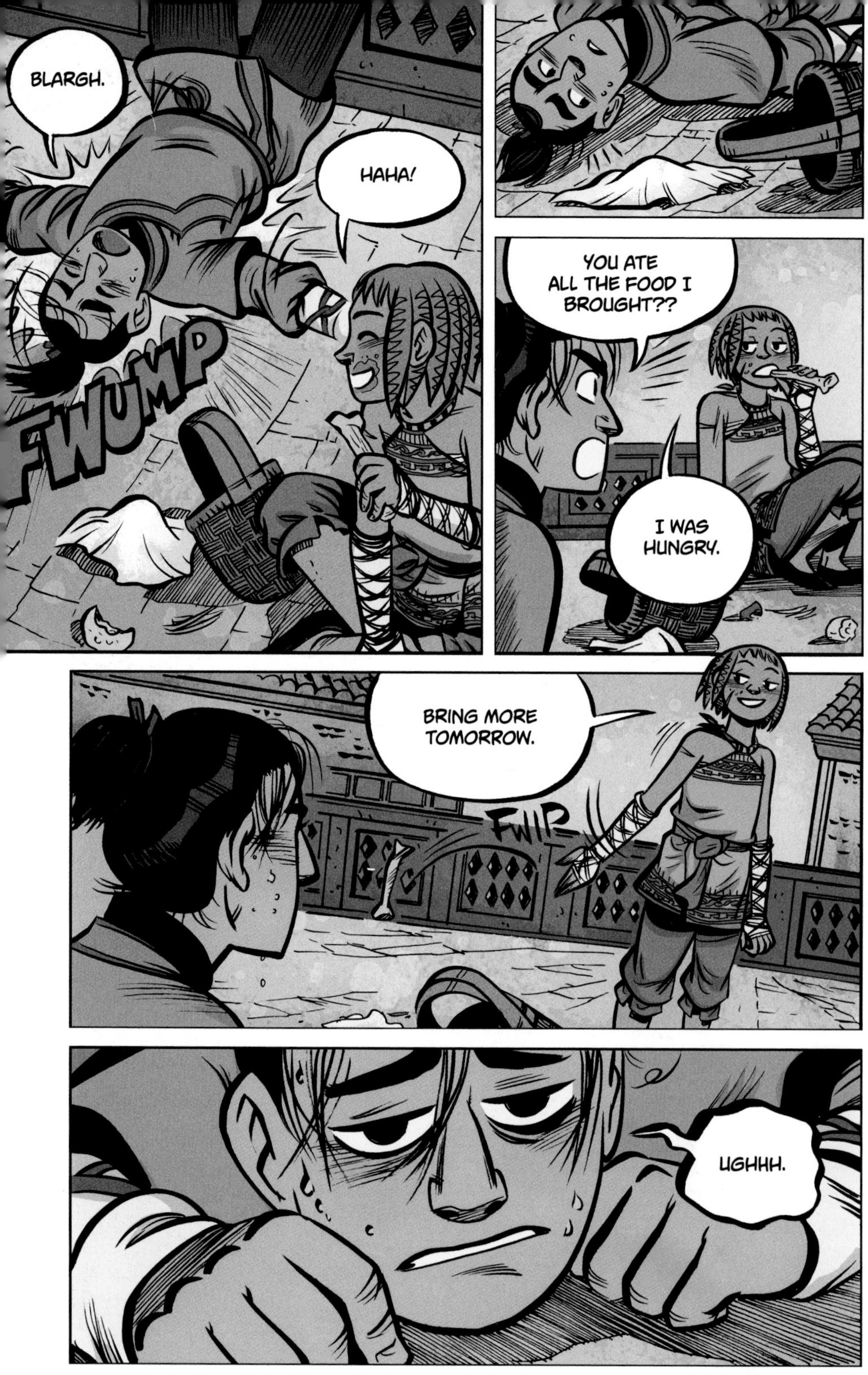
BLARGH.
HAHA!
FWUMP
YOU ATE ALL THE FOOD I BROUGHT??
I WAS HUNGRY.
BRING MORE TOMORROW.
FWIP
UGHHH.

DAY 5

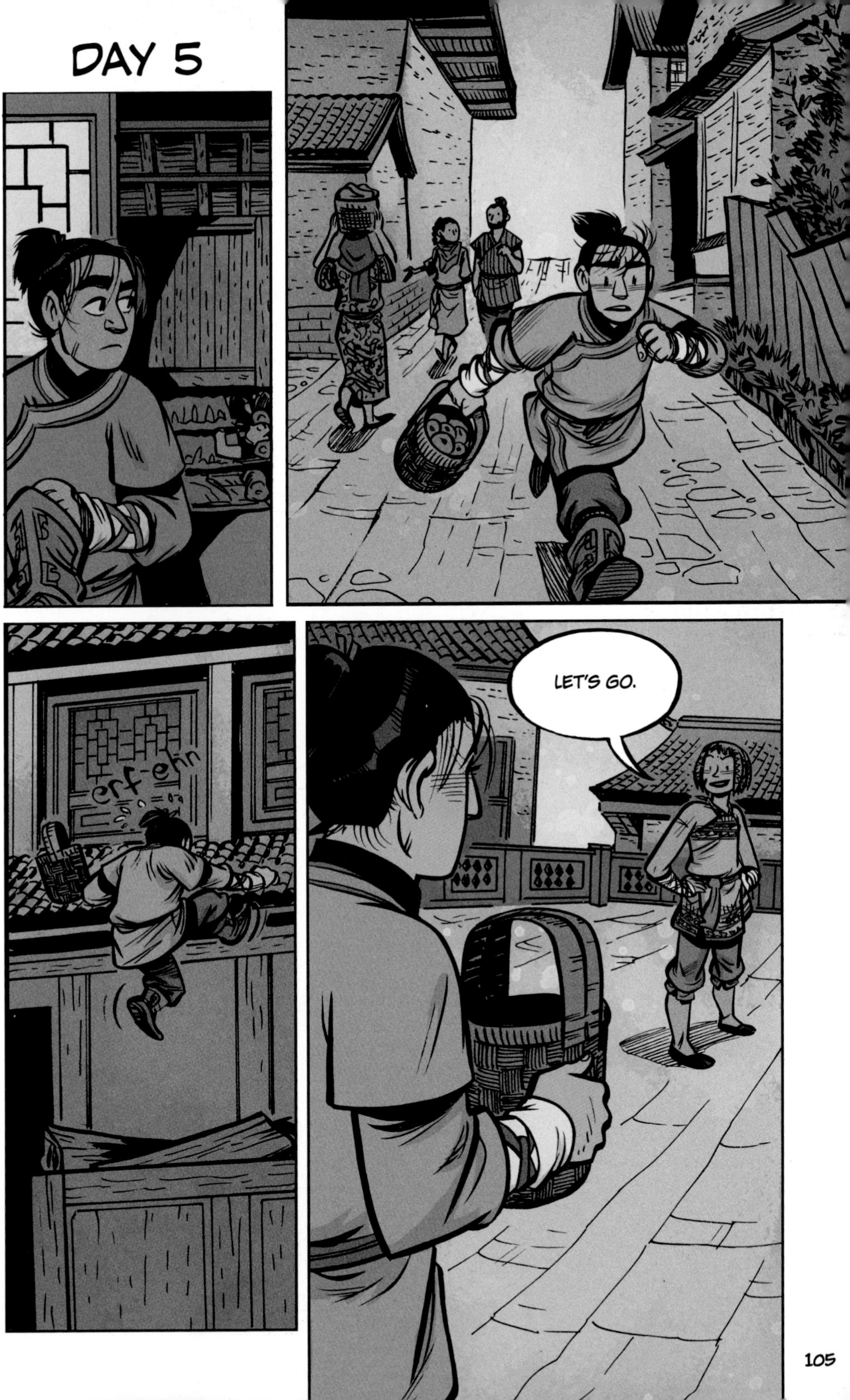
erf-ehn
LET'S GO.

DAY 6

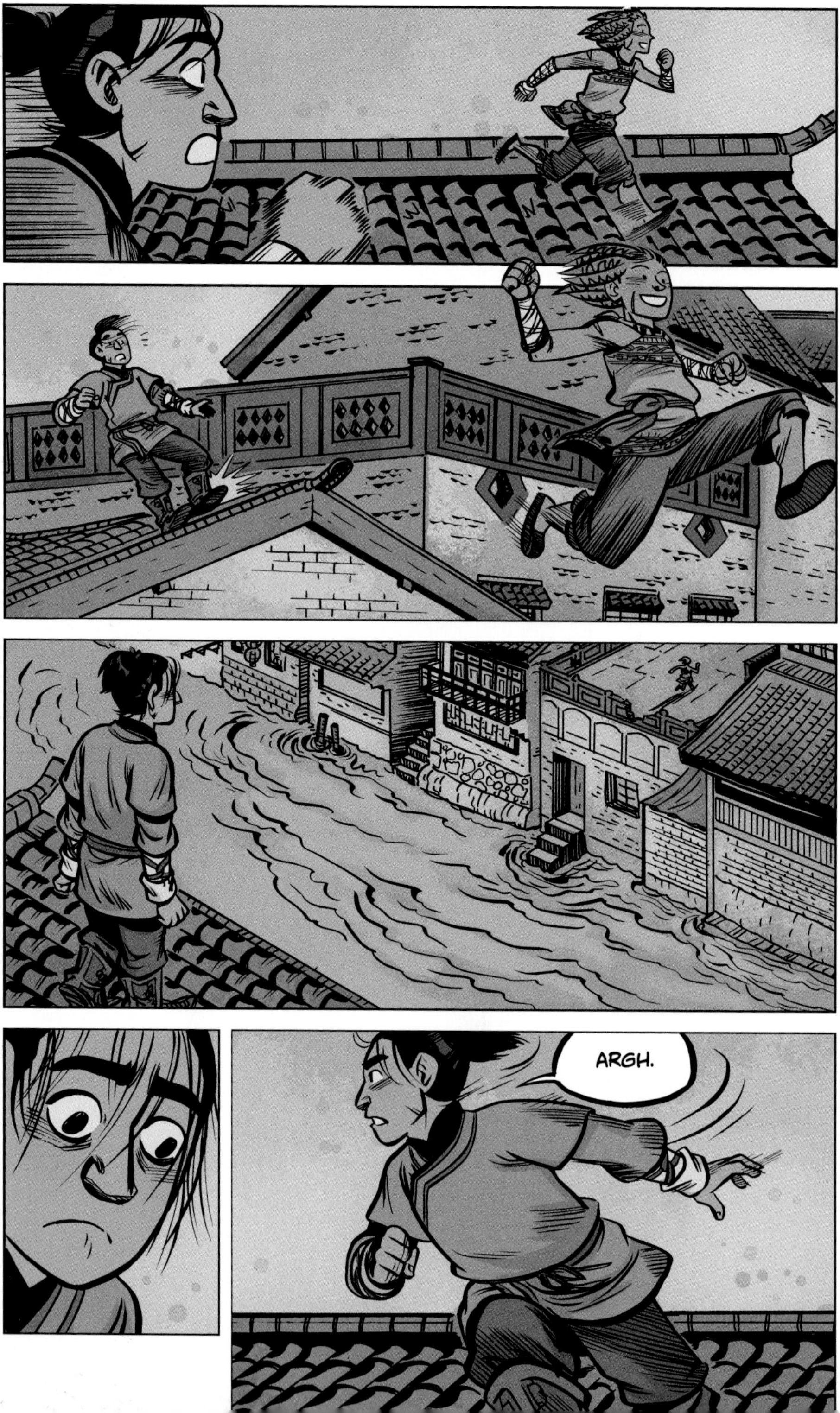
ARGH.

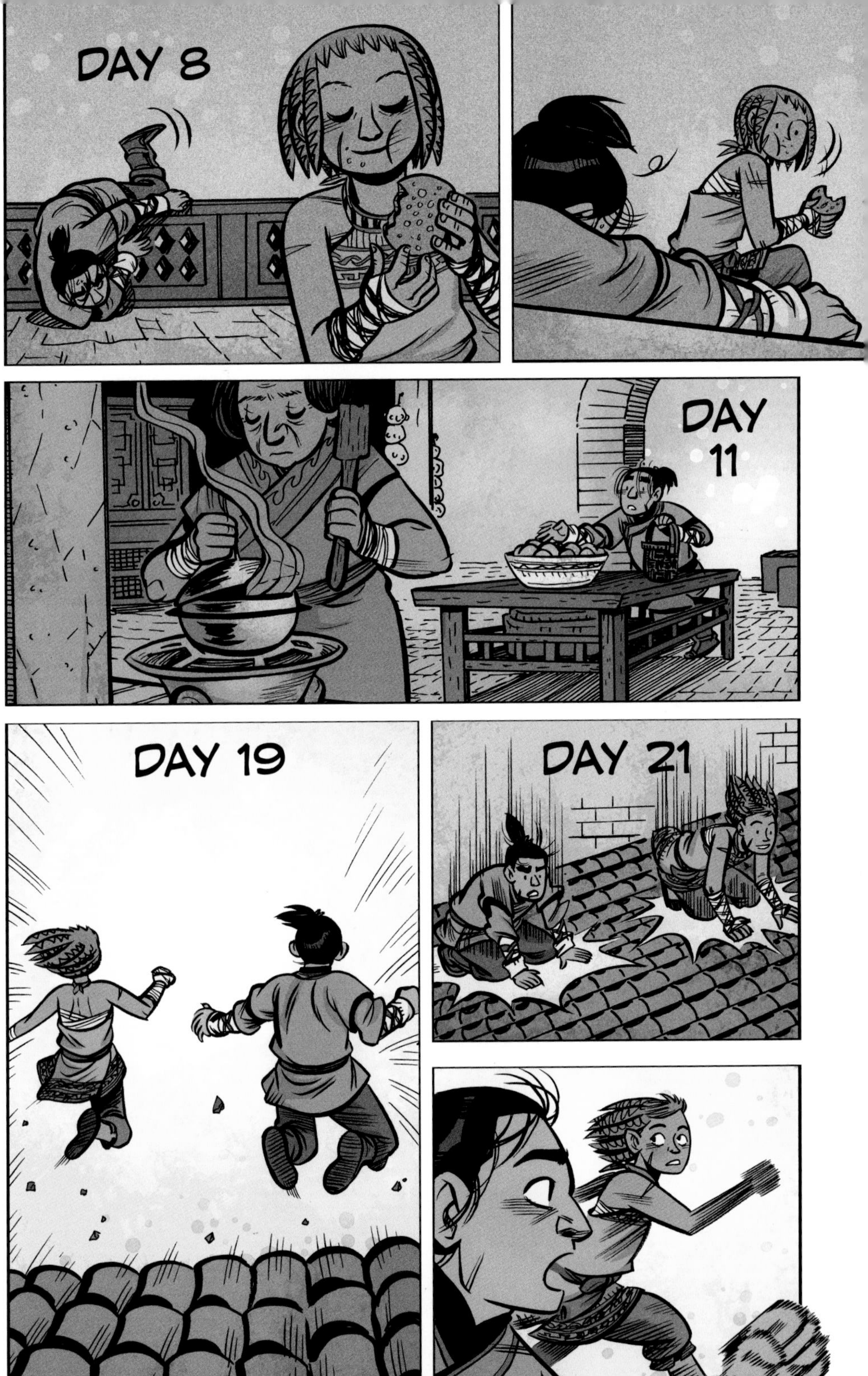
DAY 8
DAY 11
DAY 19
DAY 21

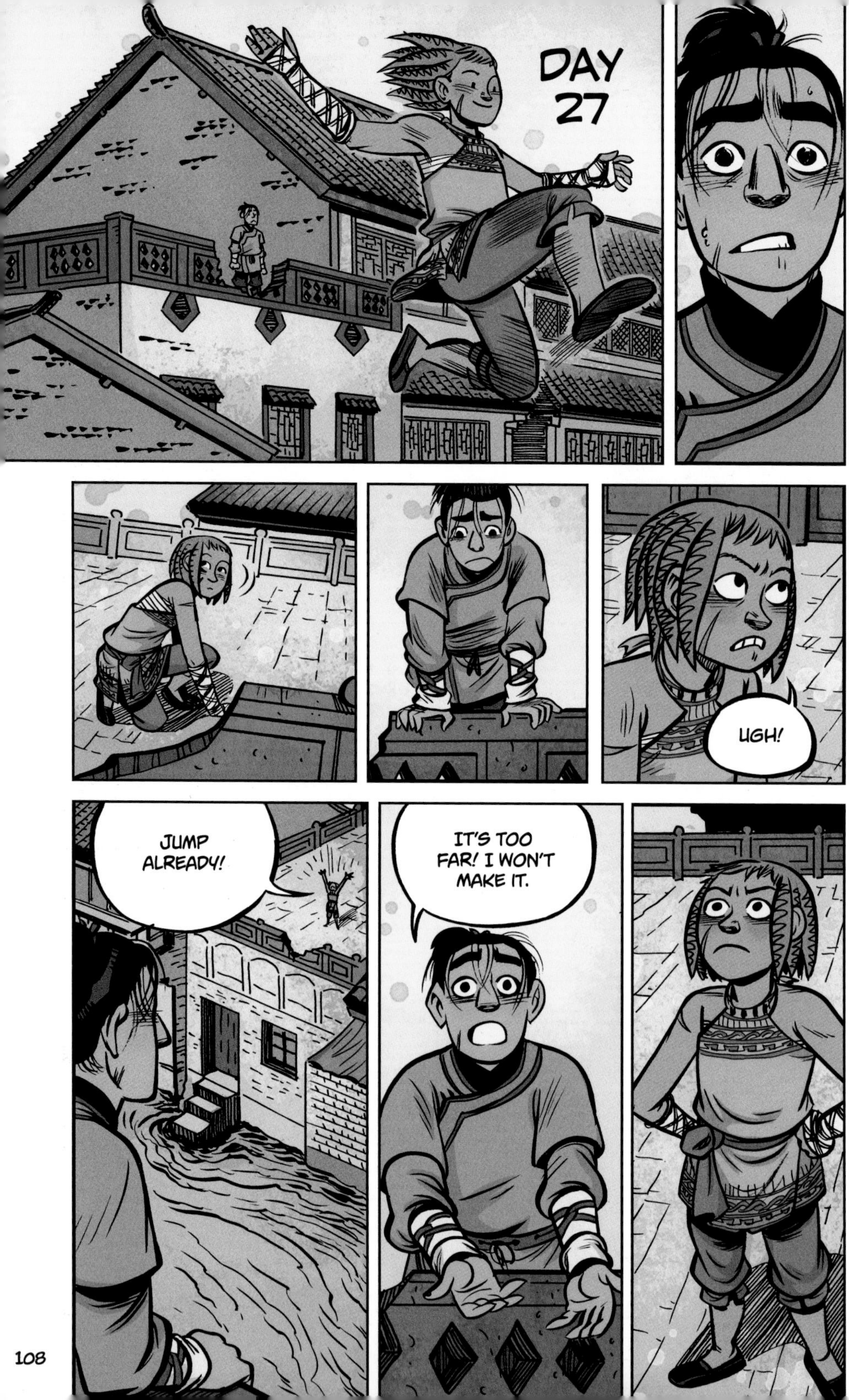
DAY
27
UGH!
JUMP
ALREADY!
IT'S TOO
FAR! I WON'T
MAKE IT.

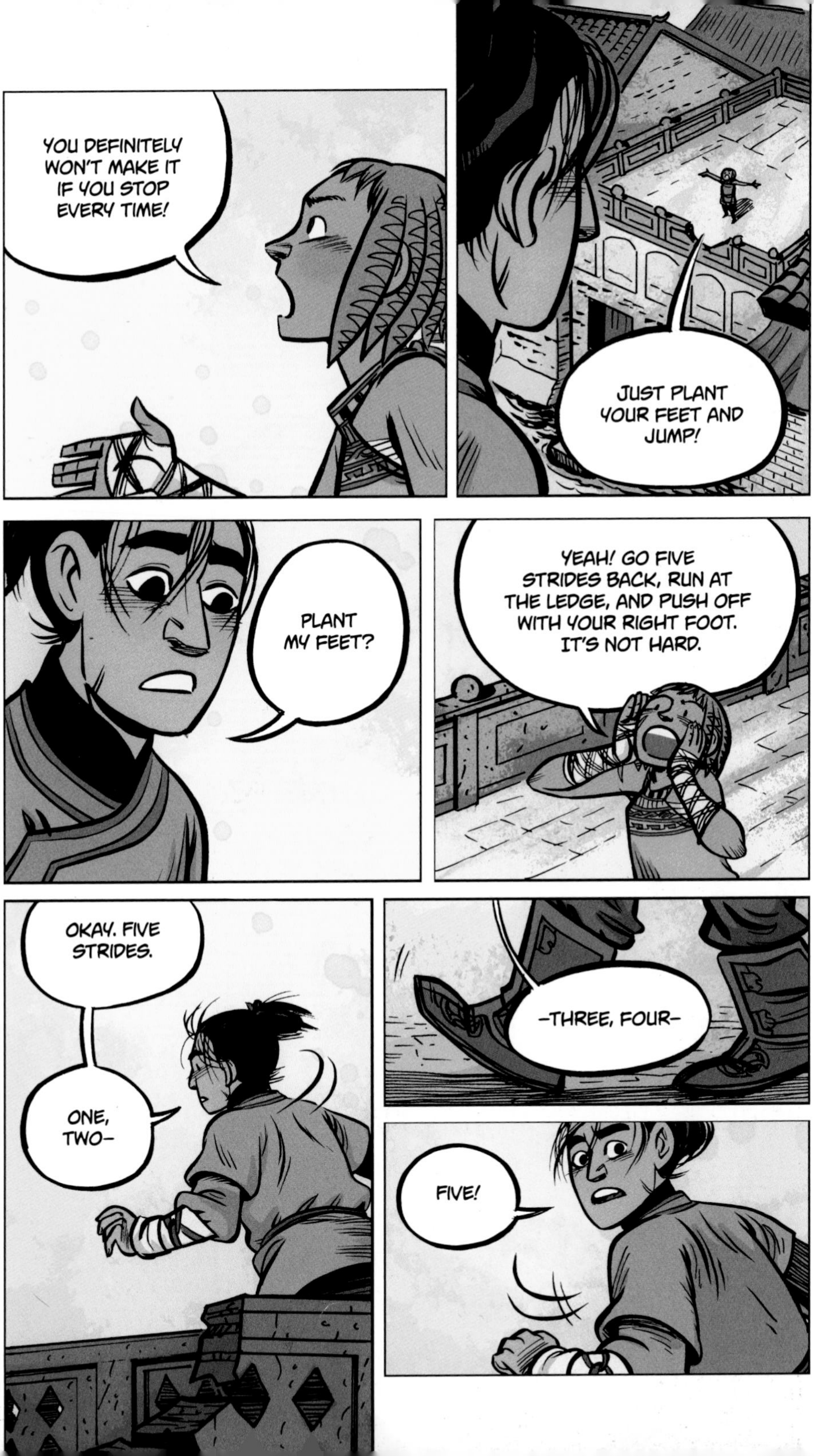
YOU DEFINITELY WON'T MAKE IT IF YOU STOP EVERY TIME!
JUST PLANT YOUR FEET AND JUMP!
PLANT MY FEET?
YEAH! GO FIVE STRIDES BACK, RUN AT THE LEDGE, AND PUSH OFF WITH YOUR RIGHT FOOT. IT'S NOT HARD.
OKAY. FIVE STRIDES.
ONE, TWO-
-THREE, FOUR-
FIVE!

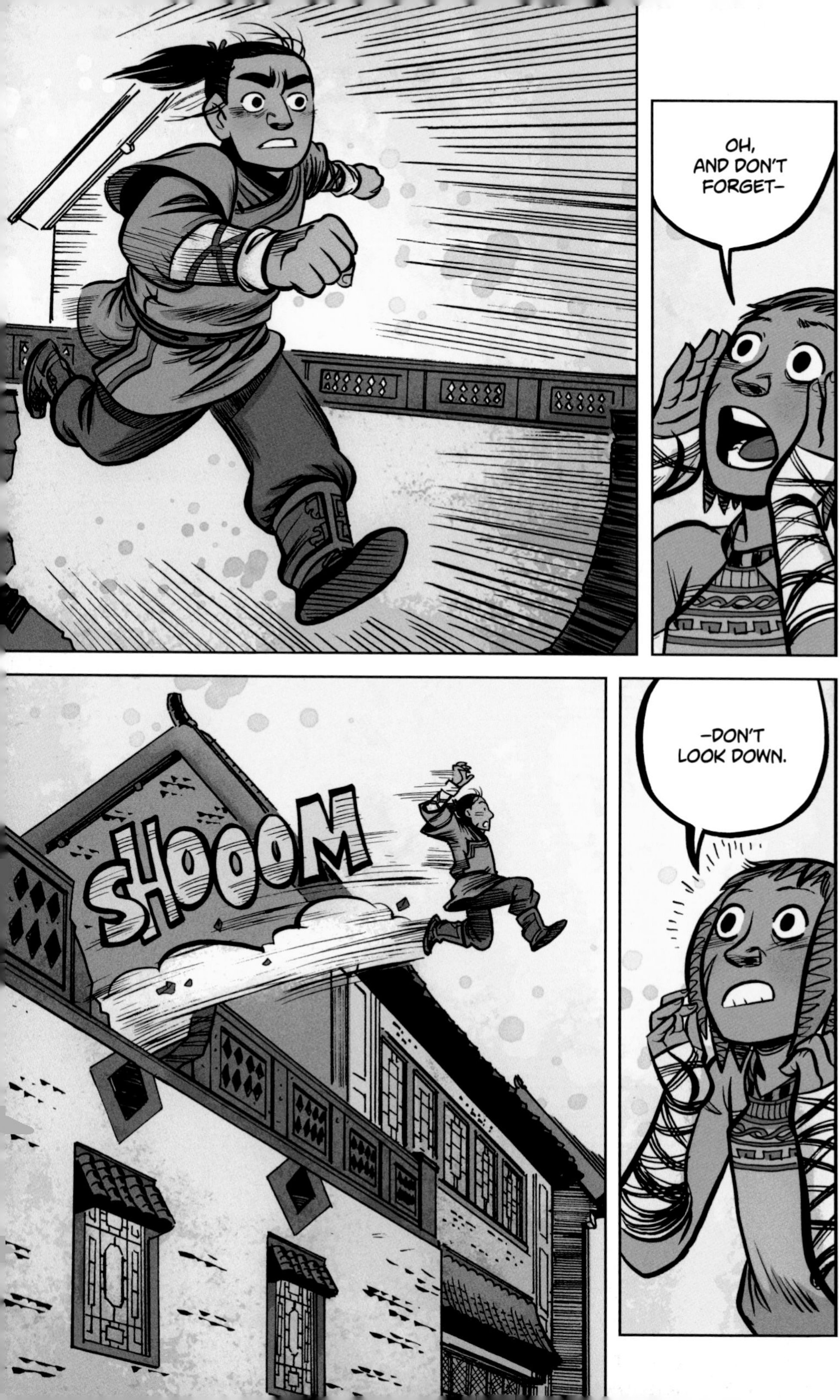
OH, AND DON'T FORGET–
SHOOOM
–DON'T LOOK DOWN.

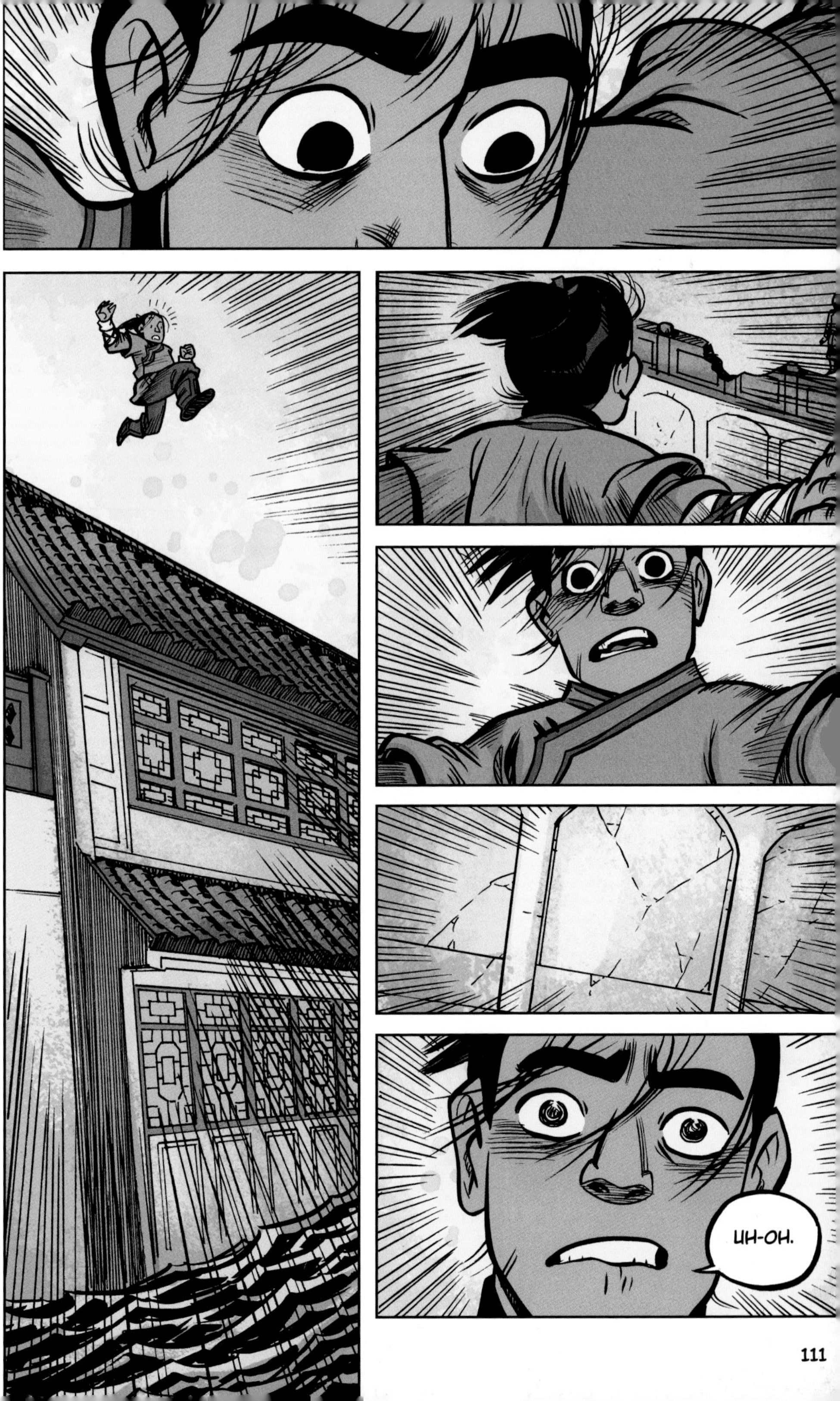
UH-OH.

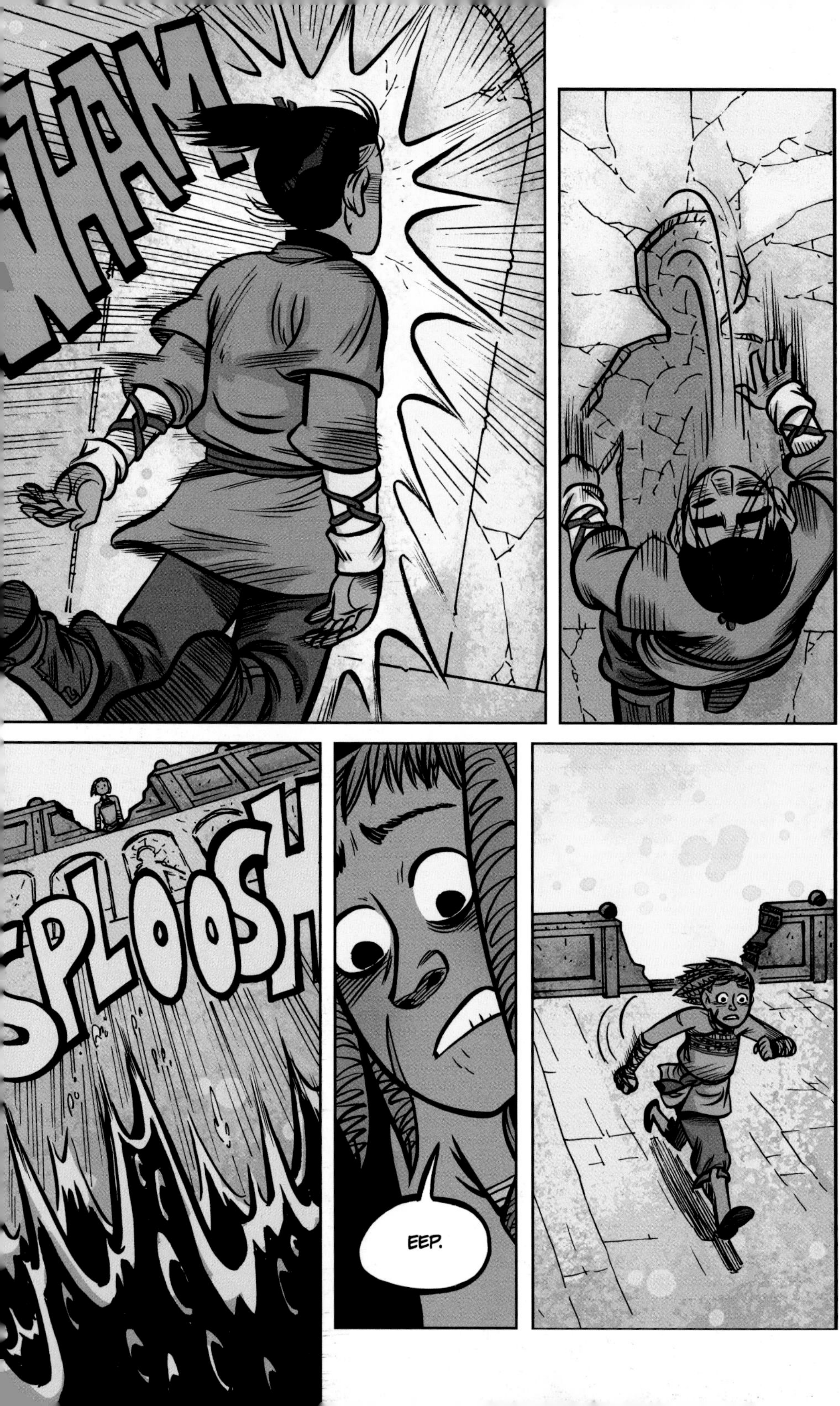
WHAM!
SPLOOSH
EEP.

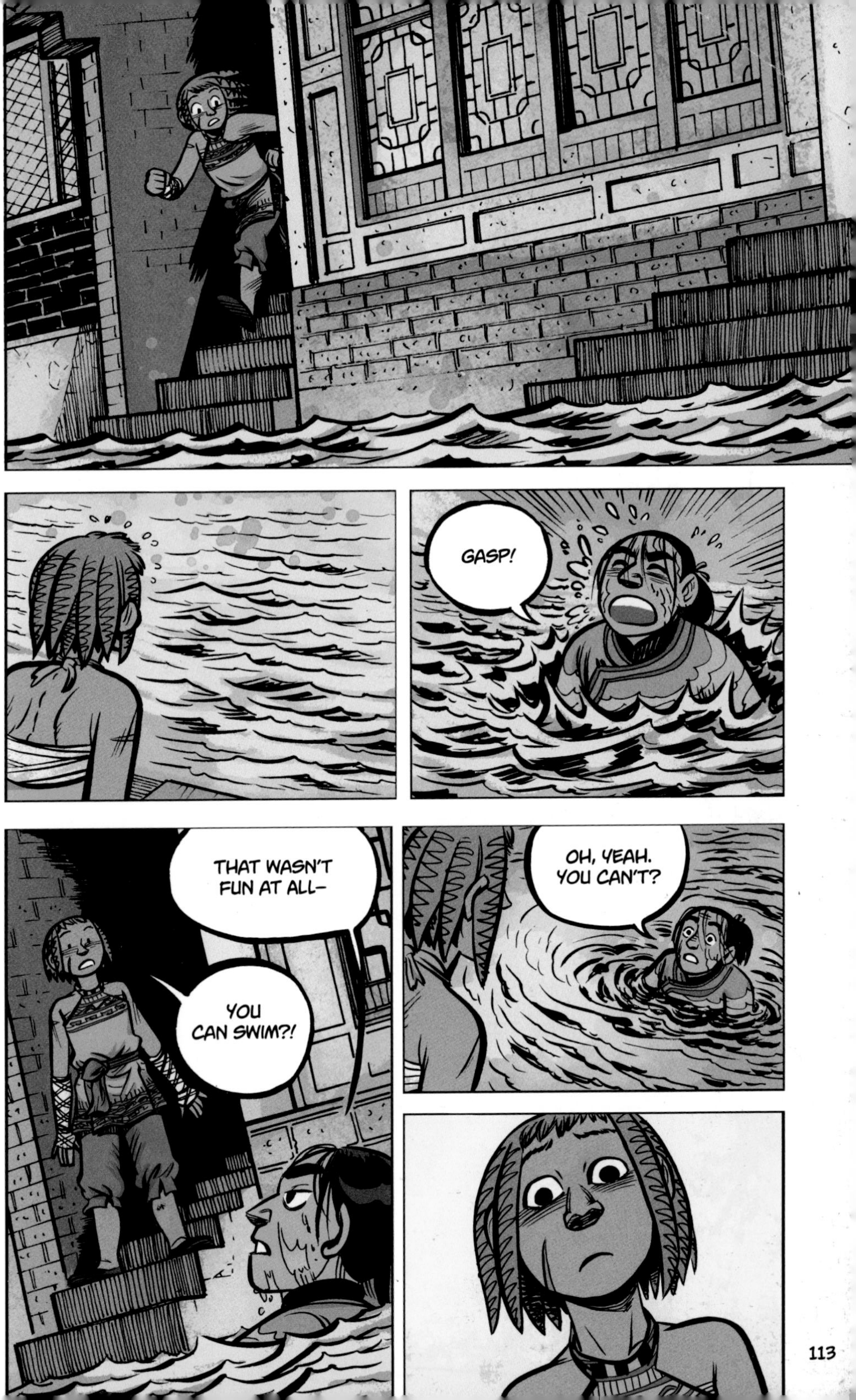
GASP!
THAT WASN'T FUN AT ALL—
YOU CAN SWIM?!
OH, YEAH. YOU CAN'T?

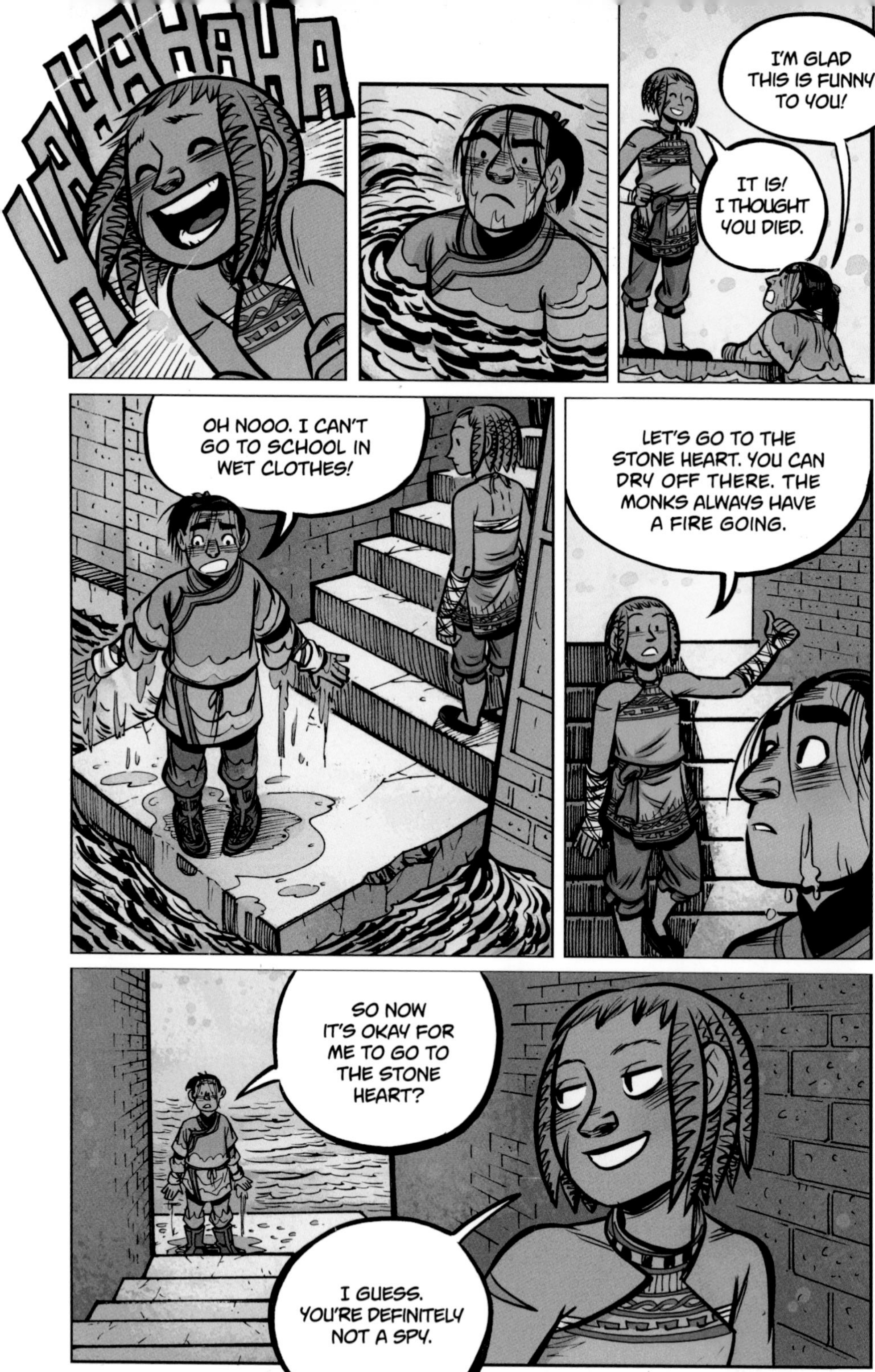
HAHAHAHAHA
I'M GLAD THIS IS FUNNY TO YOU!
IT IS! I THOUGHT YOU DIED.
OH NOOO. I CAN'T GO TO SCHOOL IN WET CLOTHES!
LET'S GO TO THE STONE HEART. YOU CAN DRY OFF THERE. THE MONKS ALWAYS HAVE A FIRE GOING.
SO NOW IT'S OKAY FOR ME TO GO TO THE STONE HEART?
I GUESS. YOU'RE DEFINITELY NOT A SPY.

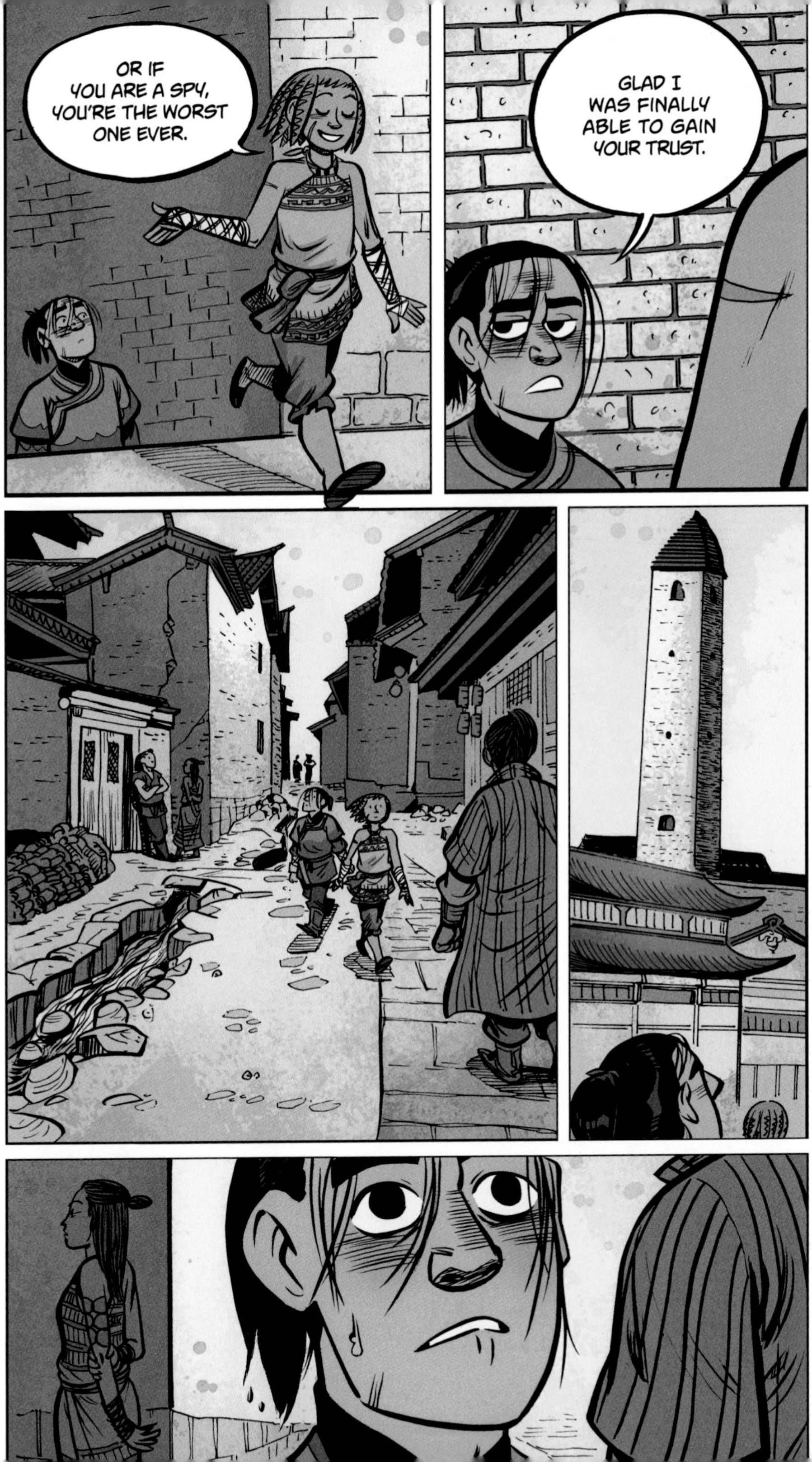
OR IF YOU ARE A SPY, YOU'RE THE WORST ONE EVER.
GLAD I WAS FINALLY ABLE TO GAIN YOUR TRUST.

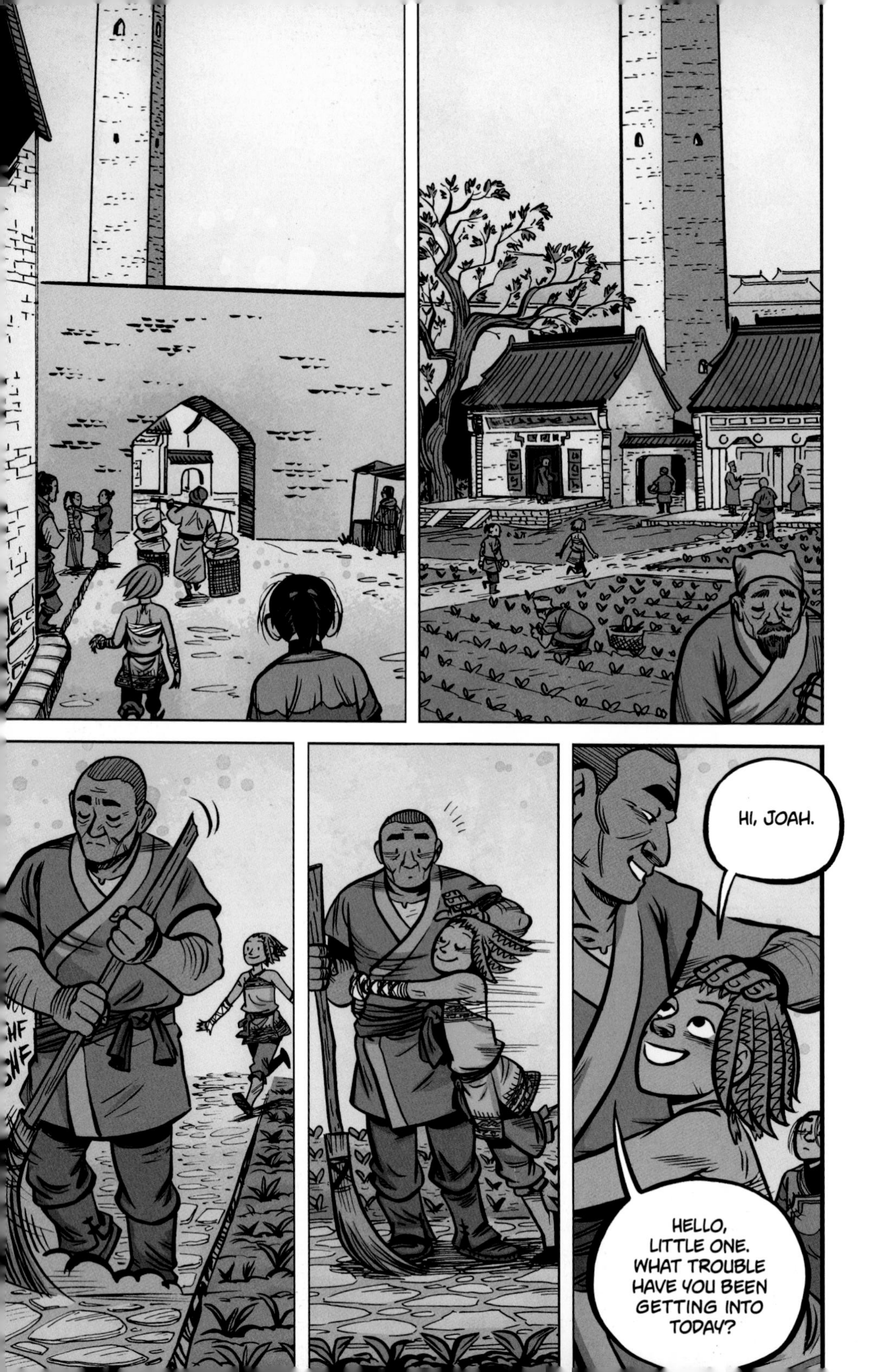
HI, JOAH.
HELLO, LITTLE ONE. WHAT TROUBLE HAVE YOU BEEN GETTING INTO TODAY?

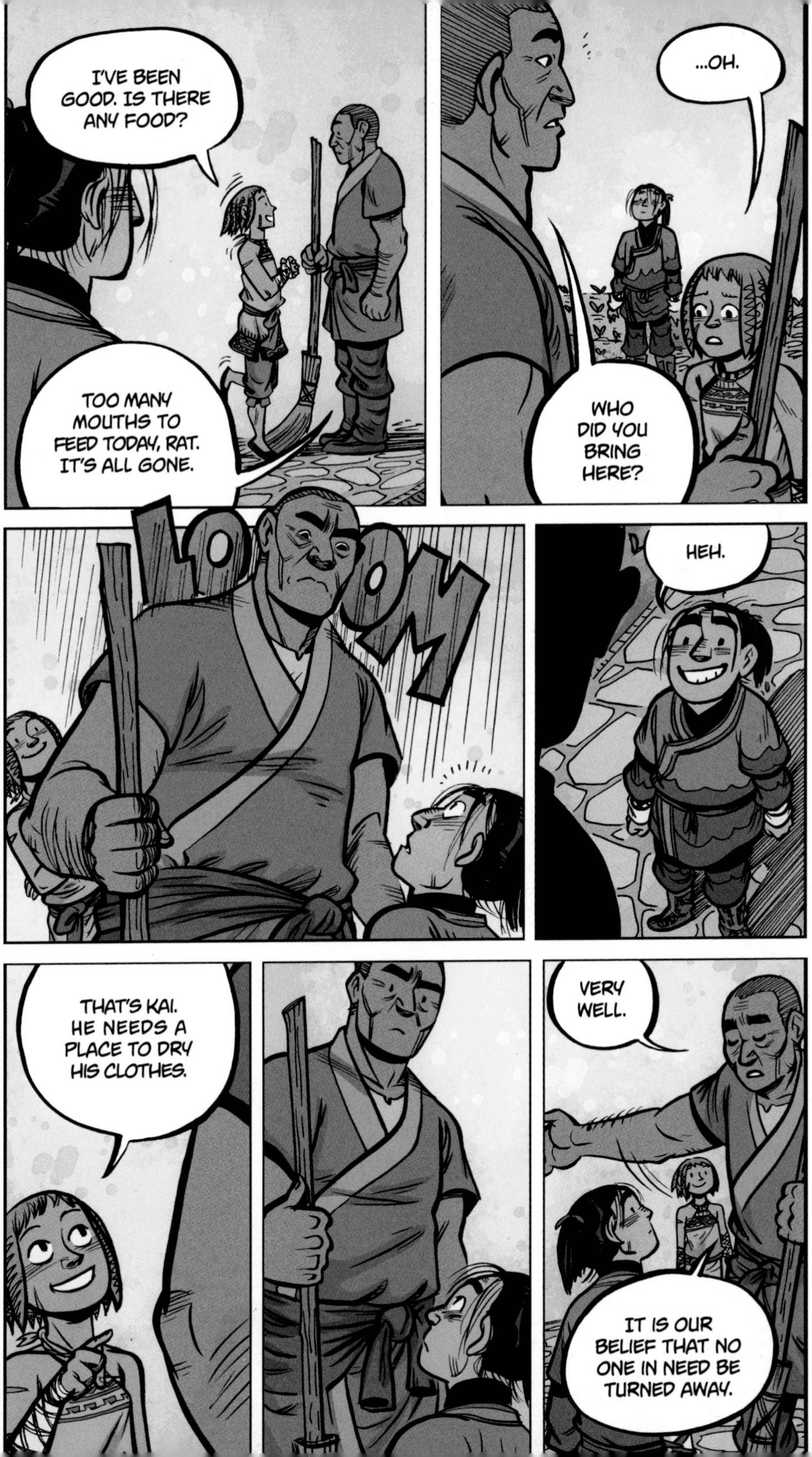
I'VE BEEN GOOD. IS THERE ANY FOOD?
TOO MANY MOUTHS TO FEED TODAY, RAT. IT'S ALL GONE.
...OH.
WHO DID YOU BRING HERE?
LOOOM
HEH.
THAT'S KAI. HE NEEDS A PLACE TO DRY HIS CLOTHES.
VERY WELL.
IT IS OUR BELIEF THAT NO ONE IN NEED BE TURNED AWAY.

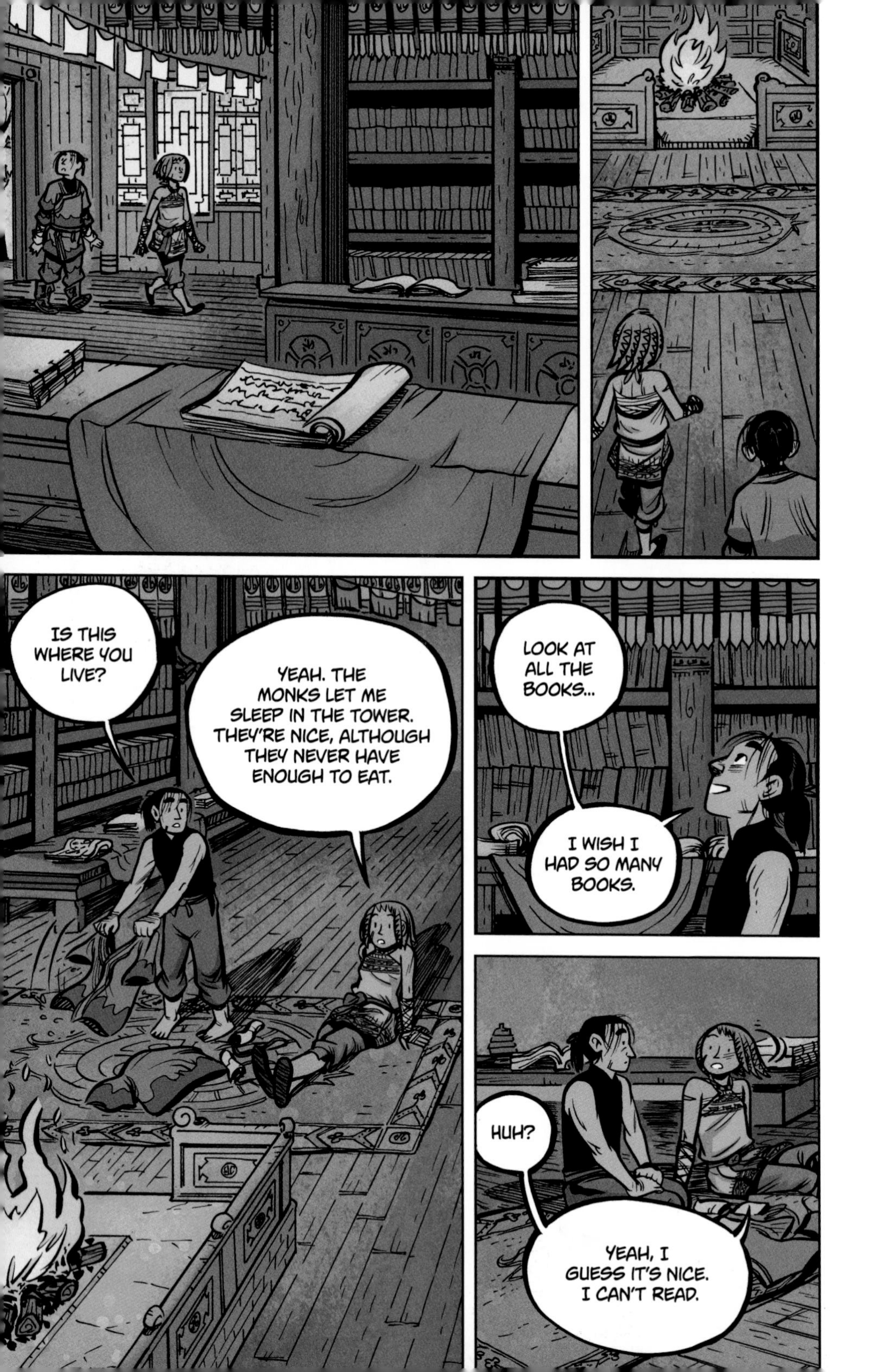
IS THIS WHERE YOU LIVE?
YEAH. THE MONKS LET ME SLEEP IN THE TOWER. THEY'RE NICE, ALTHOUGH THEY NEVER HAVE ENOUGH TO EAT.
LOOK AT ALL THE BOOKS...
I WISH I HAD SO MANY BOOKS.
HUH?
YEAH, I GUESS IT'S NICE. I CAN'T READ.

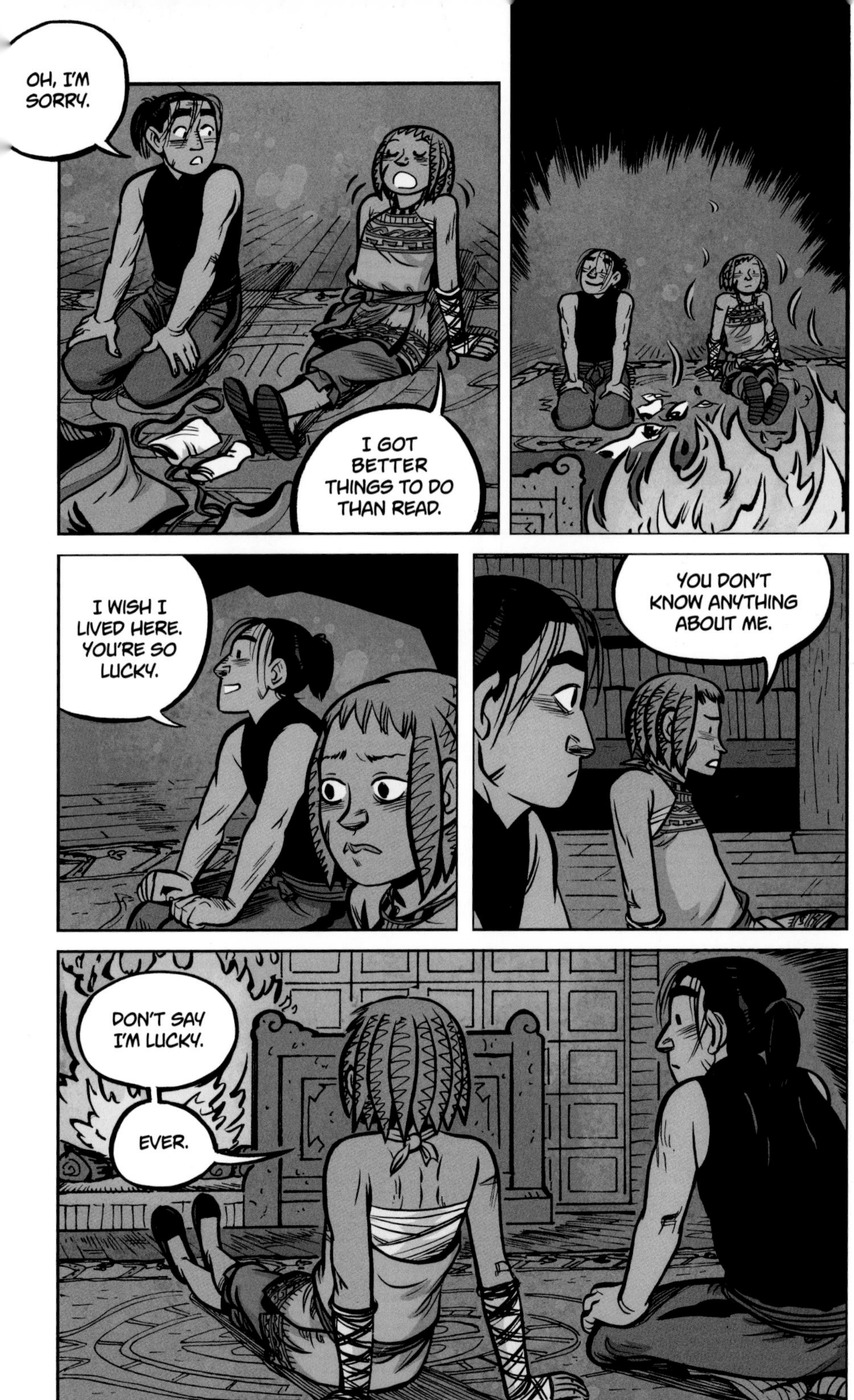
OH, I'M SORRY.
I GOT BETTER THINGS TO DO THAN READ.
I WISH I LIVED HERE. YOU'RE SO LUCKY.
YOU DON'T KNOW ANYTHING ABOUT ME.
DON'T SAY I'M LUCKY.
EVER.

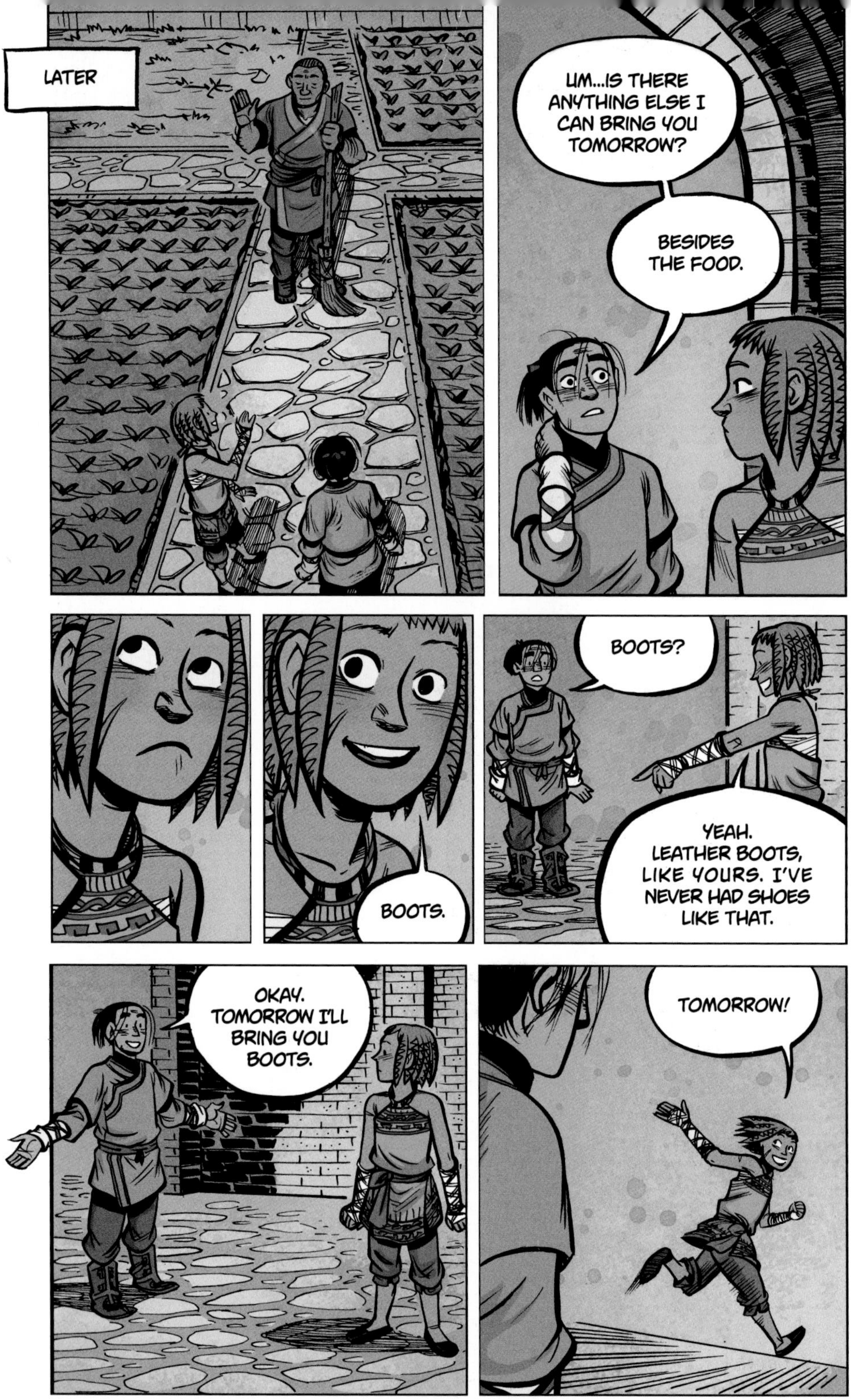
LATER
UM...IS THERE ANYTHING ELSE I CAN BRING YOU TOMORROW?
BESIDES THE FOOD.
BOOTS.
BOOTS?
YEAH. LEATHER BOOTS, LIKE YOURS. I'VE NEVER HAD SHOES LIKE THAT.
OKAY. TOMORROW I'LL BRING YOU BOOTS.
TOMORROW!

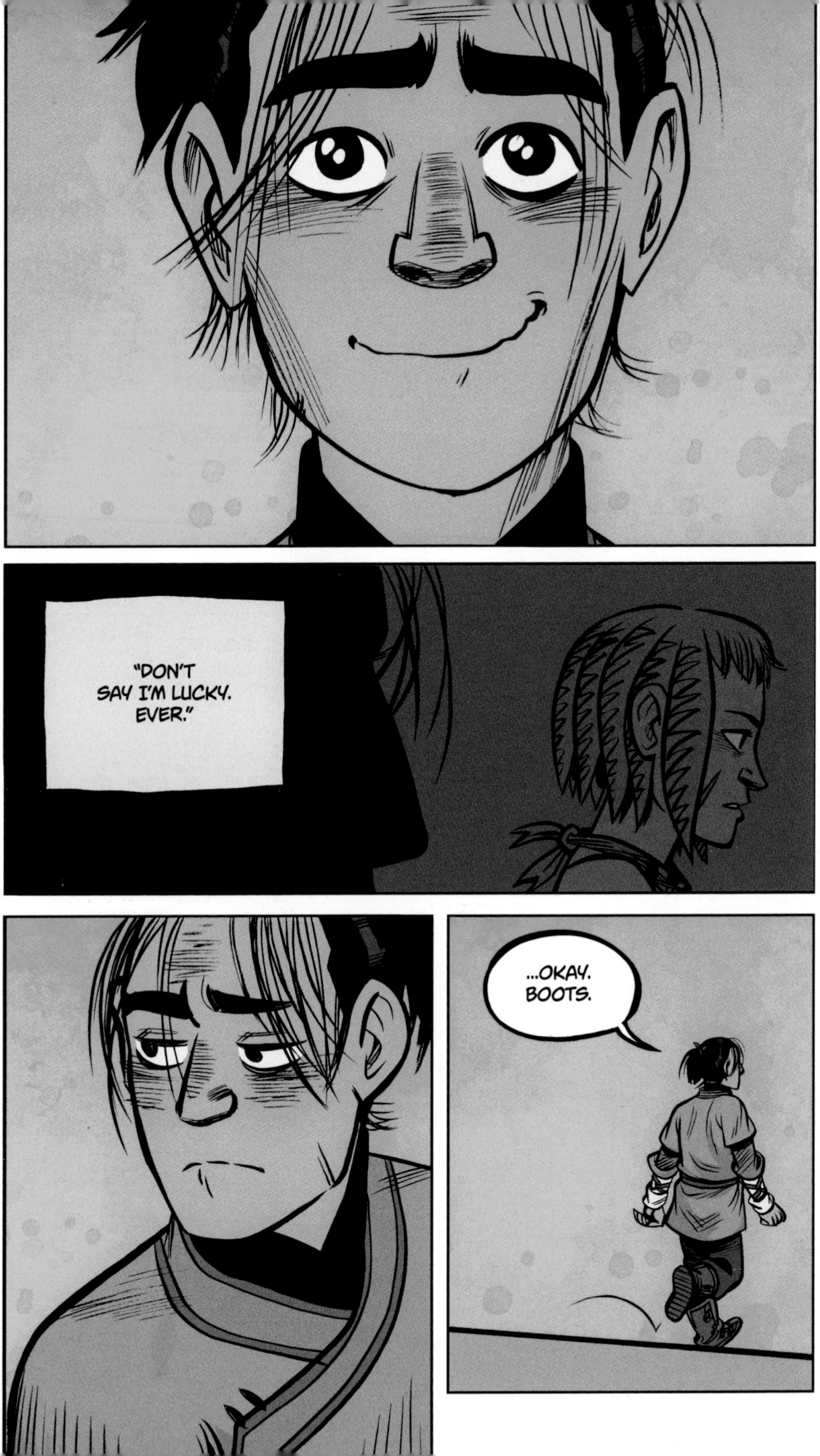
"DON'T SAY I'M LUCKY. EVER."
...OKAY. BOOTS.

DAY 28

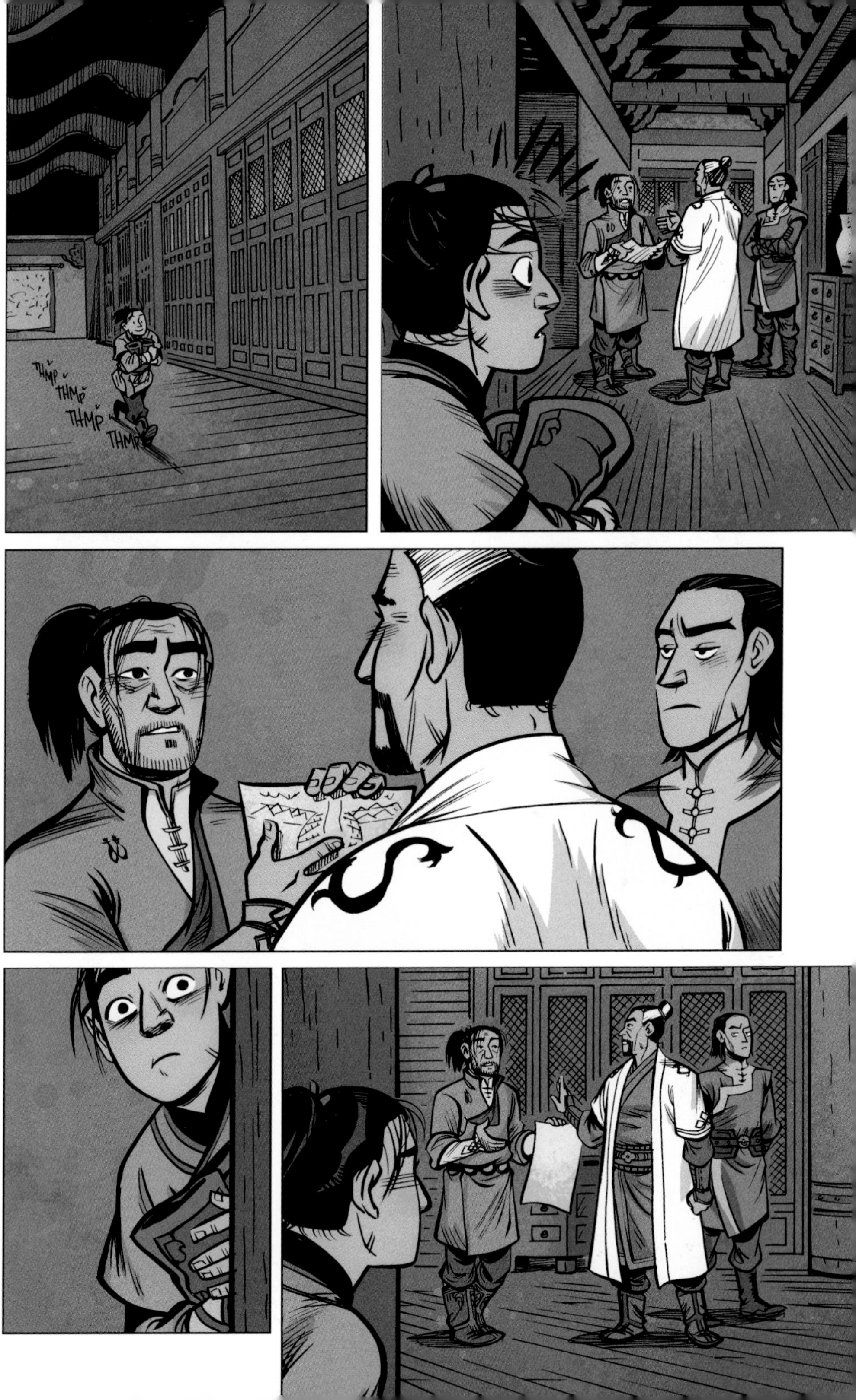
THMP
THMP
THMP
THMP

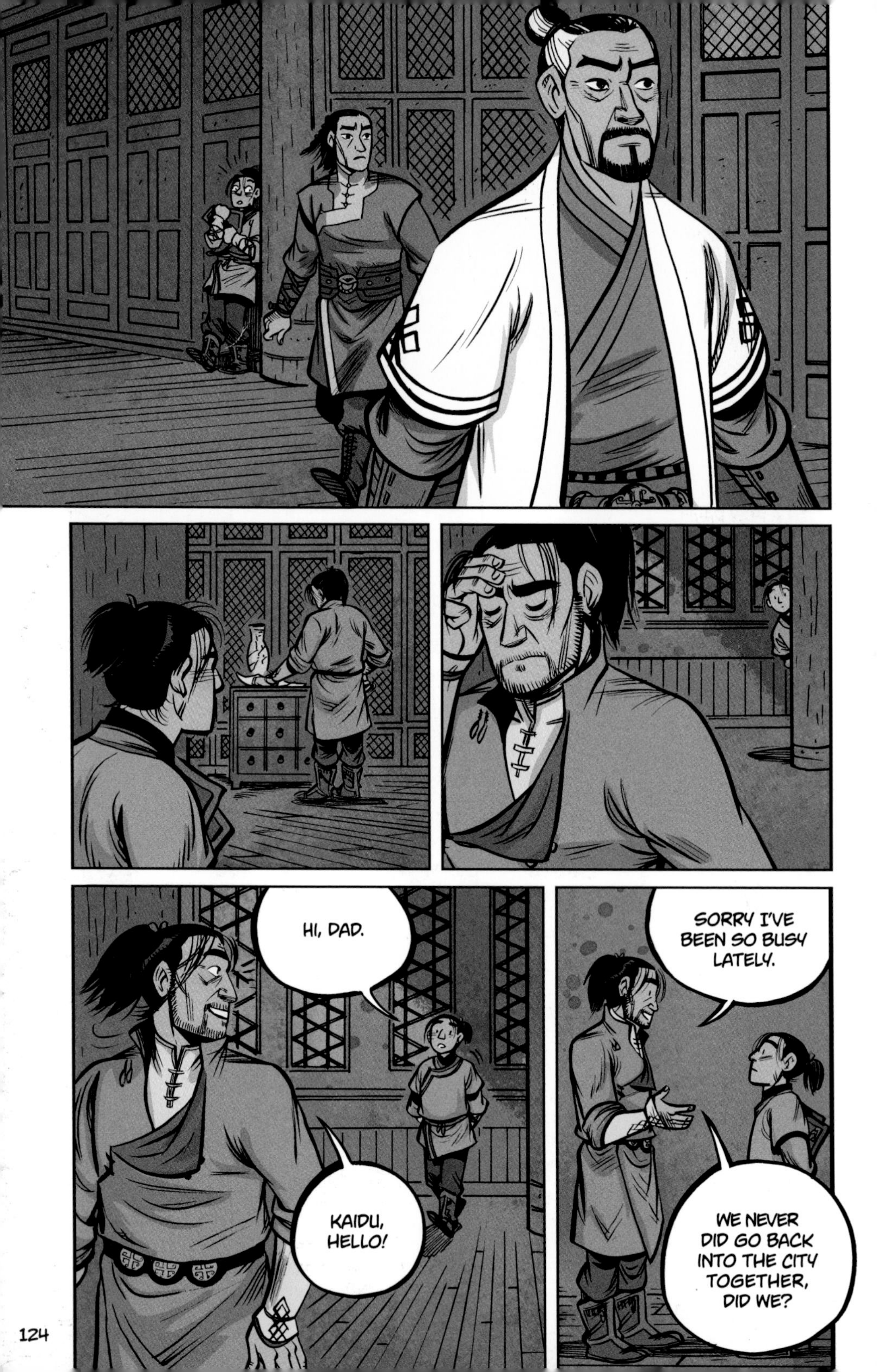
HI, DAD.
KAIDU, HELLO!
SORRY I'VE BEEN SO BUSY LATELY.
WE NEVER DID GO BACK INTO THE CITY TOGETHER, DID WE?

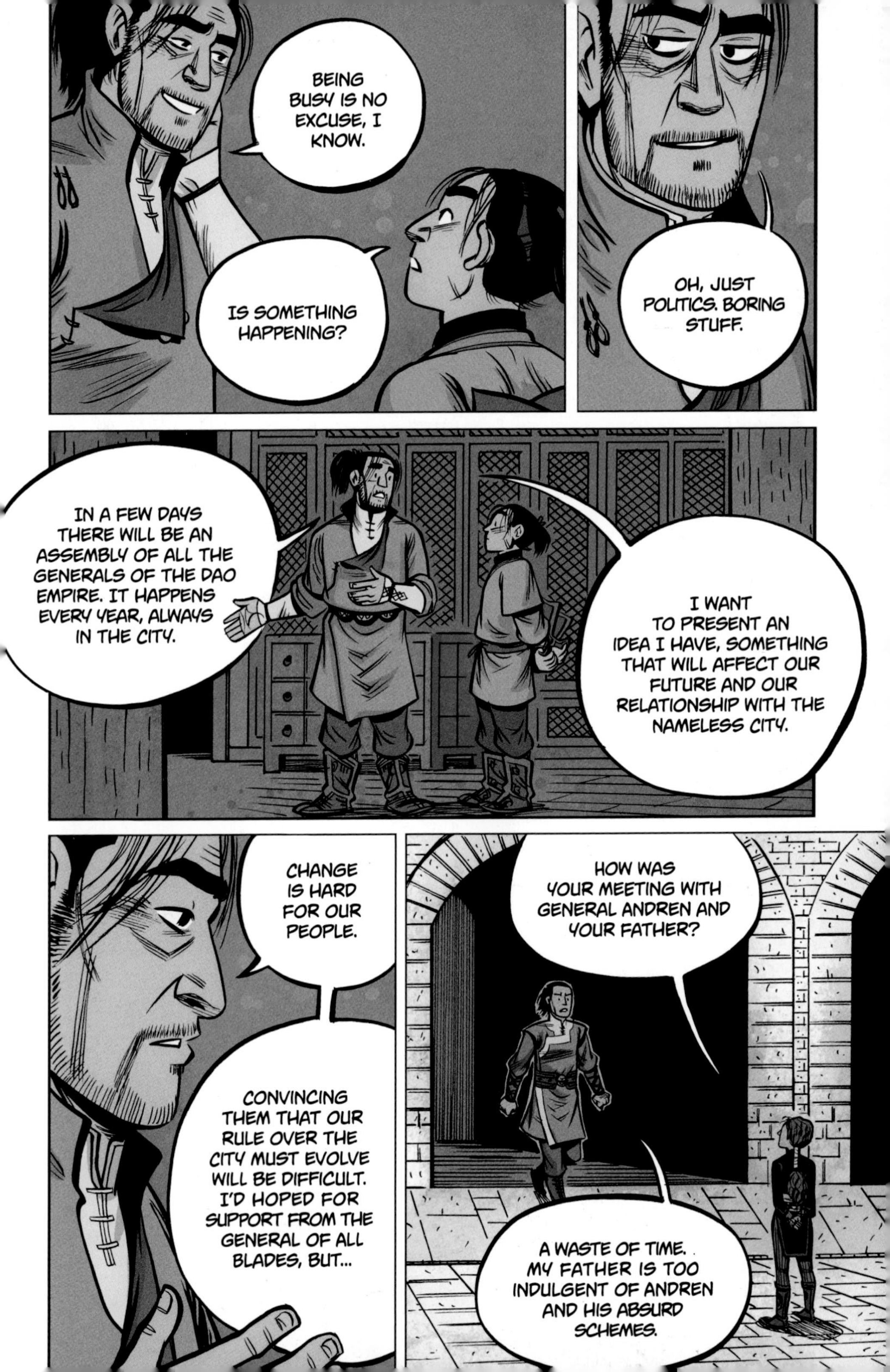
BEING BUSY IS NO EXCUSE, I KNOW.
IS SOMETHING HAPPENING?
OH, JUST POLITICS. BORING STUFF.
IN A FEW DAYS THERE WILL BE AN ASSEMBLY OF ALL THE GENERALS OF THE DAO EMPIRE. IT HAPPENS EVERY YEAR, ALWAYS IN THE CITY.
I WANT TO PRESENT AN IDEA I HAVE, SOMETHING THAT WILL AFFECT OUR FUTURE AND OUR RELATIONSHIP WITH THE NAMELESS CITY.
CHANGE IS HARD FOR OUR PEOPLE.
CONVINCING THEM THAT OUR RULE OVER THE CITY MUST EVOLVE WILL BE DIFFICULT. I'D HOPED FOR SUPPORT FROM THE GENERAL OF ALL BLADES, BUT...
HOW WAS YOUR MEETING WITH GENERAL ANDREN AND YOUR FATHER?
A WASTE OF TIME. MY FATHER IS TOO INDULGENT OF ANDREN AND HIS ABSURD SCHEMES.

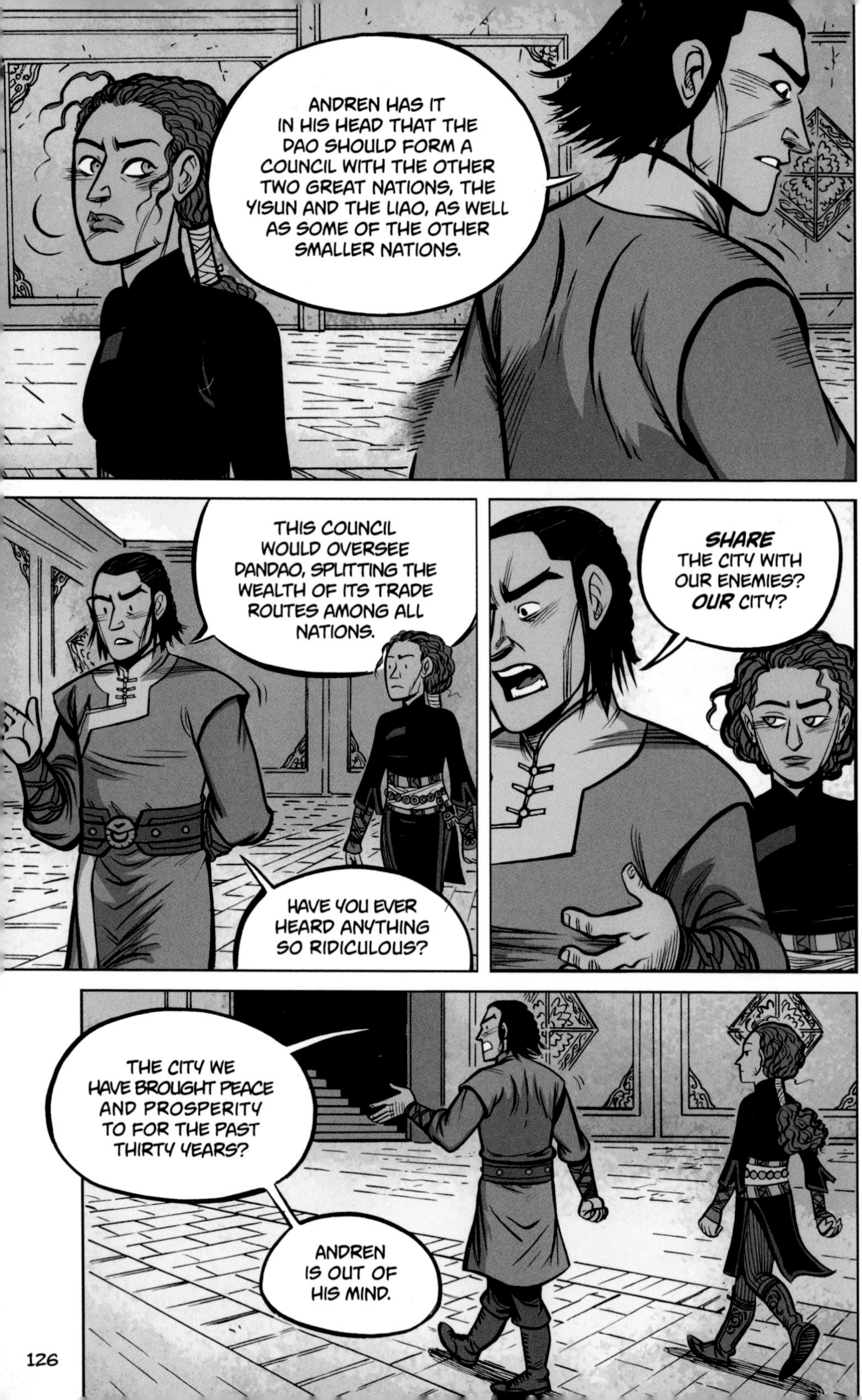
ANDREN HAS IT IN HIS HEAD THAT THE DAO SHOULD FORM A COUNCIL WITH THE OTHER TWO GREAT NATIONS, THE YISUN AND THE LIAO, AS WELL AS SOME OF THE OTHER SMALLER NATIONS.
THIS COUNCIL WOULD OVERSEE DANDAO, SPLITTING THE WEALTH OF ITS TRADE ROUTES AMONG ALL NATIONS.
HAVE YOU EVER HEARD ANYTHING SO RIDICULOUS?
SHARE THE CITY WITH OUR ENEMIES? *OUR* CITY?
THE CITY WE HAVE BROUGHT PEACE AND PROSPERITY TO FOR THE PAST THIRTY YEARS?
ANDREN IS OUT OF HIS MIND.

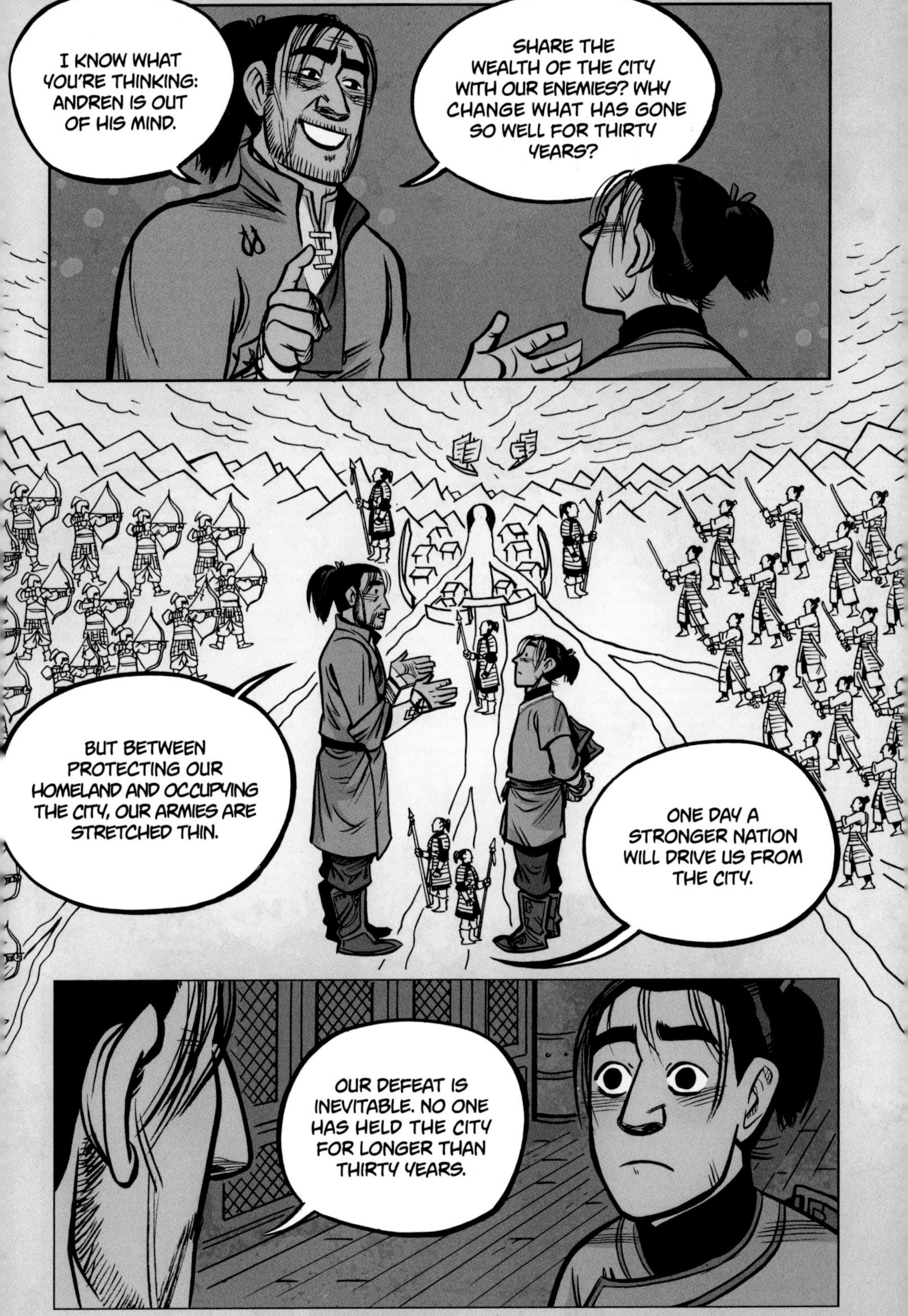
I KNOW WHAT YOU'RE THINKING: ANDREN IS OUT OF HIS MIND.
SHARE THE WEALTH OF THE CITY WITH OUR ENEMIES? WHY CHANGE WHAT HAS GONE SO WELL FOR THIRTY YEARS?
BUT BETWEEN PROTECTING OUR HOMELAND AND OCCUPYING THE CITY, OUR ARMIES ARE STRETCHED THIN.
ONE DAY A STRONGER NATION WILL DRIVE US FROM THE CITY.
OUR DEFEAT IS INEVITABLE. NO ONE HAS HELD THE CITY FOR LONGER THAN THIRTY YEARS.

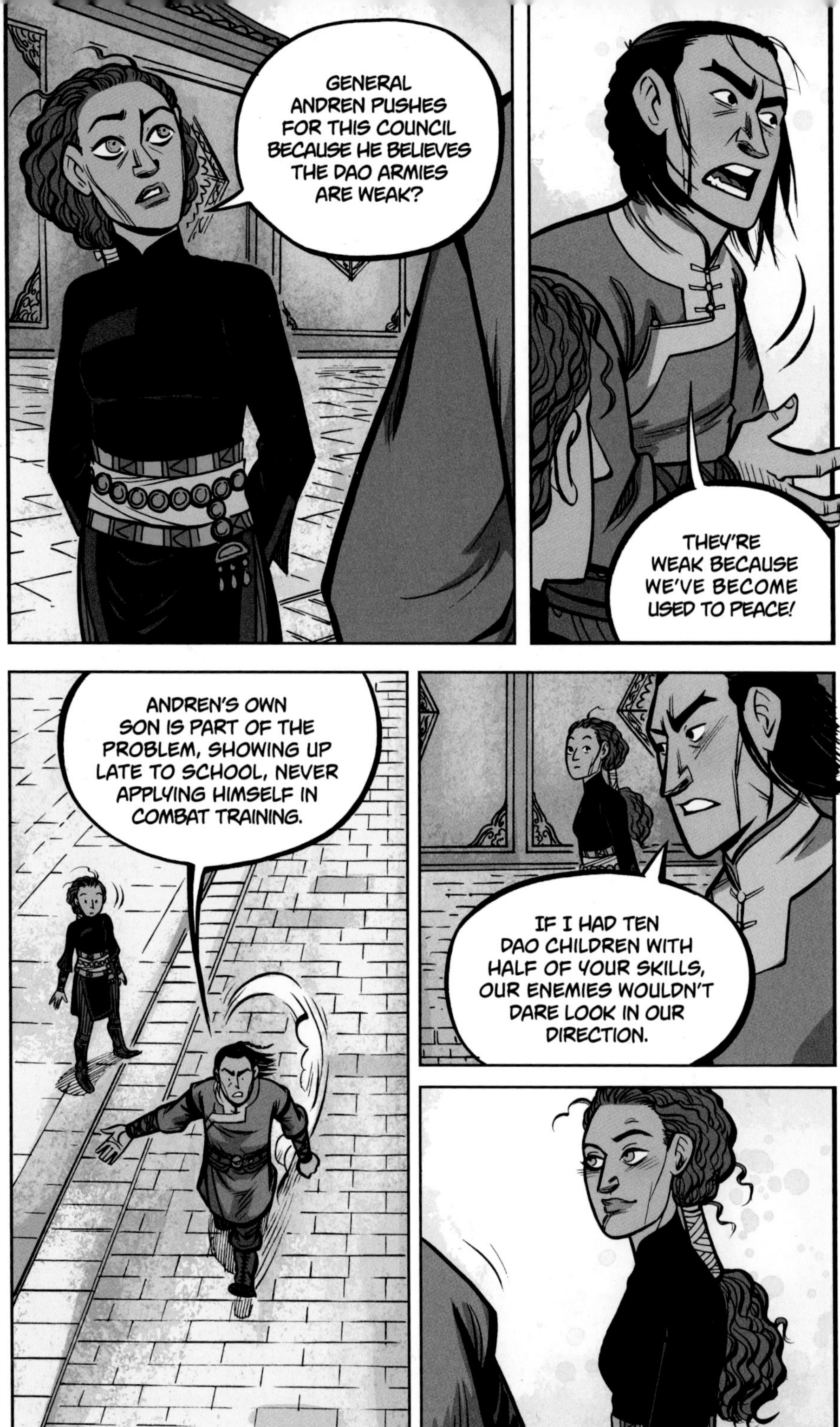
GENERAL ANDREN PUSHES FOR THIS COUNCIL BECAUSE HE BELIEVES THE DAO ARMIES ARE WEAK?
THEY'RE WEAK BECAUSE WE'VE BECOME USED TO PEACE!
ANDREN'S OWN SON IS PART OF THE PROBLEM, SHOWING UP LATE TO SCHOOL, NEVER APPLYING HIMSELF IN COMBAT TRAINING.
IF I HAD TEN DAO CHILDREN WITH HALF OF YOUR SKILLS, OUR ENEMIES WOULDN'T DARE LOOK IN OUR DIRECTION.

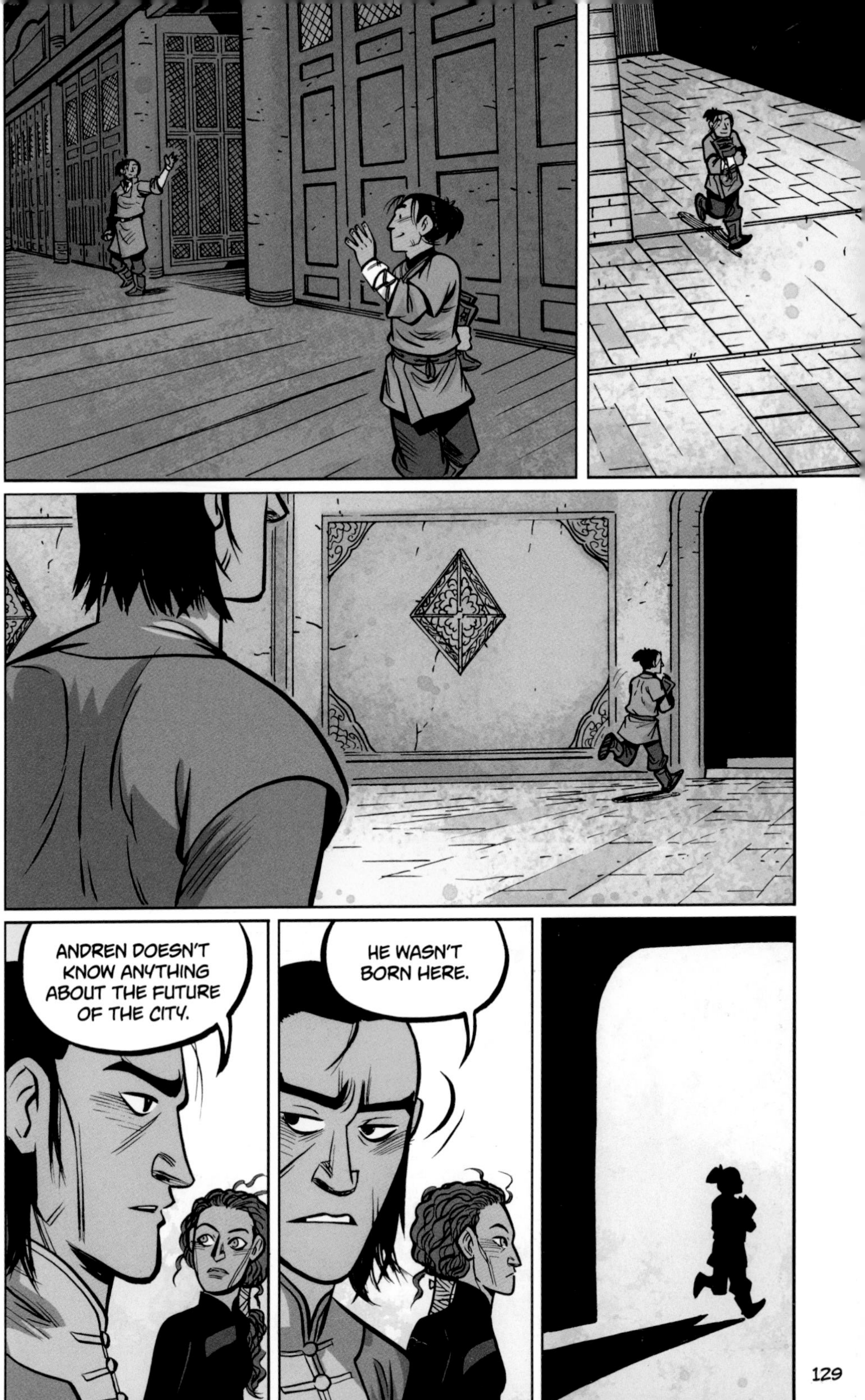
ANDREN DOESN'T KNOW ANYTHING ABOUT THE FUTURE OF THE CITY.
HE WASN'T BORN HERE.

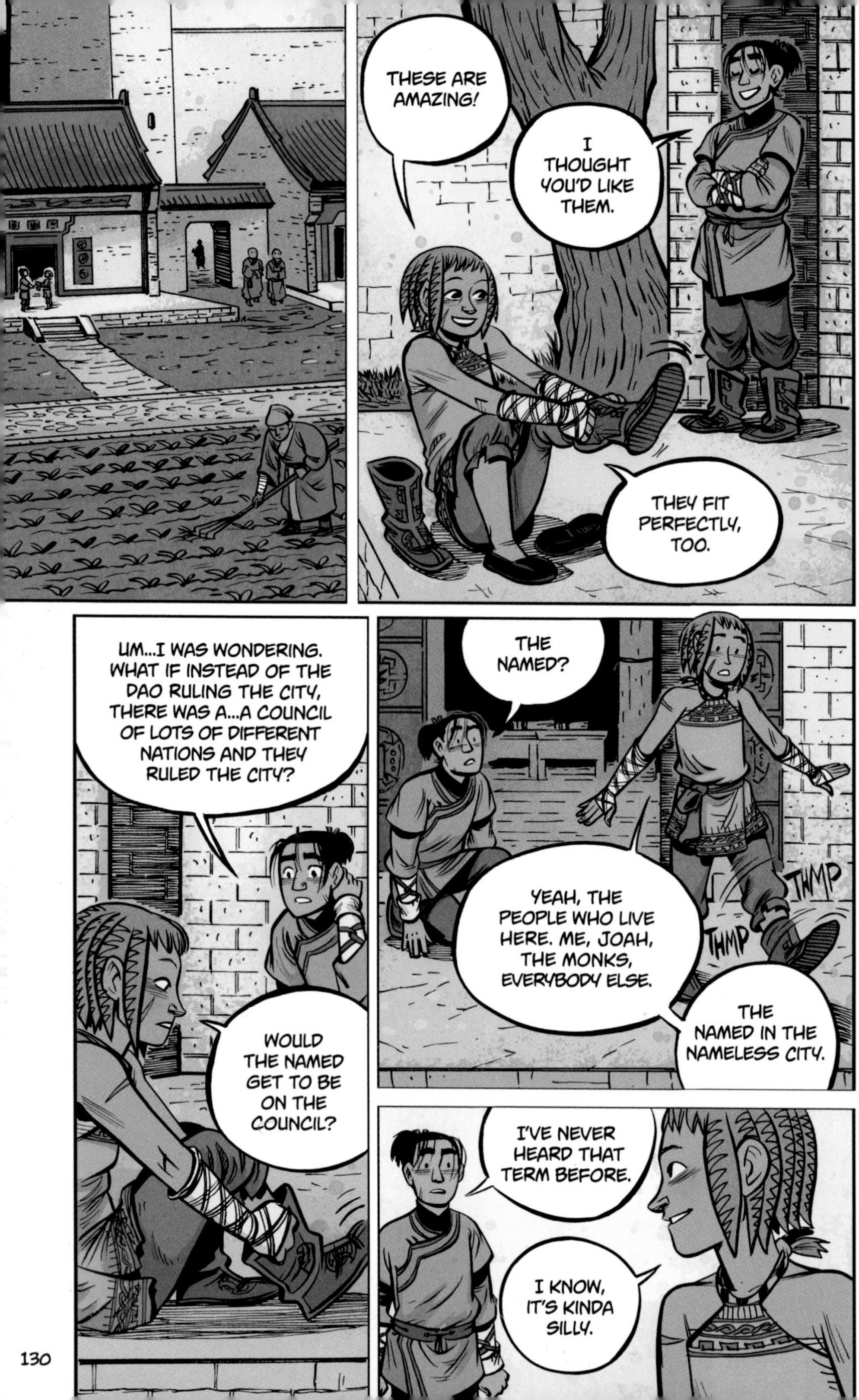
THESE ARE AMAZING!
I THOUGHT YOU'D LIKE THEM.
THEY FIT PERFECTLY, TOO.
UM...I WAS WONDERING. WHAT IF INSTEAD OF THE DAO RULING THE CITY, THERE WAS A...A COUNCIL OF LOTS OF DIFFERENT NATIONS AND THEY RULED THE CITY?
WOULD THE NAMED GET TO BE ON THE COUNCIL?
THE NAMED?
YEAH, THE PEOPLE WHO LIVE HERE. ME, JOAH, THE MONKS, EVERYBODY ELSE.
THMP
THMP
THE NAMED IN THE NAMELESS CITY.
I'VE NEVER HEARD THAT TERM BEFORE.
I KNOW, IT'S KINDA SILLY.

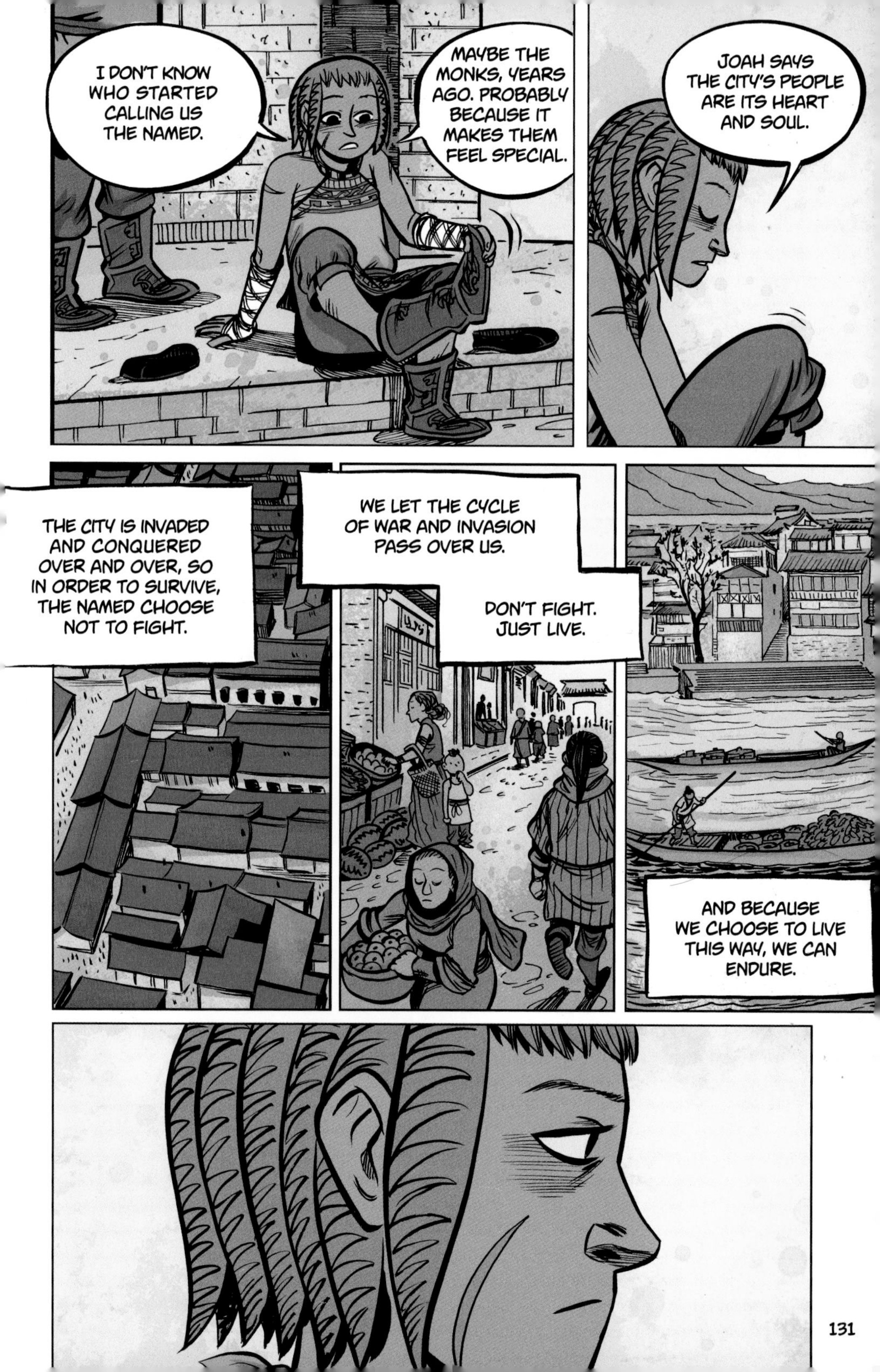

I DON'T KNOW WHO STARTED CALLING US THE NAMED.
MAYBE THE MONKS, YEARS AGO. PROBABLY BECAUSE IT MAKES THEM FEEL SPECIAL.
JOAH SAYS THE CITY'S PEOPLE ARE ITS HEART AND SOUL.
THE CITY IS INVADED AND CONQUERED OVER AND OVER, SO IN ORDER TO SURVIVE, THE NAMED CHOOSE NOT TO FIGHT.
WE LET THE CYCLE OF WAR AND INVASION PASS OVER US.
DON'T FIGHT. JUST LIVE.
AND BECAUSE WE CHOOSE TO LIVE THIS WAY, WE CAN ENDURE.

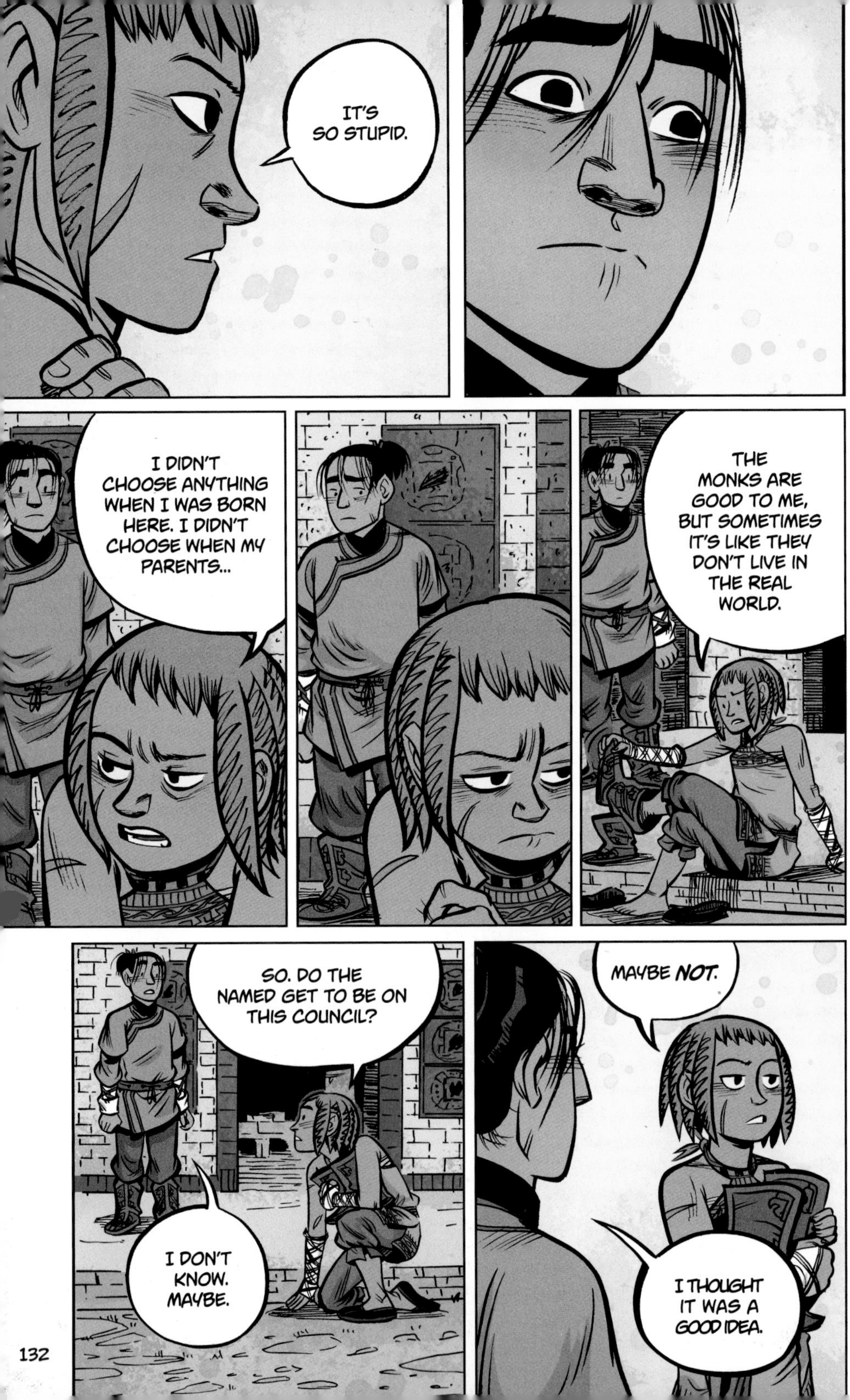
IT'S SO STUPID.
I DIDN'T CHOOSE ANYTHING WHEN I WAS BORN HERE. I DIDN'T CHOOSE WHEN MY PARENTS...
THE MONKS ARE GOOD TO ME, BUT SOMETIMES IT'S LIKE THEY DON'T LIVE IN THE REAL WORLD.
SO. DO THE NAMED GET TO BE ON THIS COUNCIL?
I DON'T KNOW. MAYBE.
MAYBE *NOT*.
I THOUGHT IT WAS A GOOD IDEA.

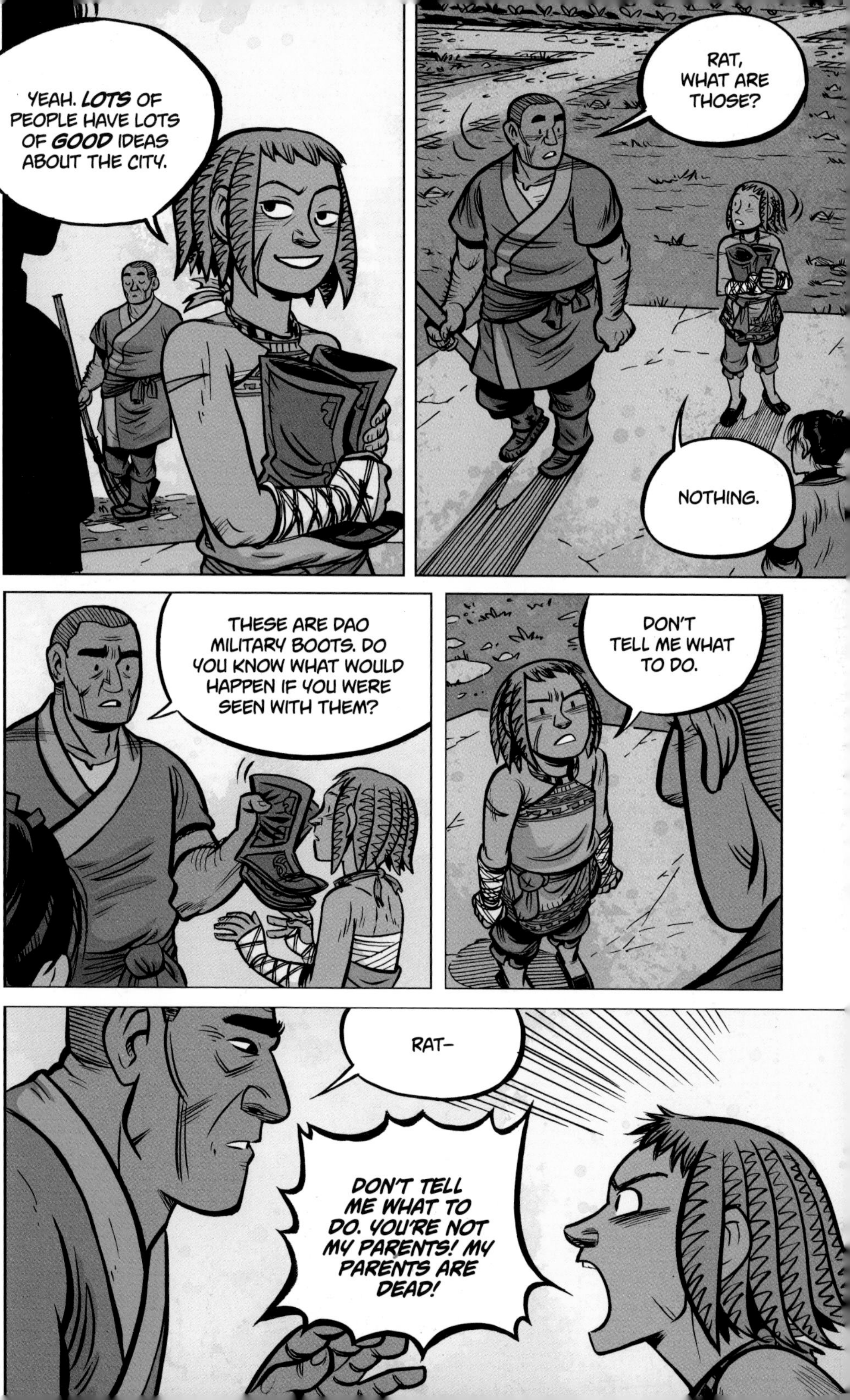
YEAH. LOTS OF PEOPLE HAVE LOTS OF GOOD IDEAS ABOUT THE CITY.
RAT, WHAT ARE THOSE?
NOTHING.
THESE ARE DAO MILITARY BOOTS. DO YOU KNOW WHAT WOULD HAPPEN IF YOU WERE SEEN WITH THEM?
DON'T TELL ME WHAT TO DO.
RAT–
DON'T TELL ME WHAT TO DO. YOU'RE NOT MY PARENTS! MY PARENTS ARE DEAD!

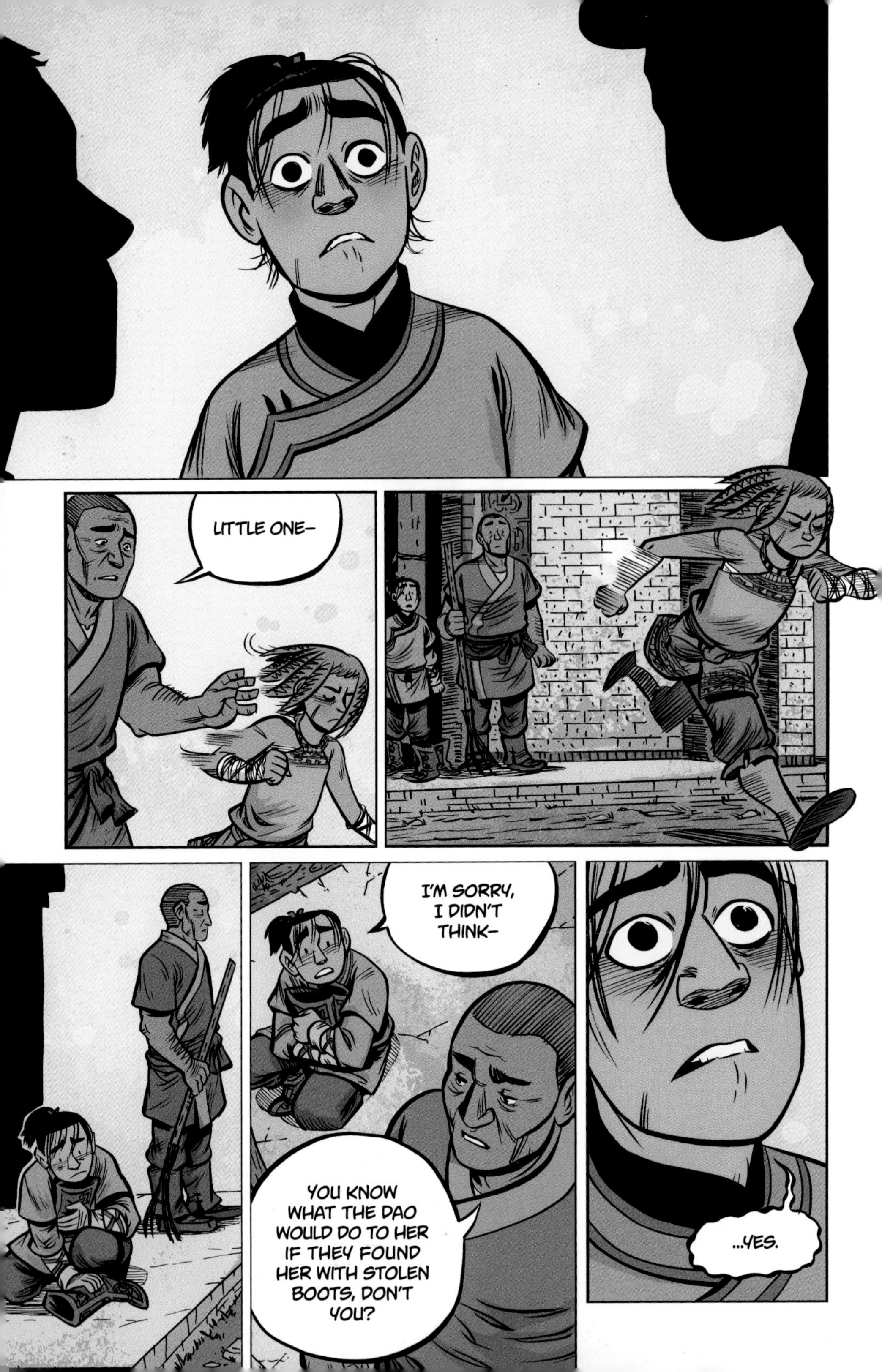
LITTLE ONE–
I'M SORRY, I DIDN'T THINK–
YOU KNOW WHAT THE DAO WOULD DO TO HER IF THEY FOUND HER WITH STOLEN BOOTS, DON'T YOU?
...YES.

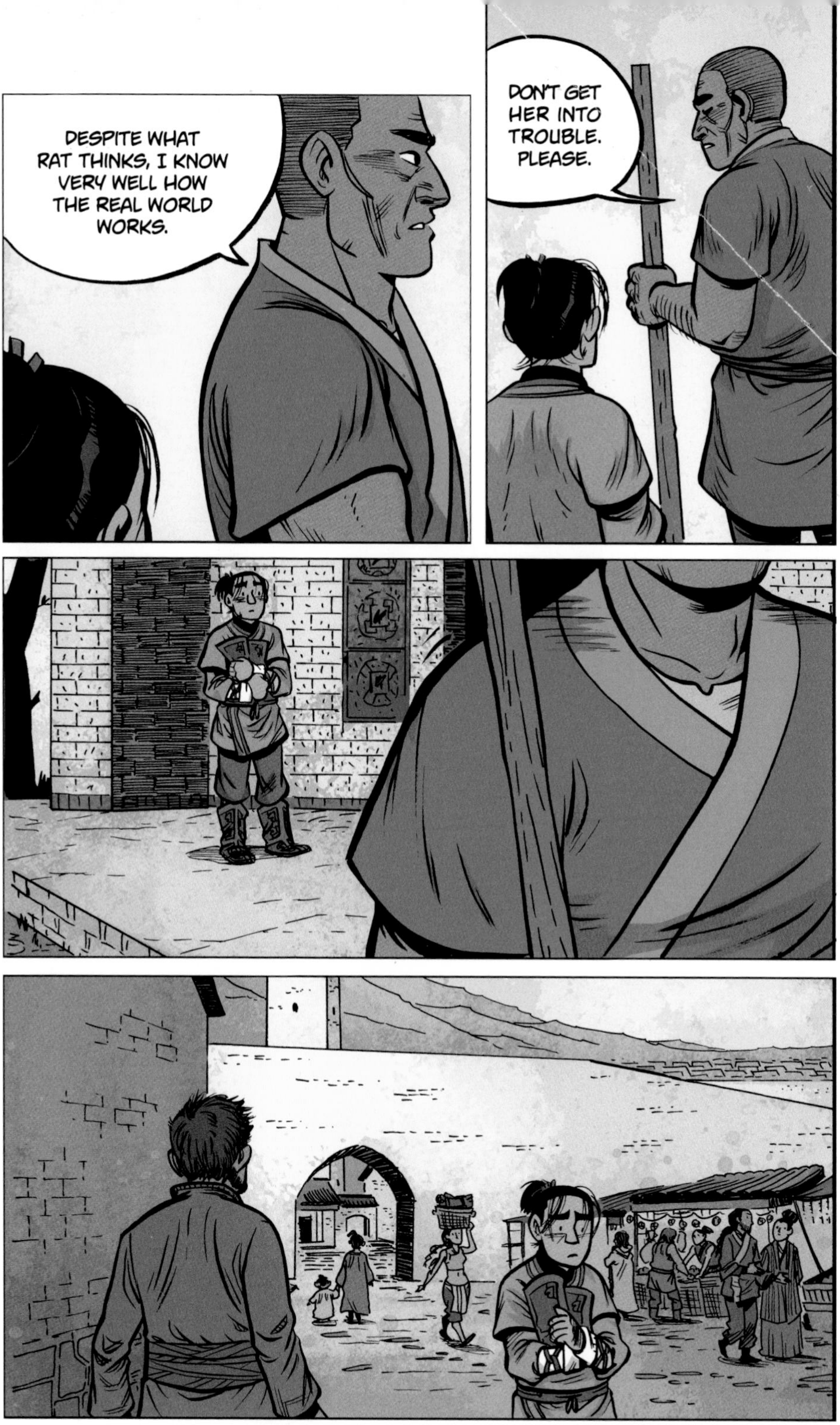
DESPITE WHAT RAT THINKS, I KNOW VERY WELL HOW THE REAL WORLD WORKS.
DON'T GET HER INTO TROUBLE. PLEASE.

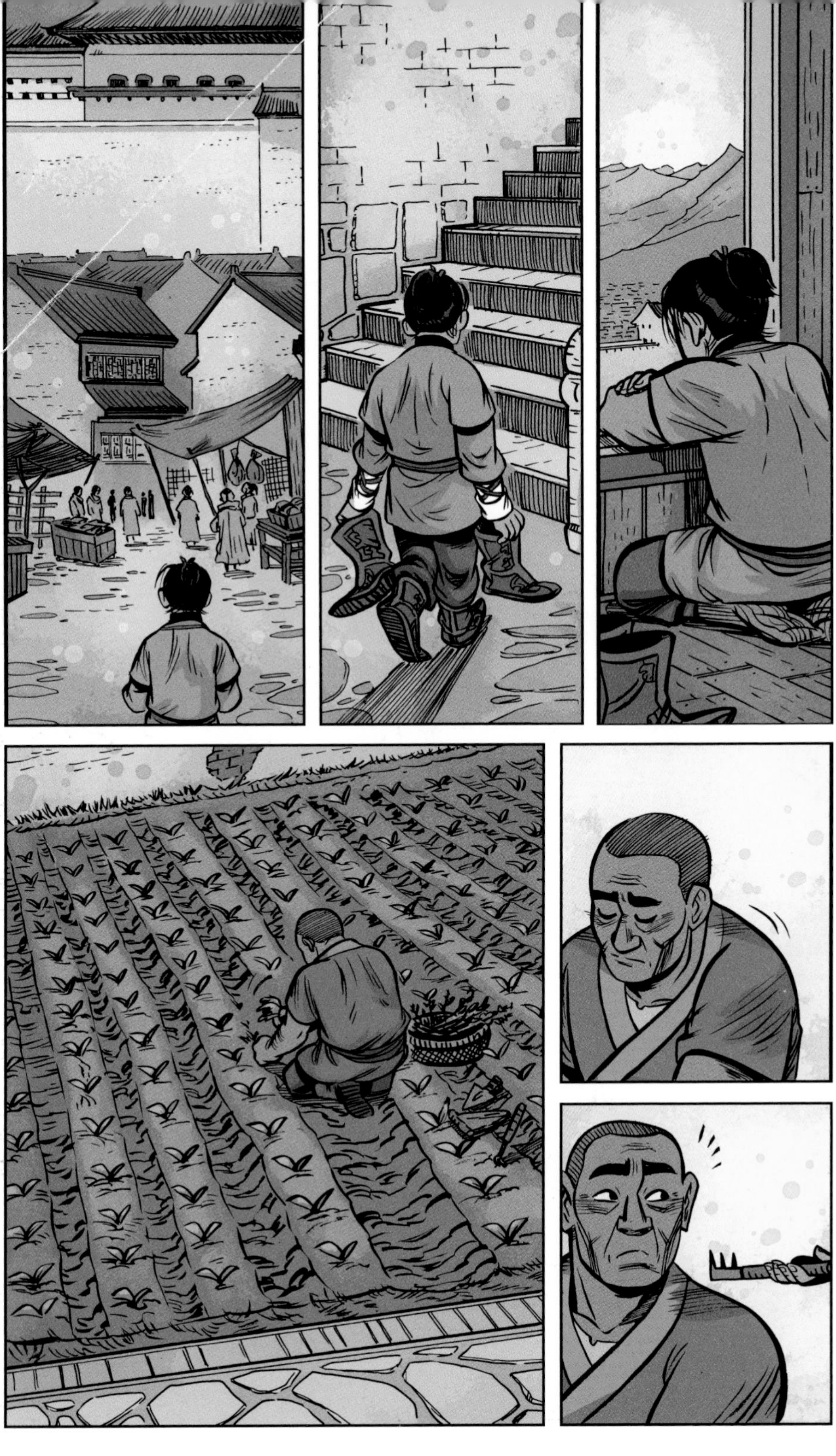

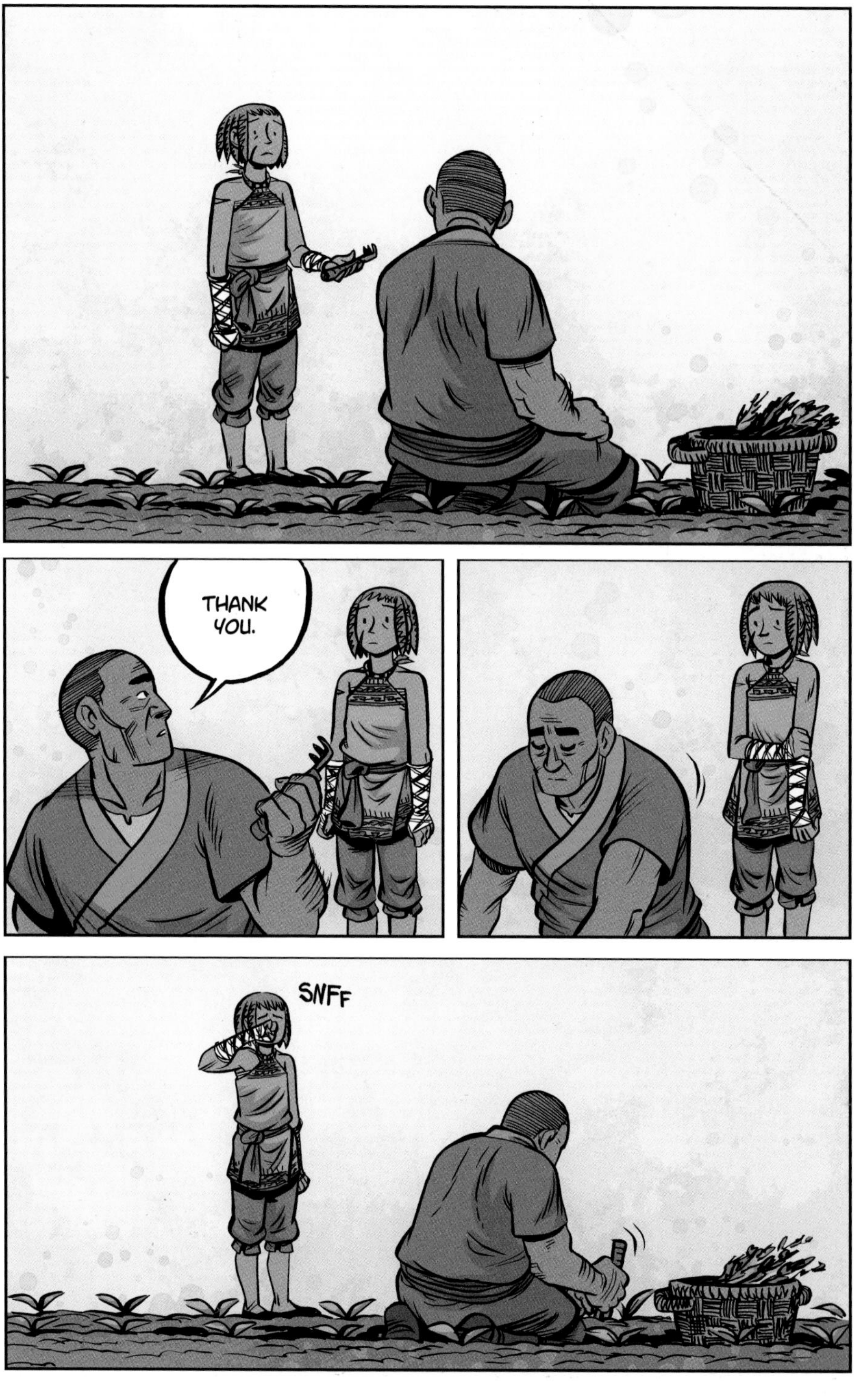
THANK YOU.
SNFF

DAY 29

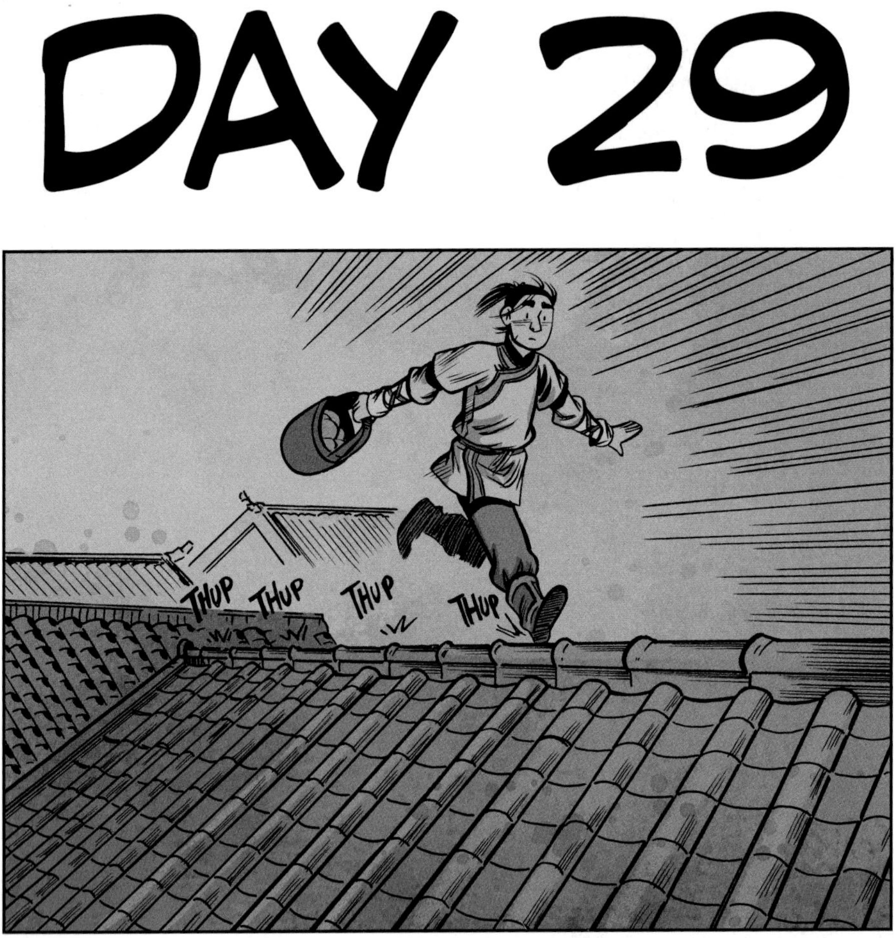
THUP
THUP
THUP
THUP

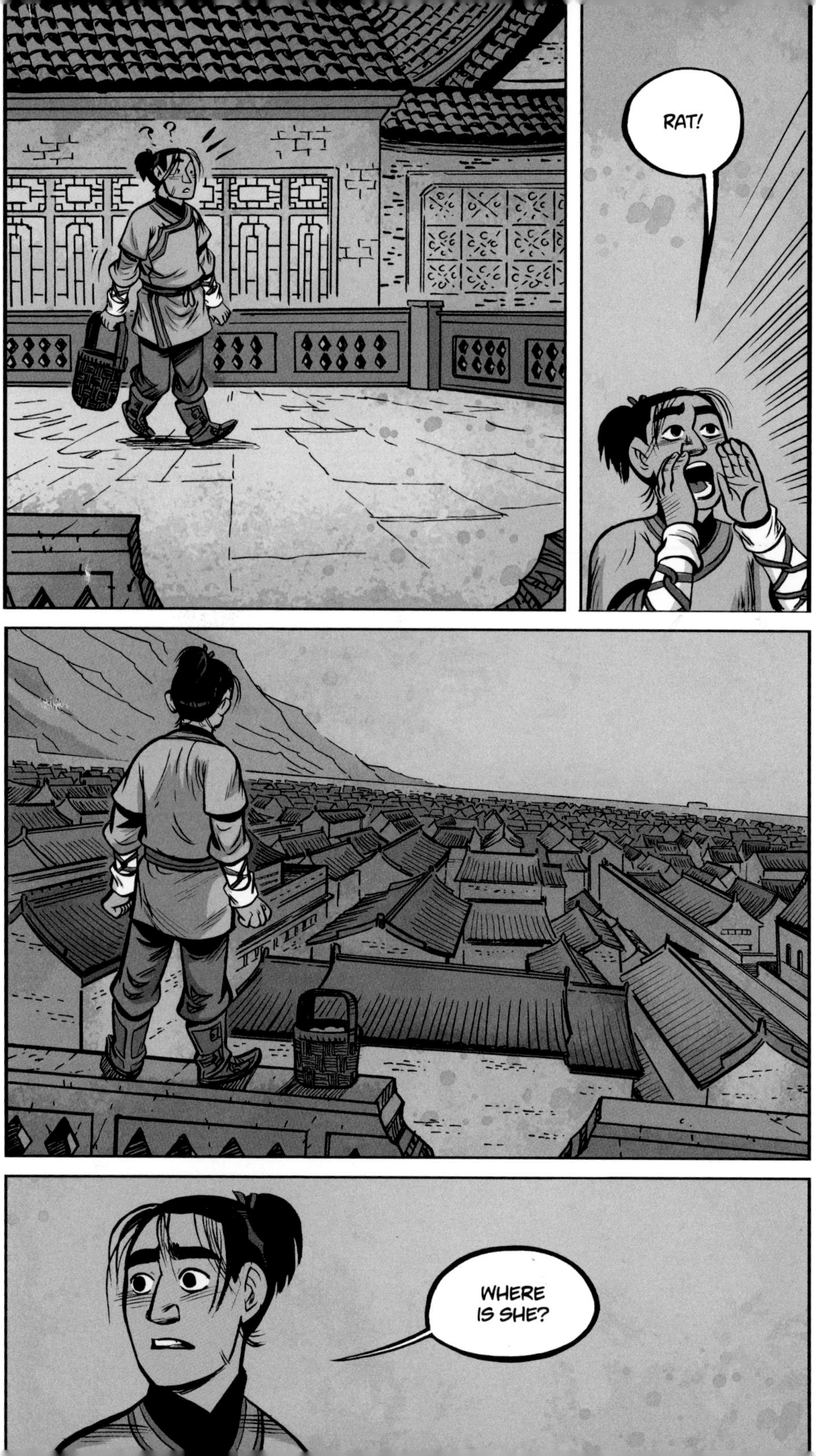
?
?
RAT!
WHERE IS SHE?

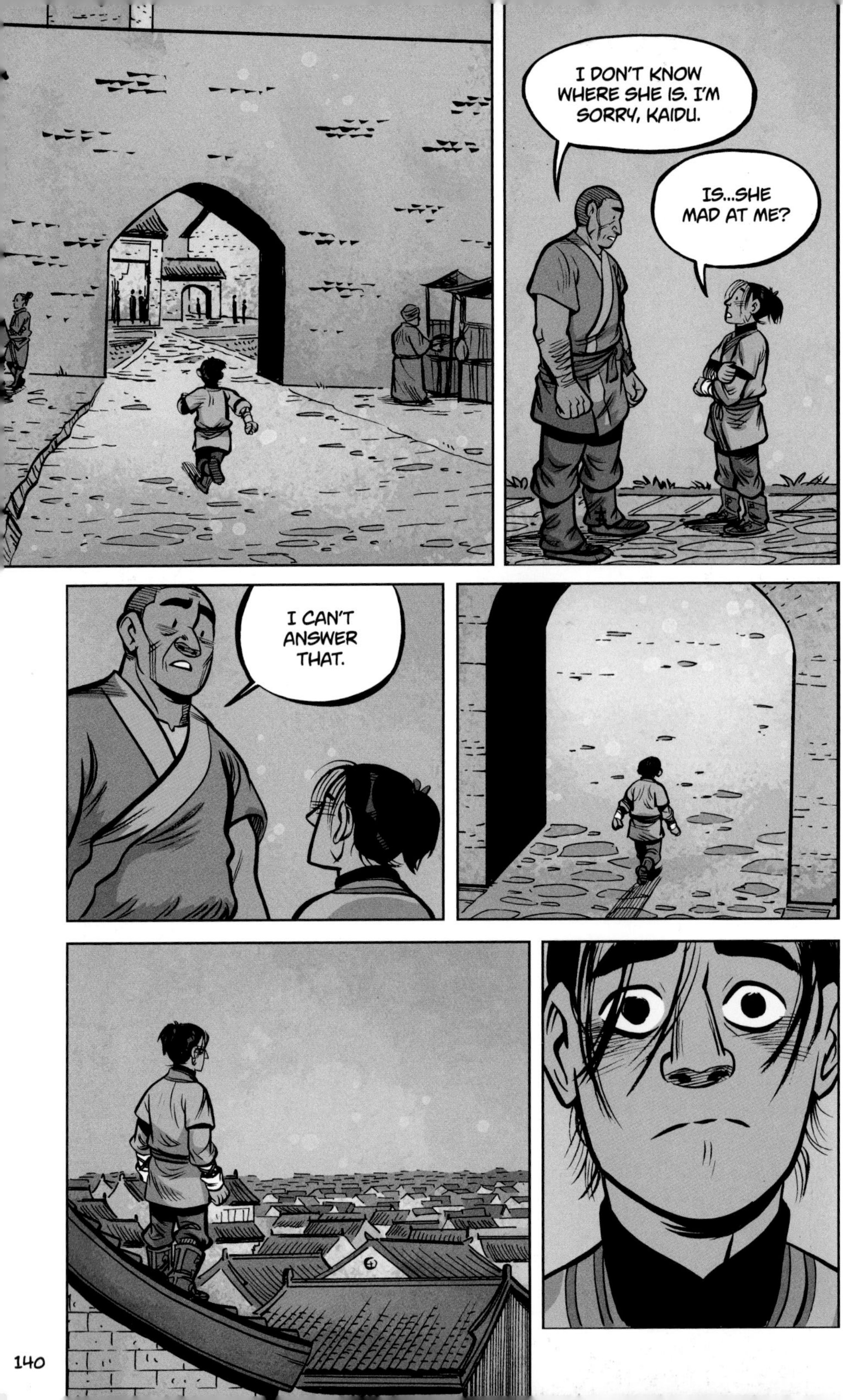
I DON'T KNOW WHERE SHE IS. I'M SORRY, KAIDU.
IS...SHE MAD AT ME?
I CAN'T ANSWER THAT.

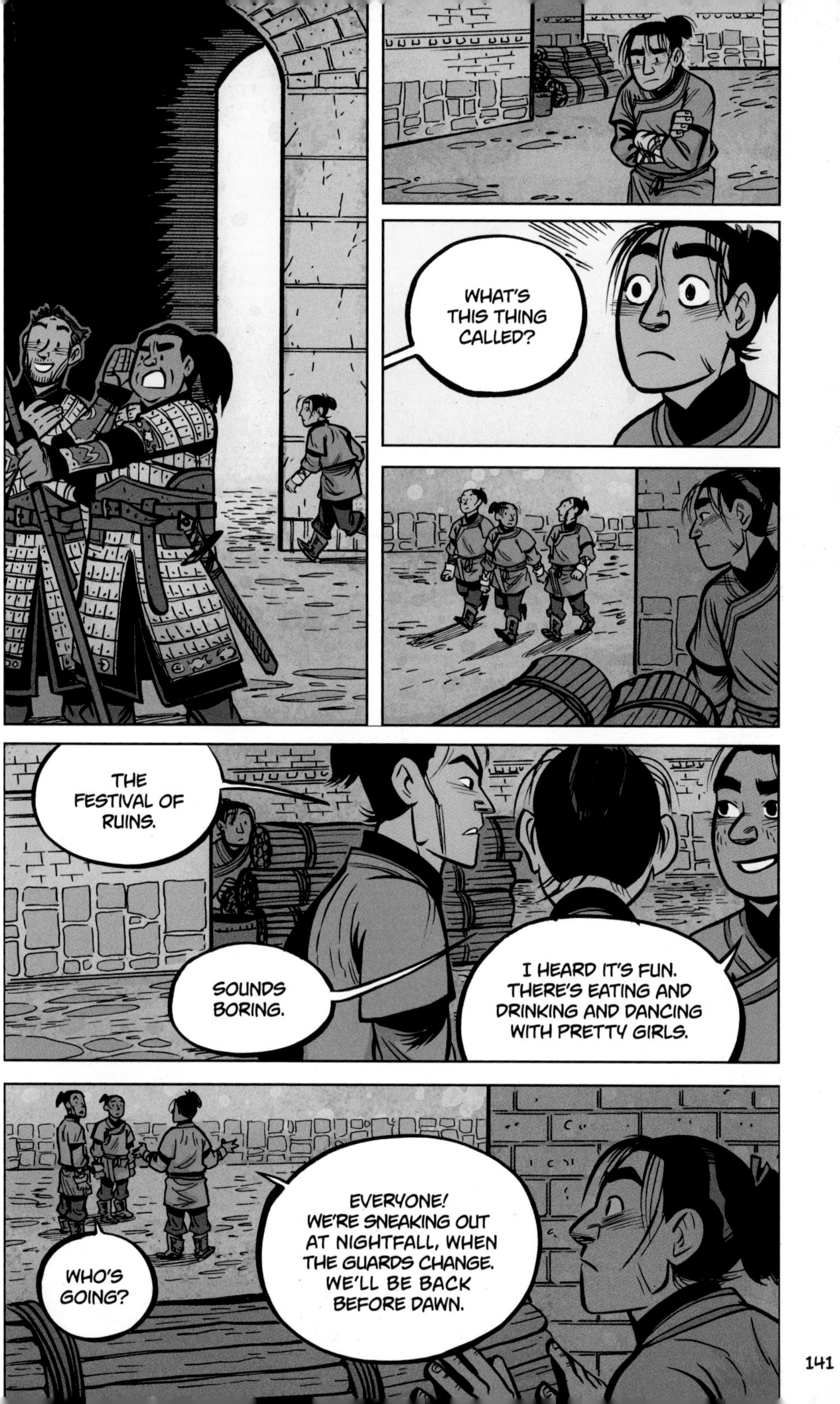
WHAT'S THIS THING CALLED?
THE FESTIVAL OF RUINS.
SOUNDS BORING.
I HEARD IT'S FUN. THERE'S EATING AND DRINKING AND DANCING WITH PRETTY GIRLS.
EVERYONE! WE'RE SNEAKING OUT AT NIGHTFALL, WHEN THE GUARDS CHANGE. WE'LL BE BACK BEFORE DAWN.
WHO'S GOING?

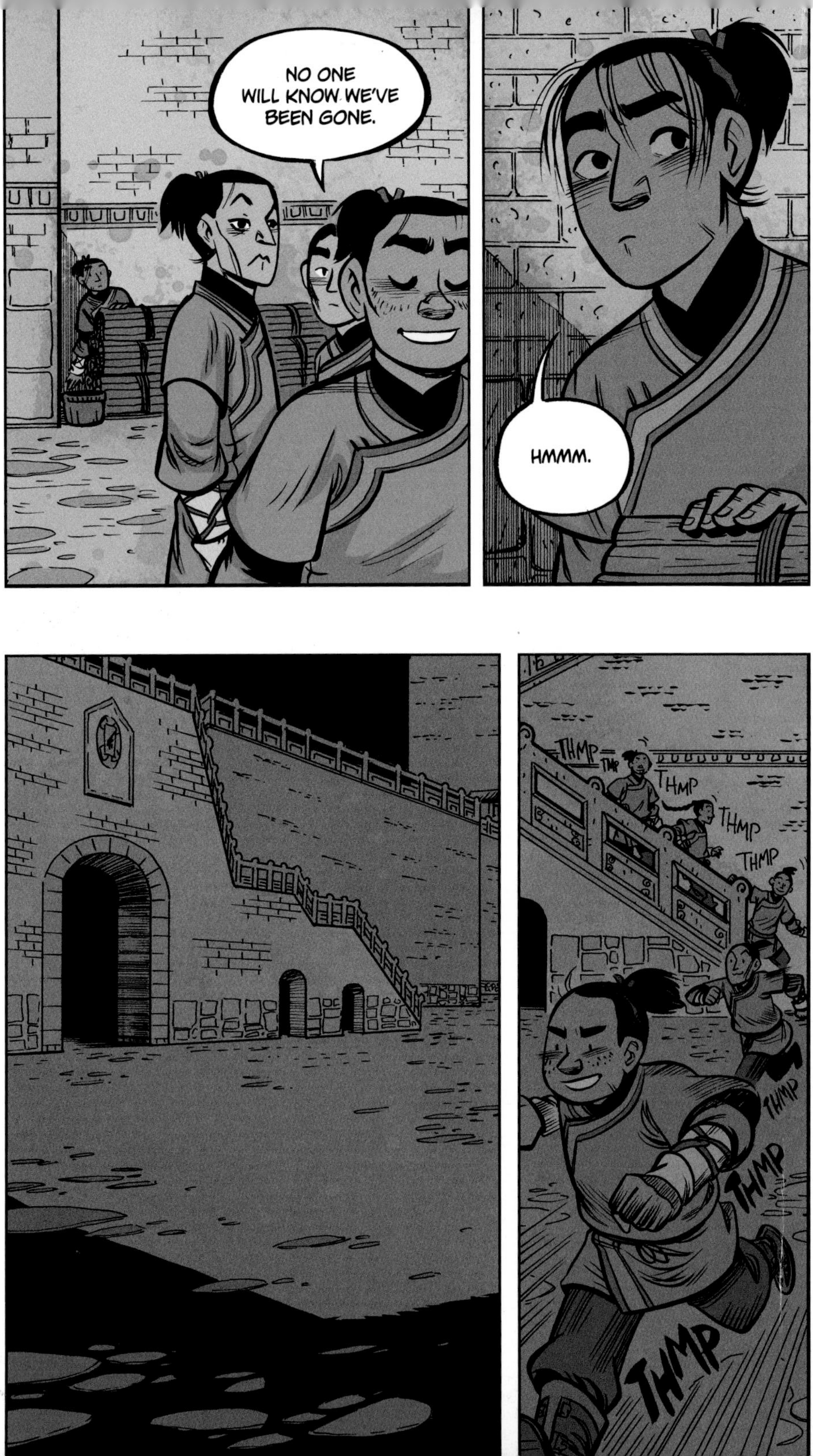
NO ONE WILL KNOW WE'VE BEEN GONE.
HMMM.
THMP
THMP
THMP
THMP
THMP
THMP
THMP
THMP
THMP

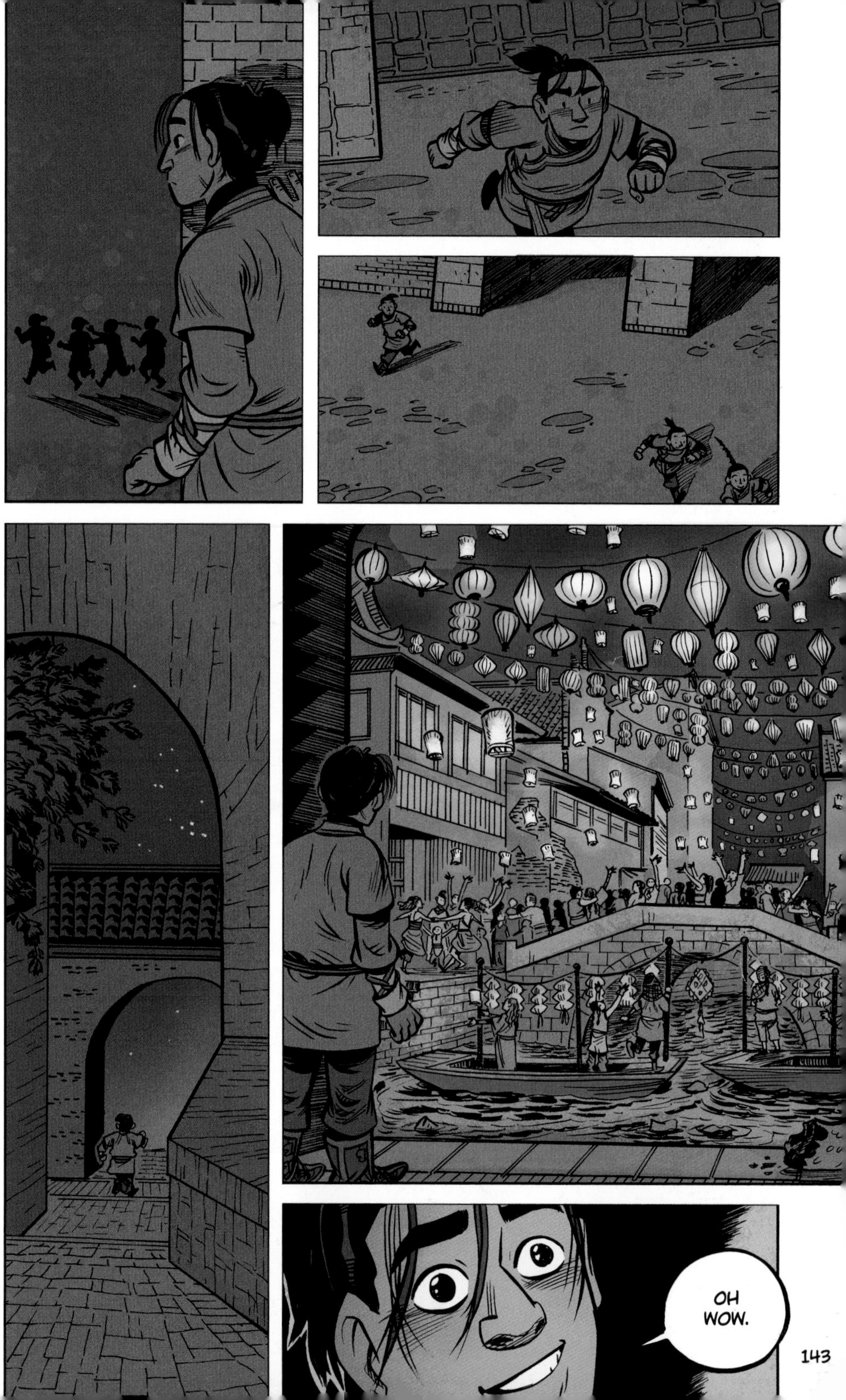
OH
WOW.

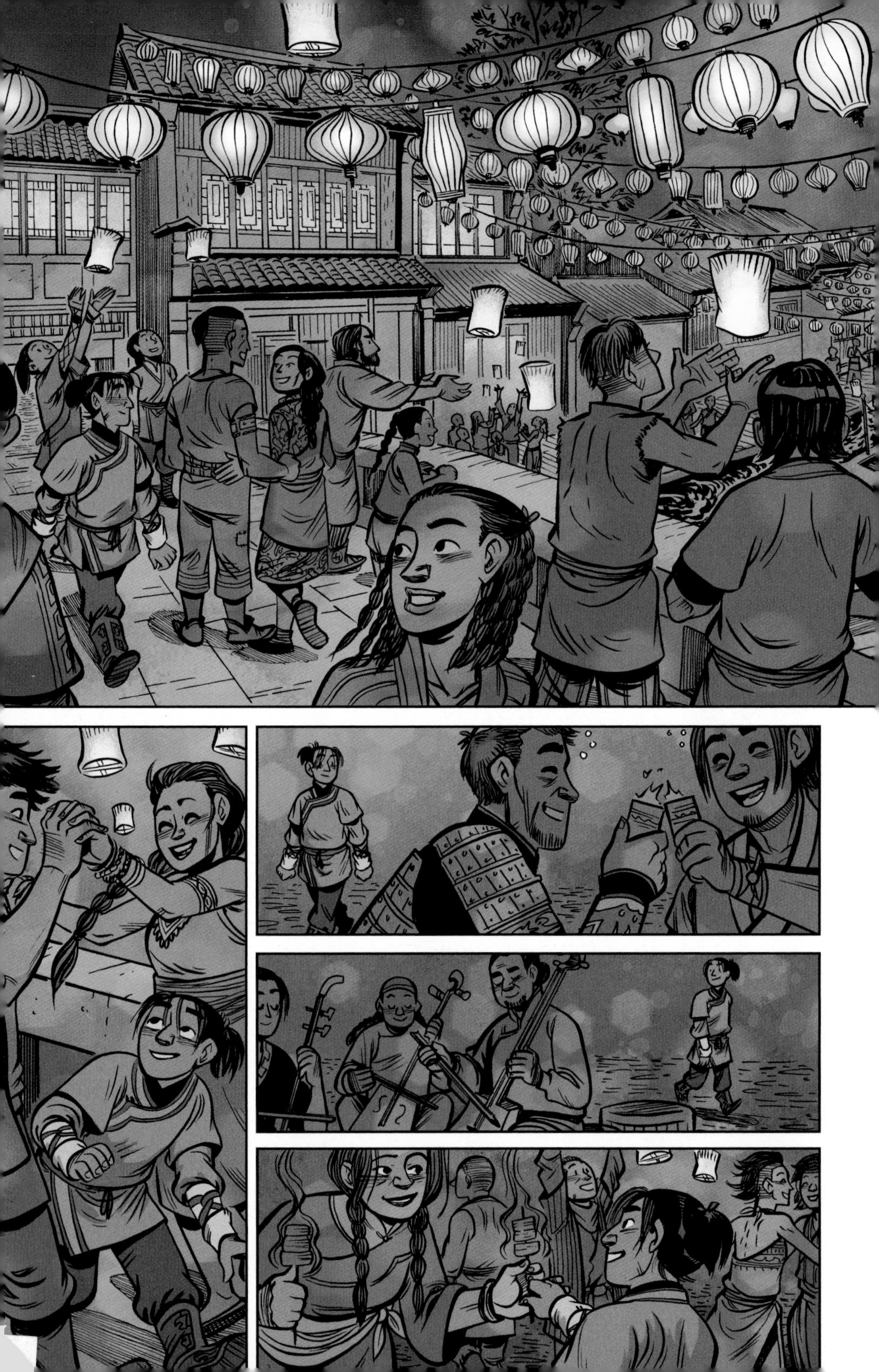

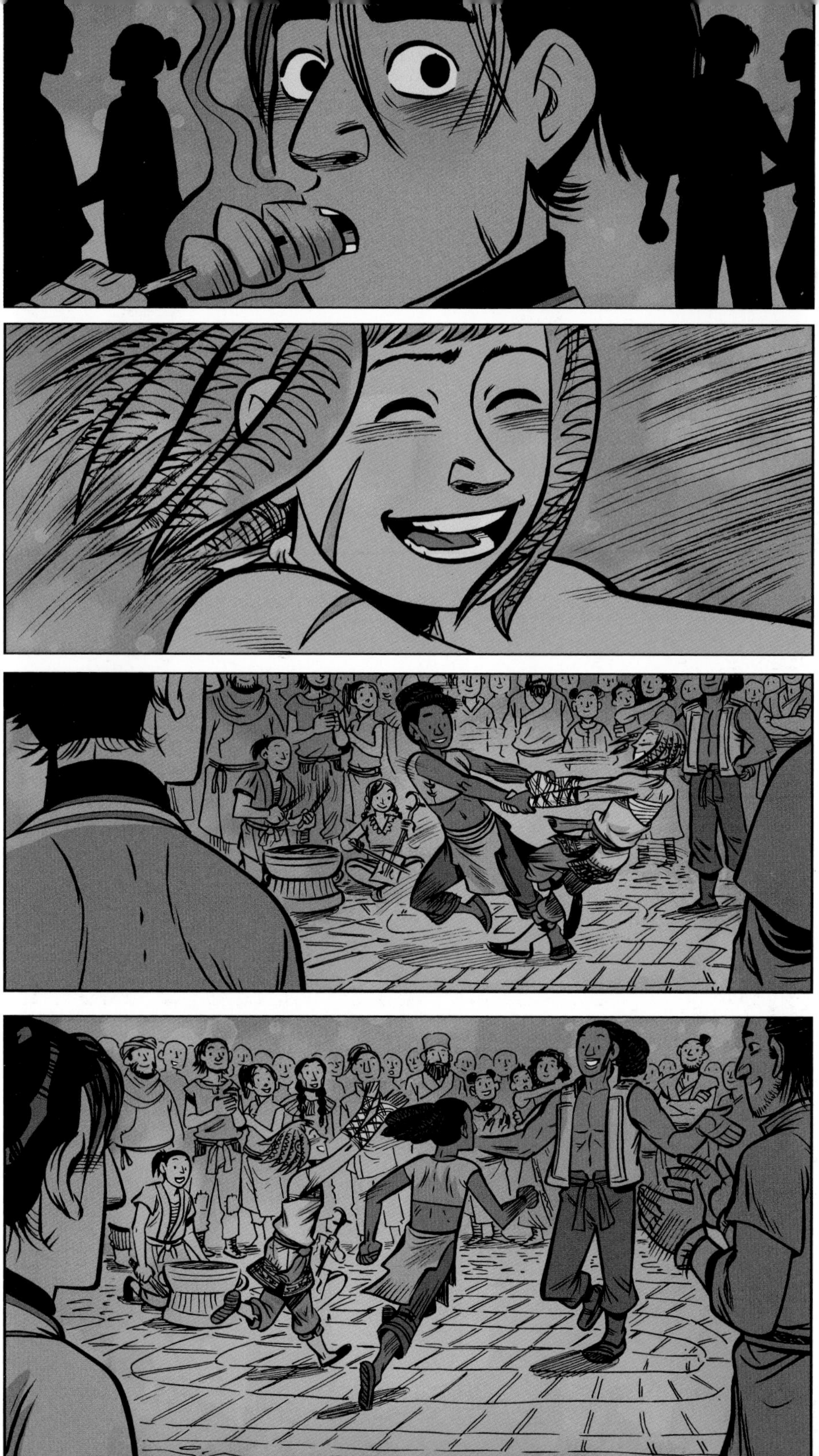

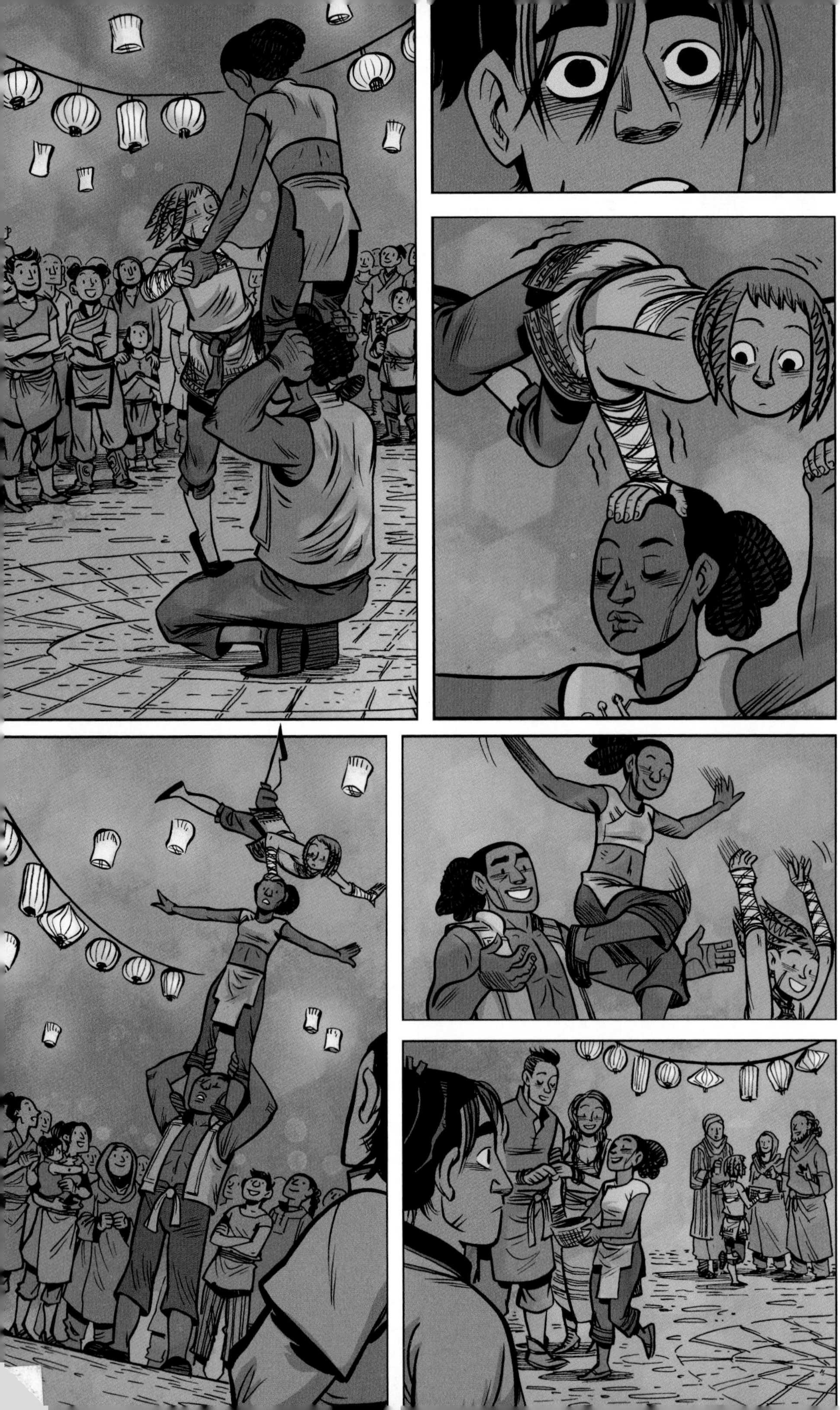

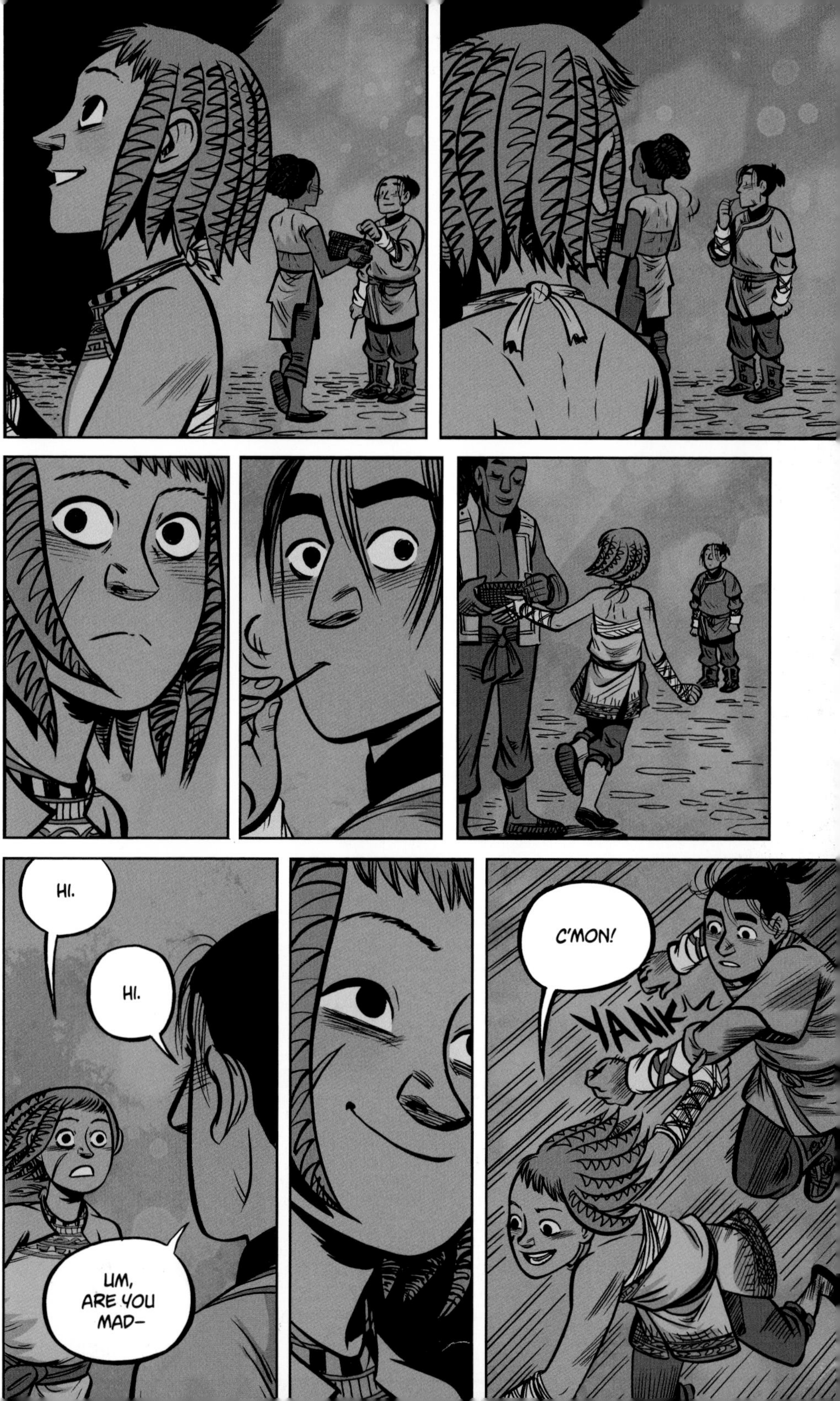
HI.
HI.
UM, ARE YOU MAD–
C'MON!
YANK

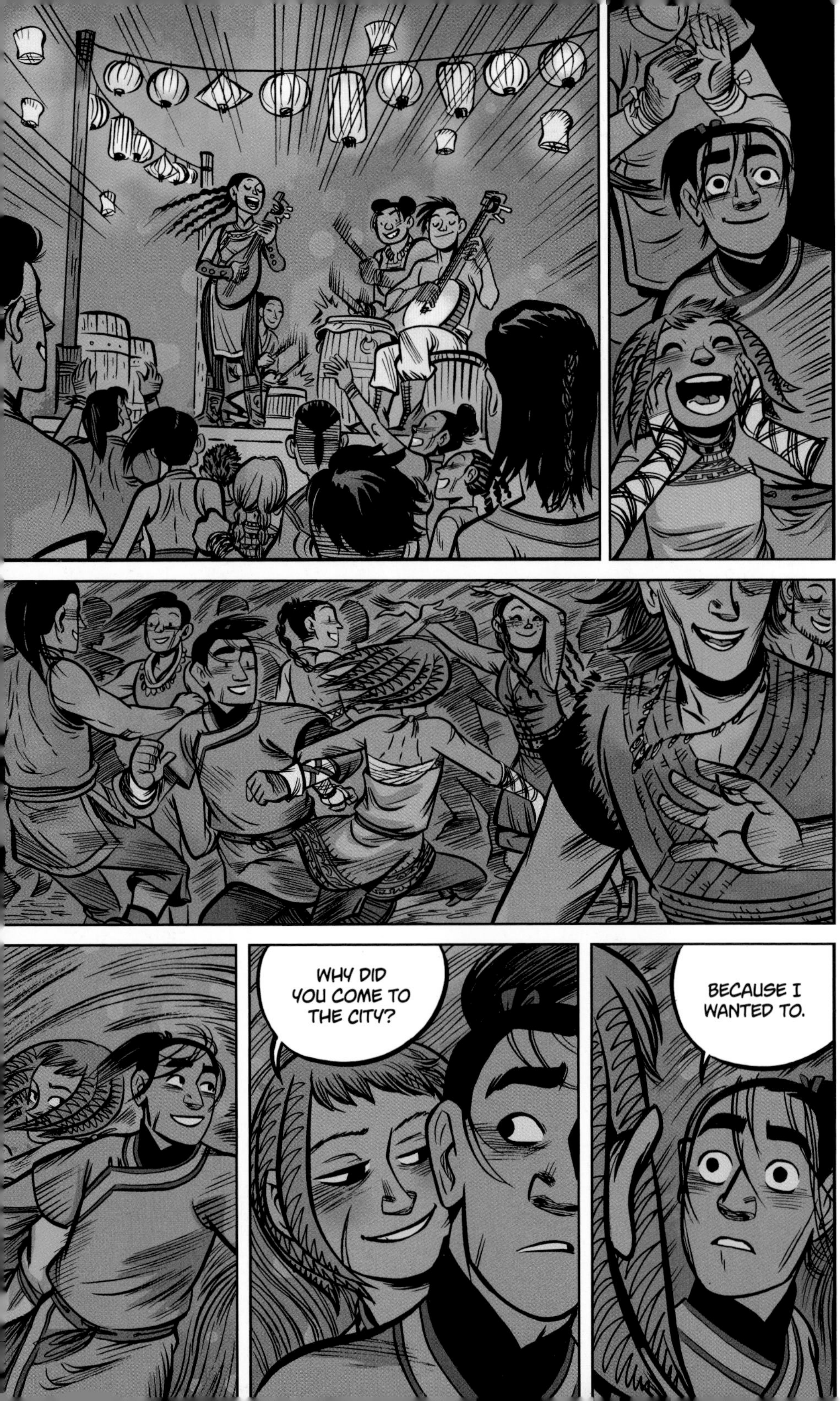
WHY DID YOU COME TO THE CITY?
BECAUSE I WANTED TO.

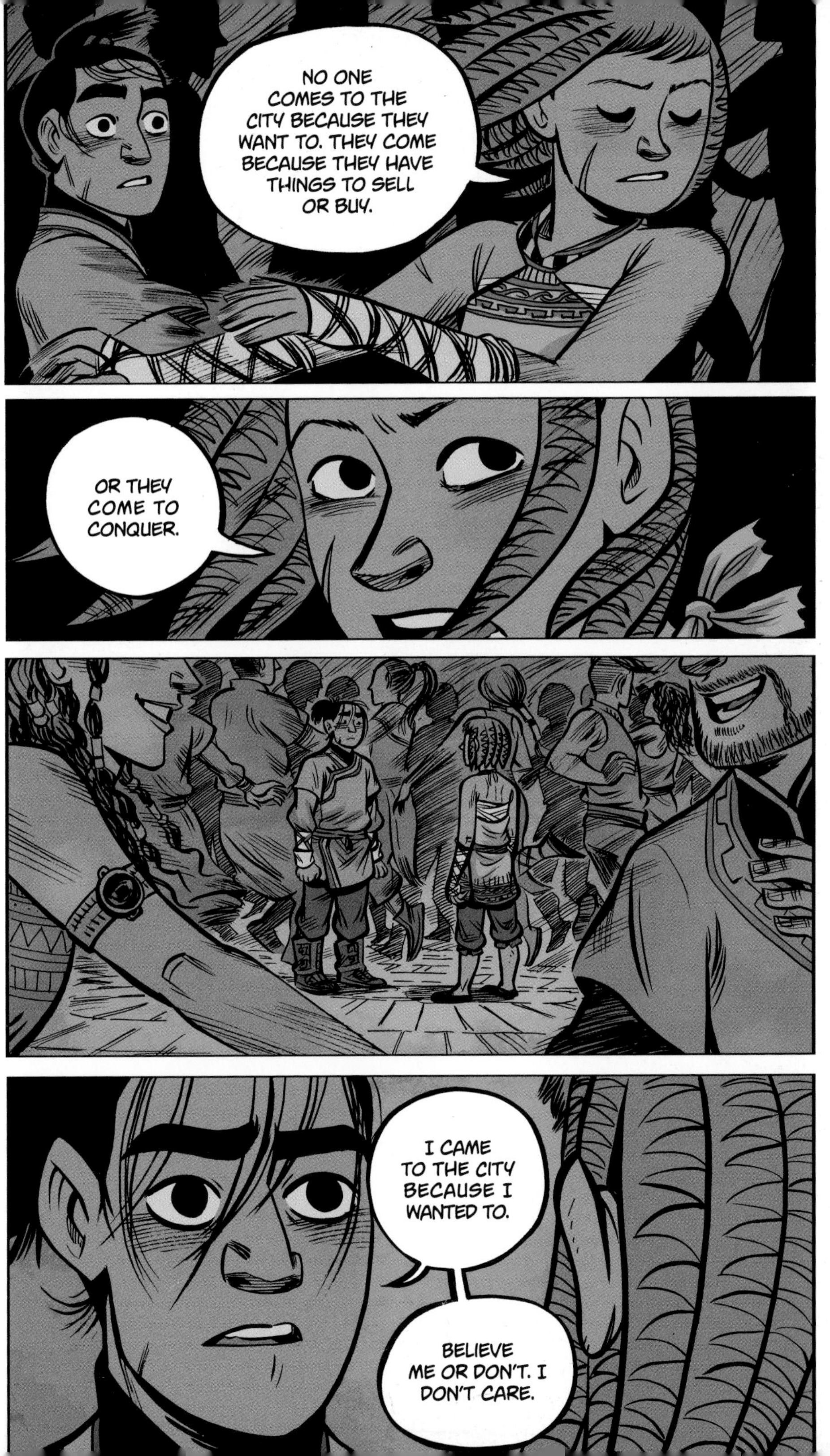
NO ONE COMES TO THE CITY BECAUSE THEY WANT TO. THEY COME BECAUSE THEY HAVE THINGS TO SELL OR BUY.
OR THEY COME TO CONQUER.
I CAME TO THE CITY BECAUSE I WANTED TO.
BELIEVE ME OR DON'T. I DON'T CARE.

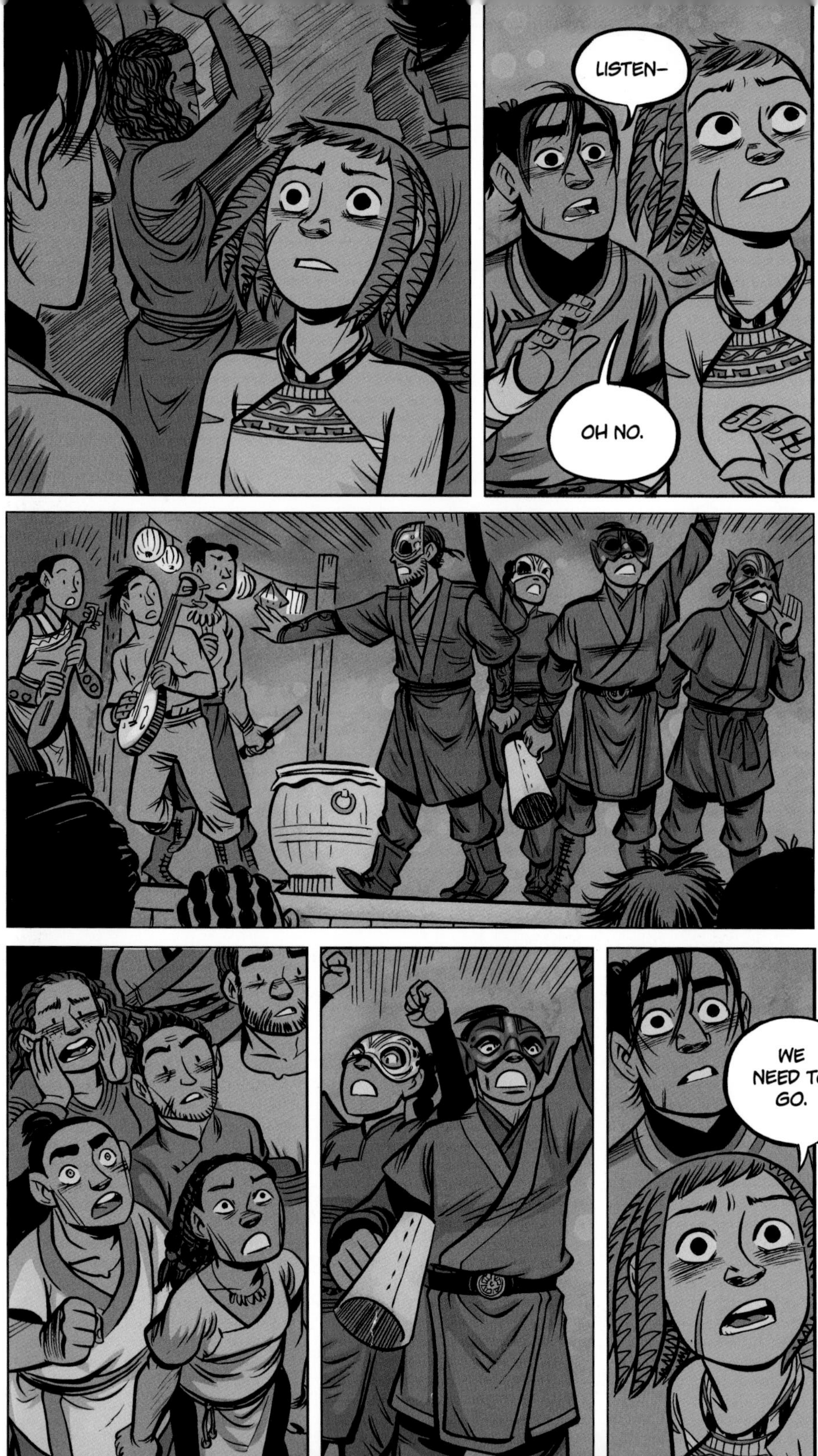
LISTEN–
OH NO.
WE NEED TO GO.

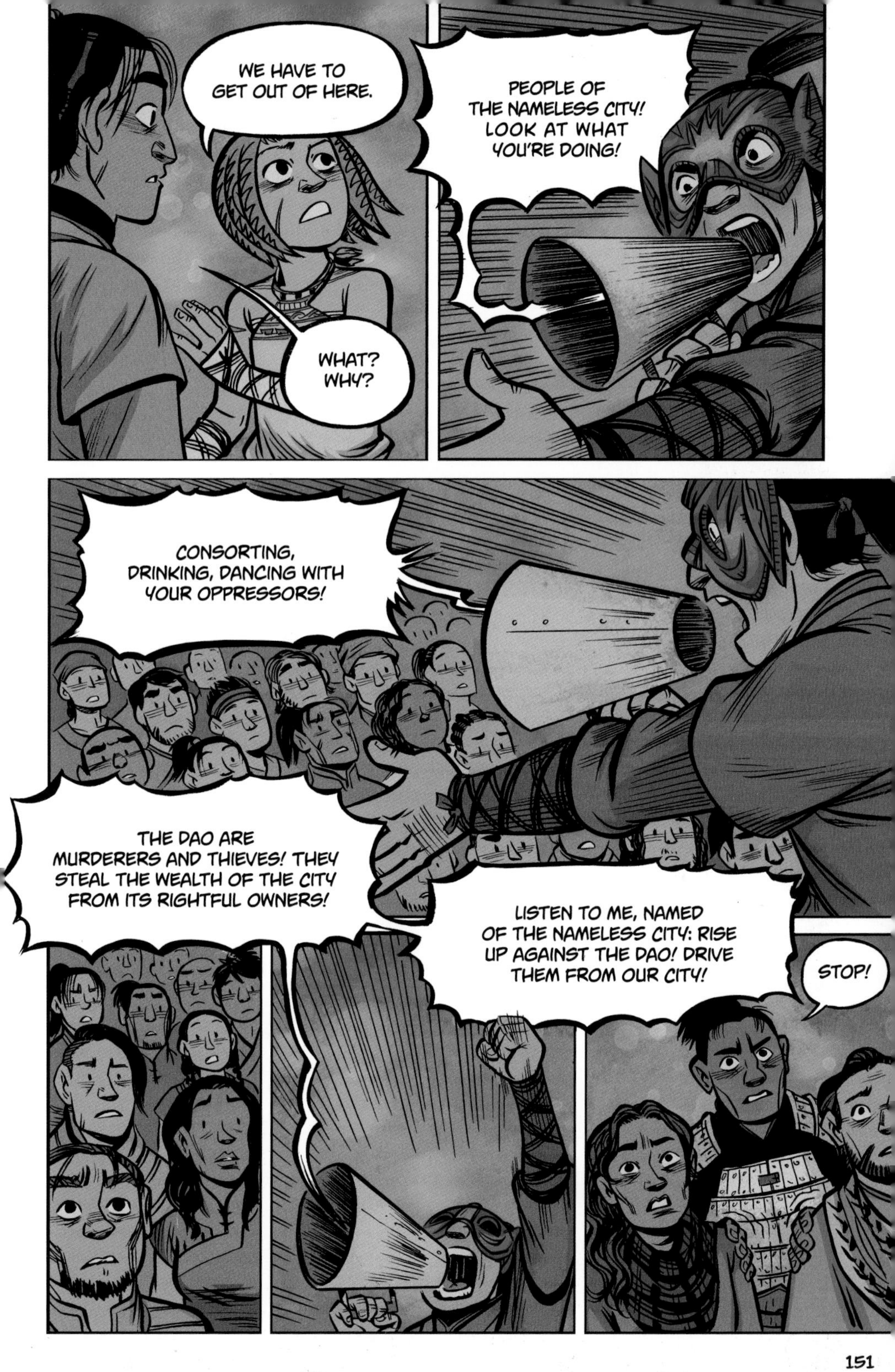
WE HAVE TO GET OUT OF HERE.
WHAT? WHY?
PEOPLE OF THE NAMELESS CITY! LOOK AT WHAT YOU'RE DOING!
CONSORTING, DRINKING, DANCING WITH YOUR OPPRESSORS!
THE DAO ARE MURDERERS AND THIEVES! THEY STEAL THE WEALTH OF THE CITY FROM ITS RIGHTFUL OWNERS!
LISTEN TO ME, NAMED OF THE NAMELESS CITY: RISE UP AGAINST THE DAO! DRIVE THEM FROM OUR CITY!
STOP!

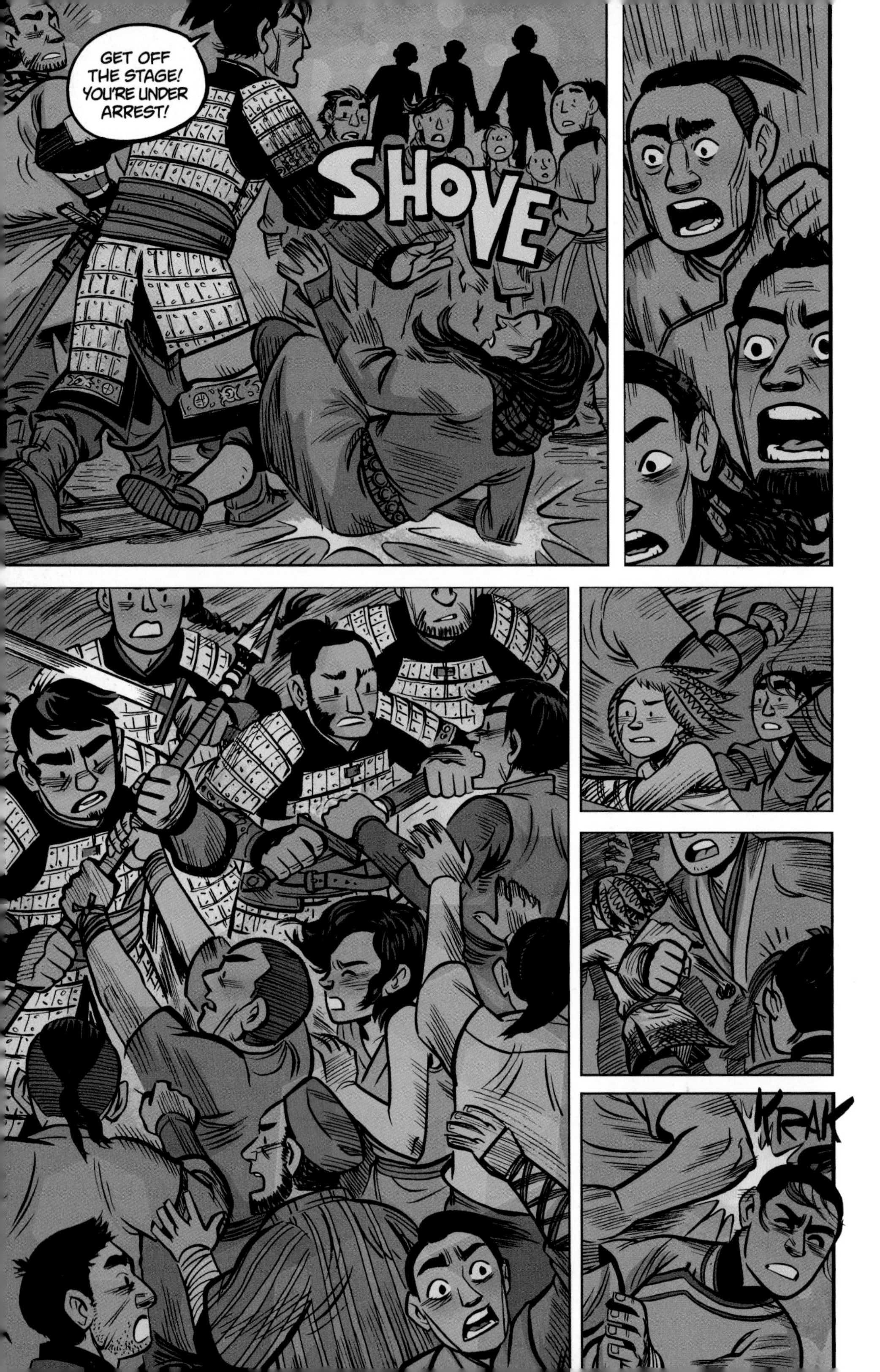
GET OFF THE STAGE! YOU'RE UNDER ARREST!
SHOVE
KRAK

WHAMM

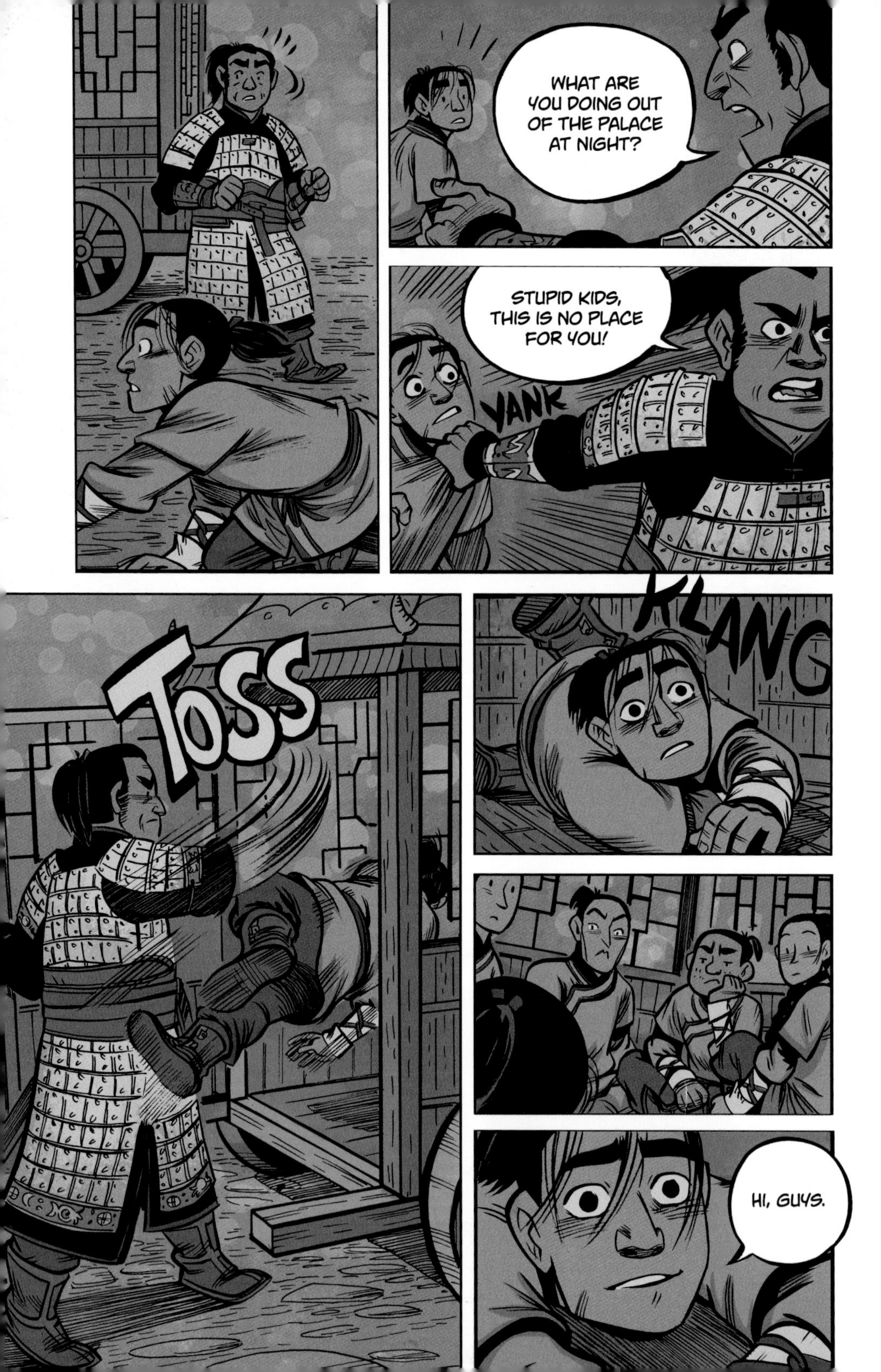
WHAT ARE YOU DOING OUT OF THE PALACE AT NIGHT?
STUPID KIDS, THIS IS NO PLACE FOR YOU!
YANK
TOSS
KLANG
HI, GUYS.

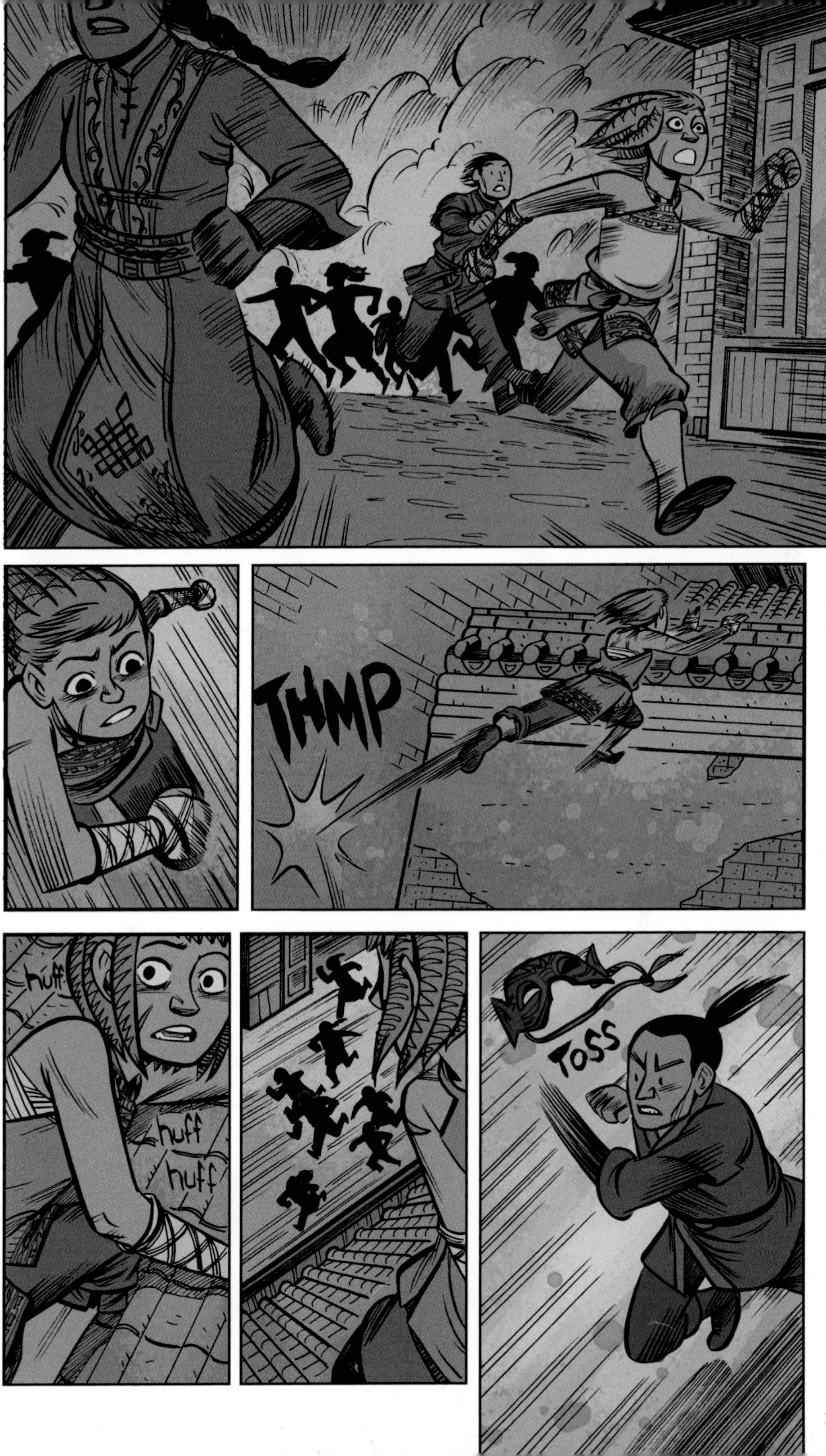
THMP
huff
huff
huff
TOSS

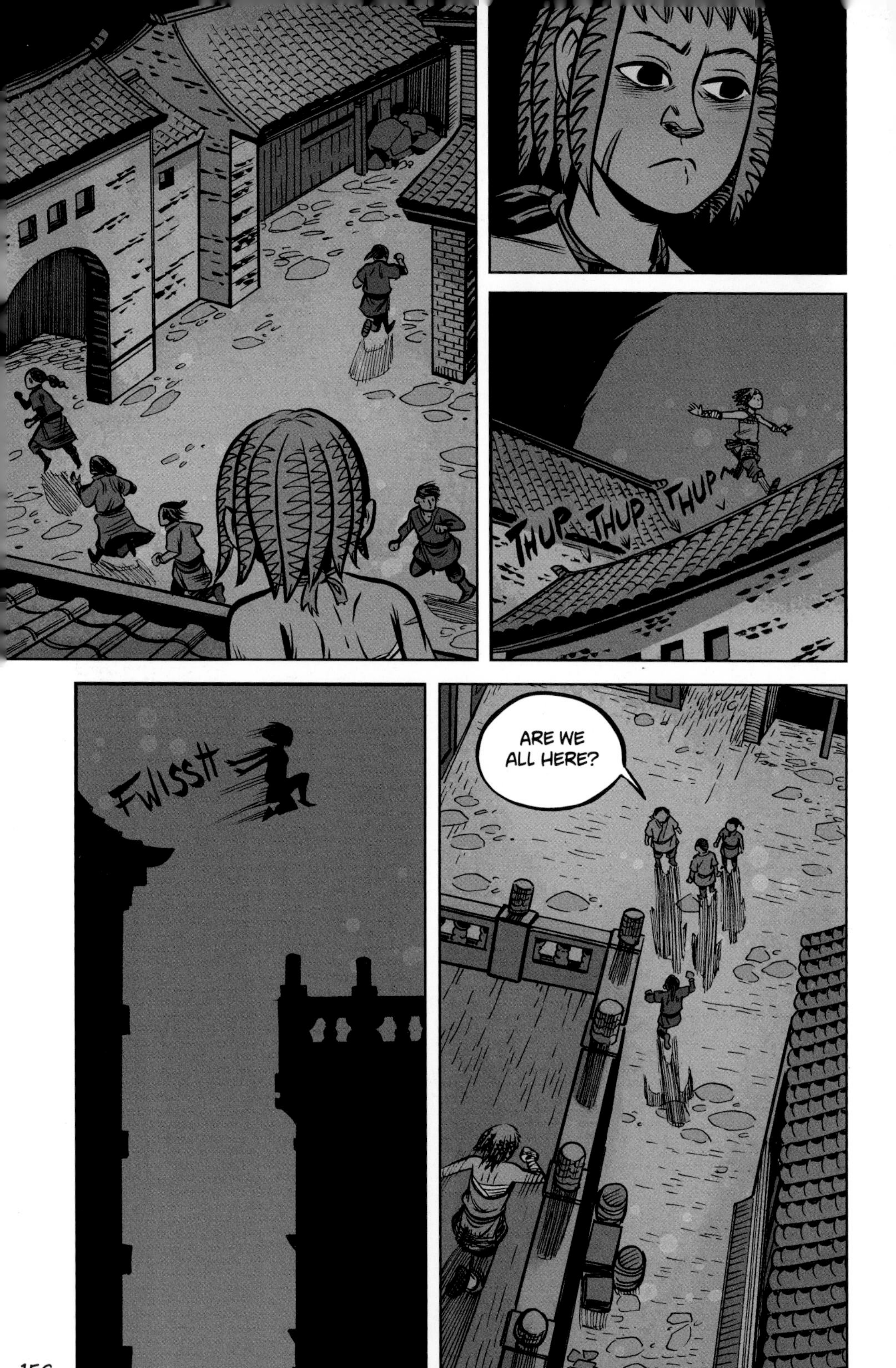
THUP THUP THUP
FWISSH
ARE WE ALL HERE?

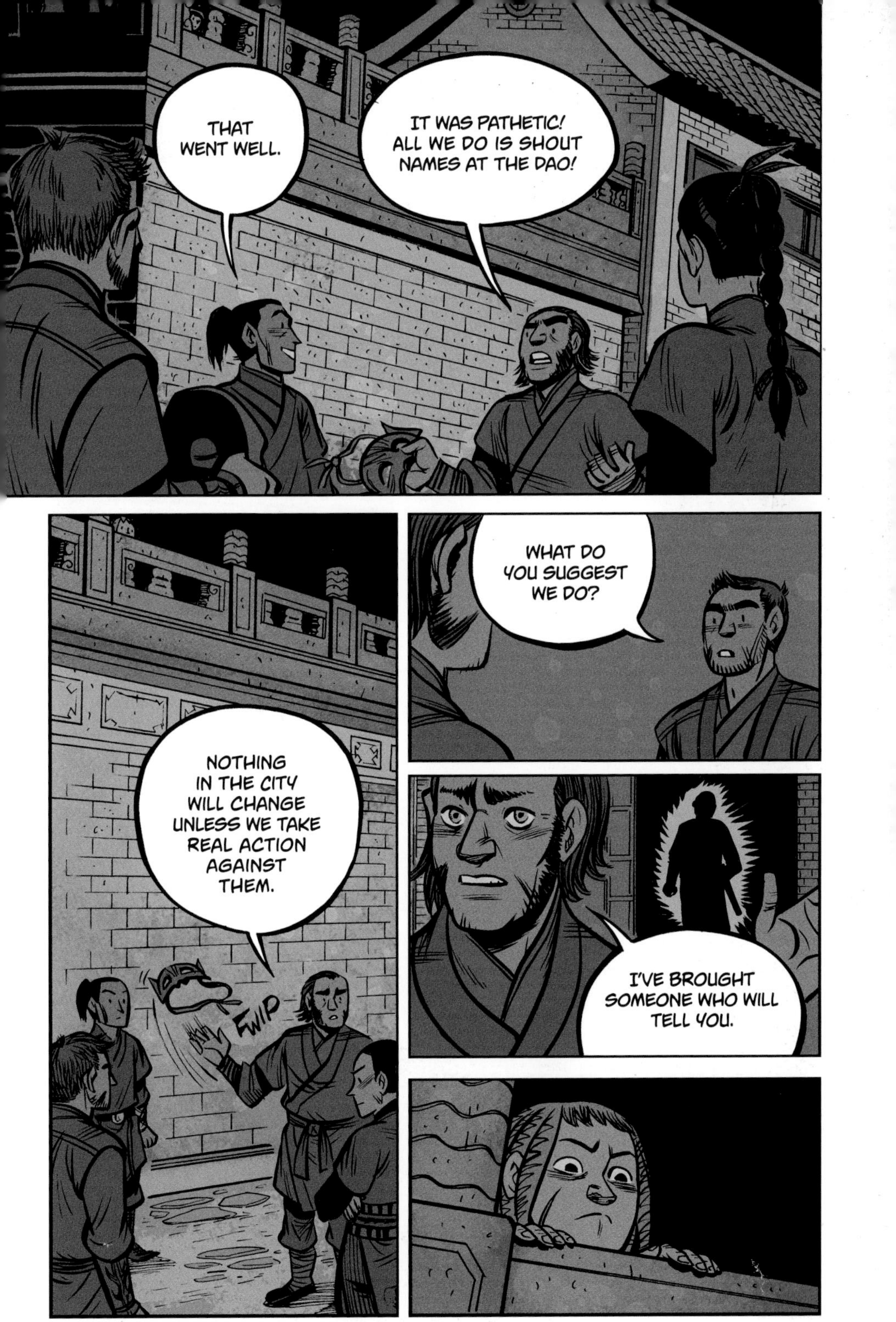
THAT WENT WELL.
IT WAS PATHETIC! ALL WE DO IS SHOUT NAMES AT THE DAO!
WHAT DO YOU SUGGEST WE DO?
NOTHING IN THE CITY WILL CHANGE UNLESS WE TAKE REAL ACTION AGAINST THEM.
FWIP
I'VE BROUGHT SOMEONE WHO WILL TELL YOU.

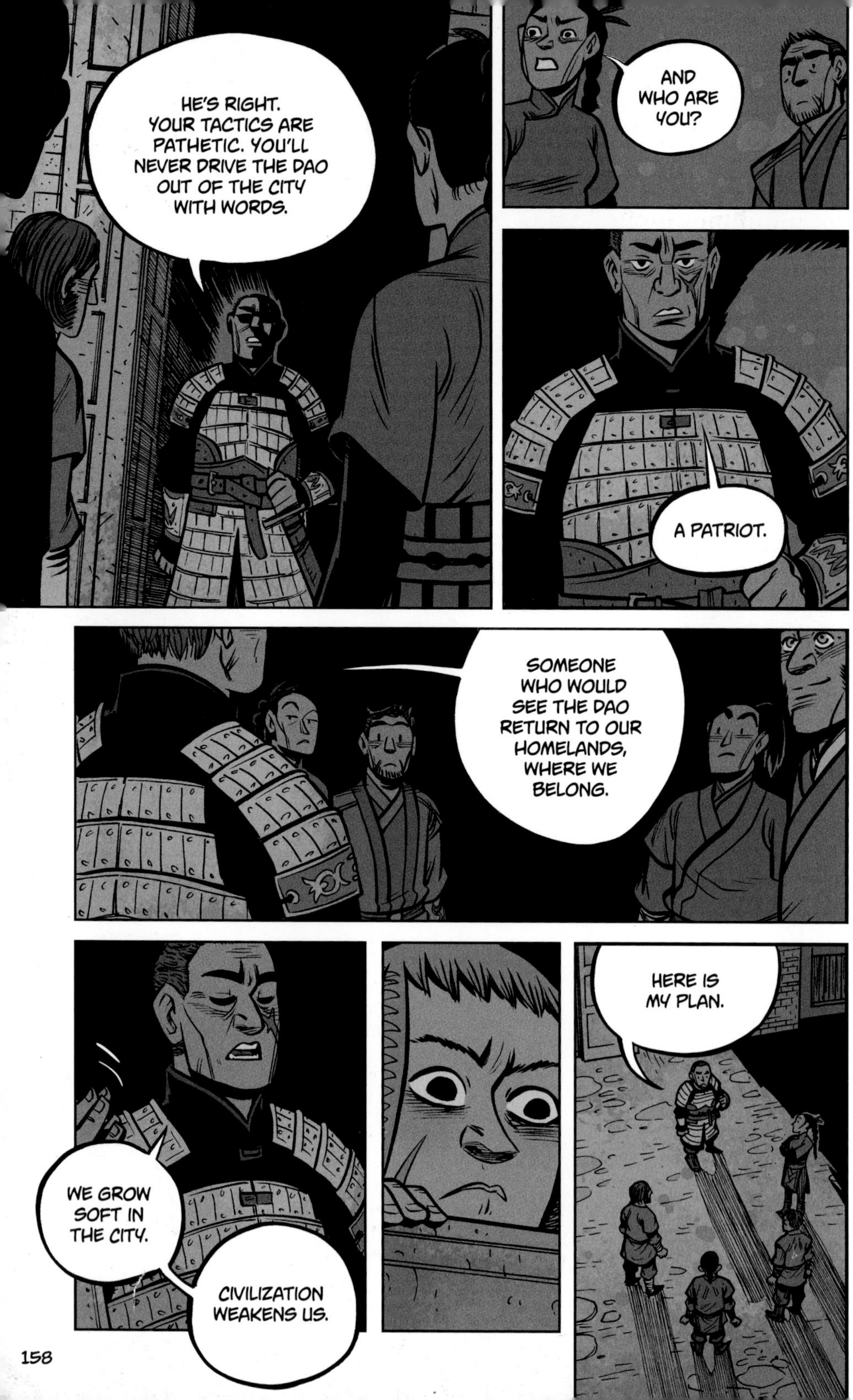
HE'S RIGHT. YOUR TACTICS ARE PATHETIC. YOU'LL NEVER DRIVE THE DAO OUT OF THE CITY WITH WORDS.
AND WHO ARE YOU?
A PATRIOT.
SOMEONE WHO WOULD SEE THE DAO RETURN TO OUR HOMELANDS, WHERE WE BELONG.
WE GROW SOFT IN THE CITY.
CIVILIZATION WEAKENS US.
HERE IS MY PLAN.

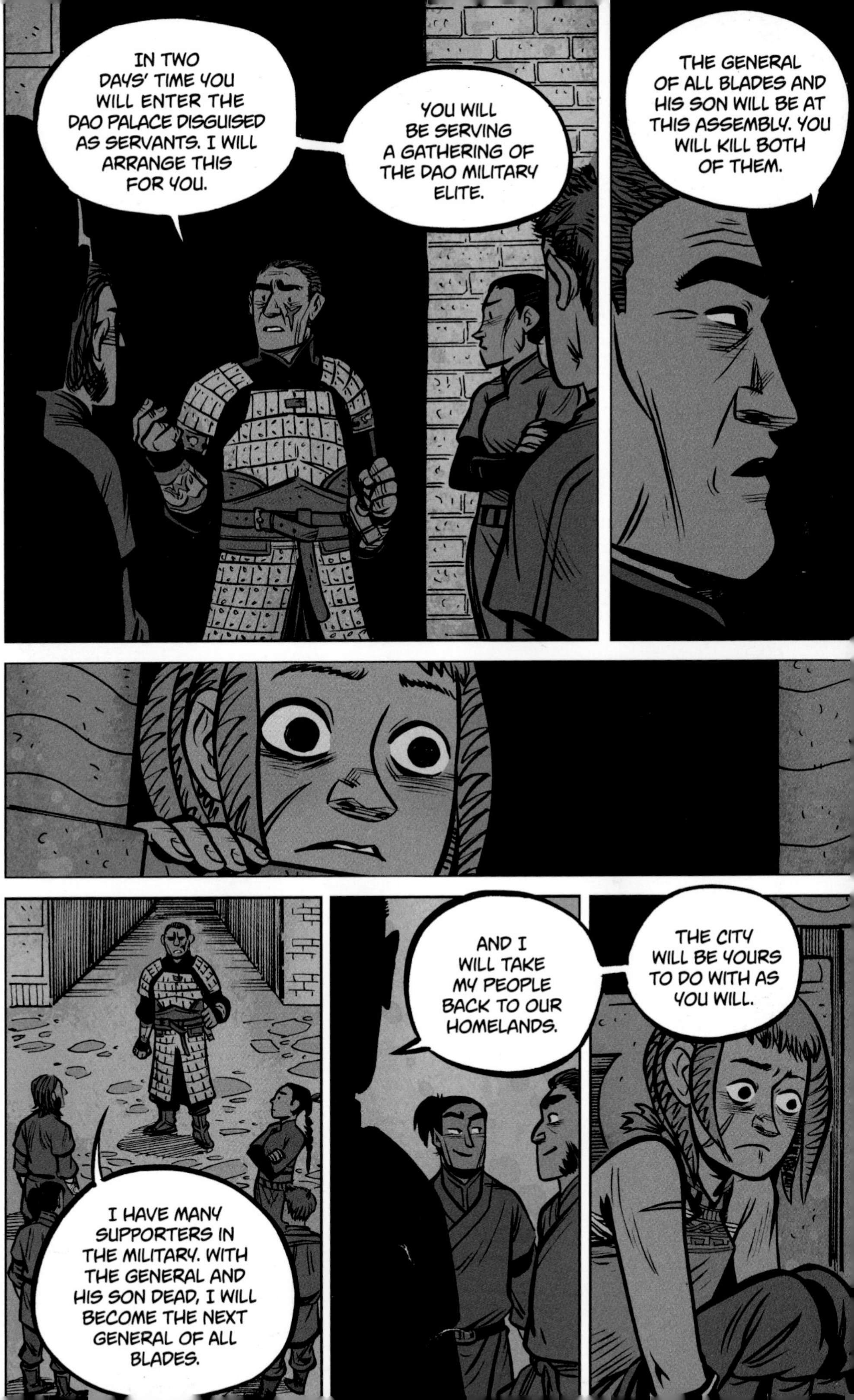
IN TWO DAYS' TIME YOU WILL ENTER THE DAO PALACE DISGUISED AS SERVANTS. I WILL ARRANGE THIS FOR YOU.
YOU WILL BE SERVING A GATHERING OF THE DAO MILITARY ELITE.
THE GENERAL OF ALL BLADES AND HIS SON WILL BE AT THIS ASSEMBLY. YOU WILL KILL BOTH OF THEM.
I HAVE MANY SUPPORTERS IN THE MILITARY. WITH THE GENERAL AND HIS SON DEAD, I WILL BECOME THE NEXT GENERAL OF ALL BLADES.
AND I WILL TAKE MY PEOPLE BACK TO OUR HOMELANDS.
THE CITY WILL BE YOURS TO DO WITH AS YOU WILL.

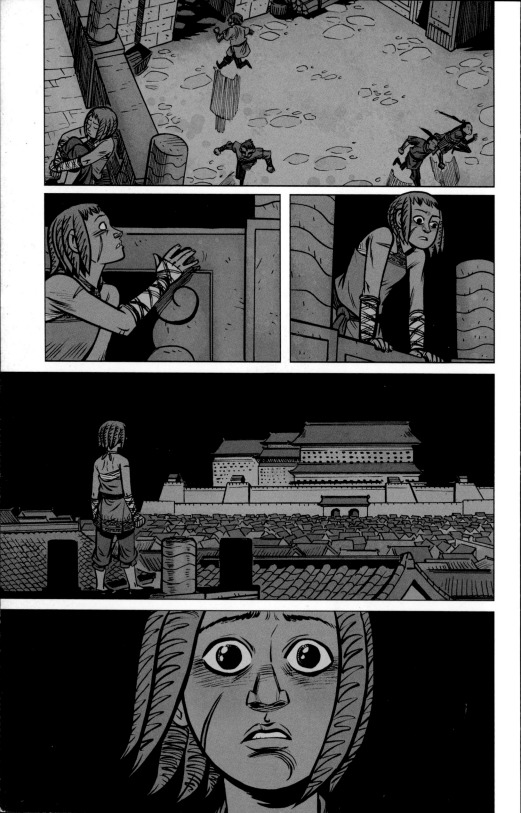

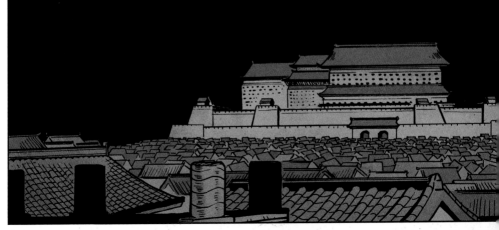

DAY 30

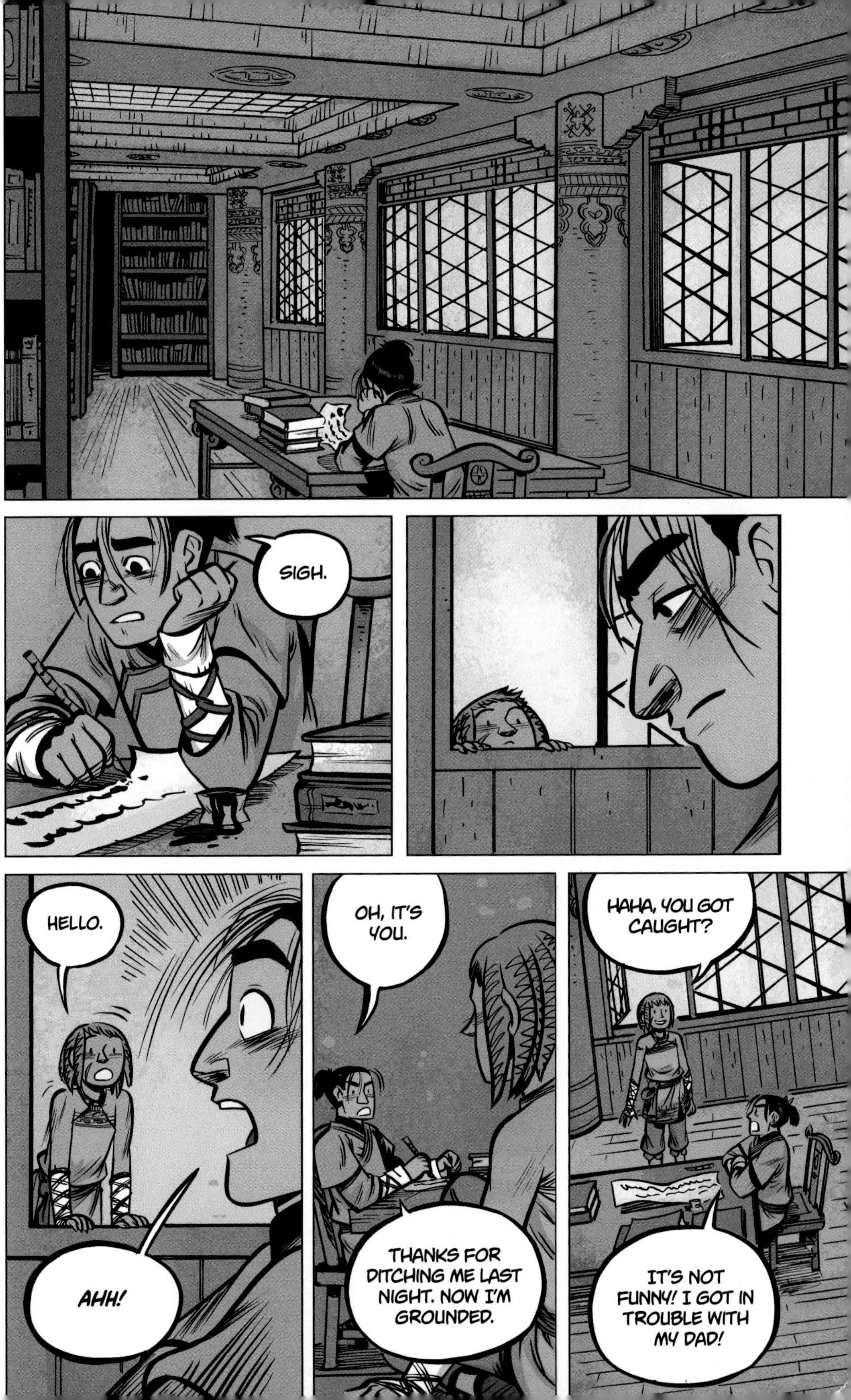
SIGH.
HELLO.
AHH!
OH, IT'S YOU.
THANKS FOR DITCHING ME LAST NIGHT. NOW I'M GROUNDED.
HAHA, YOU GOT CAUGHT?
IT'S NOT FUNNY! I GOT IN TROUBLE WITH MY DAD!

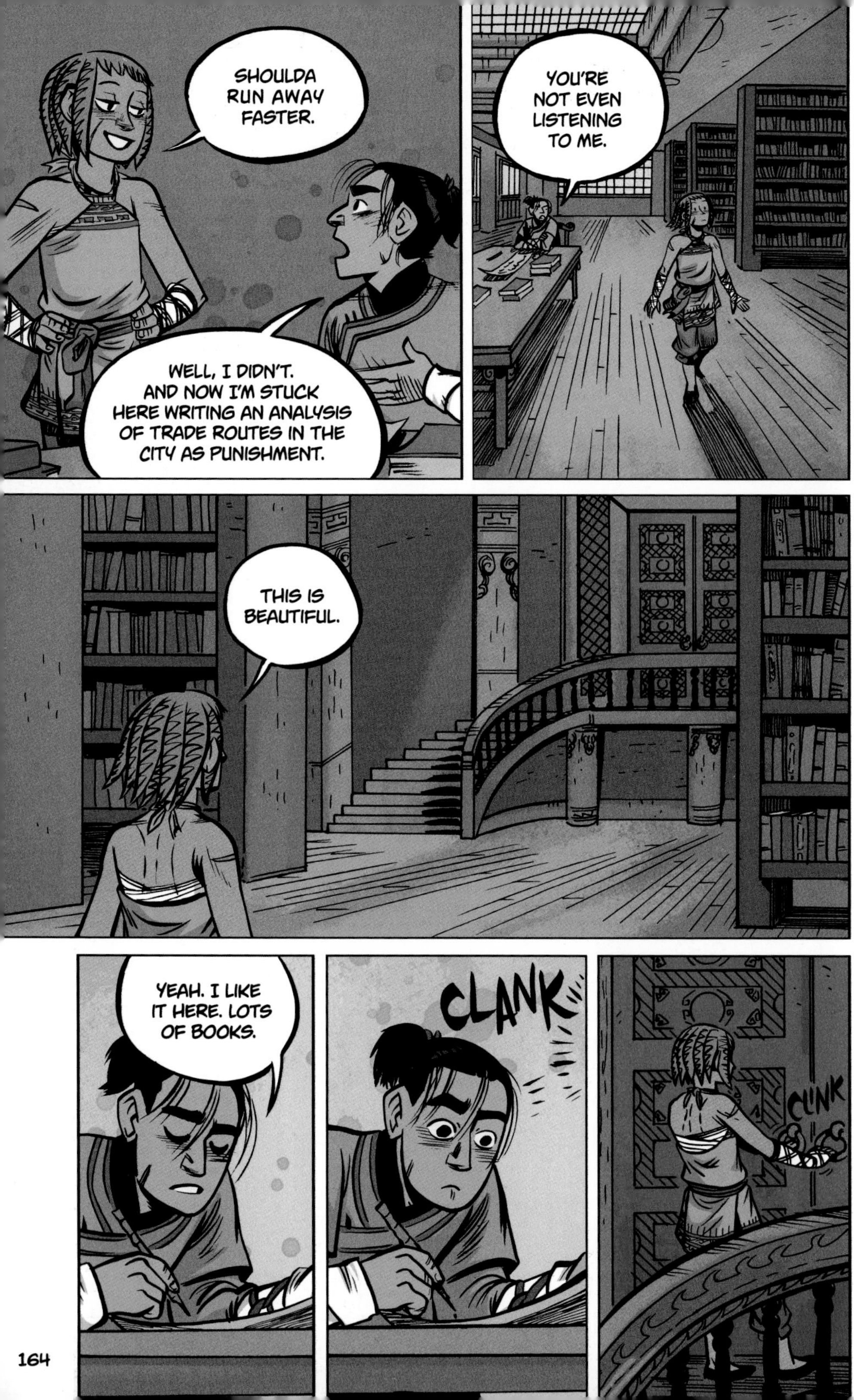
SHOULDA RUN AWAY FASTER.
WELL, I DIDN'T. AND NOW I'M STUCK HERE WRITING AN ANALYSIS OF TRADE ROUTES IN THE CITY AS PUNISHMENT.
YOU'RE NOT EVEN LISTENING TO ME.
THIS IS BEAUTIFUL.
YEAH. I LIKE IT HERE. LOTS OF BOOKS.
CLANK
CLINK

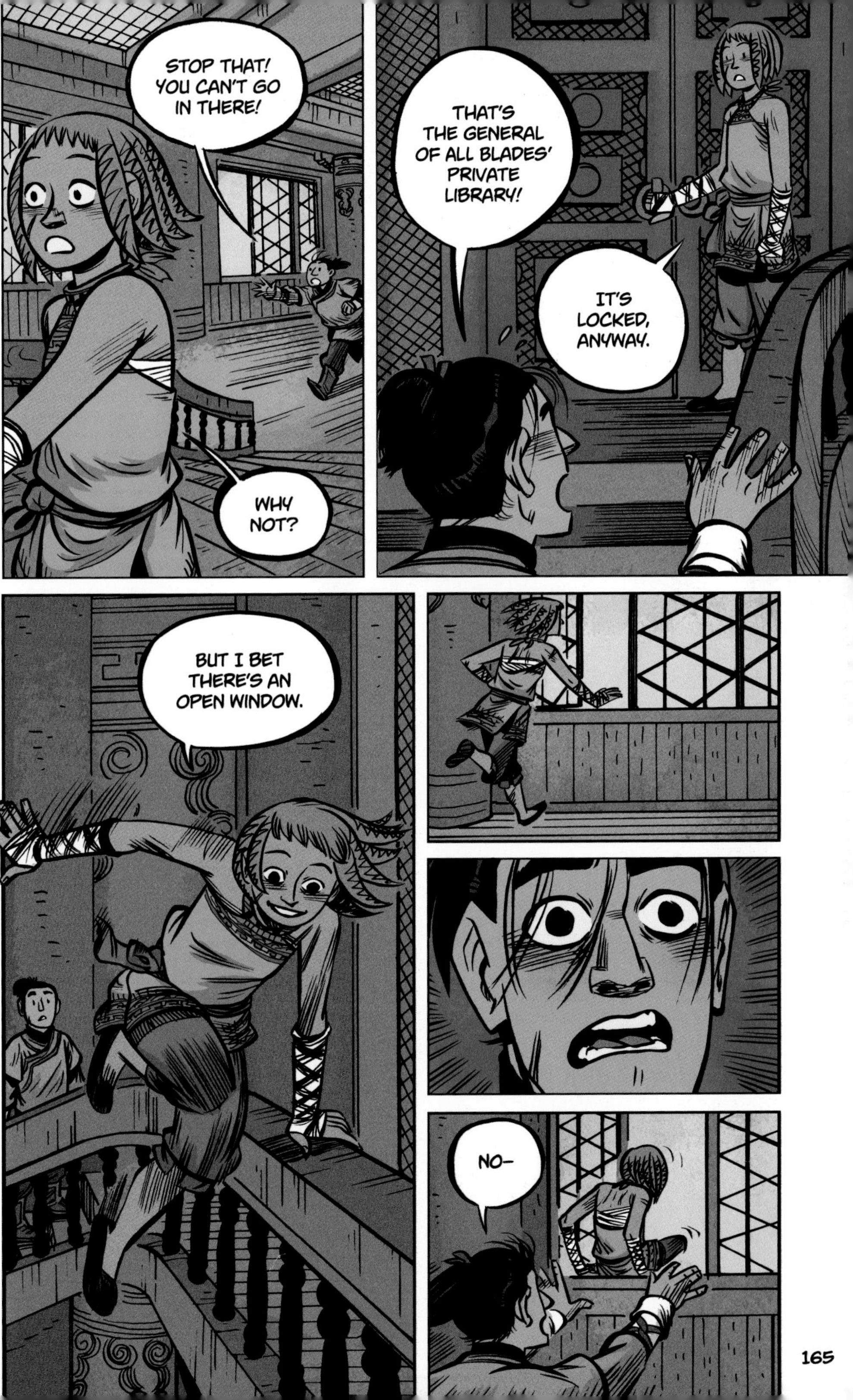
STOP THAT! YOU CAN'T GO IN THERE!
WHY NOT?
THAT'S THE GENERAL OF ALL BLADES' PRIVATE LIBRARY!
IT'S LOCKED, ANYWAY.
BUT I BET THERE'S AN OPEN WINDOW.
NO–

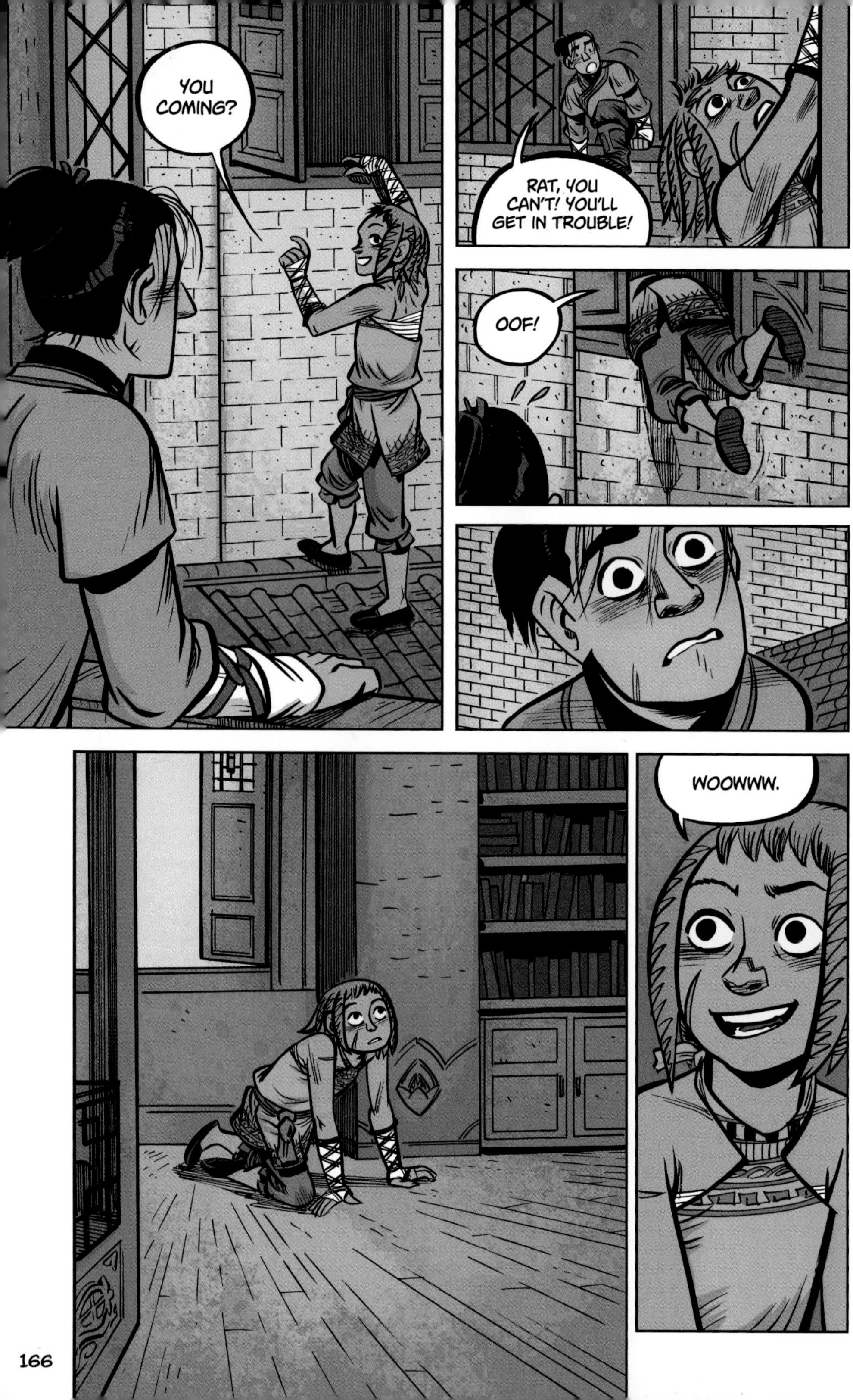
YOU COMING?
RAT, YOU CAN'T! YOU'LL GET IN TROUBLE!
OOF!
WOOWWW.

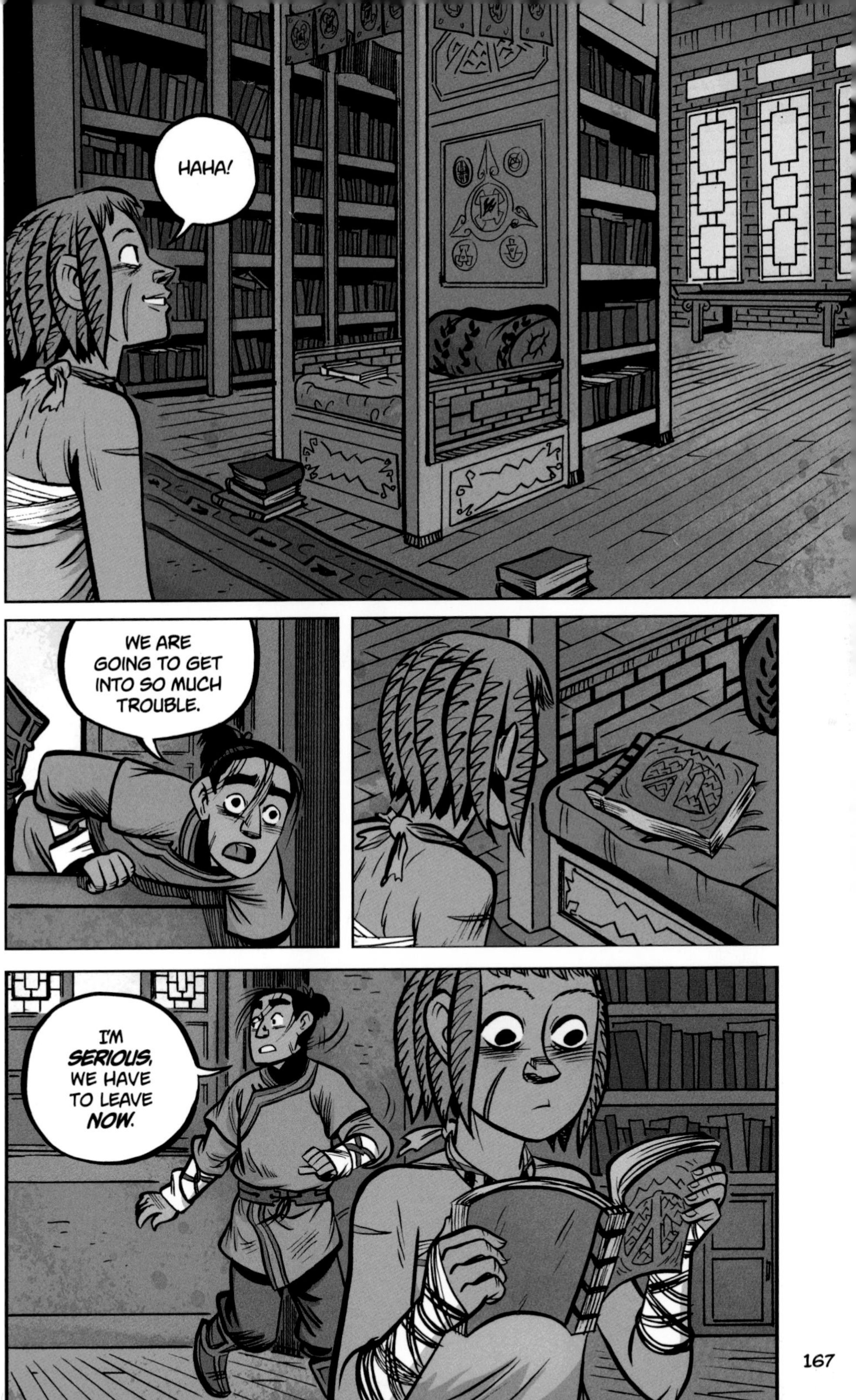
HAHA!
WE ARE GOING TO GET INTO SO MUCH TROUBLE.
I'M SERIOUS, WE HAVE TO LEAVE NOW.

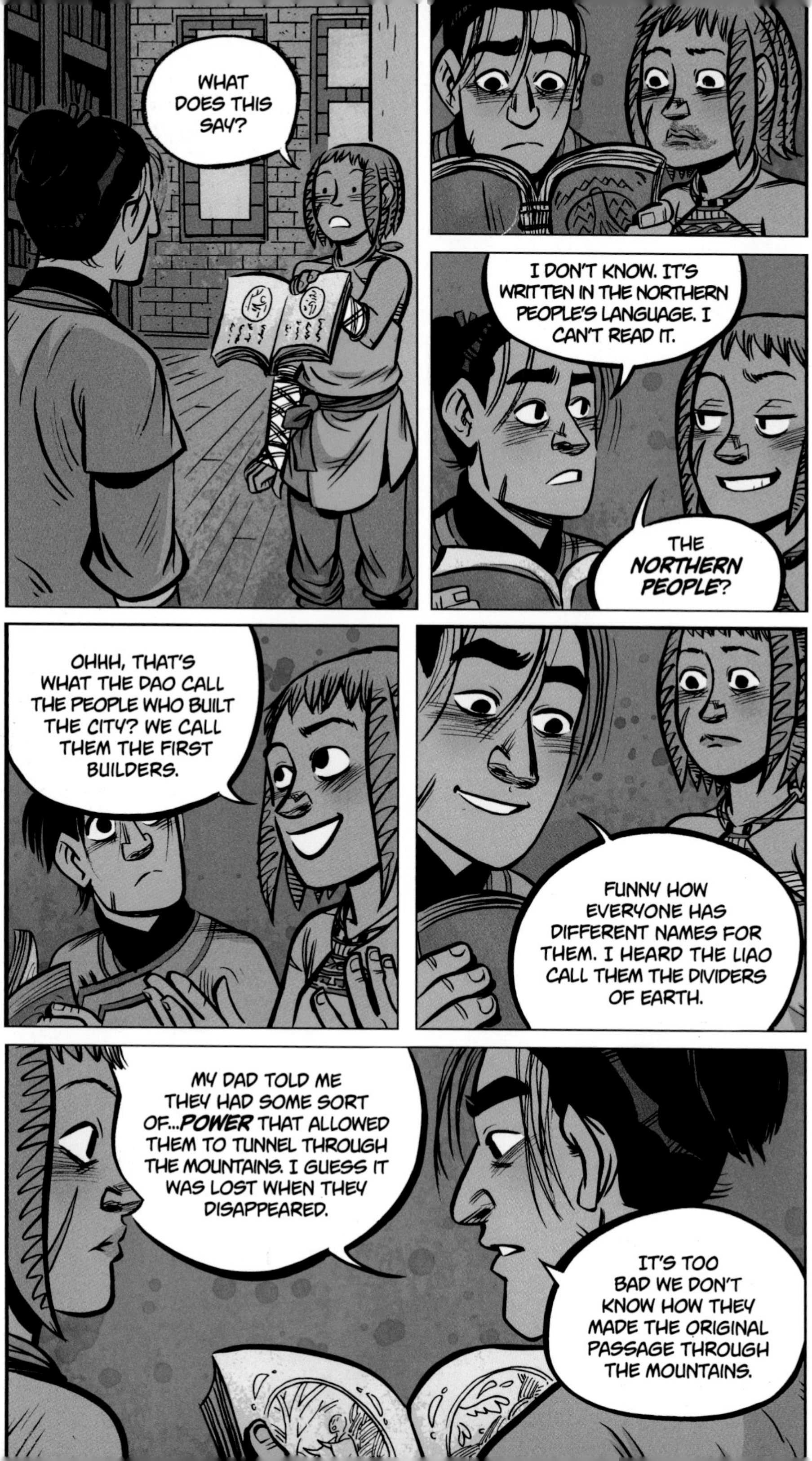
WHAT DOES THIS SAY?
I DON'T KNOW. IT'S WRITTEN IN THE NORTHERN PEOPLE'S LANGUAGE. I CAN'T READ IT.
THE *NORTHERN PEOPLE*?
OHHH, THAT'S WHAT THE DAO CALL THE PEOPLE WHO BUILT THE CITY? WE CALL THEM THE FIRST BUILDERS.
FUNNY HOW EVERYONE HAS DIFFERENT NAMES FOR THEM. I HEARD THE LIAO CALL THEM THE DIVIDERS OF EARTH.
MY DAD TOLD ME THEY HAD SOME SORT OF...*POWER* THAT ALLOWED THEM TO TUNNEL THROUGH THE MOUNTAINS. I GUESS IT WAS LOST WHEN THEY DISAPPEARED.
IT'S TOO BAD WE DON'T KNOW HOW THEY MADE THE ORIGINAL PASSAGE THROUGH THE MOUNTAINS.

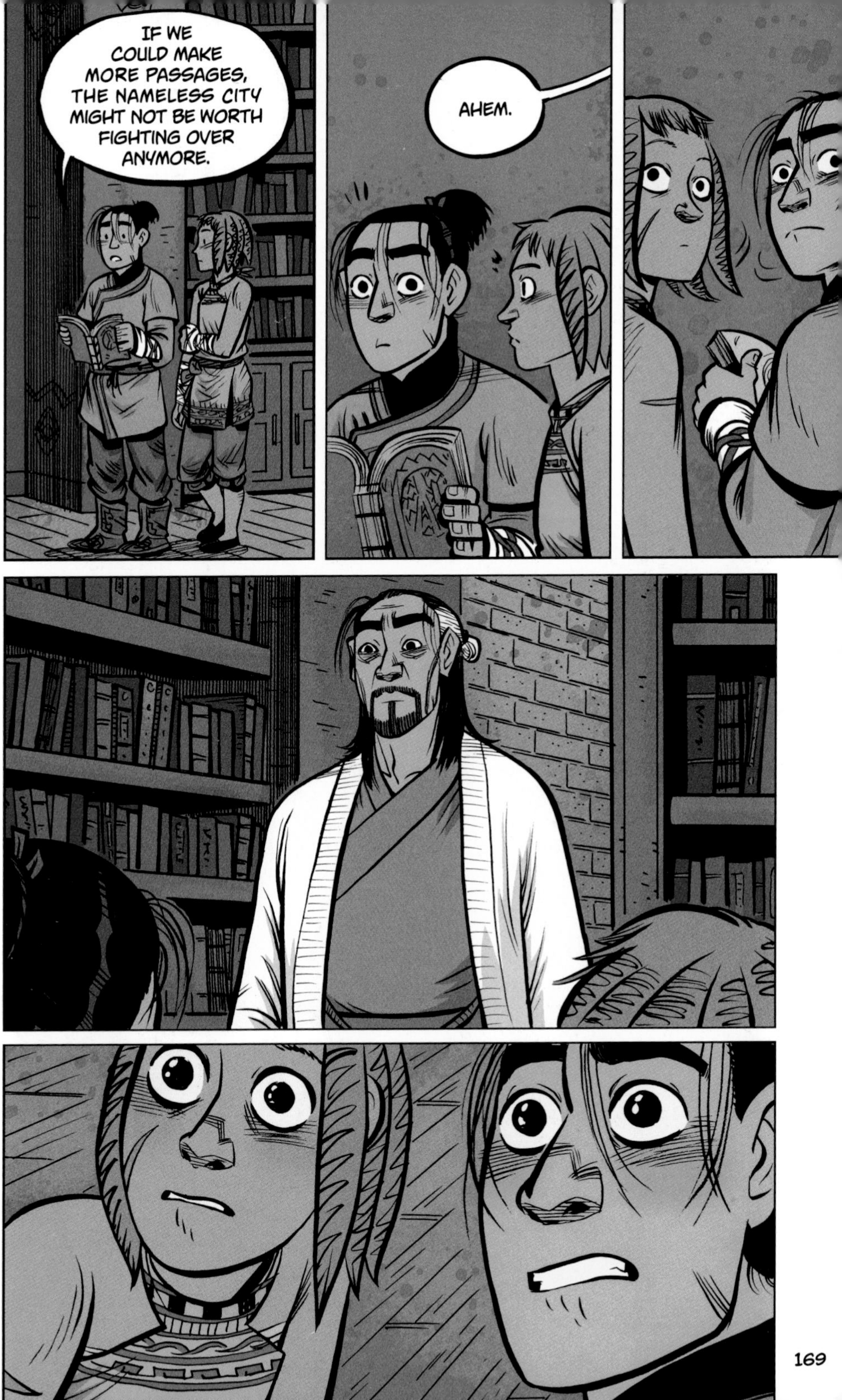
IF WE COULD MAKE MORE PASSAGES, THE NAMELESS CITY MIGHT NOT BE WORTH FIGHTING OVER ANYMORE.
AHEM.

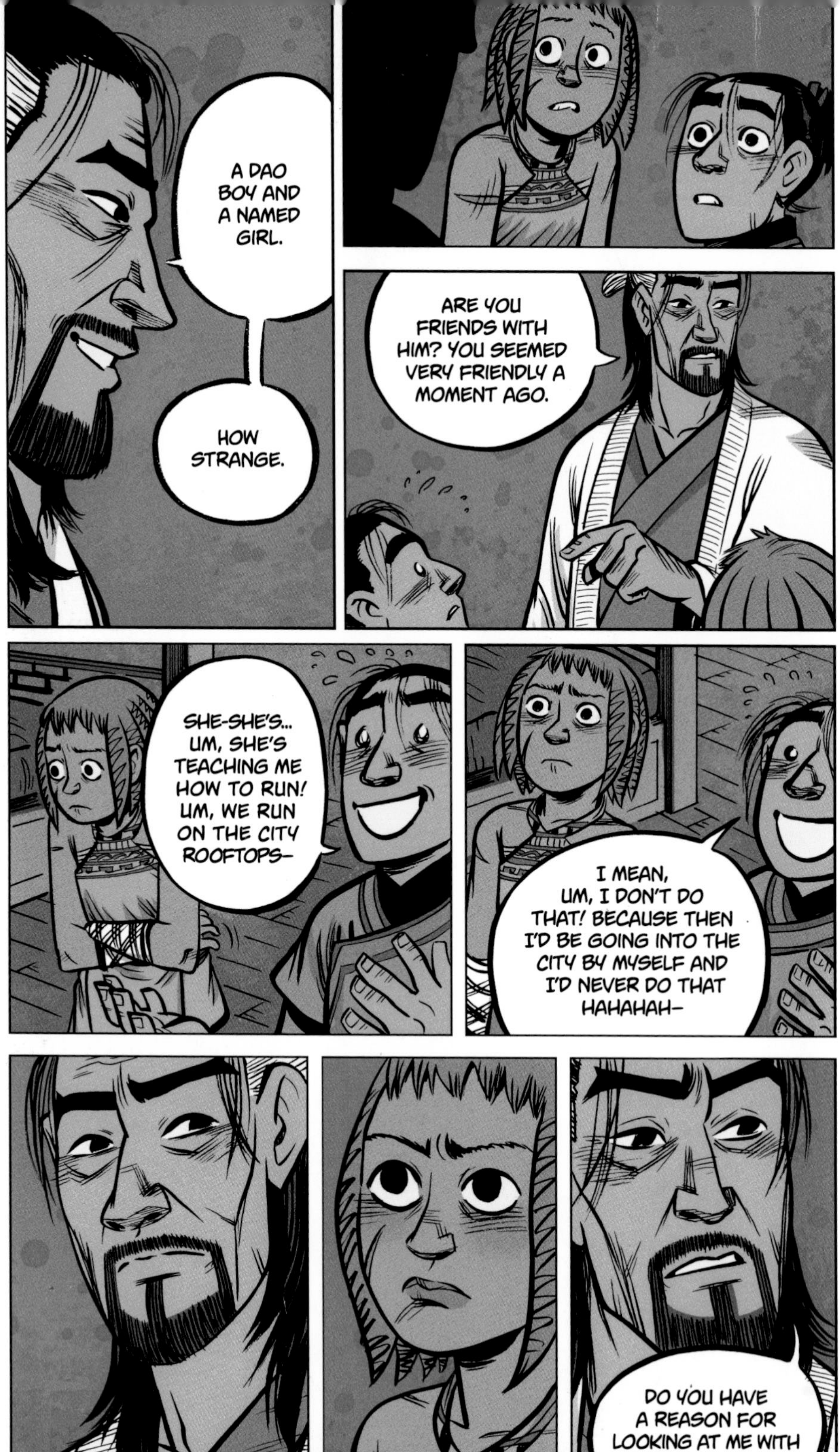
A DAO BOY AND A NAMED GIRL.
HOW STRANGE.
ARE YOU FRIENDS WITH HIM? YOU SEEMED VERY FRIENDLY A MOMENT AGO.
SHE-SHE'S... UM, SHE'S TEACHING ME HOW TO RUN! UM, WE RUN ON THE CITY ROOFTOPS—
I MEAN, UM, I DON'T DO THAT! BECAUSE THEN I'D BE GOING INTO THE CITY BY MYSELF AND I'D NEVER DO THAT HAHAHAH—
DO YOU HAVE A REASON FOR LOOKING AT ME WITH SUCH ANGER?

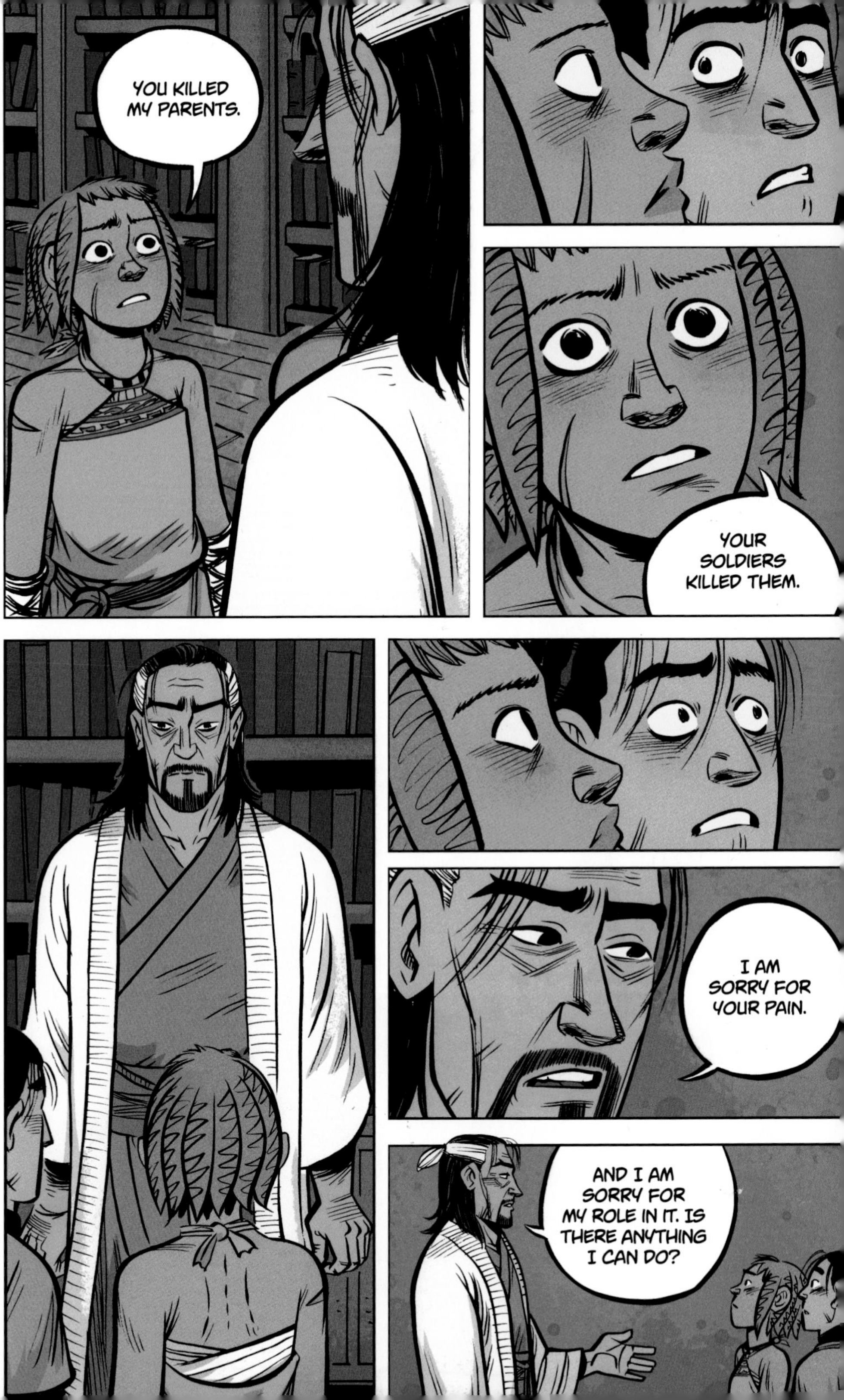
YOU KILLED MY PARENTS.
YOUR SOLDIERS KILLED THEM.
I AM SORRY FOR YOUR PAIN.
AND I AM SORRY FOR MY ROLE IN IT. IS THERE ANYTHING I CAN DO?

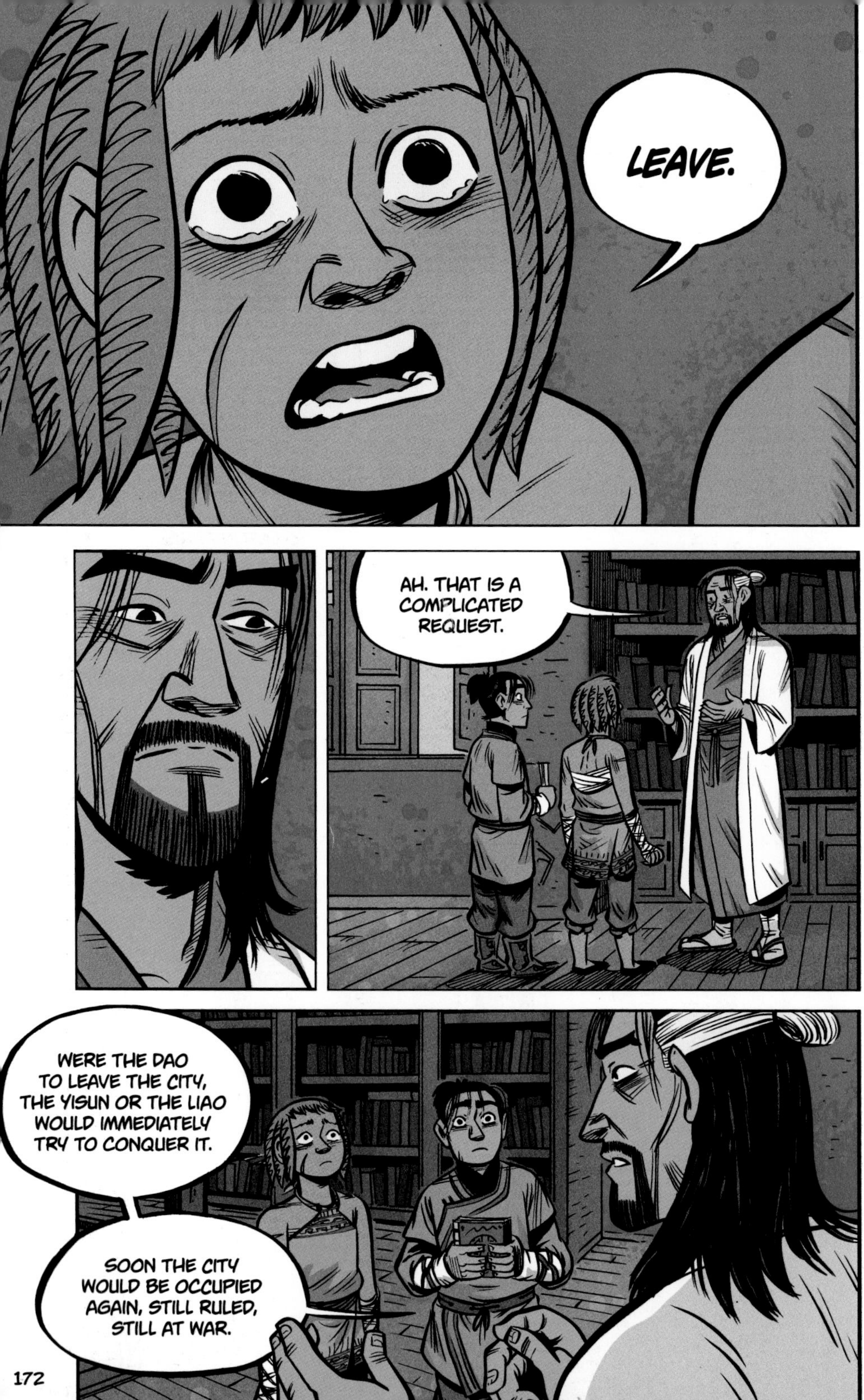
LEAVE.
AH. THAT IS A COMPLICATED REQUEST.
WERE THE DAO TO LEAVE THE CITY, THE YISUN OR THE LIAO WOULD IMMEDIATELY TRY TO CONQUER IT.
SOON THE CITY WOULD BE OCCUPIED AGAIN, STILL RULED, STILL AT WAR.

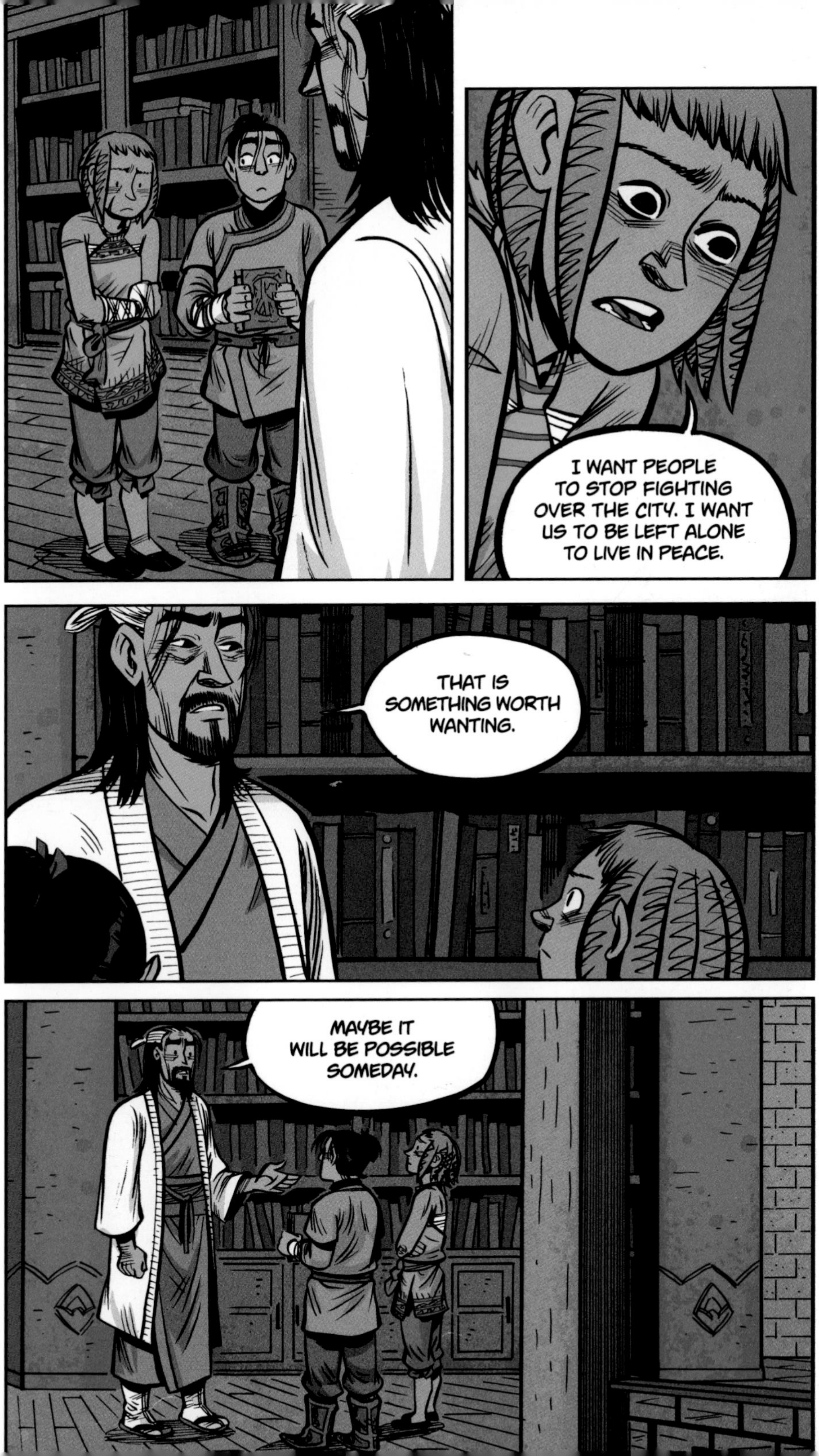

I WANT PEOPLE TO STOP FIGHTING OVER THE CITY. I WANT US TO BE LEFT ALONE TO LIVE IN PEACE.
THAT IS SOMETHING WORTH WANTING.
MAYBE IT WILL BE POSSIBLE SOMEDAY.

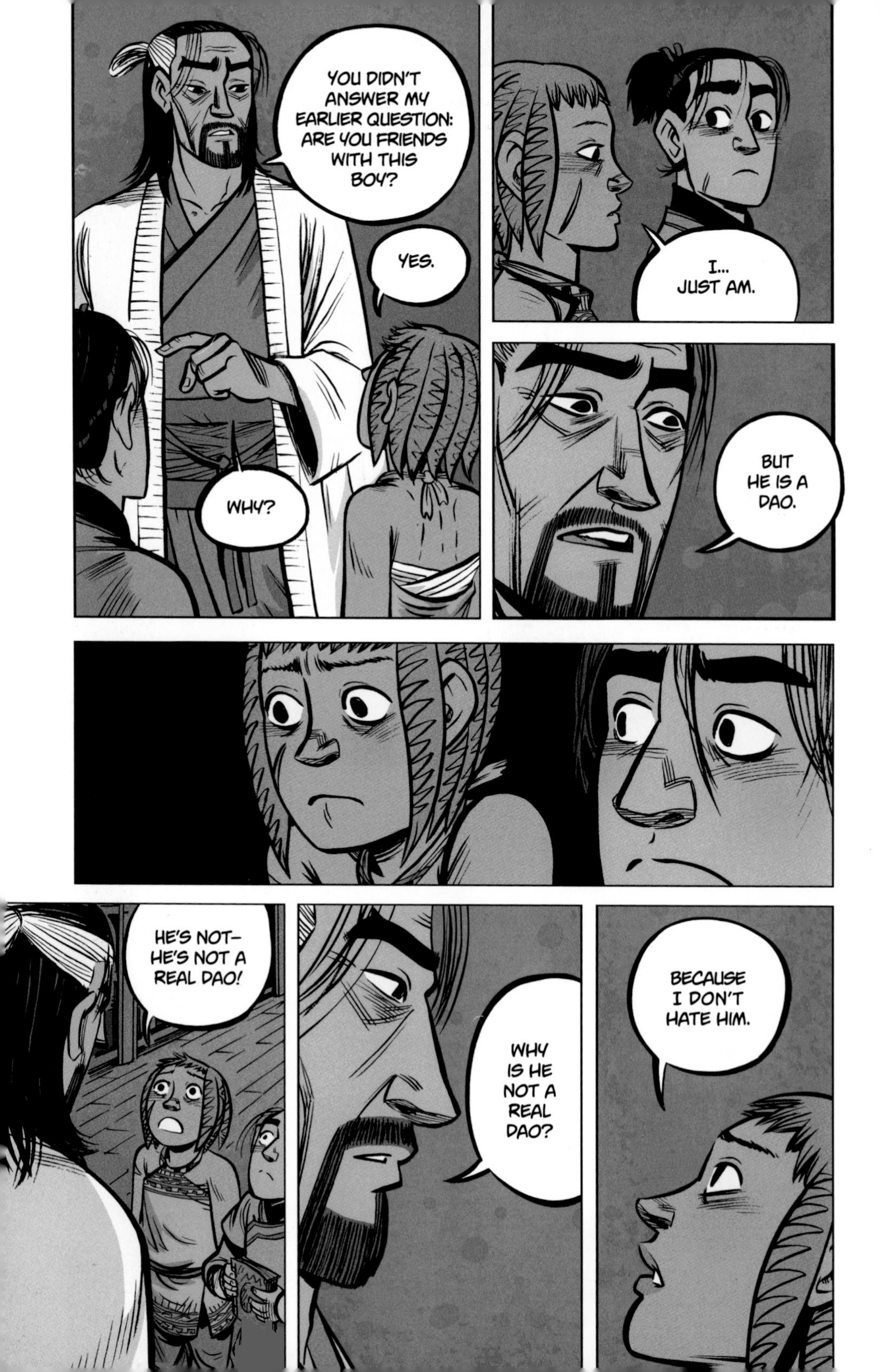
YOU DIDN'T ANSWER MY EARLIER QUESTION: ARE YOU FRIENDS WITH THIS BOY?
YES.
WHY?
I... JUST AM.
BUT HE IS A DAO.
HE'S NOT— HE'S NOT A REAL DAO!
WHY IS HE NOT A REAL DAO?
BECAUSE I DON'T HATE HIM.

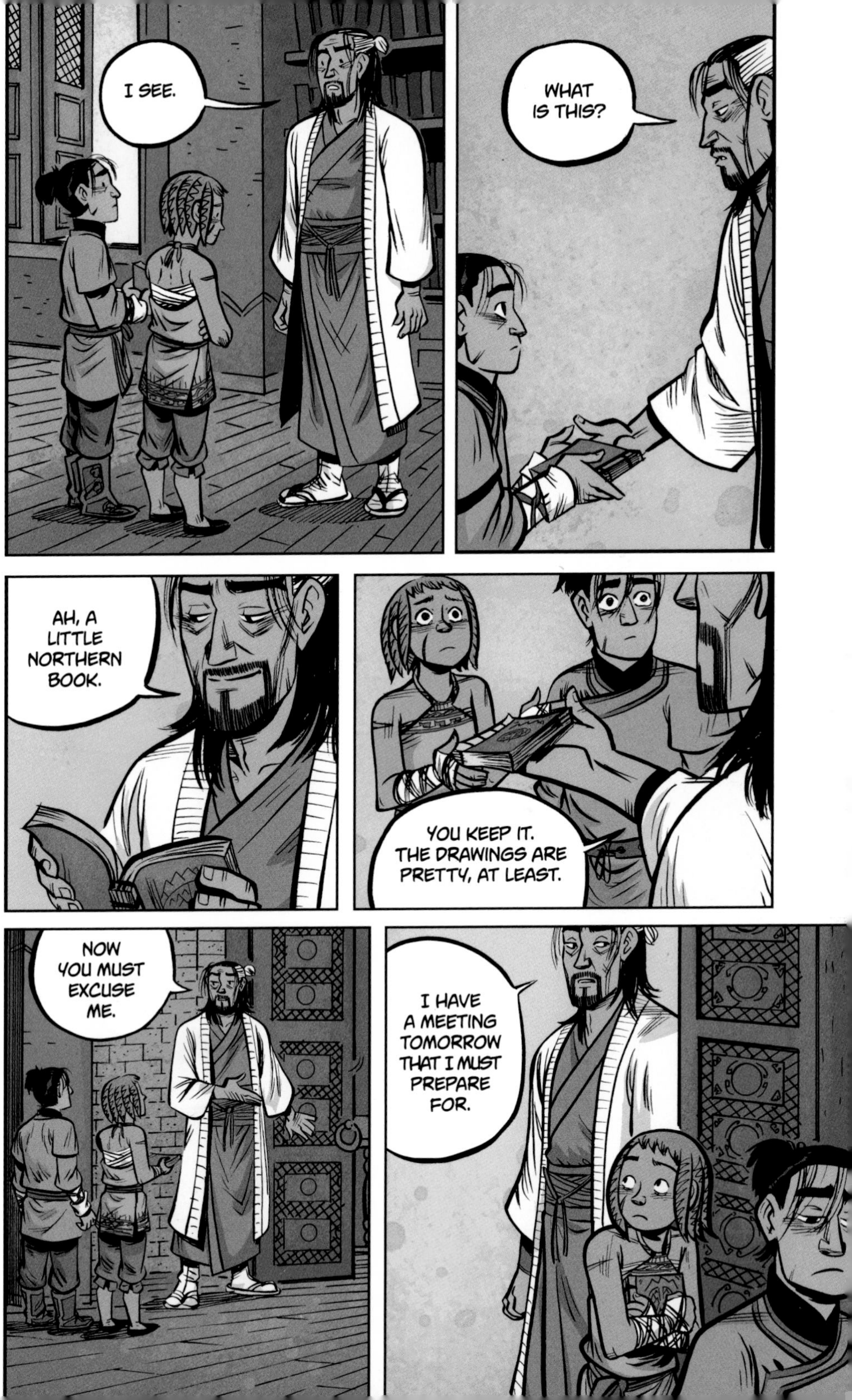
I SEE.
WHAT IS THIS?
AH, A LITTLE NORTHERN BOOK.
YOU KEEP IT. THE DRAWINGS ARE PRETTY, AT LEAST.
NOW YOU MUST EXCUSE ME.
I HAVE A MEETING TOMORROW THAT I MUST PREPARE FOR.

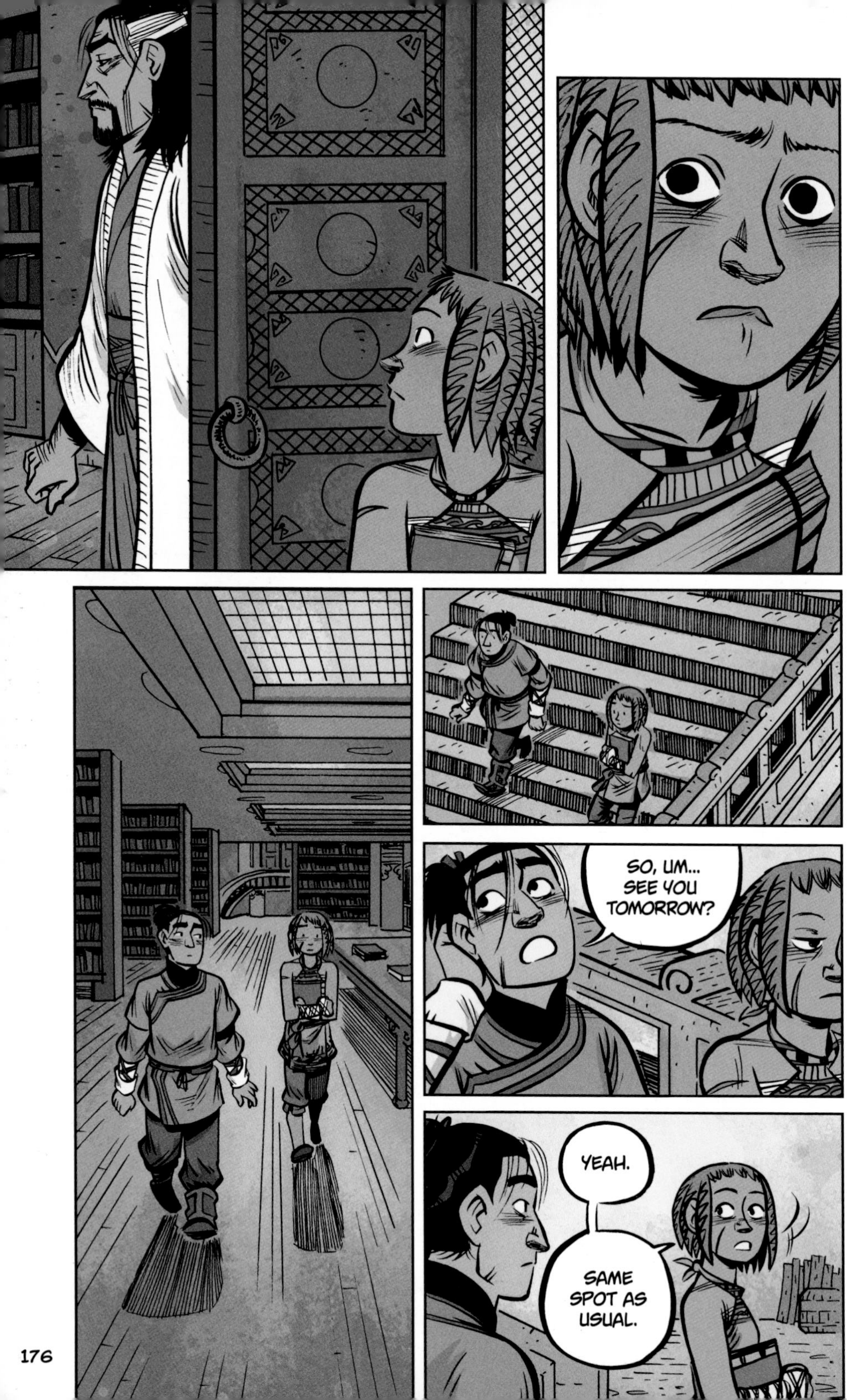
SO, UM...
SEE YOU
TOMORROW?
YEAH.
SAME
SPOT AS
USUAL.

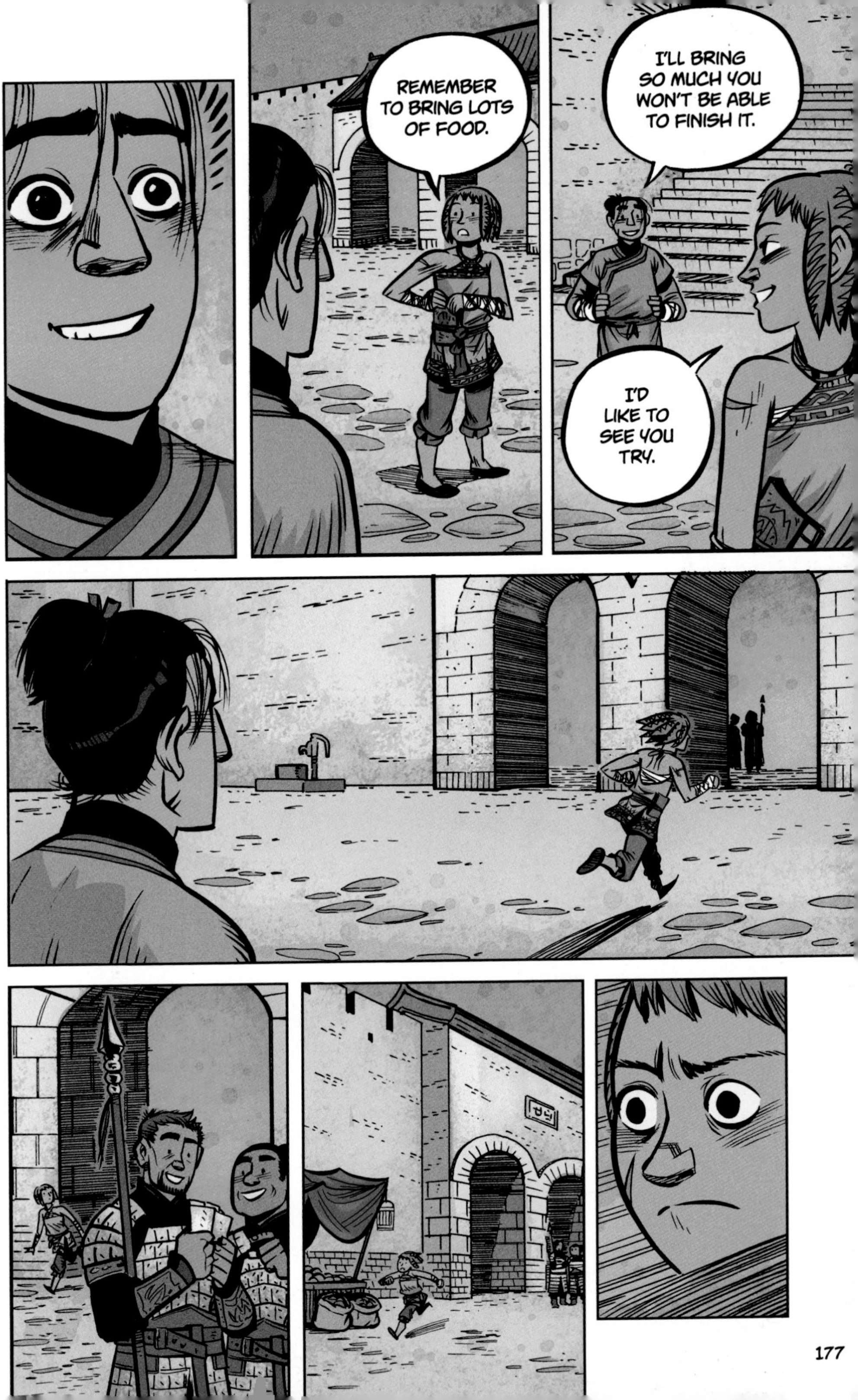
REMEMBER TO BRING LOTS OF FOOD.
I'LL BRING SO MUCH YOU WON'T BE ABLE TO FINISH IT.
I'D LIKE TO SEE YOU TRY.

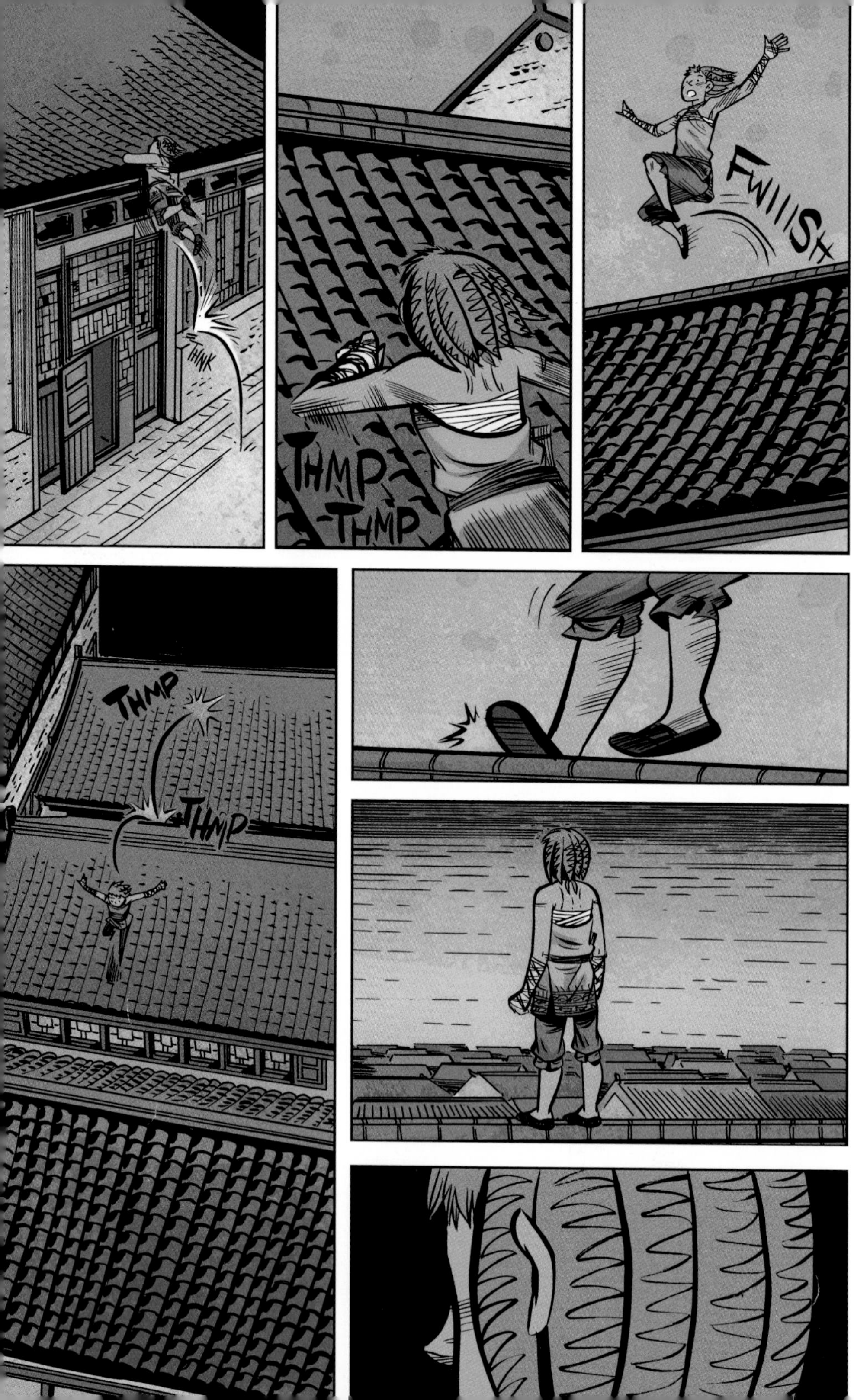
THNK
THMP
THMP
FWIIISH
THMP
THMP

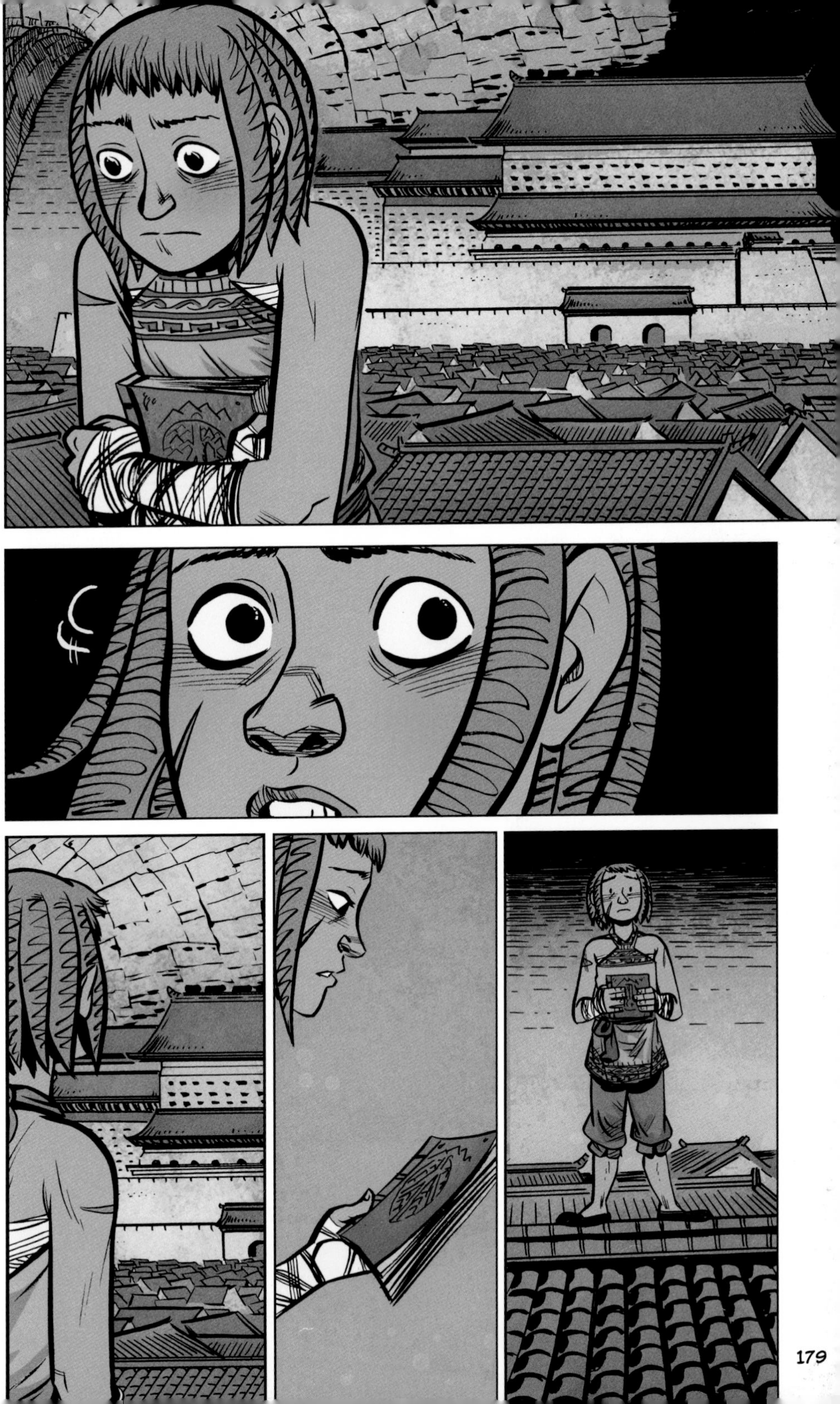

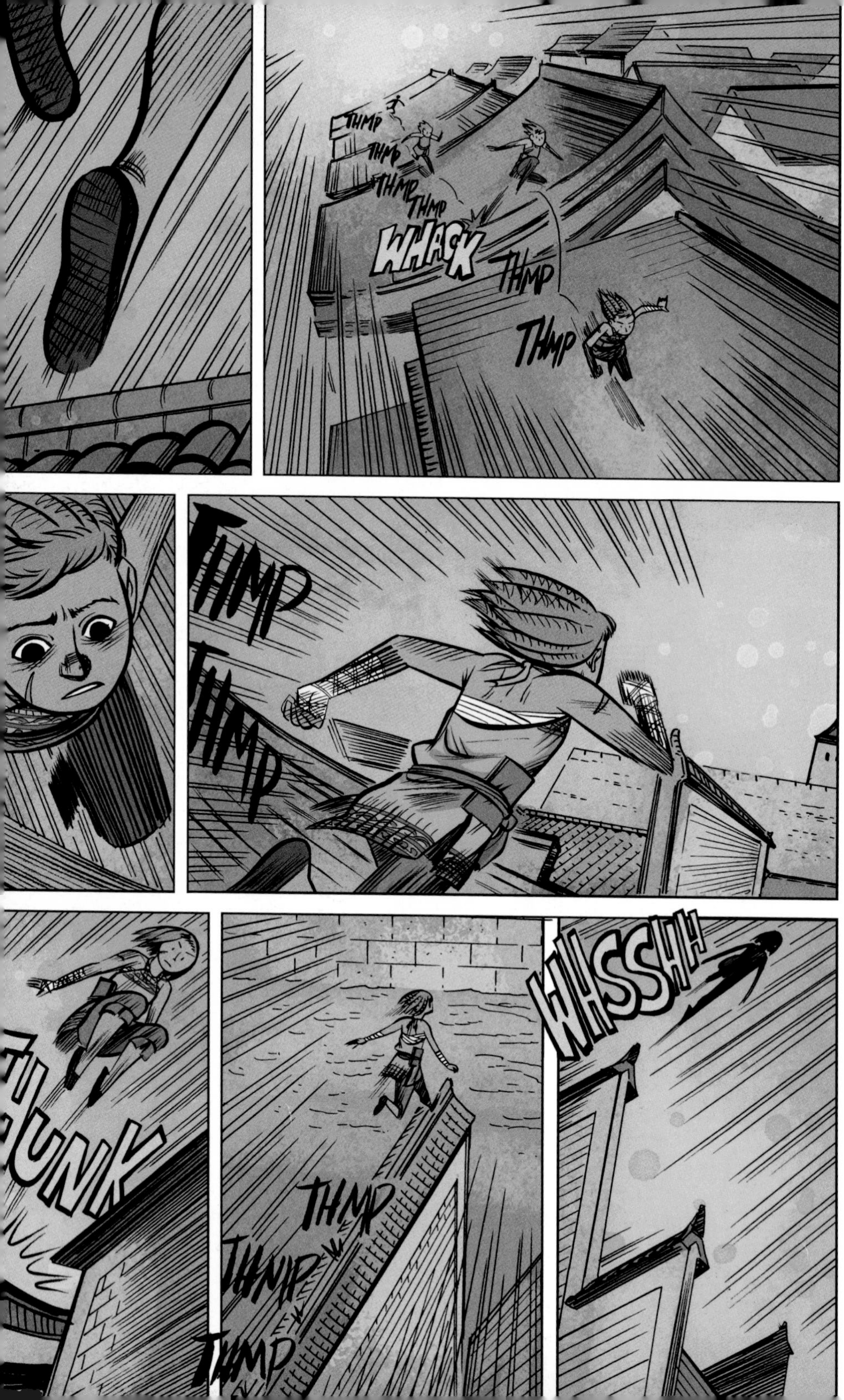
THMP
THMP
THMP
THMP
WHACK
THMP
THMP
THMP
THMP
THMP
THUNK
THMP
THMP
THMP
WHSSHH

WHSSSSH

THNK

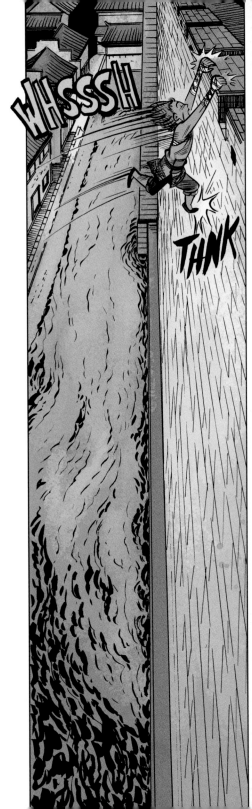

hff hff hff

EHNN.

HUFF
HUFF
HUFF

HALT!

WHO ARE YOU?

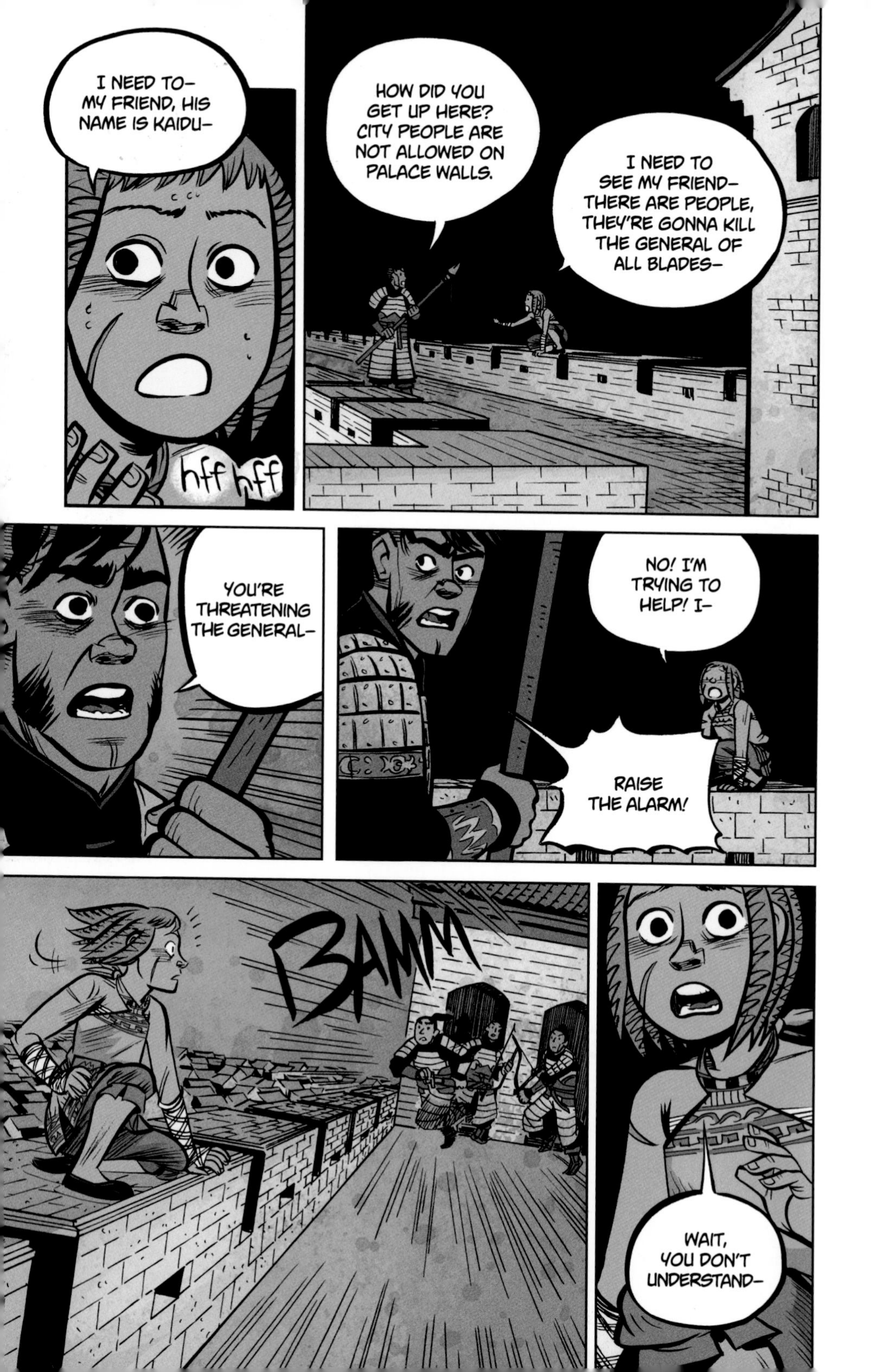
I NEED TO—
MY FRIEND, HIS
NAME IS KAIDU—
hff hff
HOW DID YOU
GET UP HERE?
CITY PEOPLE ARE
NOT ALLOWED ON
PALACE WALLS.
I NEED TO
SEE MY FRIEND—
THERE ARE PEOPLE,
THEY'RE GONNA KILL
THE GENERAL OF
ALL BLADES—
YOU'RE
THREATENING
THE GENERAL—
NO! I'M
TRYING TO
HELP! I—
RAISE
THE ALARM!
BAMM
WAIT,
YOU DON'T
UNDERSTAND—

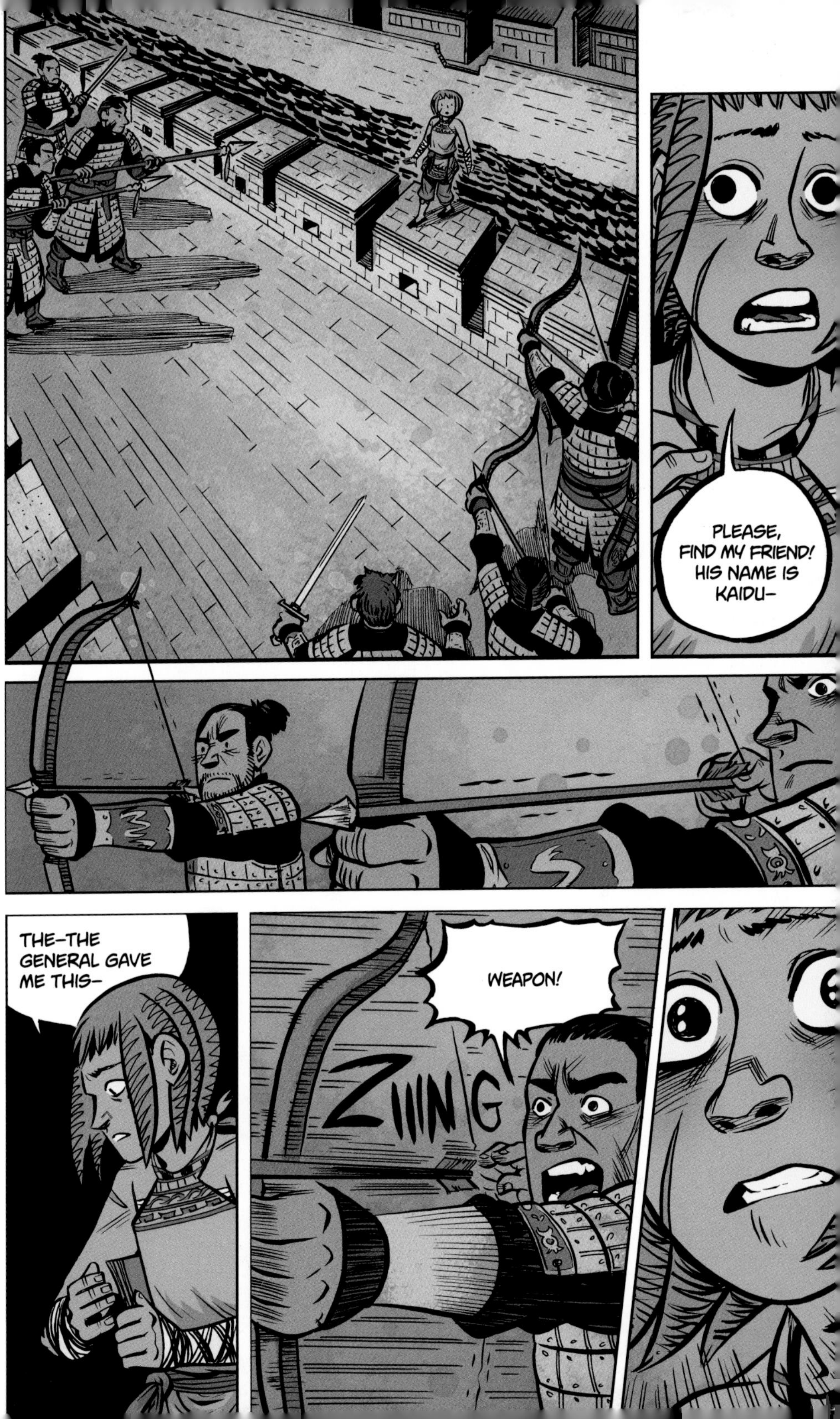
PLEASE, FIND MY FRIEND! HIS NAME IS KAIDU-
THE-THE GENERAL GAVE ME THIS-
WEAPON!
ZIIING

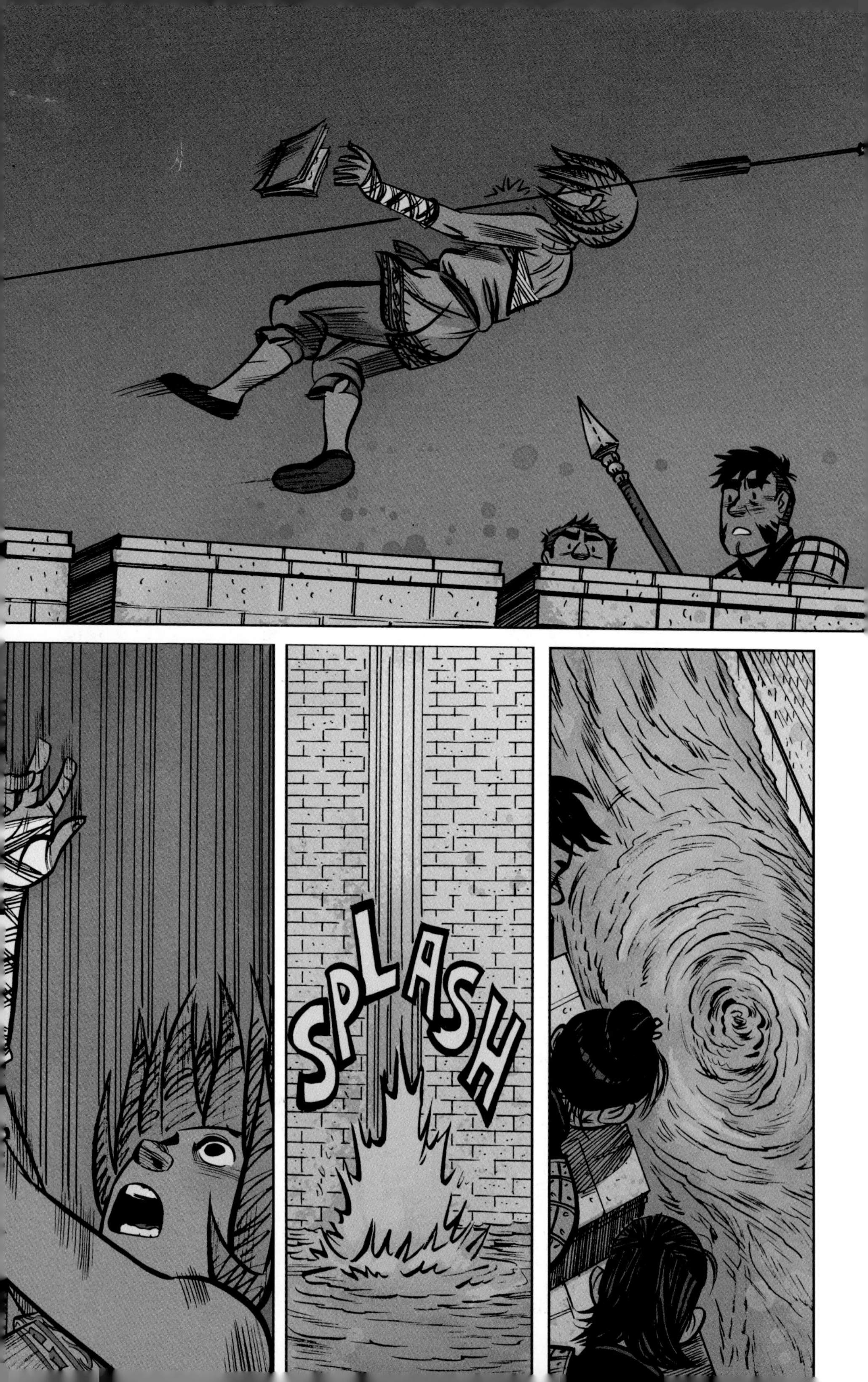
SPLASH

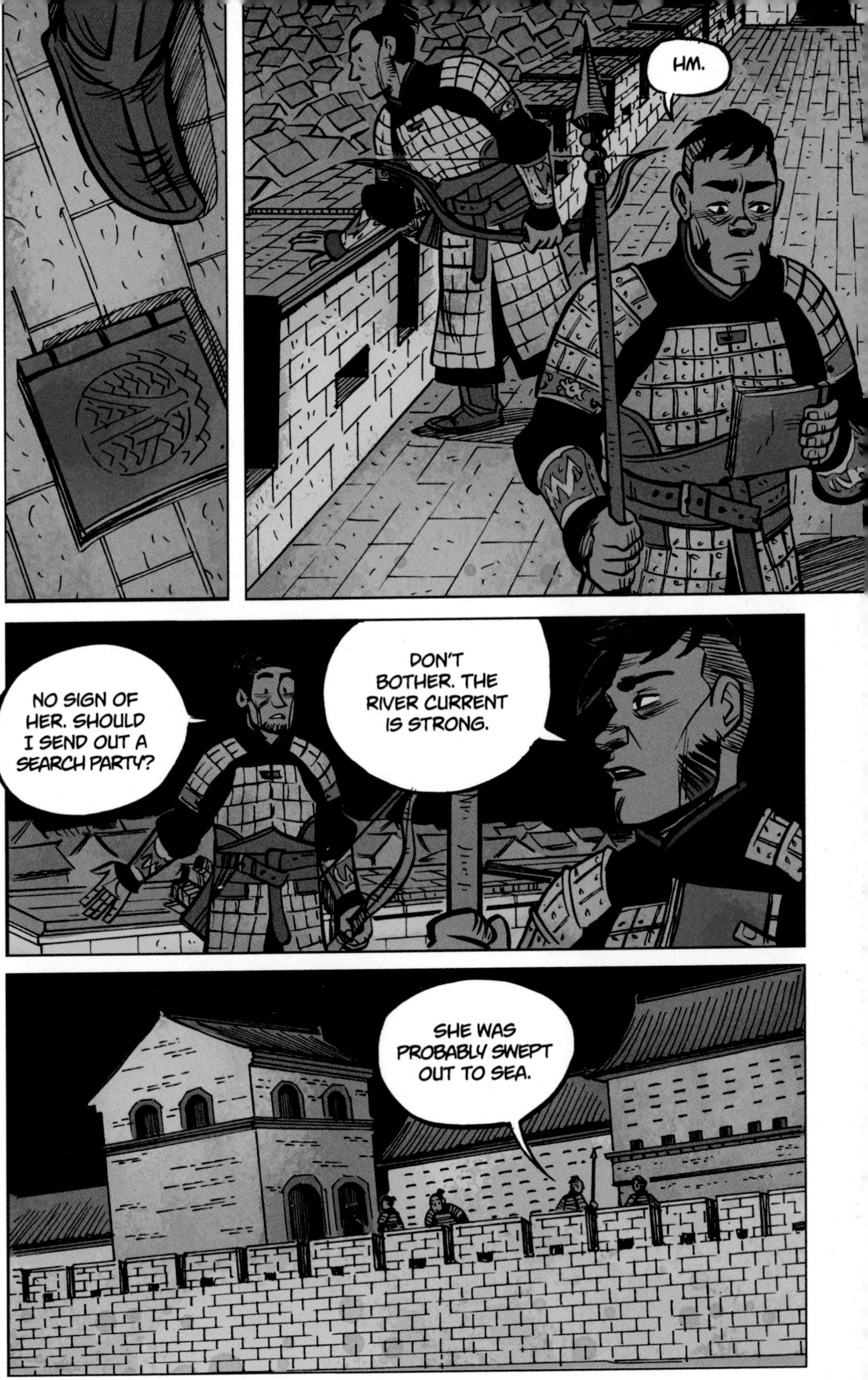
HM.
NO SIGN OF HER. SHOULD I SEND OUT A SEARCH PARTY?
DON'T BOTHER. THE RIVER CURRENT IS STRONG.
SHE WAS PROBABLY SWEPT OUT TO SEA.

DAY 31

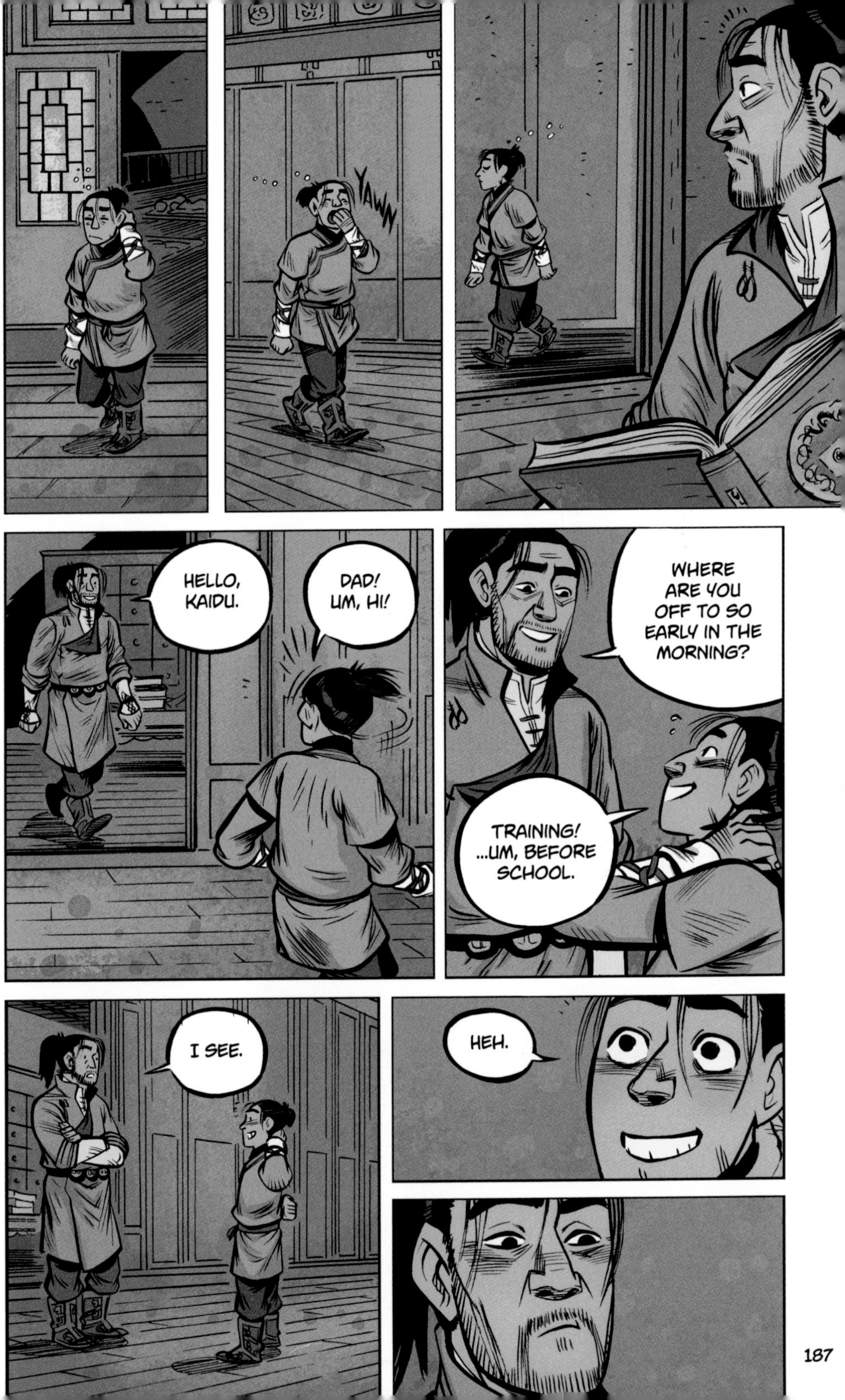
YAWN
HELLO, KAIDU.
DAD! UM, HI!
WHERE ARE YOU OFF TO SO EARLY IN THE MORNING?
TRAINING! ...UM, BEFORE SCHOOL.
I SEE.
HEH.

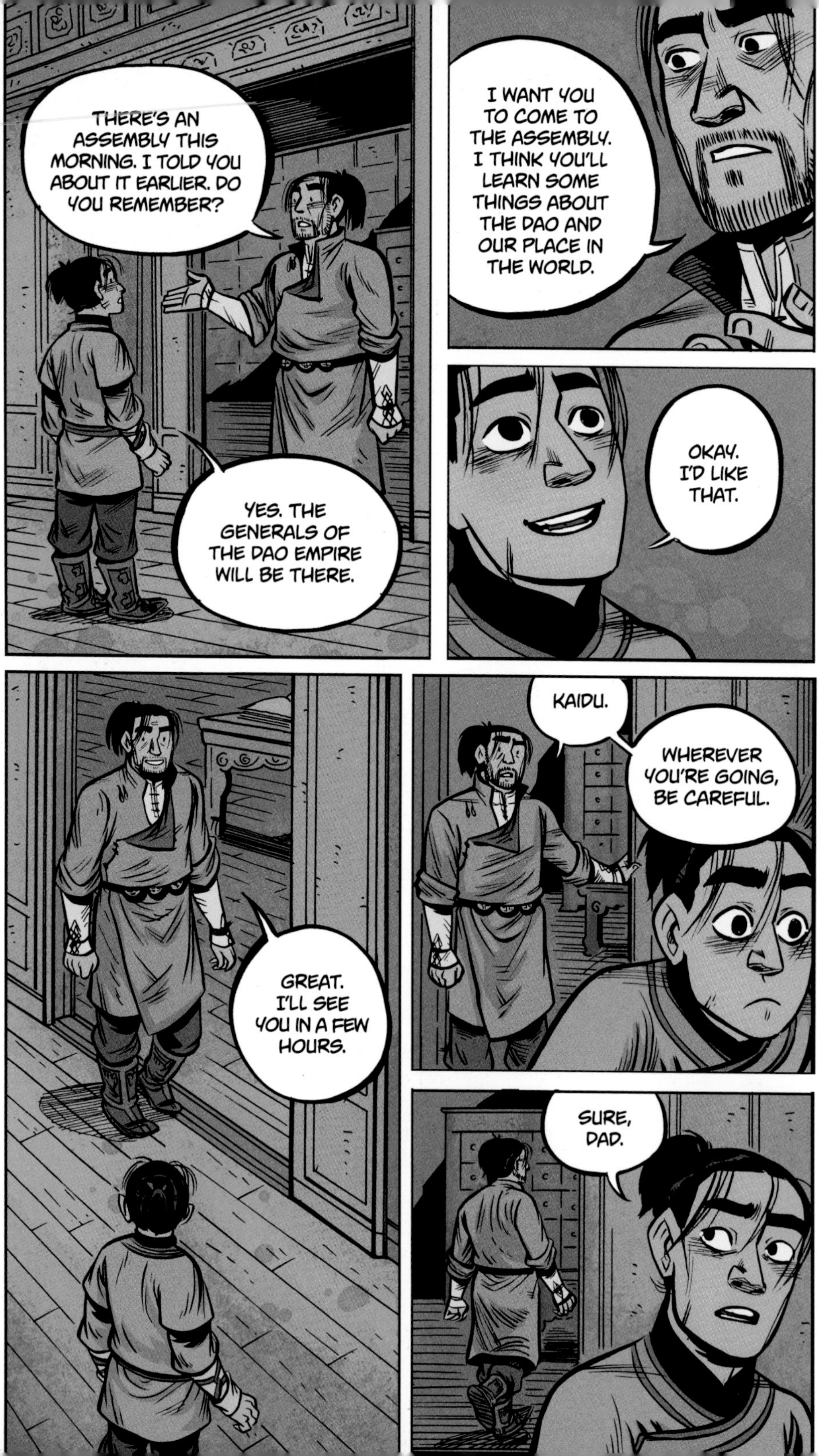
THERE'S AN ASSEMBLY THIS MORNING. I TOLD YOU ABOUT IT EARLIER. DO YOU REMEMBER?
YES. THE GENERALS OF THE DAO EMPIRE WILL BE THERE.
I WANT YOU TO COME TO THE ASSEMBLY. I THINK YOU'LL LEARN SOME THINGS ABOUT THE DAO AND OUR PLACE IN THE WORLD.
OKAY. I'D LIKE THAT.
GREAT. I'LL SEE YOU IN A FEW HOURS.
KAIDU.
WHEREVER YOU'RE GOING, BE CAREFUL.
SURE, DAD.

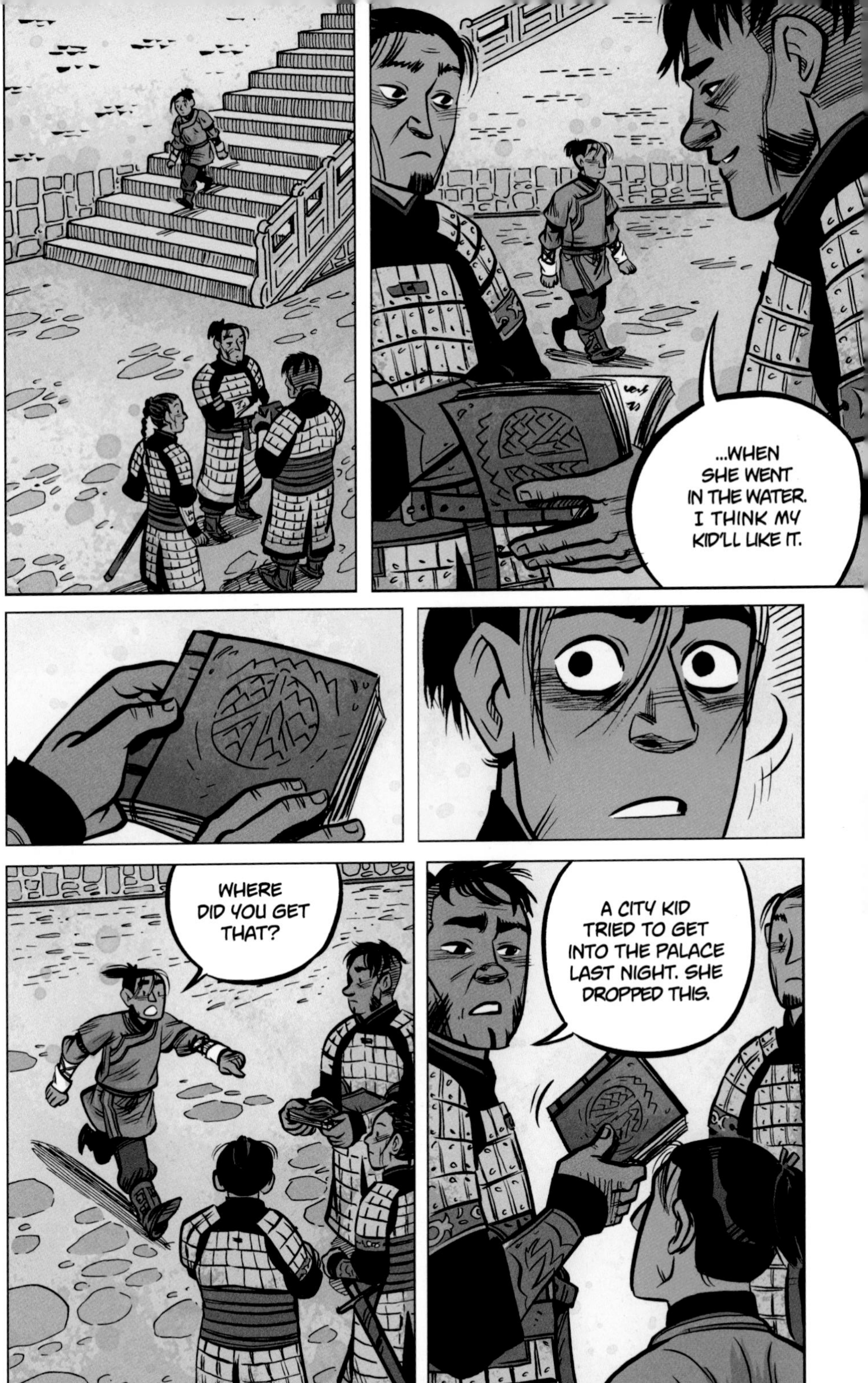
...WHEN SHE WENT IN THE WATER. I THINK MY KID'LL LIKE IT.
WHERE DID YOU GET THAT?
A CITY KID TRIED TO GET INTO THE PALACE LAST NIGHT. SHE DROPPED THIS.

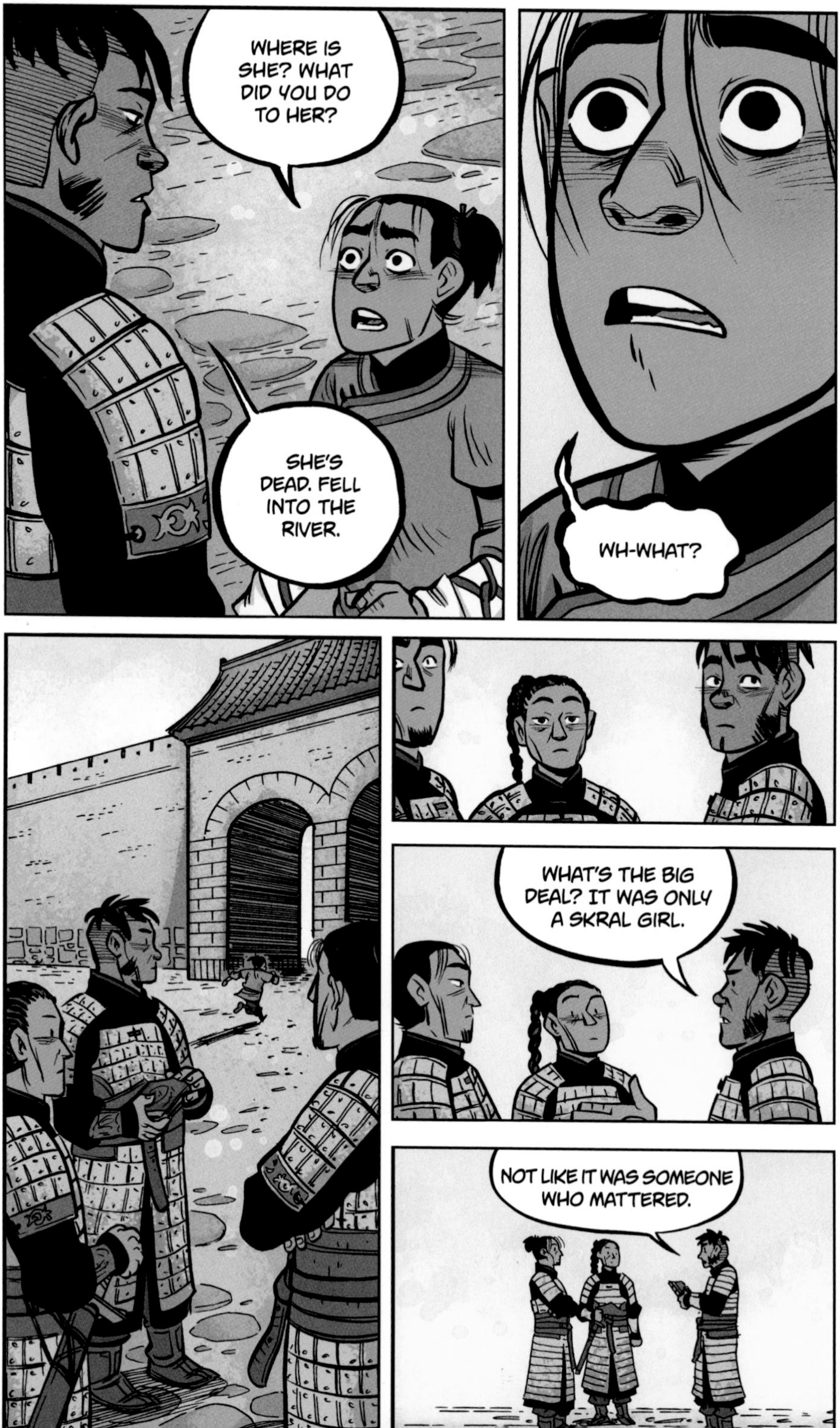
WHERE IS SHE? WHAT DID YOU DO TO HER?
SHE'S DEAD. FELL INTO THE RIVER.
WH-WHAT?
WHAT'S THE BIG DEAL? IT WAS ONLY A SKRAL GIRL.
NOT LIKE IT WAS SOMEONE WHO MATTERED.

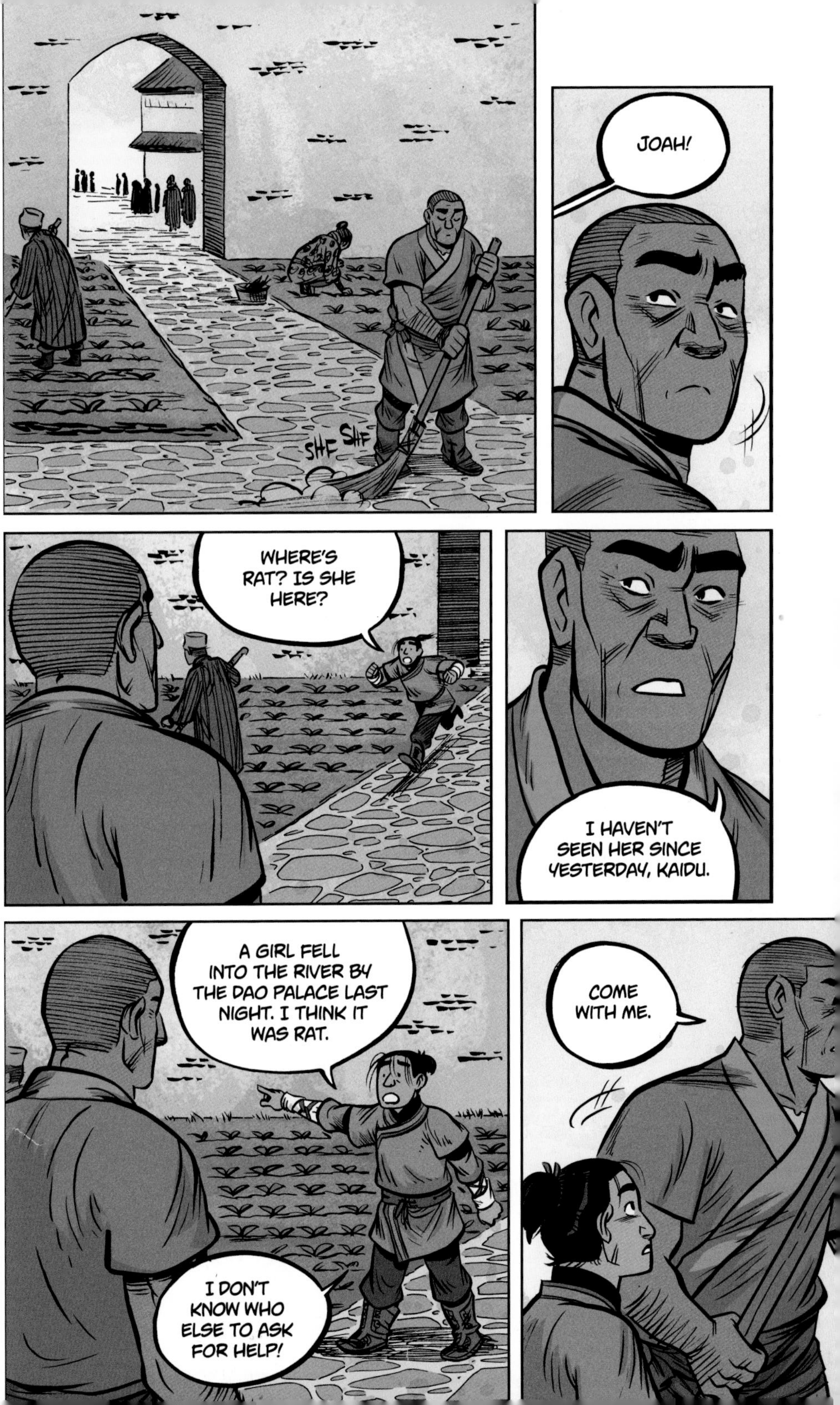
SHF SHF
JOAH!
WHERE'S RAT? IS SHE HERE?
I HAVEN'T SEEN HER SINCE YESTERDAY, KAIDU.
A GIRL FELL INTO THE RIVER BY THE DAO PALACE LAST NIGHT. I THINK IT WAS RAT.
I DON'T KNOW WHO ELSE TO ASK FOR HELP!
COME WITH ME.

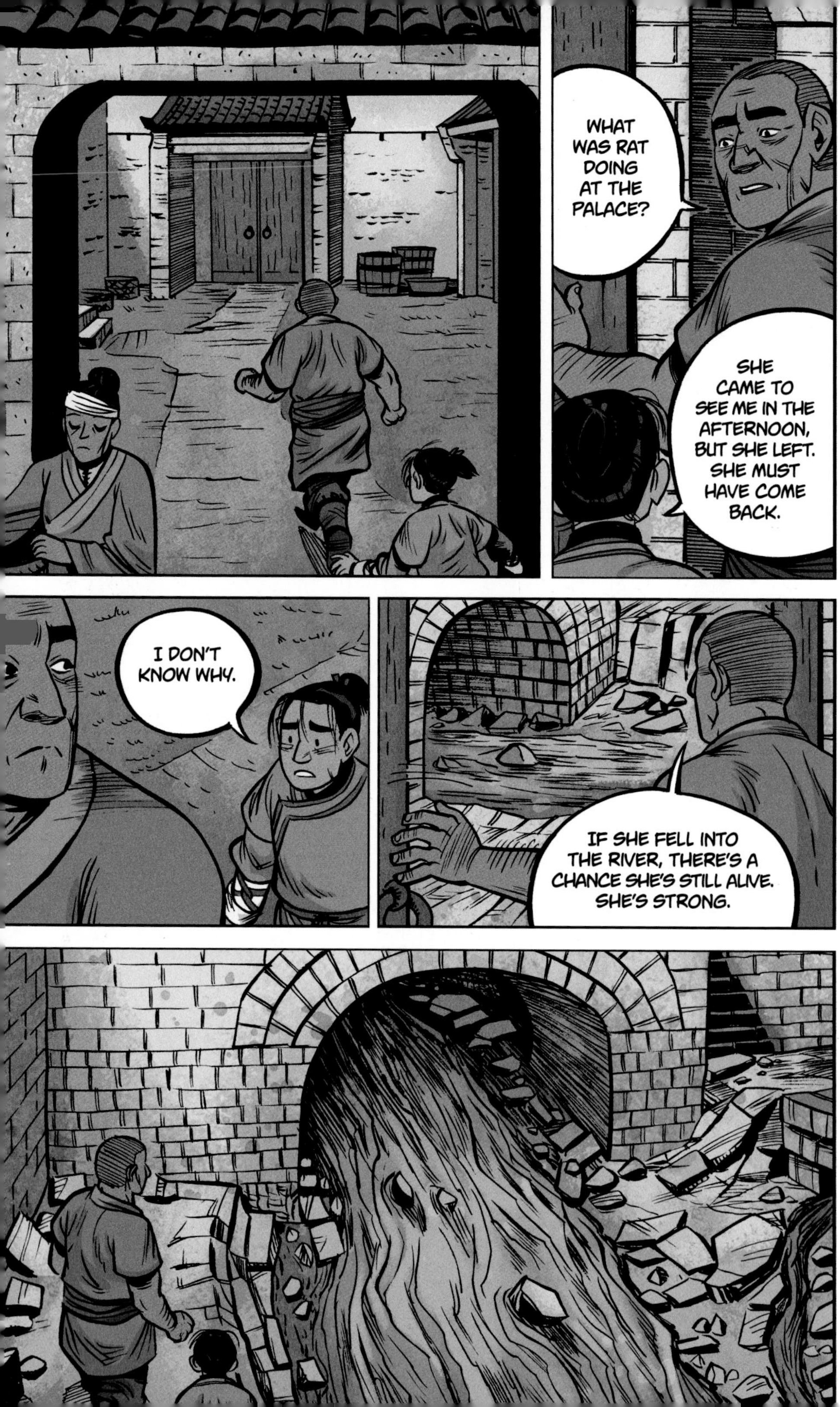
WHAT WAS RAT DOING AT THE PALACE?
SHE CAME TO SEE ME IN THE AFTERNOON, BUT SHE LEFT. SHE MUST HAVE COME BACK.
I DON'T KNOW WHY.
IF SHE FELL INTO THE RIVER, THERE'S A CHANCE SHE'S STILL ALIVE. SHE'S STRONG.

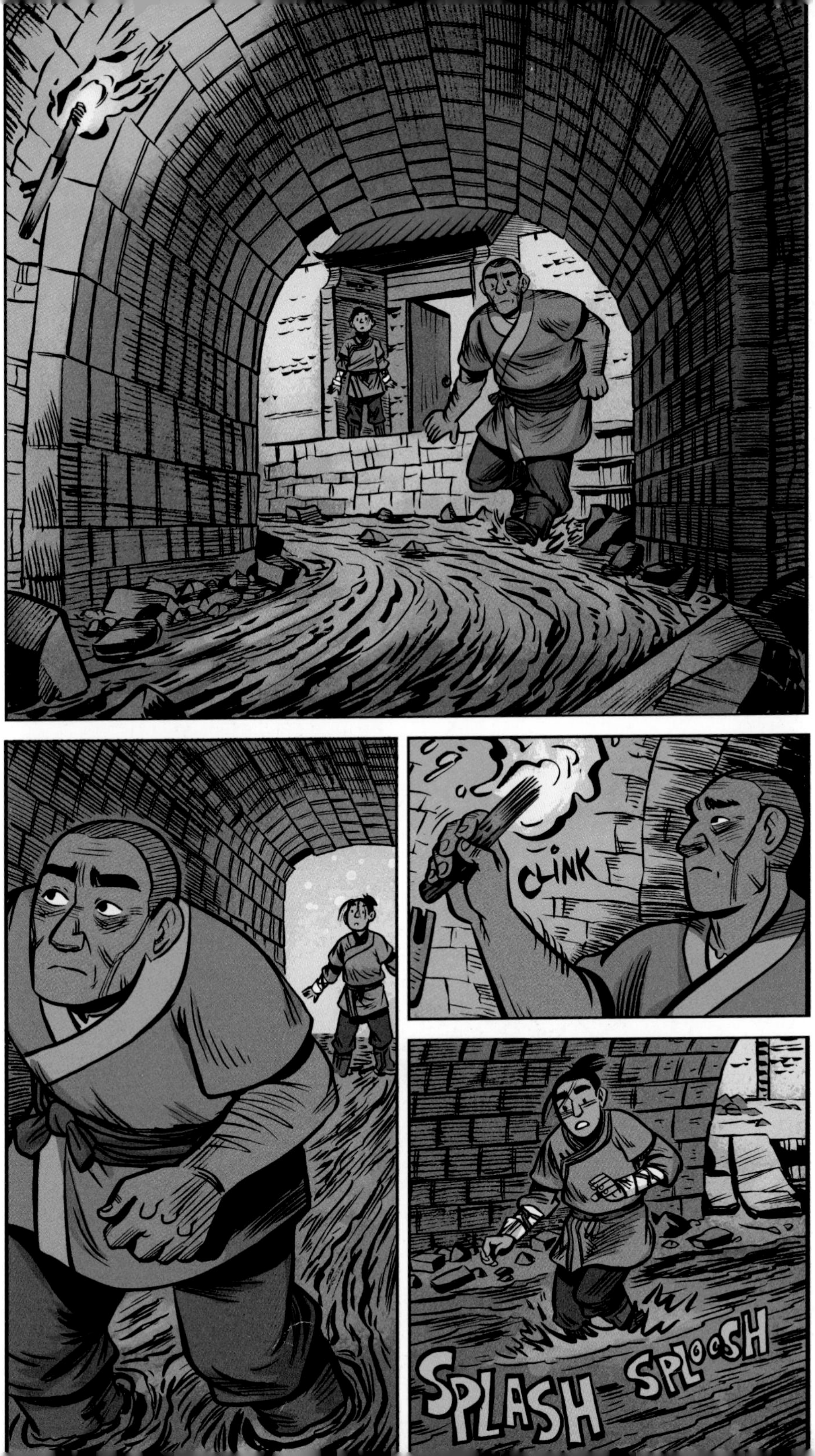
CLINK
SPLASH
SPLOOSH

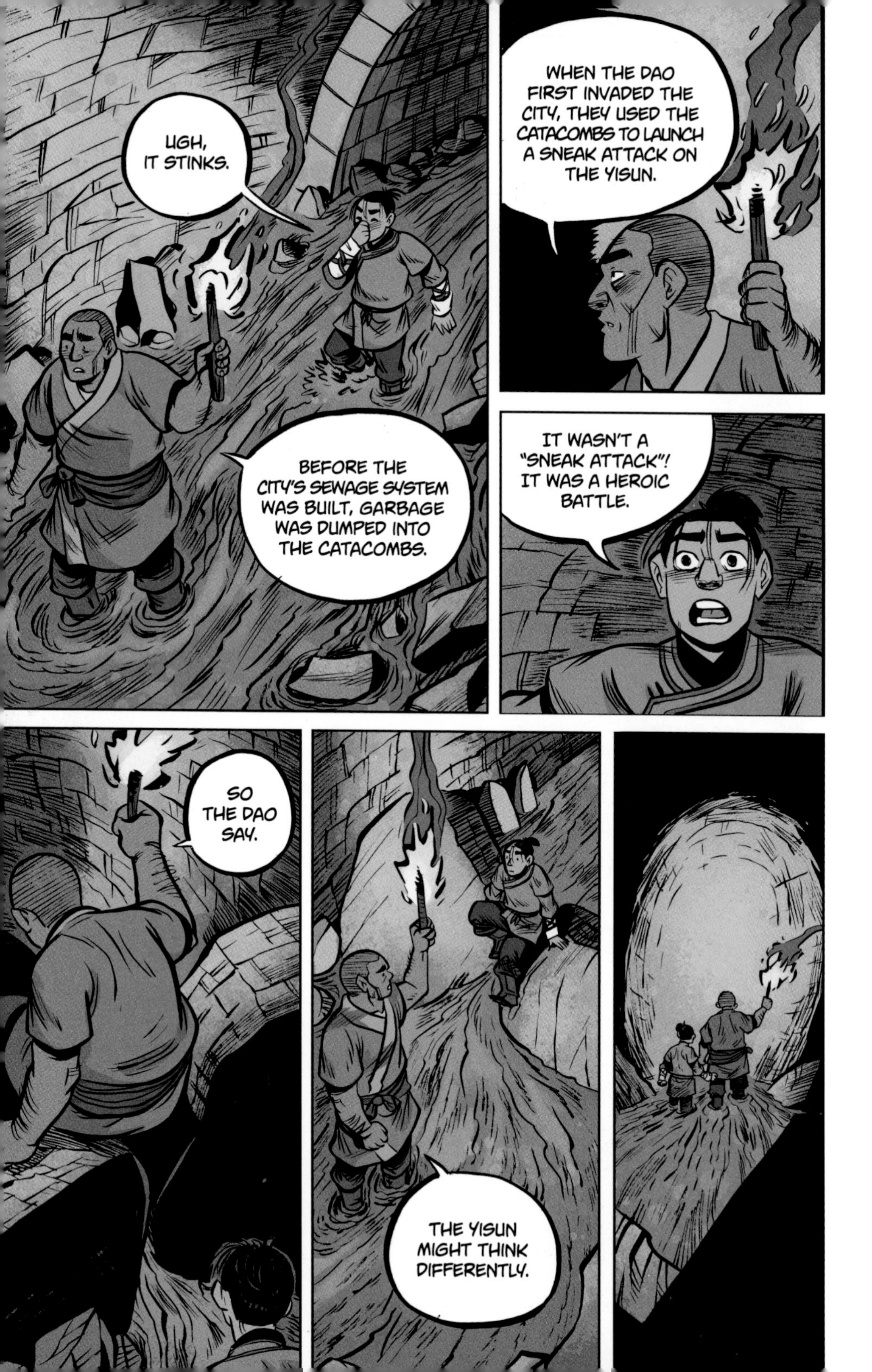
UGH, IT STINKS.
BEFORE THE CITY'S SEWAGE SYSTEM WAS BUILT, GARBAGE WAS DUMPED INTO THE CATACOMBS.
WHEN THE DAO FIRST INVADED THE CITY, THEY USED THE CATACOMBS TO LAUNCH A SNEAK ATTACK ON THE YISUN.
IT WASN'T A "SNEAK ATTACK"! IT WAS A HEROIC BATTLE.
SO THE DAO SAY.
THE YISUN MIGHT THINK DIFFERENTLY.

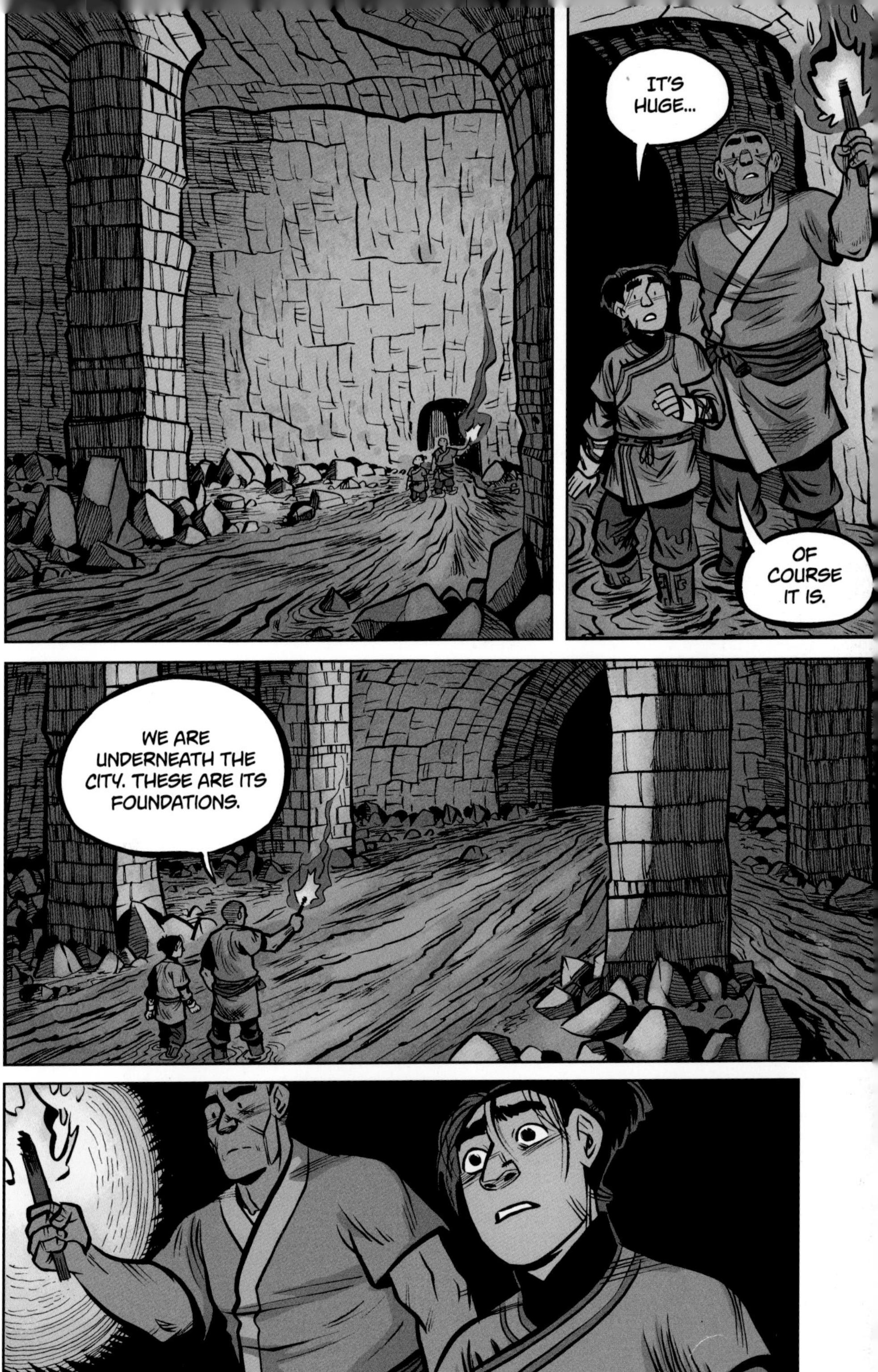
IT'S HUGE...
OF COURSE IT IS.
WE ARE UNDERNEATH THE CITY. THESE ARE ITS FOUNDATIONS.

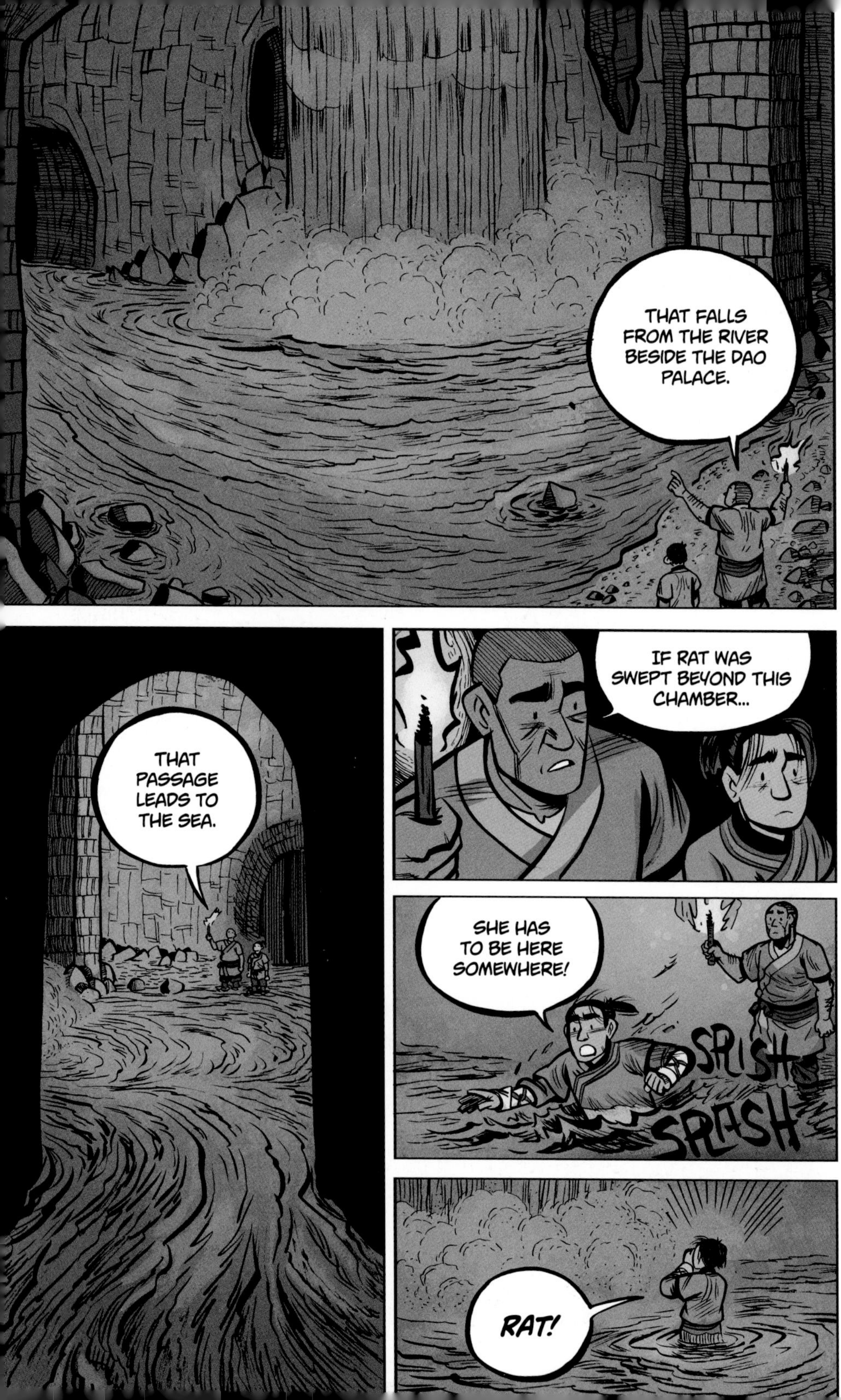
THAT FALLS FROM THE RIVER BESIDE THE DAO PALACE.
THAT PASSAGE LEADS TO THE SEA.
IF RAT WAS SWEPT BEYOND THIS CHAMBER...
SHE HAS TO BE HERE SOMEWHERE!
SPLISH
SPLASH
RAT!

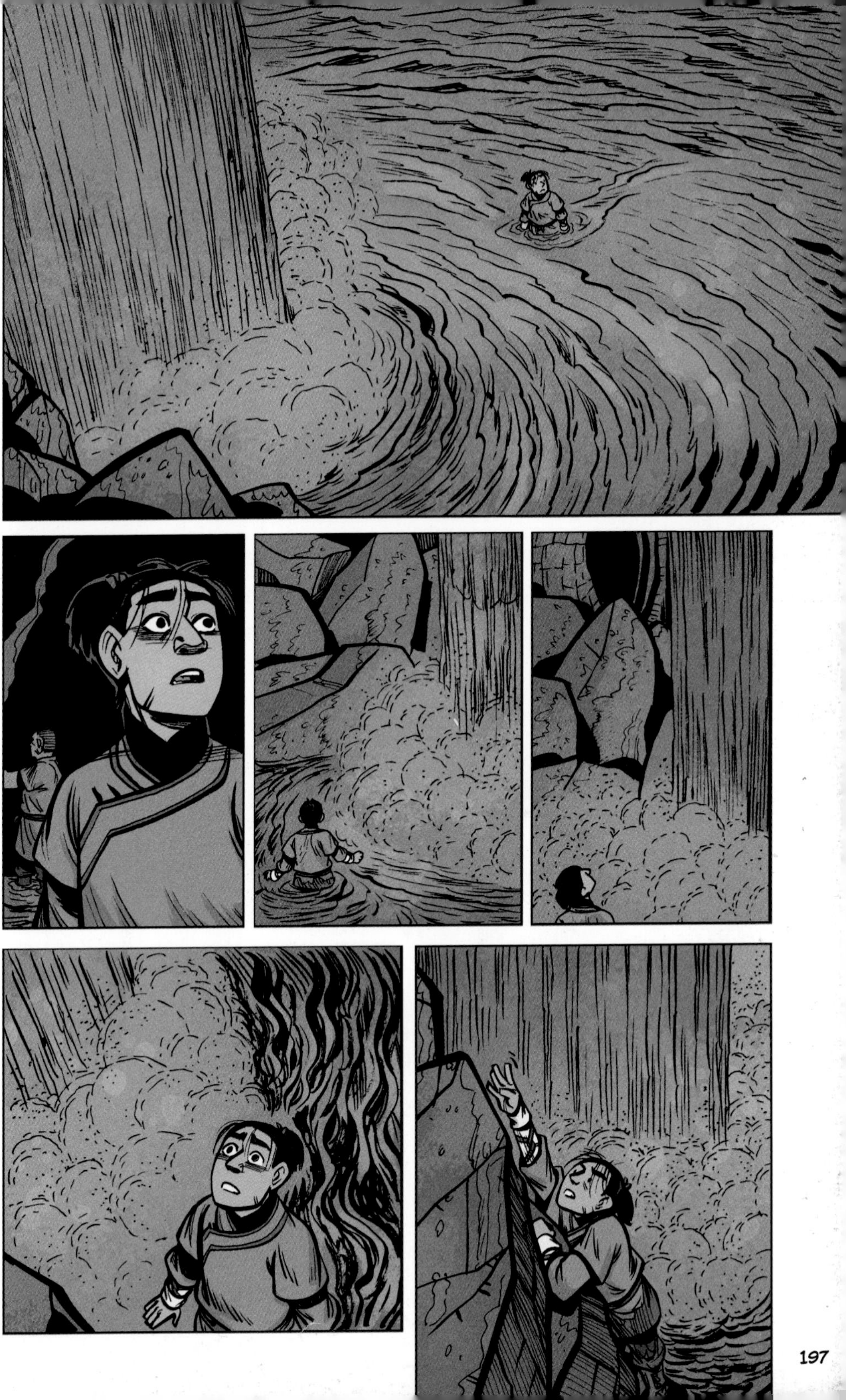

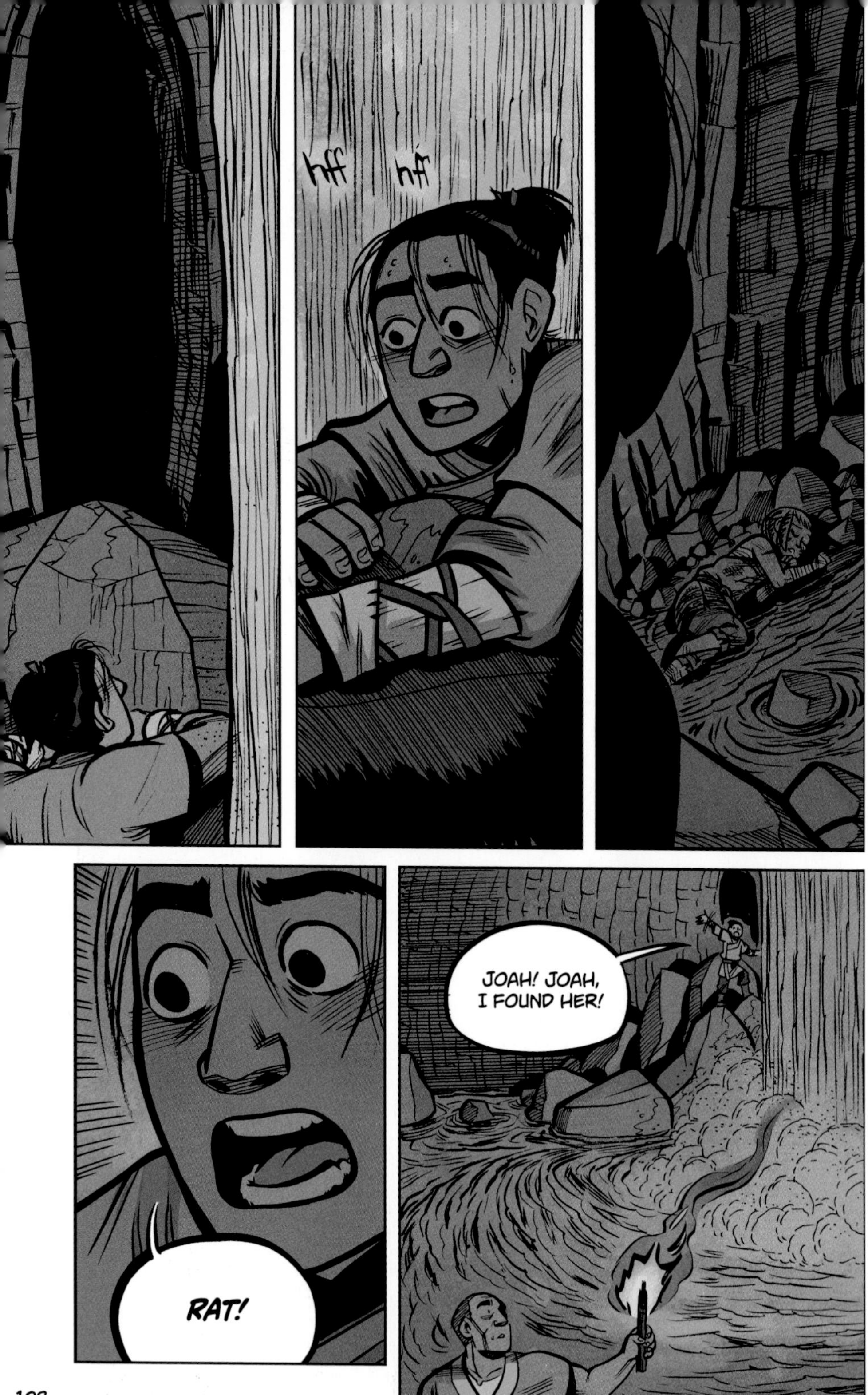
hff hff
JOAH! JOAH, I FOUND HER!
RAT!

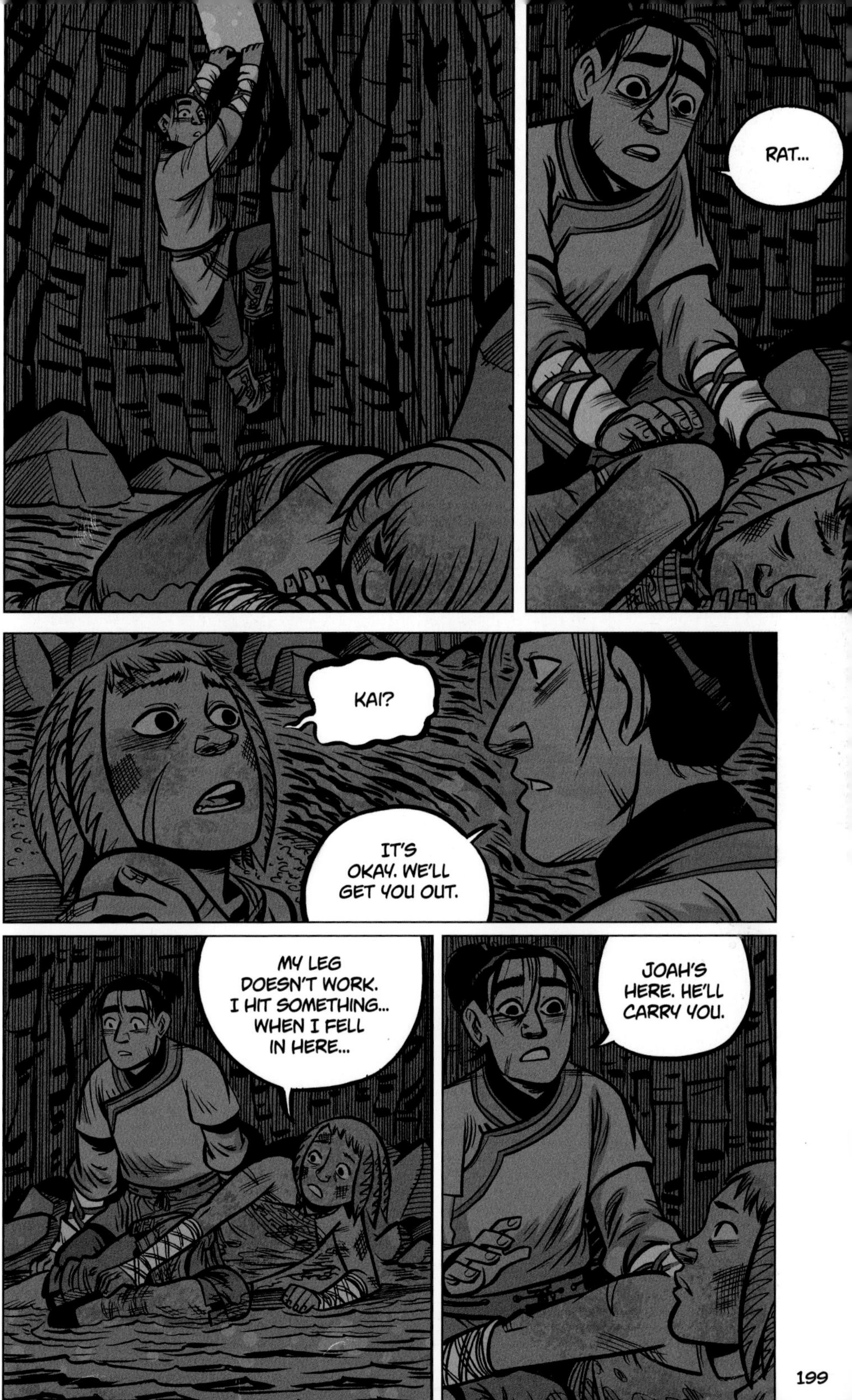
RAT...
KAI?
IT'S OKAY. WE'LL GET YOU OUT.
MY LEG DOESN'T WORK. I HIT SOMETHING... WHEN I FELL IN HERE...
JOAH'S HERE. HE'LL CARRY YOU.

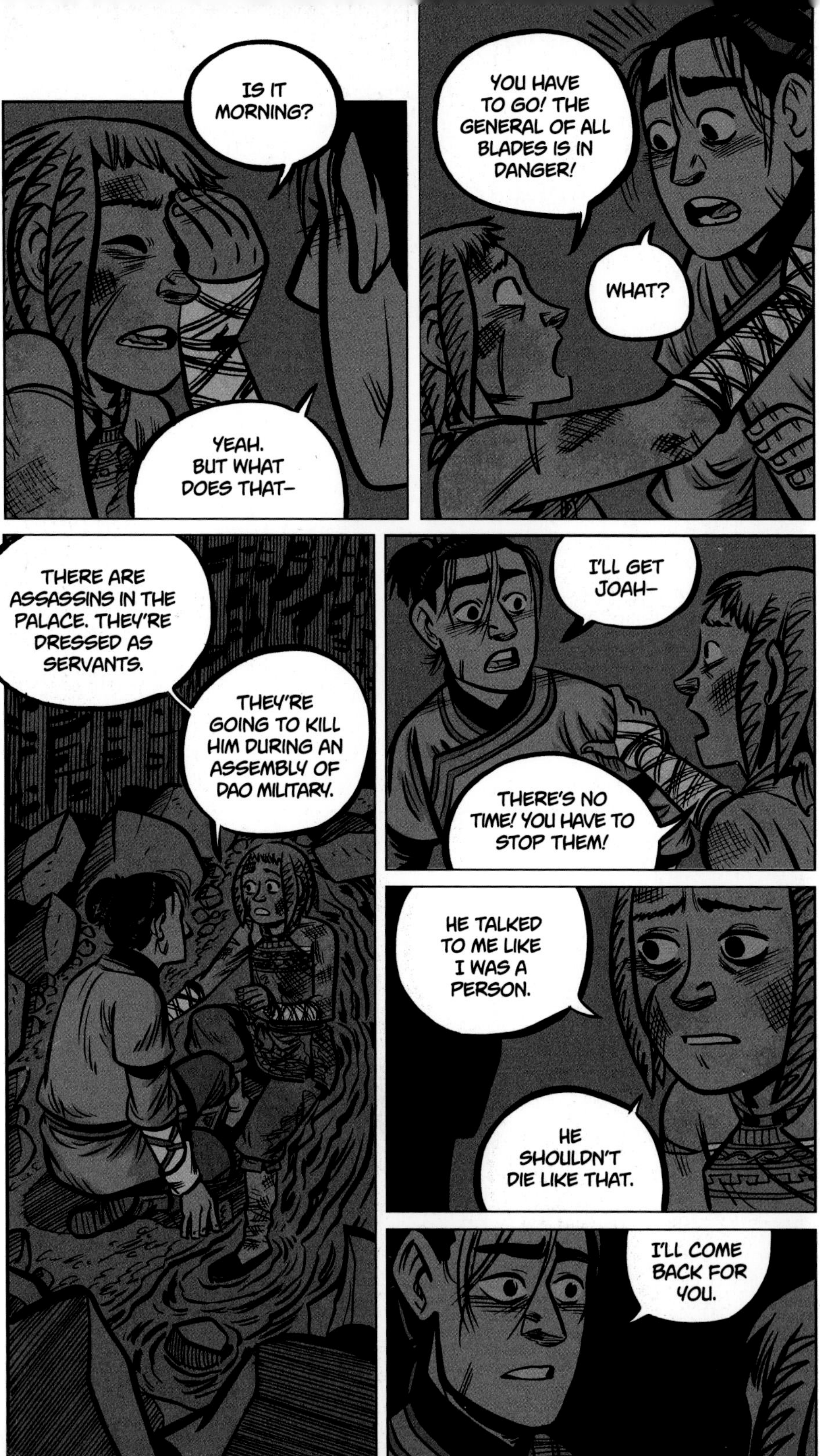
IS IT MORNING?
YEAH. BUT WHAT DOES THAT–
YOU HAVE TO GO! THE GENERAL OF ALL BLADES IS IN DANGER!
WHAT?
THERE ARE ASSASSINS IN THE PALACE. THEY'RE DRESSED AS SERVANTS.
THEY'RE GOING TO KILL HIM DURING AN ASSEMBLY OF DAO MILITARY.
I'LL GET JOAH–
THERE'S NO TIME! YOU HAVE TO STOP THEM!
HE TALKED TO ME LIKE I WAS A PERSON.
HE SHOULDN'T DIE LIKE THAT.
I'LL COME BACK FOR YOU.

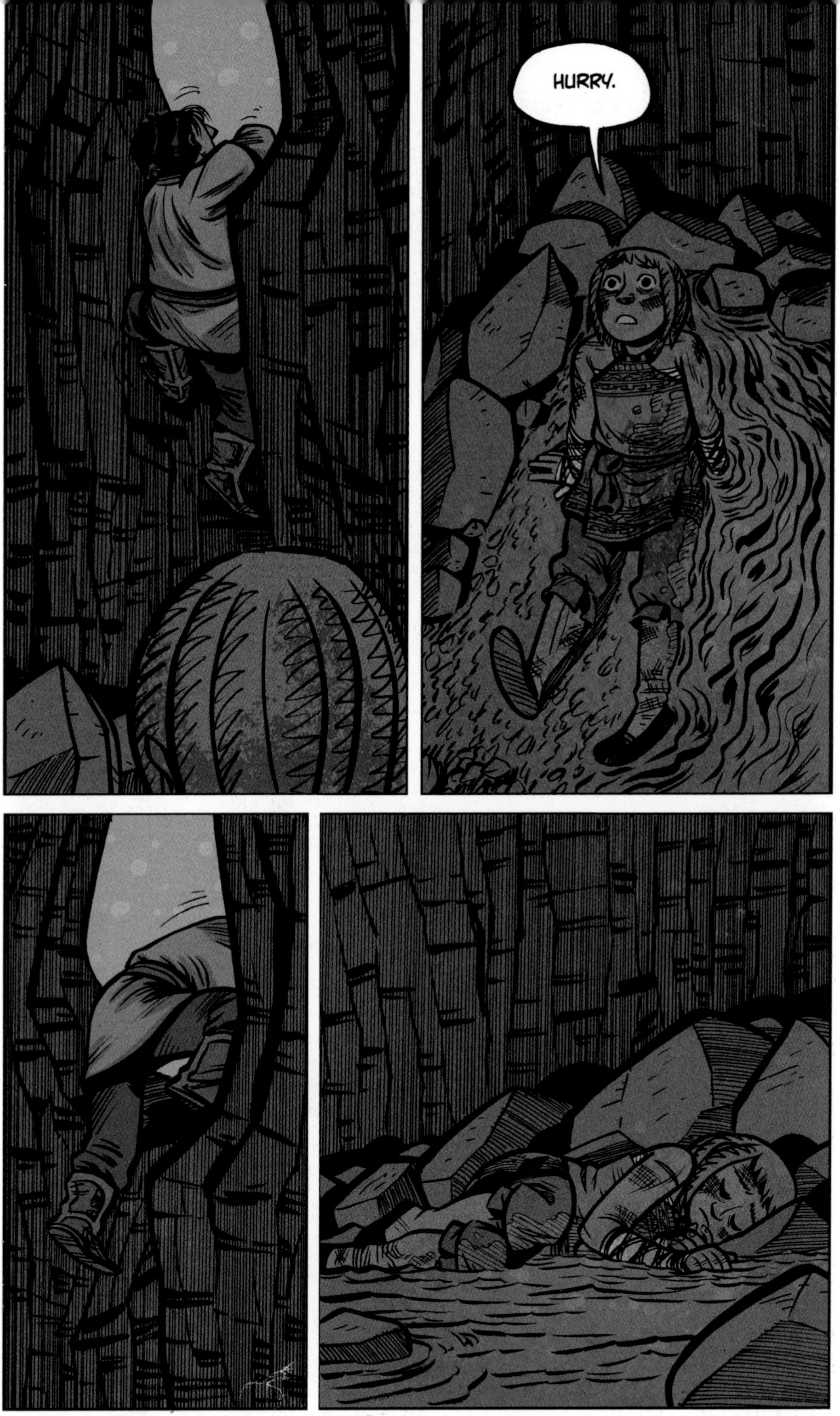
HURRY.

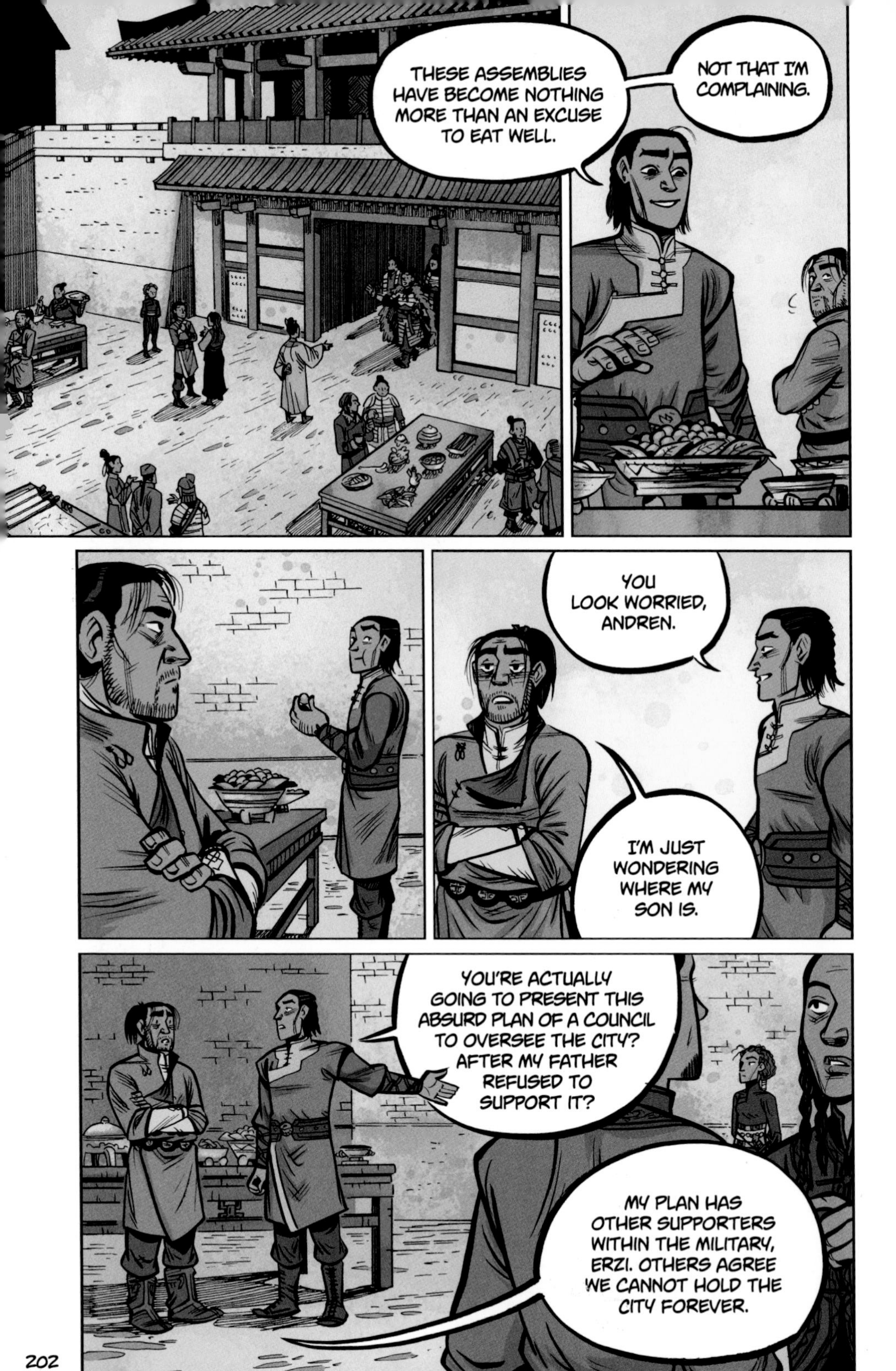
THESE ASSEMBLIES HAVE BECOME NOTHING MORE THAN AN EXCUSE TO EAT WELL.
NOT THAT I'M COMPLAINING.
YOU LOOK WORRIED, ANDREN.
I'M JUST WONDERING WHERE MY SON IS.
YOU'RE ACTUALLY GOING TO PRESENT THIS ABSURD PLAN OF A COUNCIL TO OVERSEE THE CITY? AFTER MY FATHER REFUSED TO SUPPORT IT?
MY PLAN HAS OTHER SUPPORTERS WITHIN THE MILITARY, ERZI. OTHERS AGREE WE CANNOT HOLD THE CITY FOREVER.

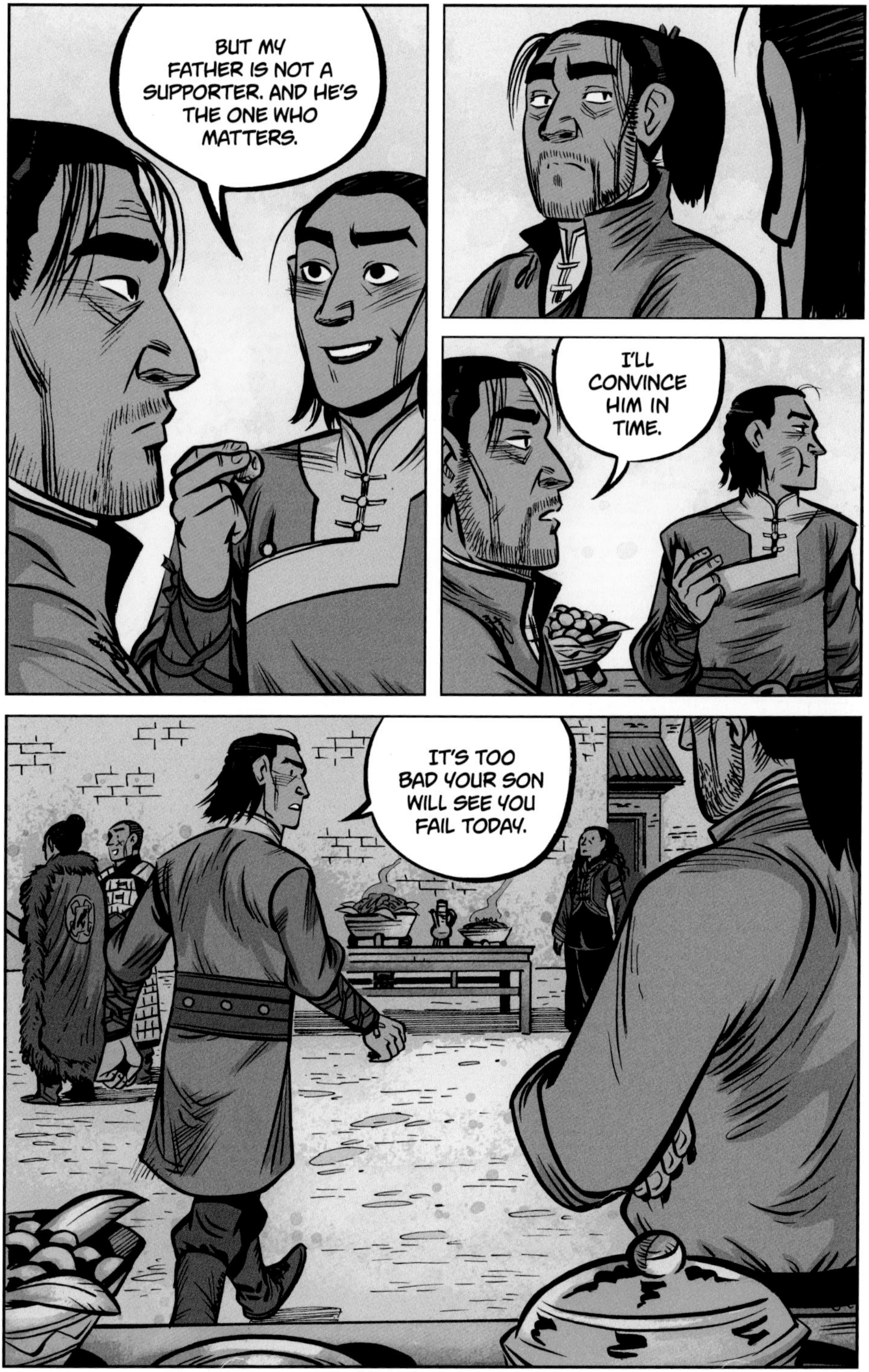
BUT MY FATHER IS NOT A SUPPORTER. AND HE'S THE ONE WHO MATTERS.
I'LL CONVINCE HIM IN TIME.
IT'S TOO BAD YOUR SON WILL SEE YOU FAIL TODAY.

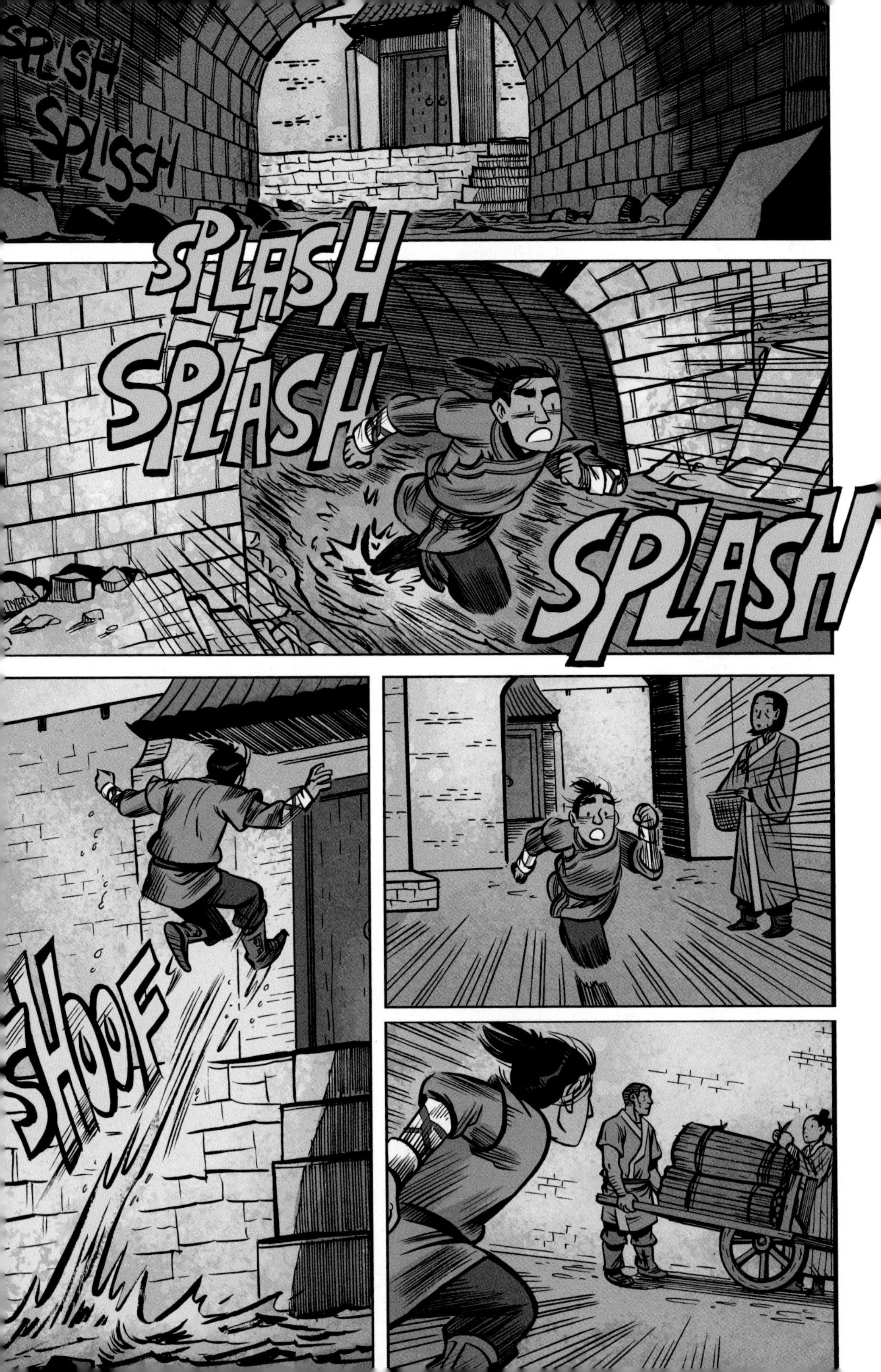
SPLISH
SPLISSH
SPLASH
SPLASH
SPLASH
SHOOF

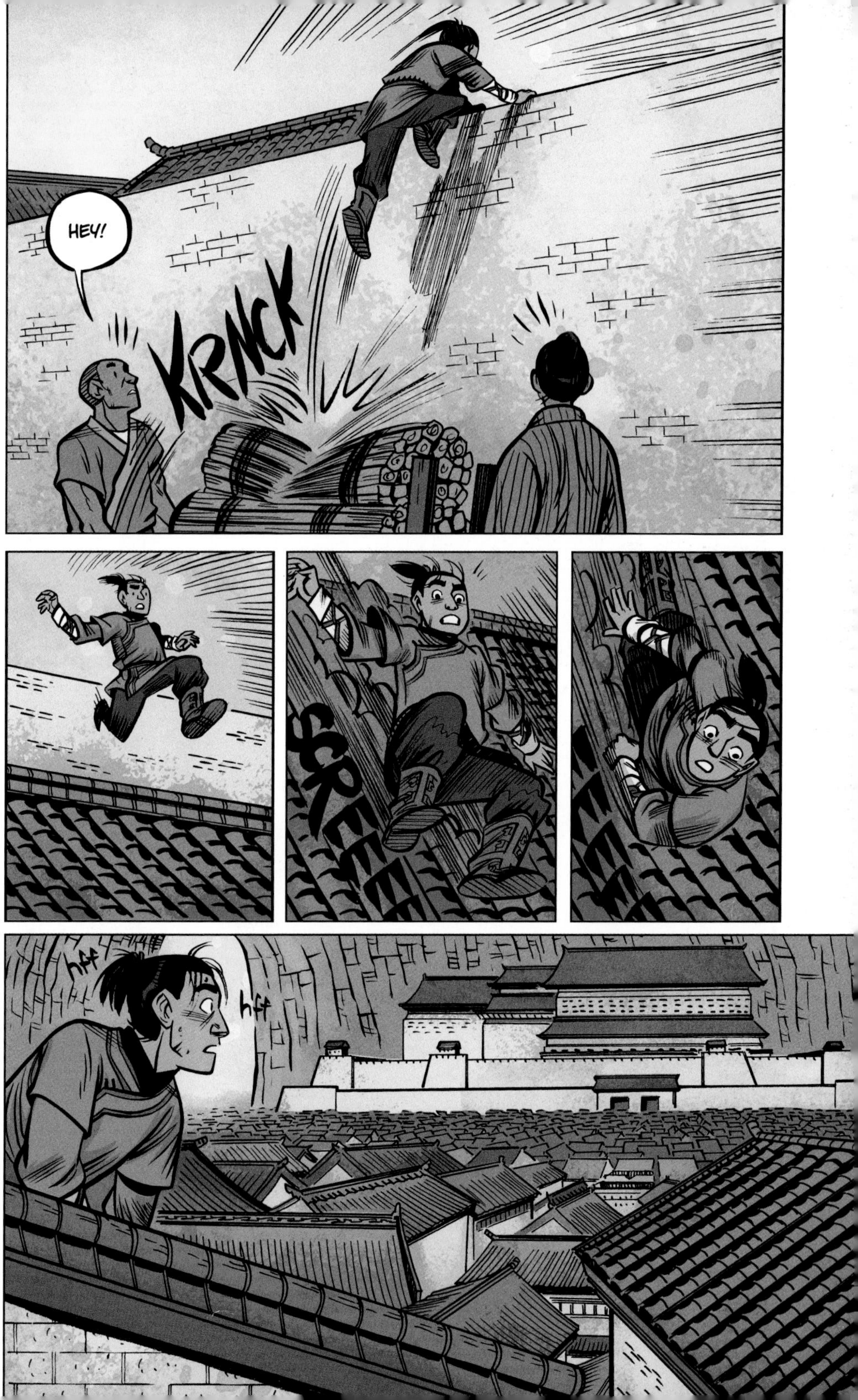
HEY!
KRACK
SCREEE
hff
hff

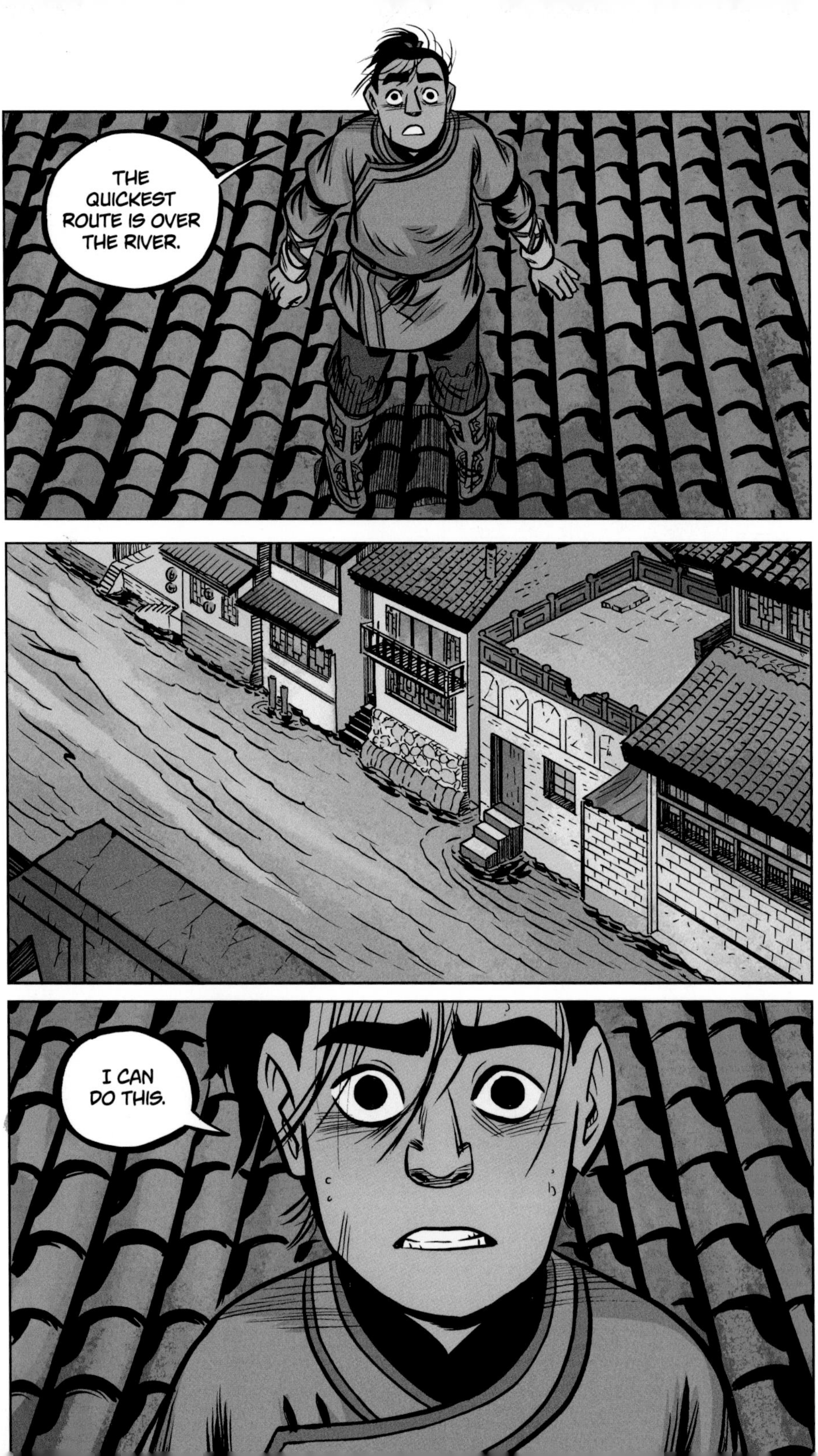
THE QUICKEST ROUTE IS OVER THE RIVER.
I CAN DO THIS.

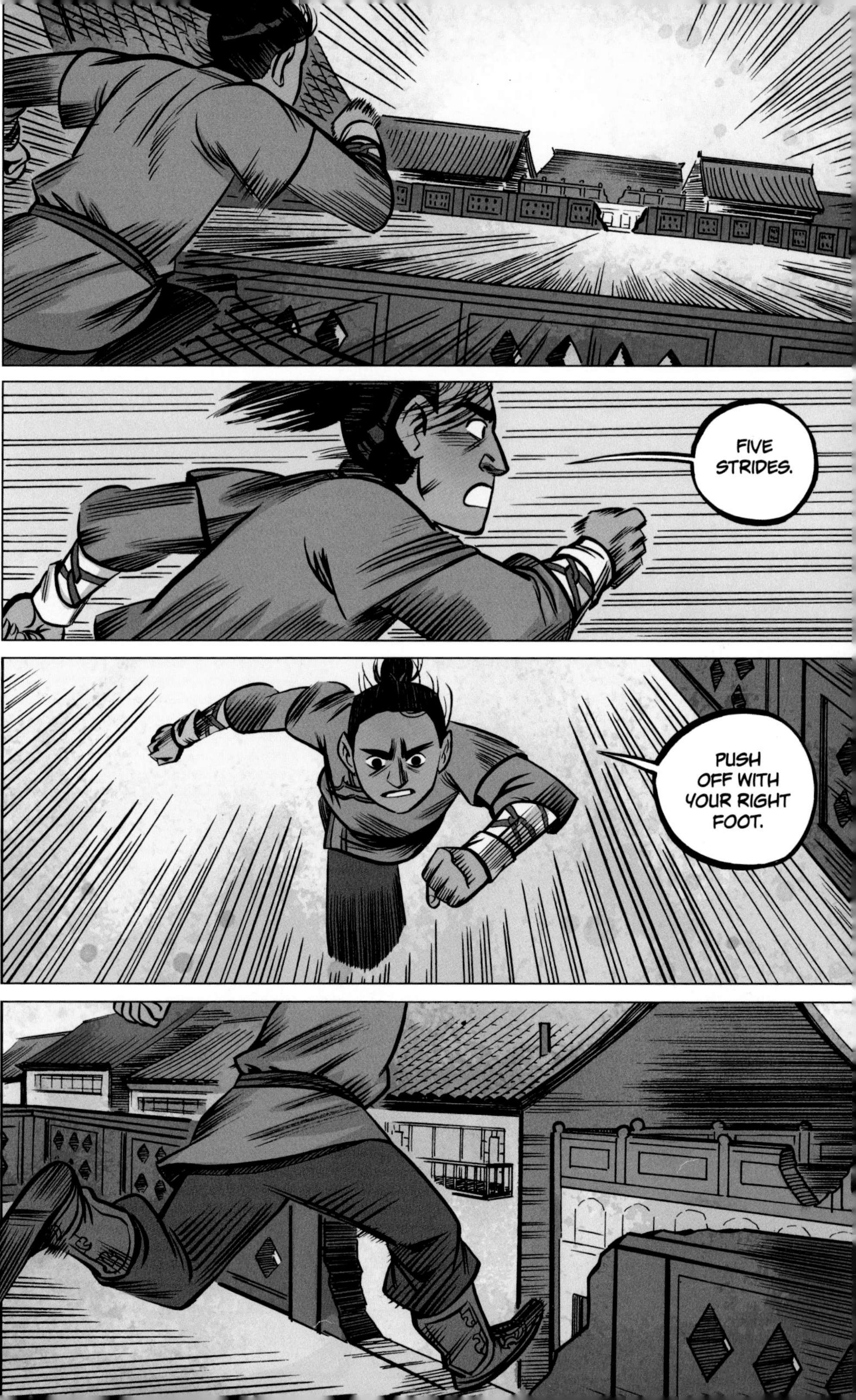
FIVE STRIDES.
PUSH OFF WITH YOUR RIGHT FOOT.

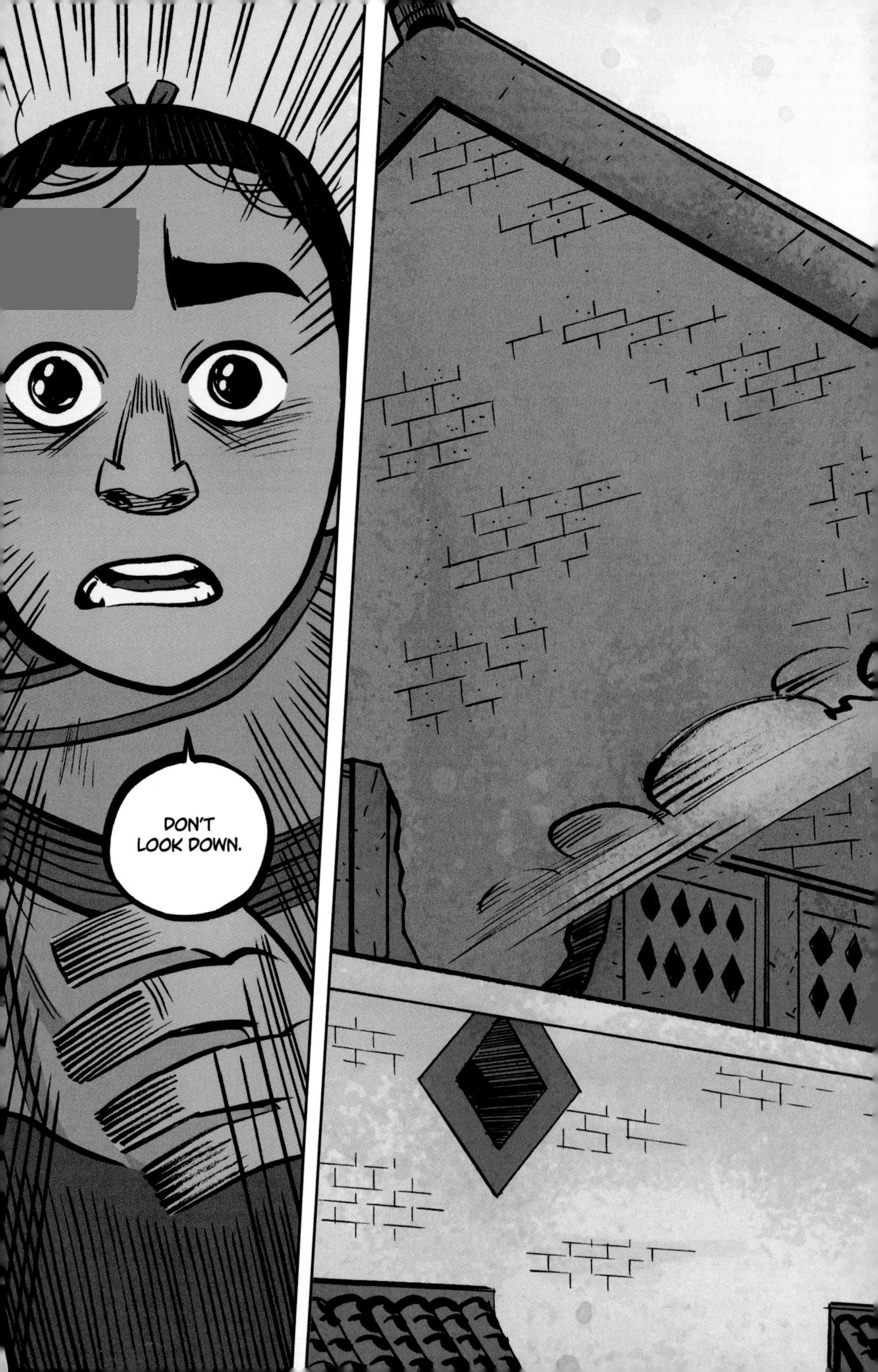
DON'T LOOK DOWN.

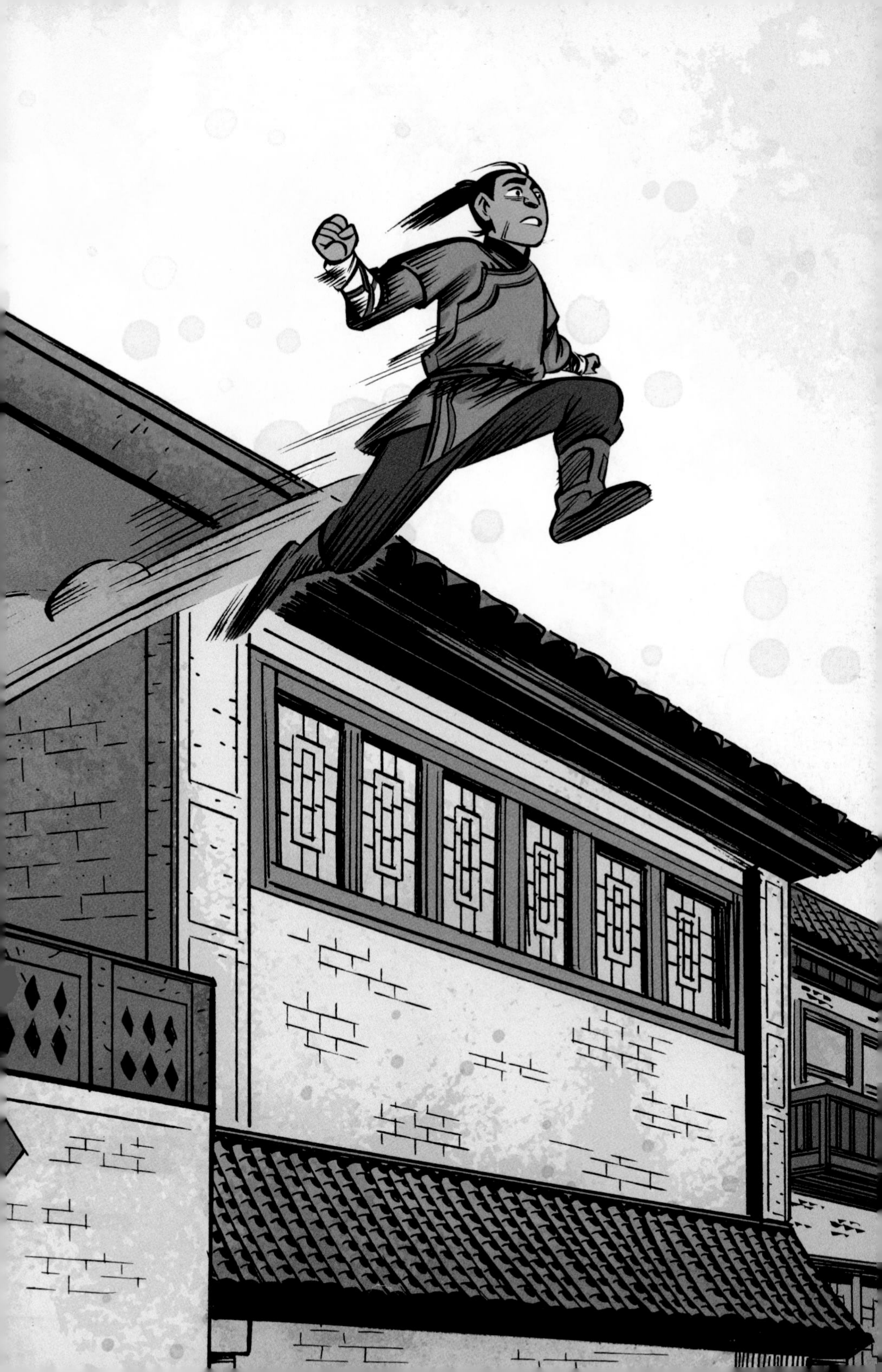

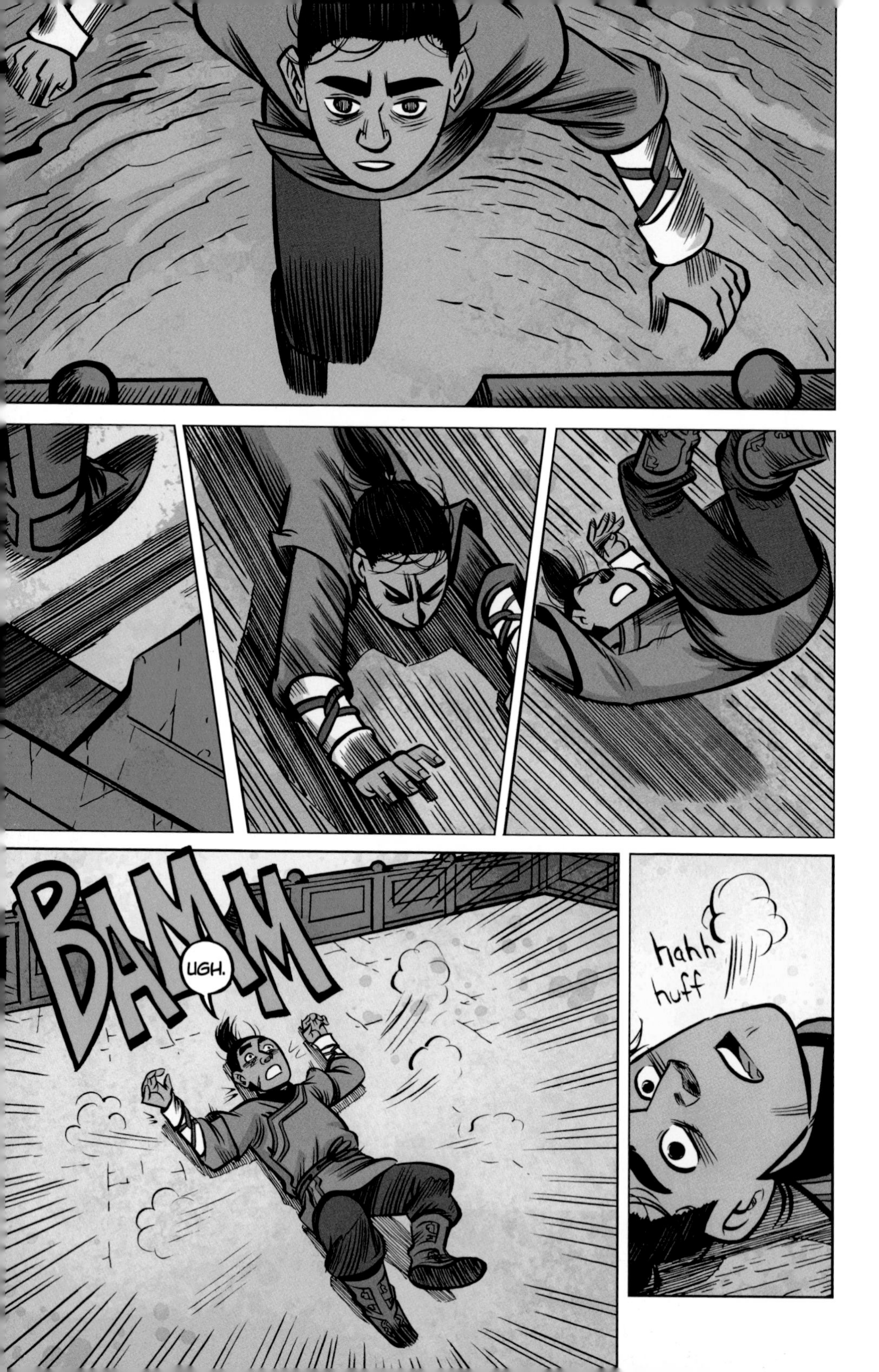
BAMM
UGH.
hahh
huff

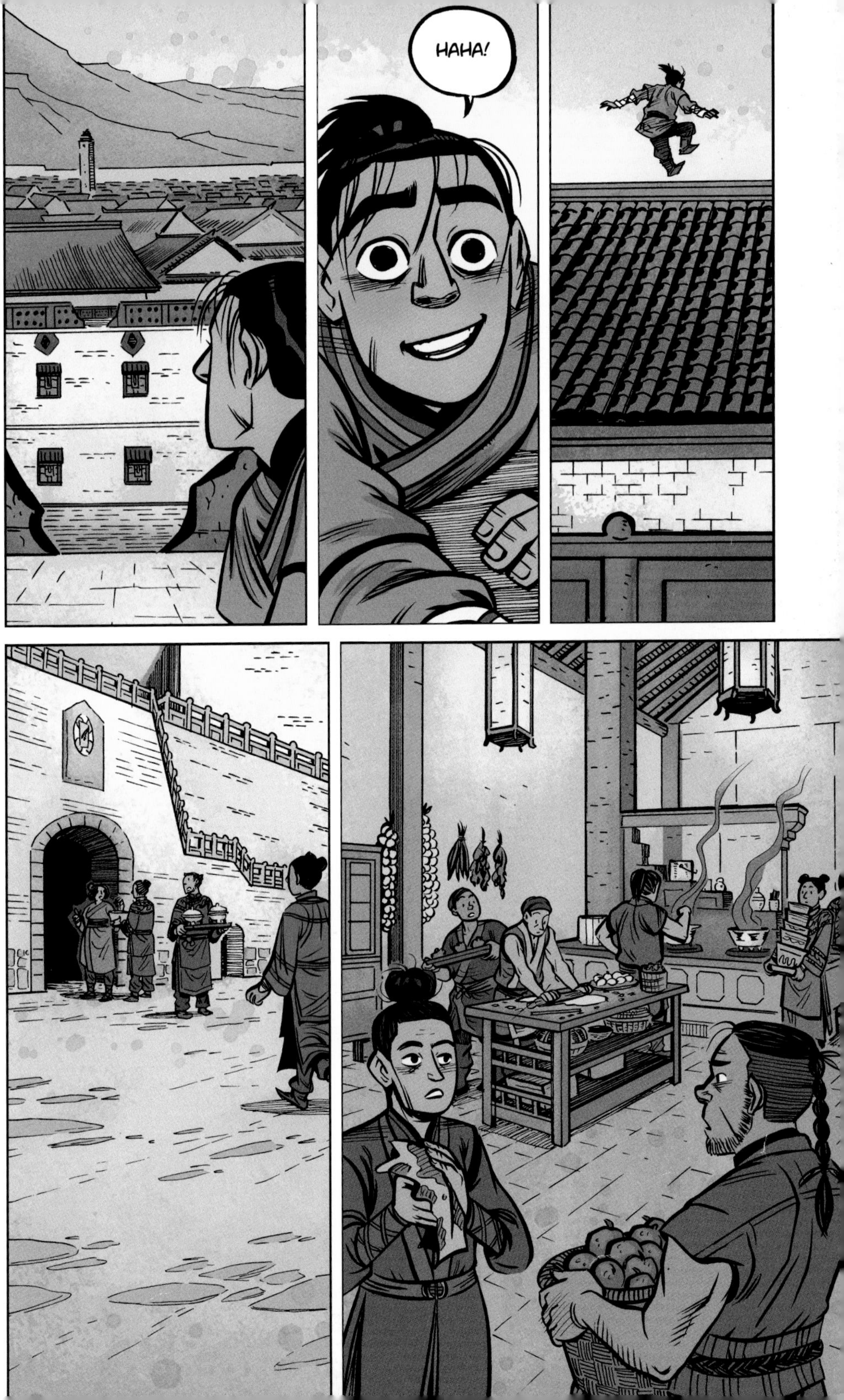
HAHA!

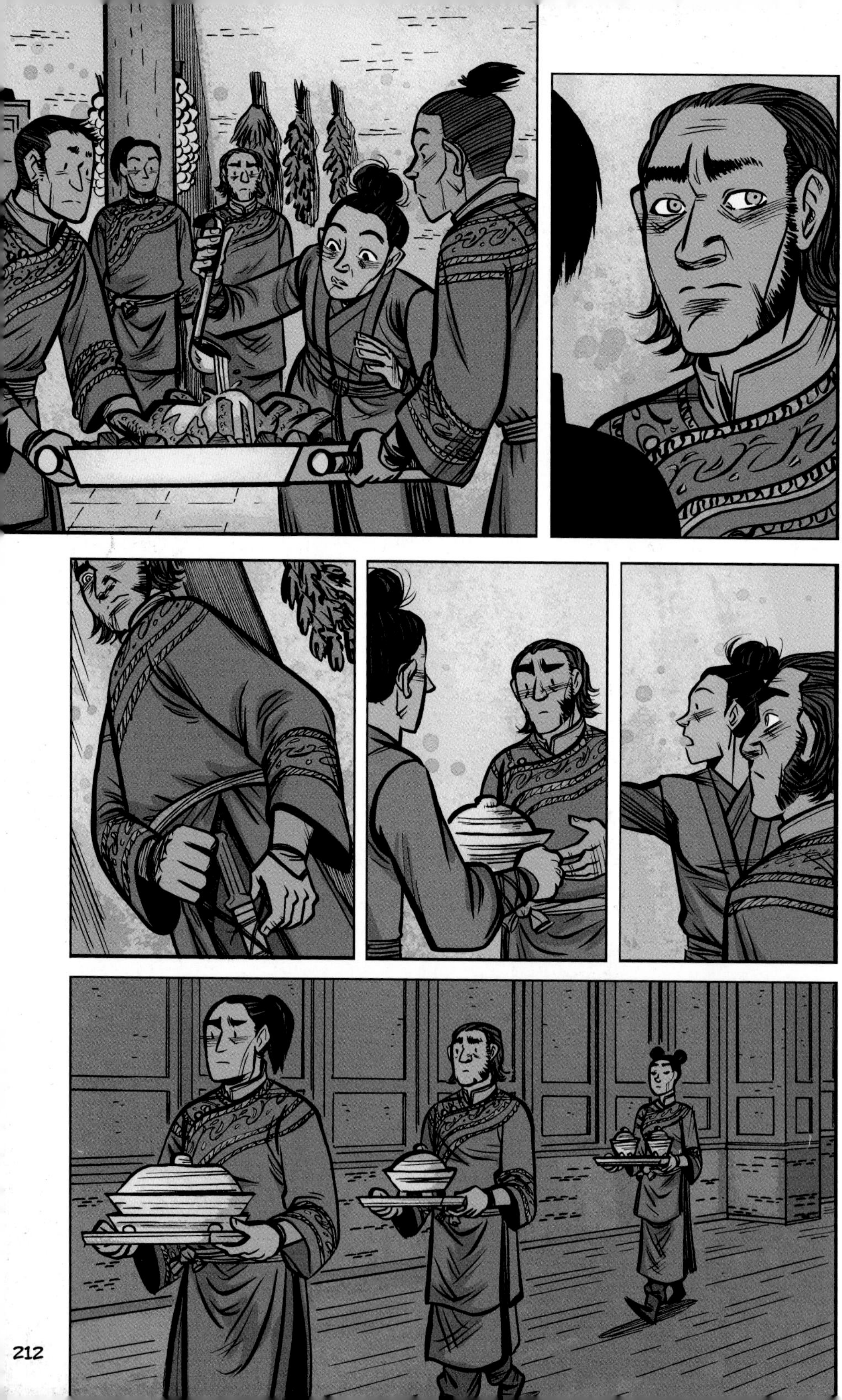

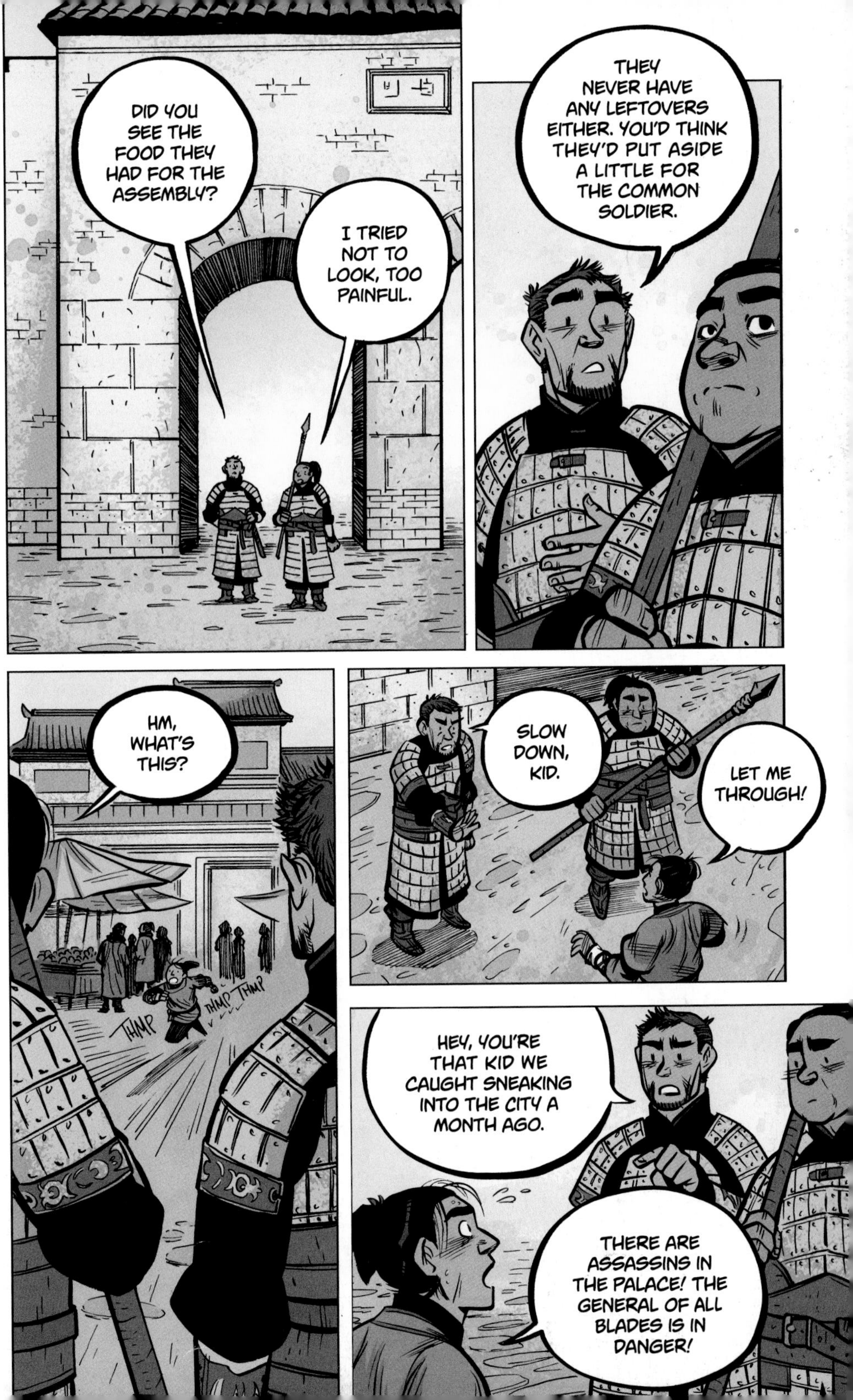
DID YOU SEE THE FOOD THEY HAD FOR THE ASSEMBLY?
I TRIED NOT TO LOOK, TOO PAINFUL.
THEY NEVER HAVE ANY LEFTOVERS EITHER. YOU'D THINK THEY'D PUT ASIDE A LITTLE FOR THE COMMON SOLDIER.
HM, WHAT'S THIS?
THMP
THMP THMP THMP
SLOW DOWN, KID.
LET ME THROUGH!
HEY, YOU'RE THAT KID WE CAUGHT SNEAKING INTO THE CITY A MONTH AGO.
THERE ARE ASSASSINS IN THE PALACE! THE GENERAL OF ALL BLADES IS IN DANGER!

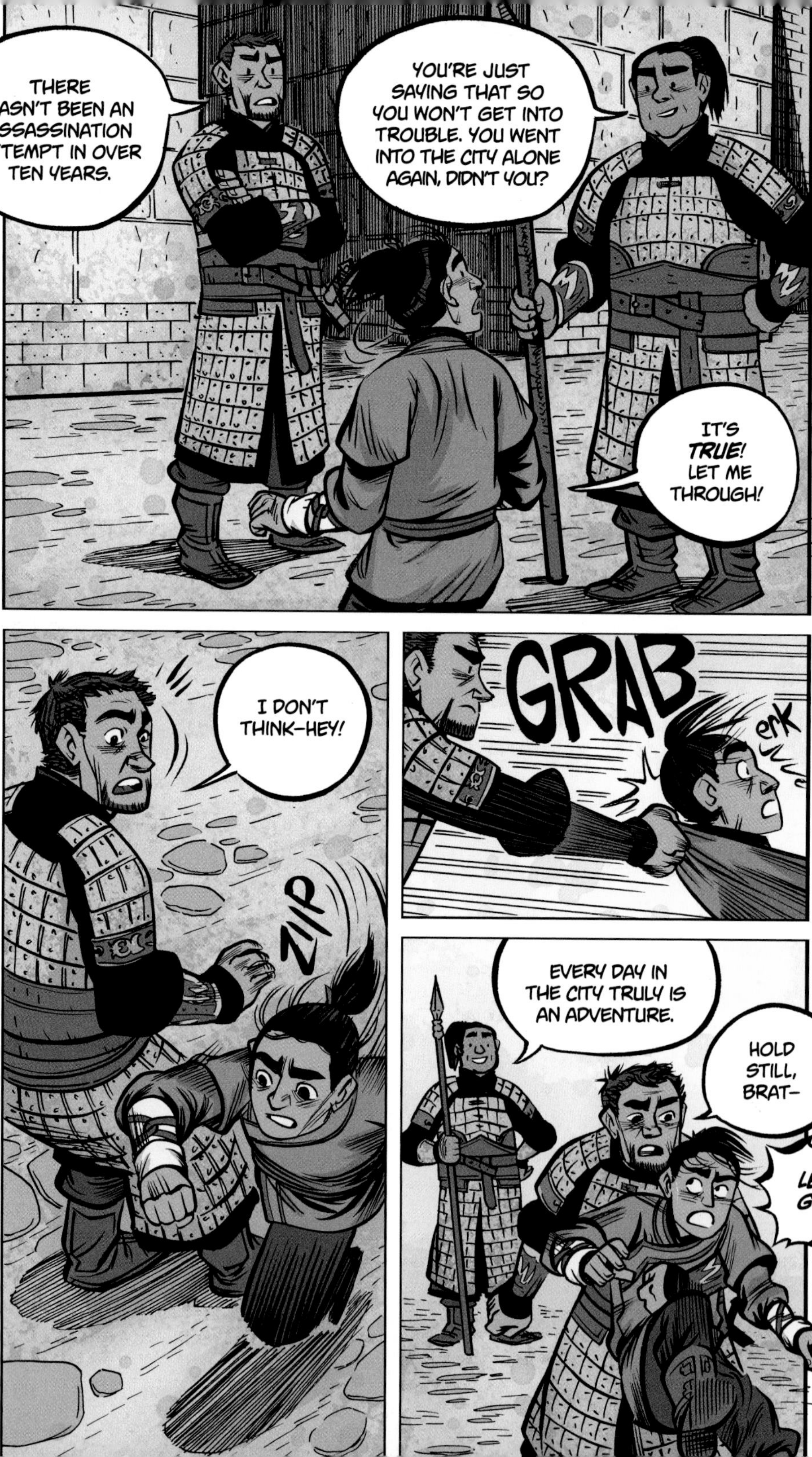
THERE HASN'T BEEN AN ASSASSINATION ATTEMPT IN OVER TEN YEARS.
YOU'RE JUST SAYING THAT SO YOU WON'T GET INTO TROUBLE. YOU WENT INTO THE CITY ALONE AGAIN, DIDN'T YOU?
IT'S *TRUE*! LET ME THROUGH!
I DON'T THINK—HEY!
ZIP
GRAB
erk
EVERY DAY IN THE CITY TRULY IS AN ADVENTURE.
HOLD STILL, BRAT—
LET GO!!

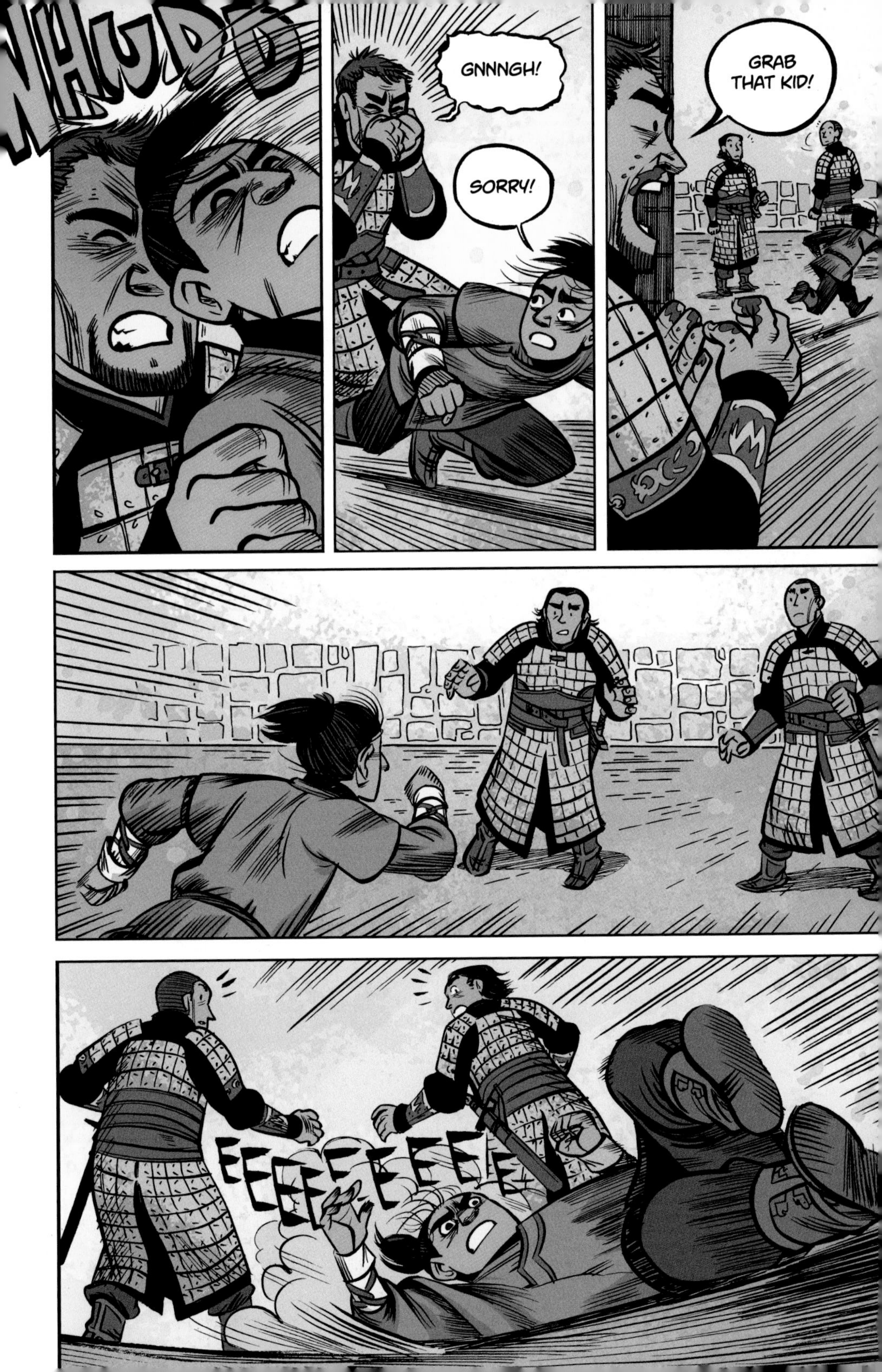
WHUD
GNNNGH!
SORRY!
GRAB THAT KID!
EEEEEEEEEEEEE

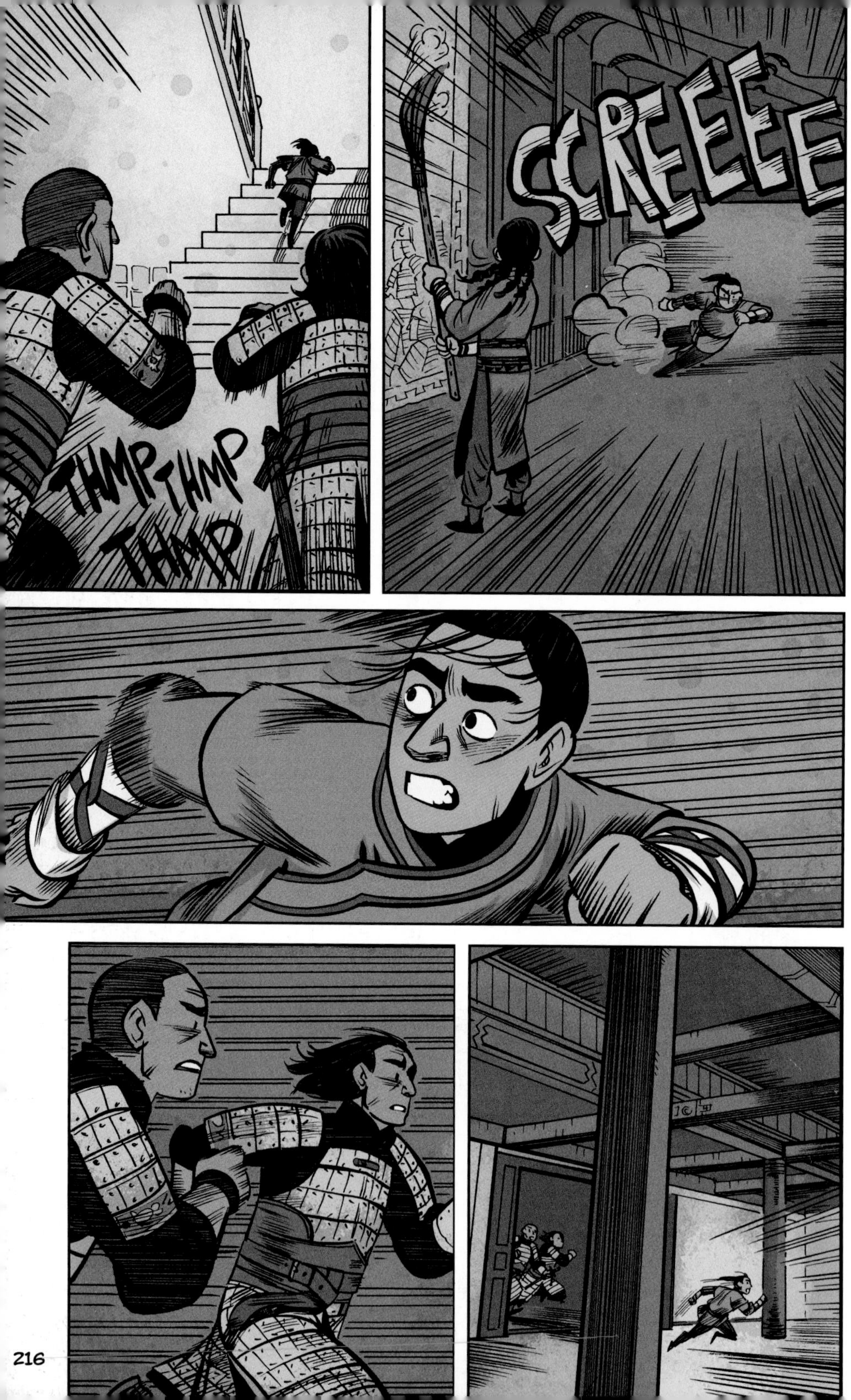
THMP THMP
THMP
SCREEEE

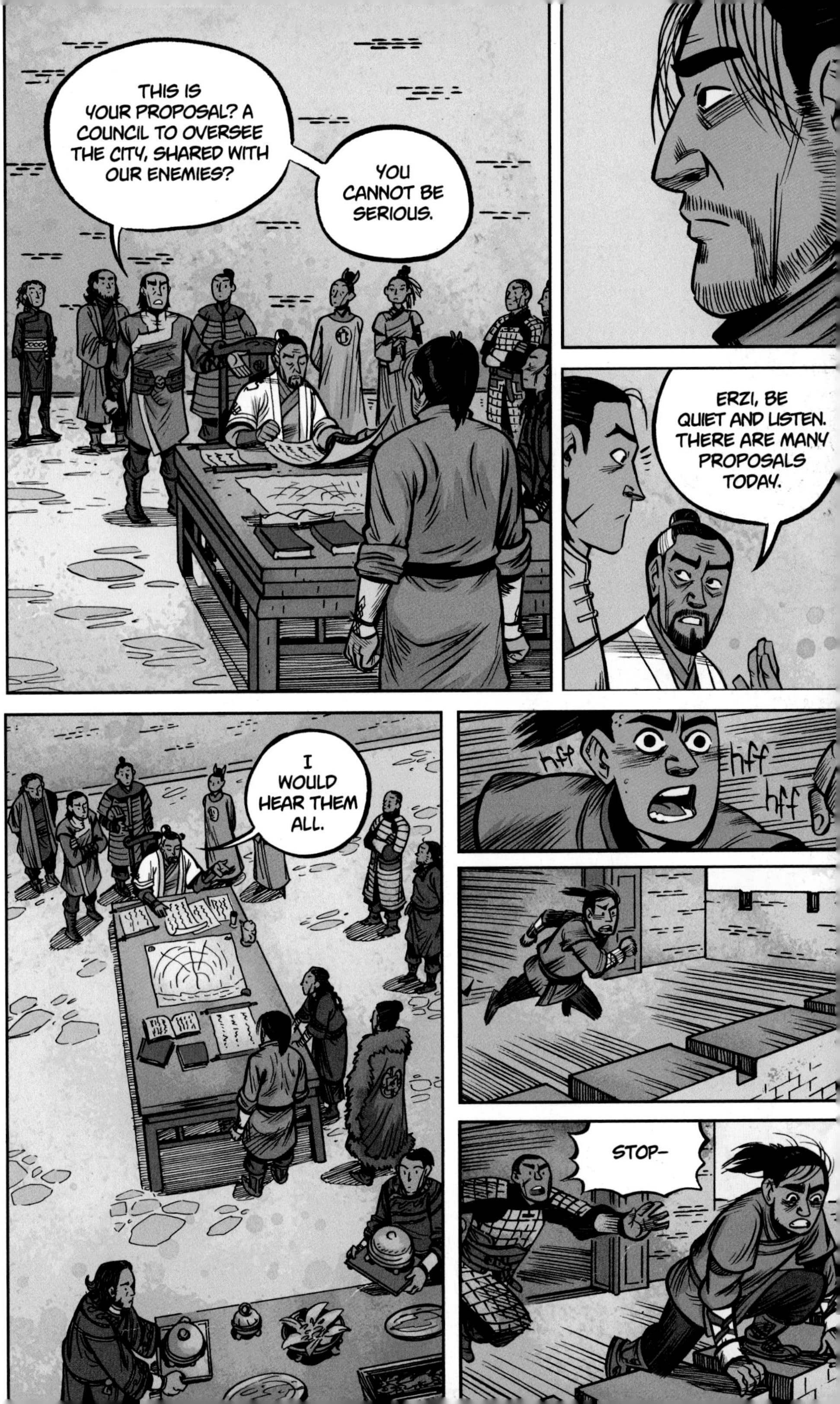
THIS IS YOUR PROPOSAL? A COUNCIL TO OVERSEE THE CITY, SHARED WITH OUR ENEMIES?
YOU CANNOT BE SERIOUS.
ERZI, BE QUIET AND LISTEN. THERE ARE MANY PROPOSALS TODAY.
I WOULD HEAR THEM ALL.
hff
hff
hff
STOP-

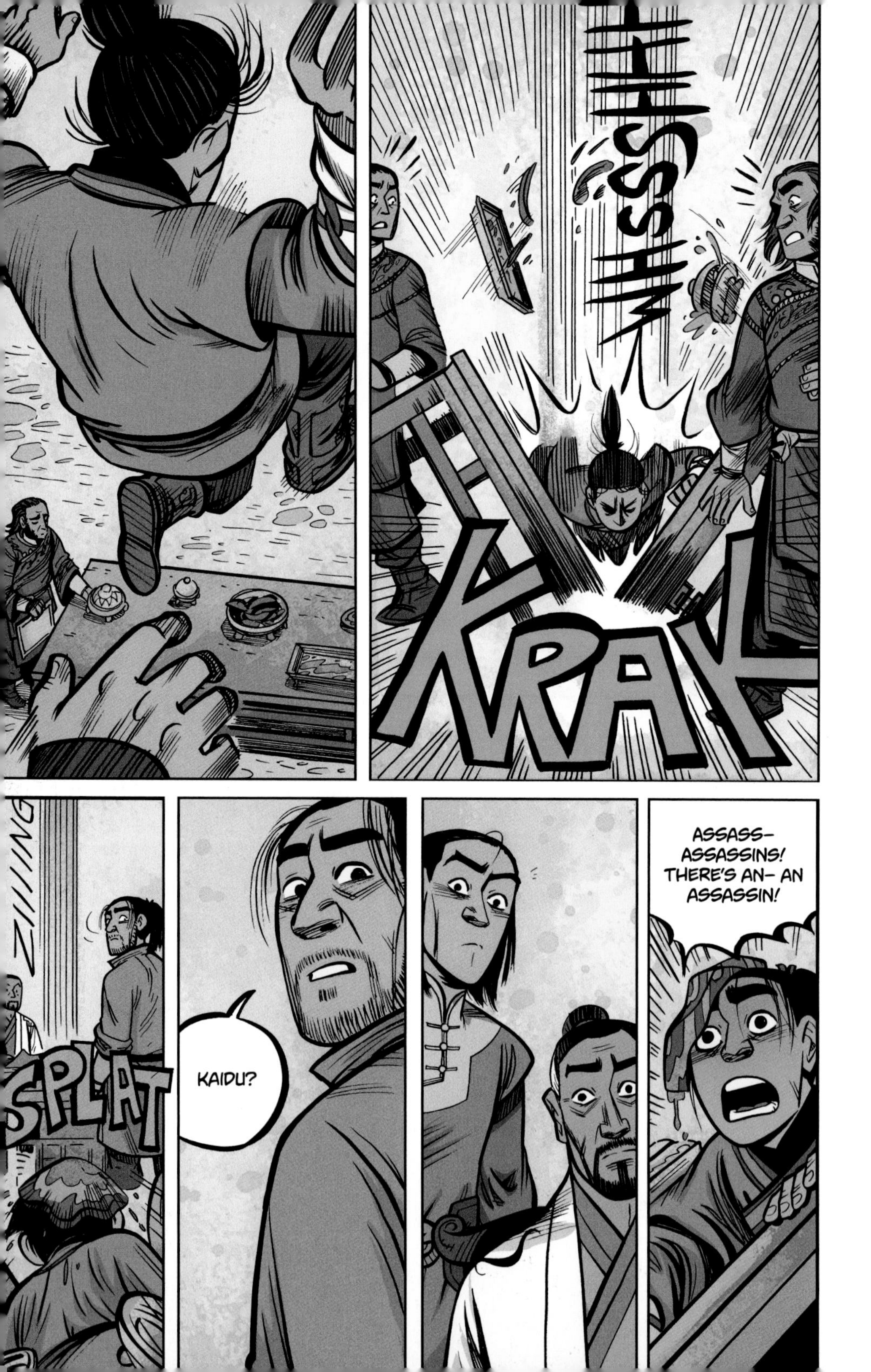

KRAK
ZIIIIING
SPLAT
KAIDU?
ASSASS-
ASSASSINS! THERE'S AN- AN ASSASSIN!

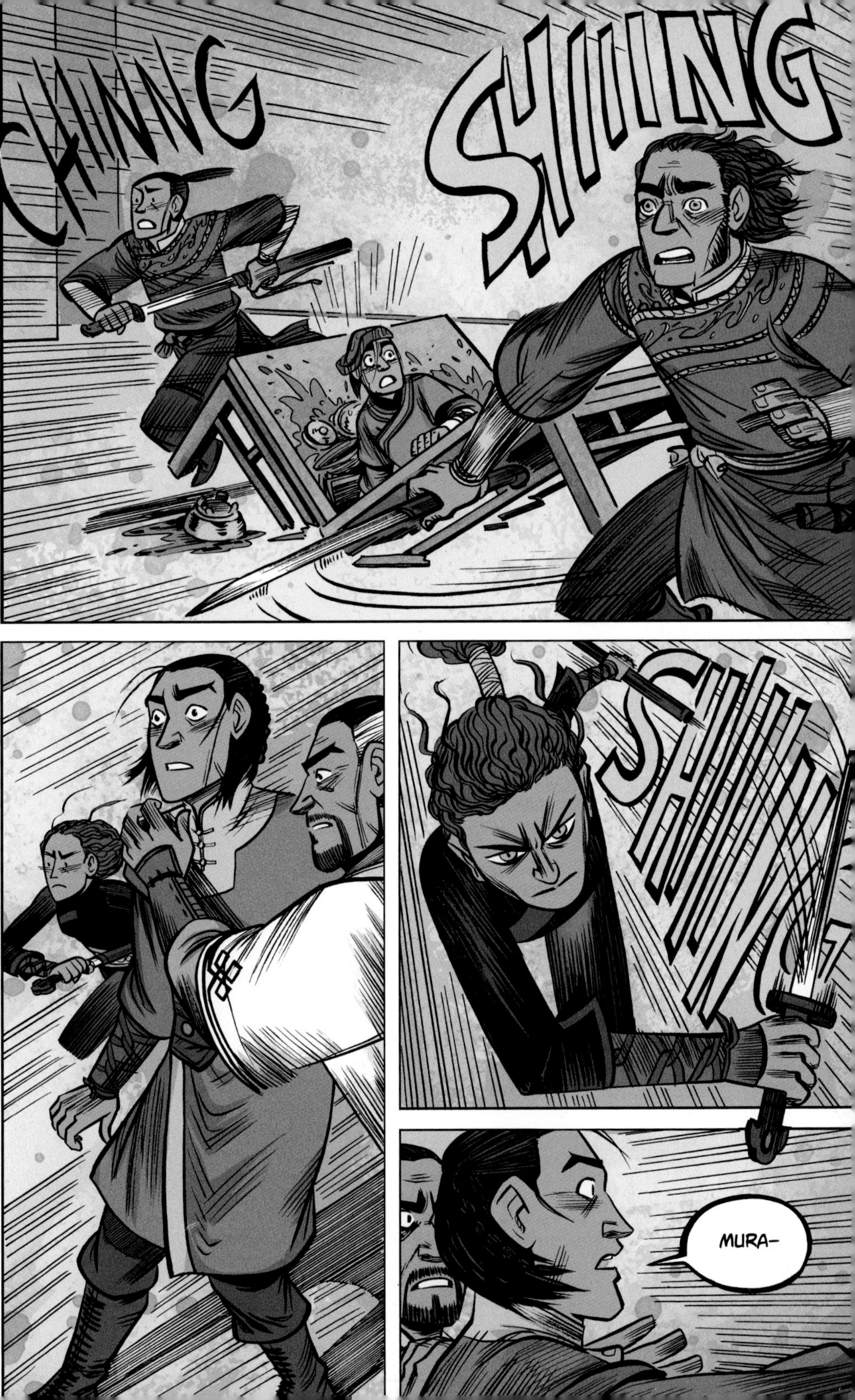
CHING
SHING
SHING
MURA-

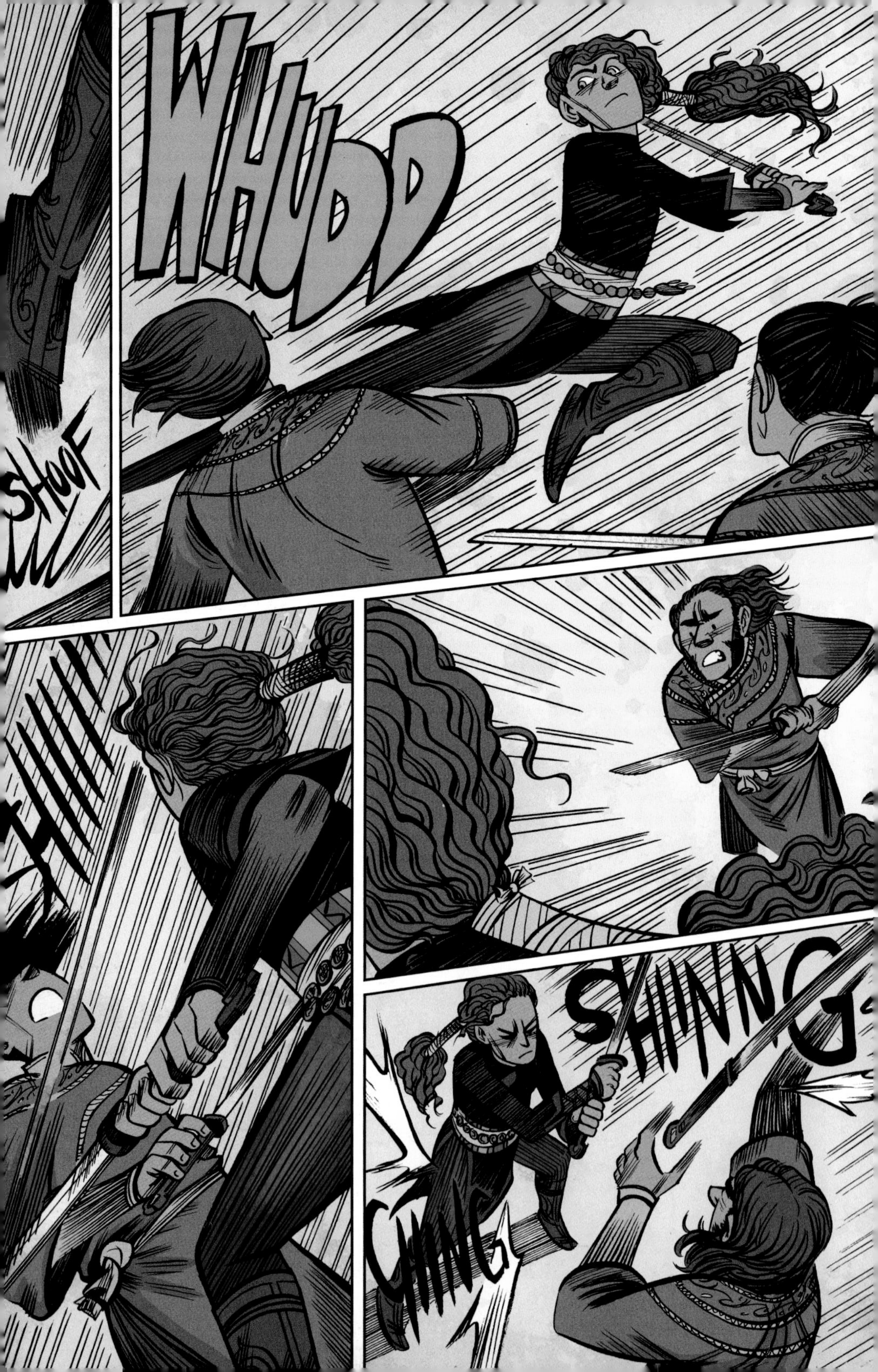
WHUDD
SHOOF
SHINNG
CHING

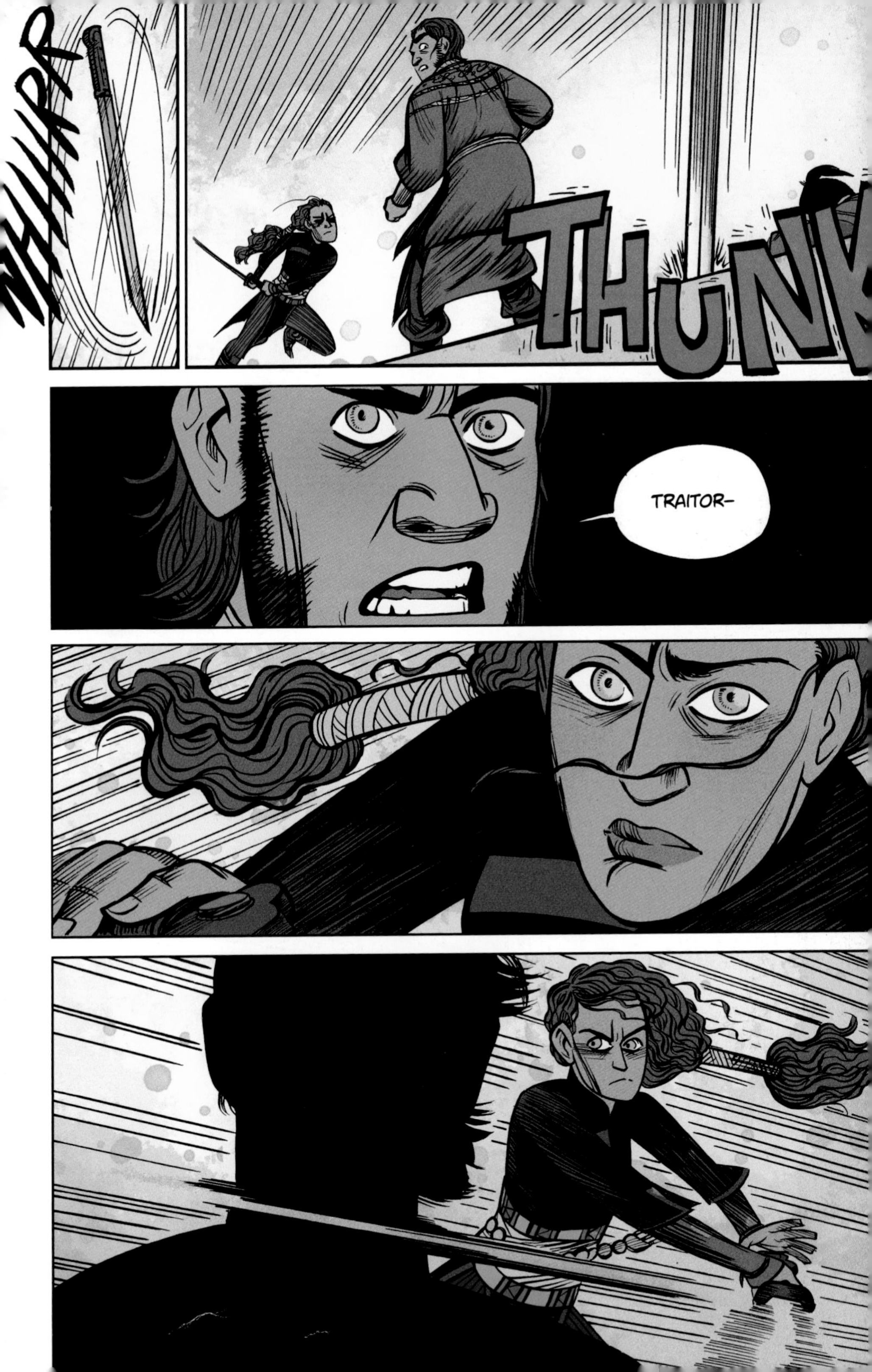
THHIIPR
THUNK
TRAITOR-

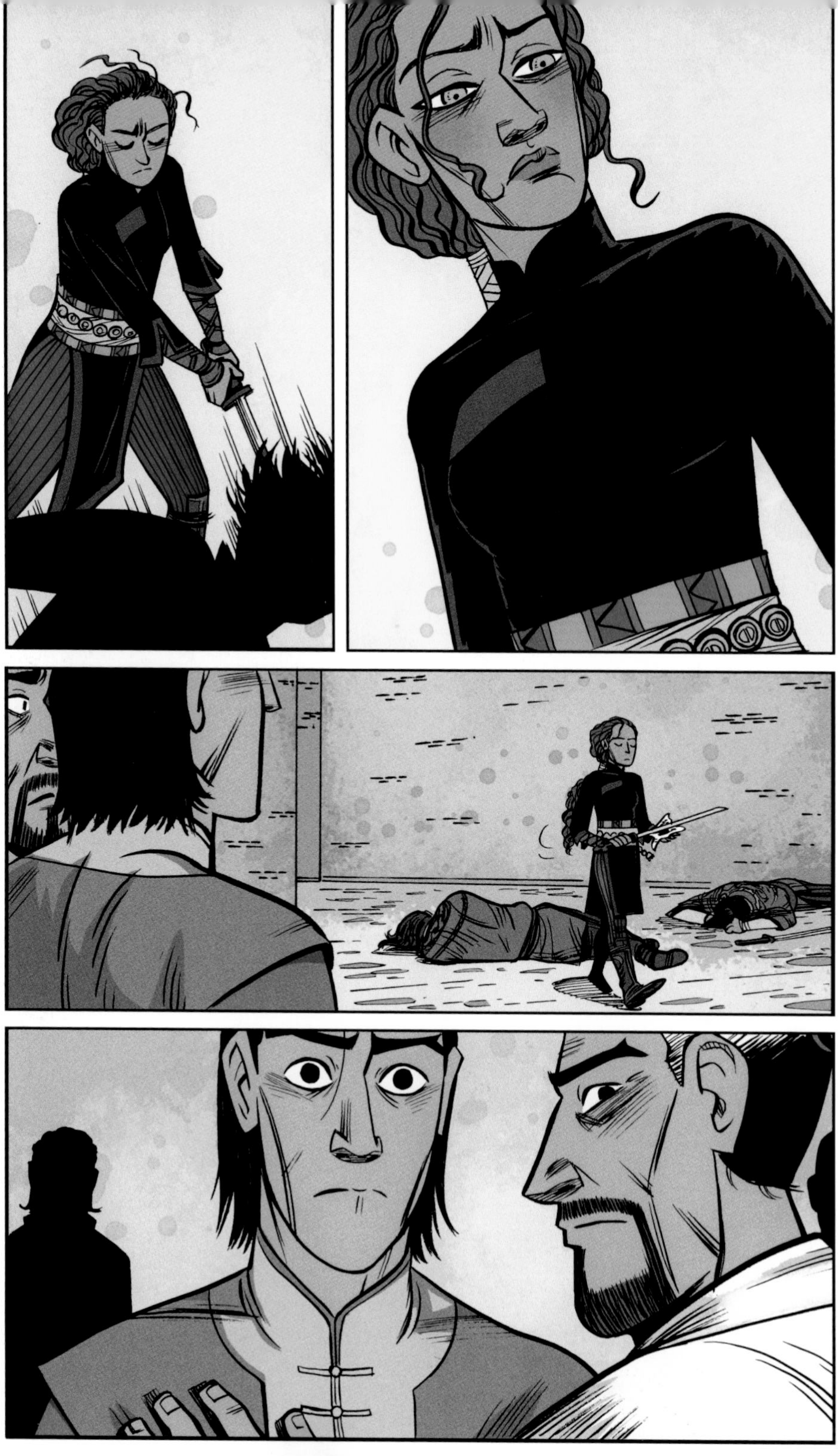

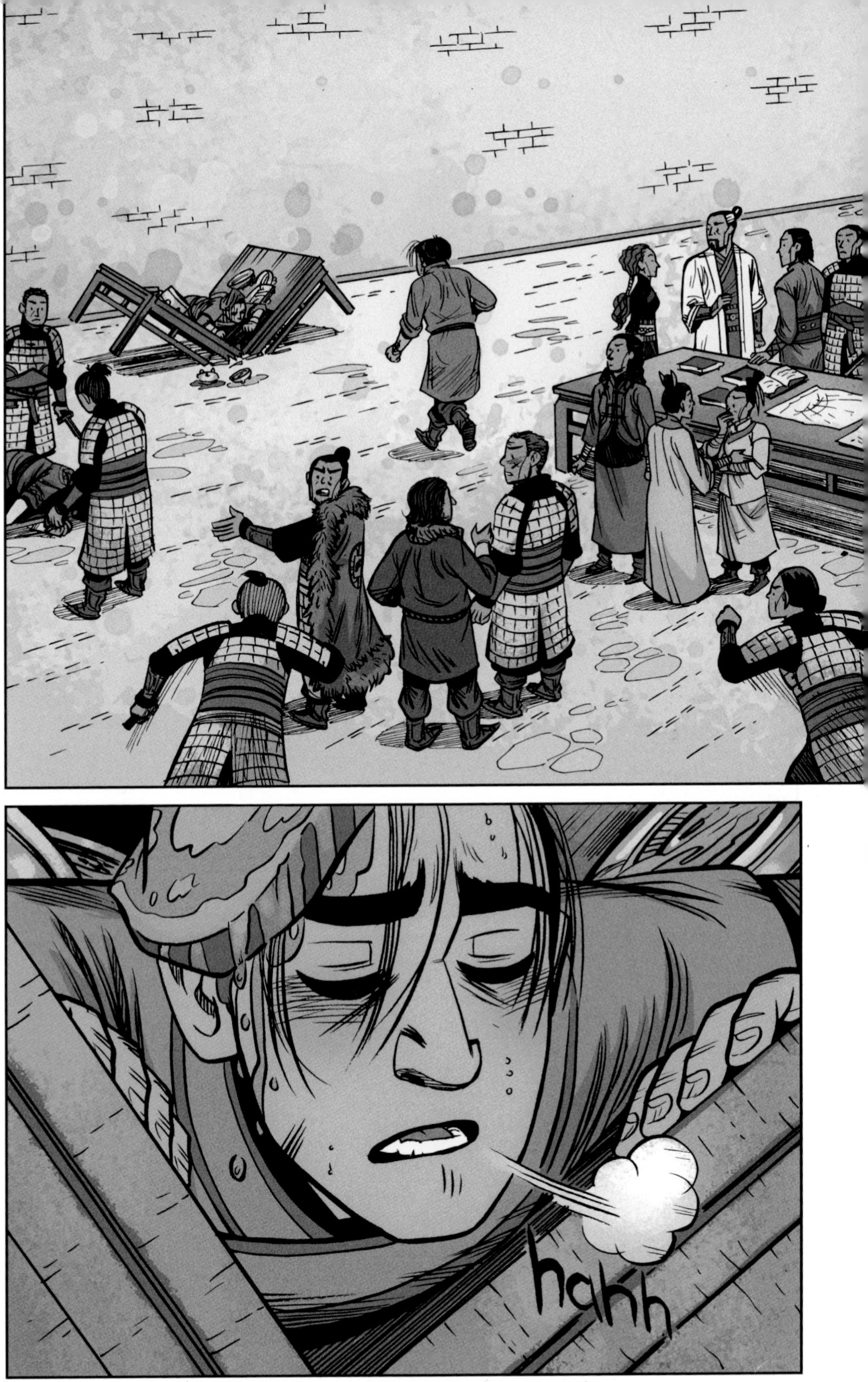
hahh

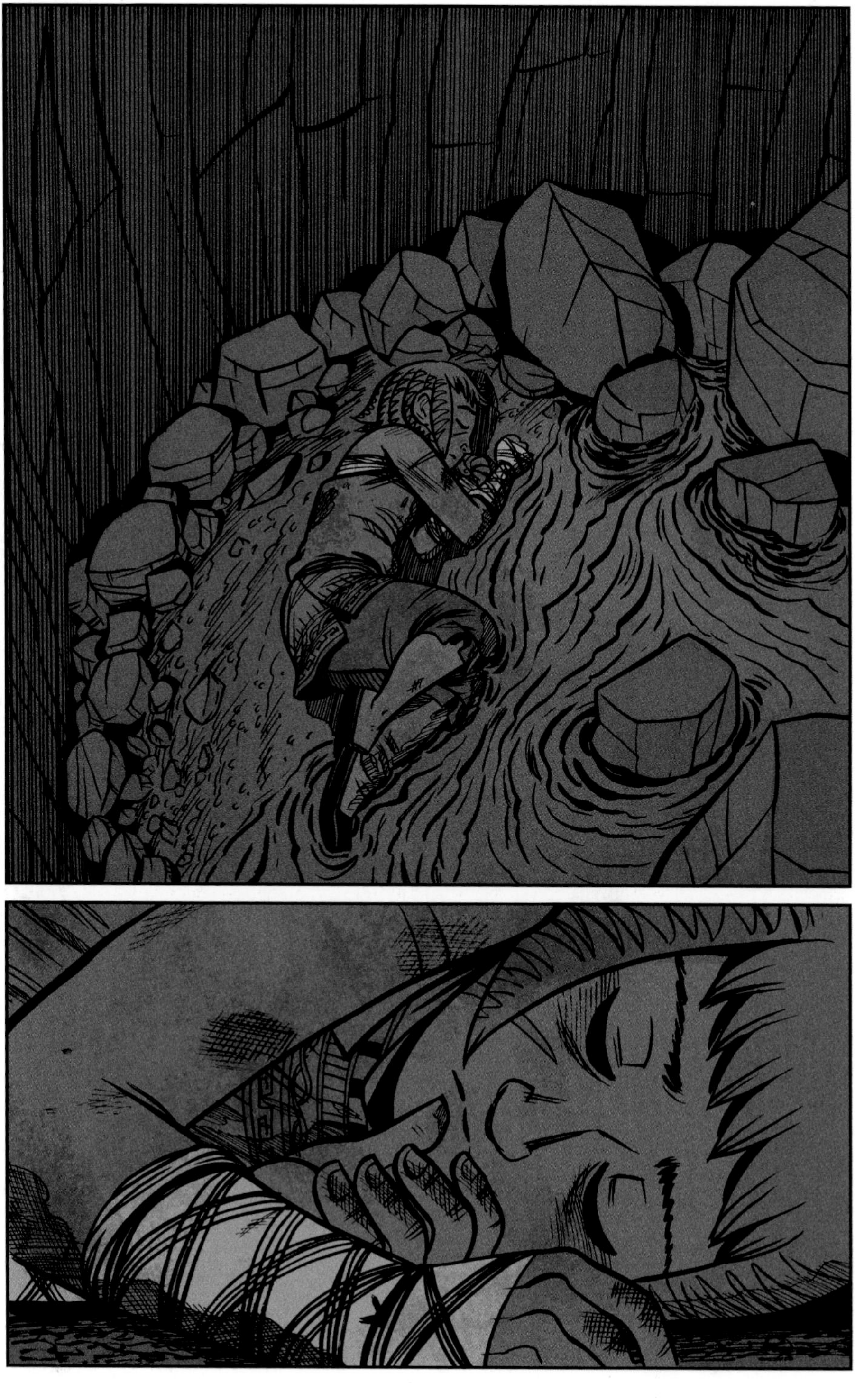

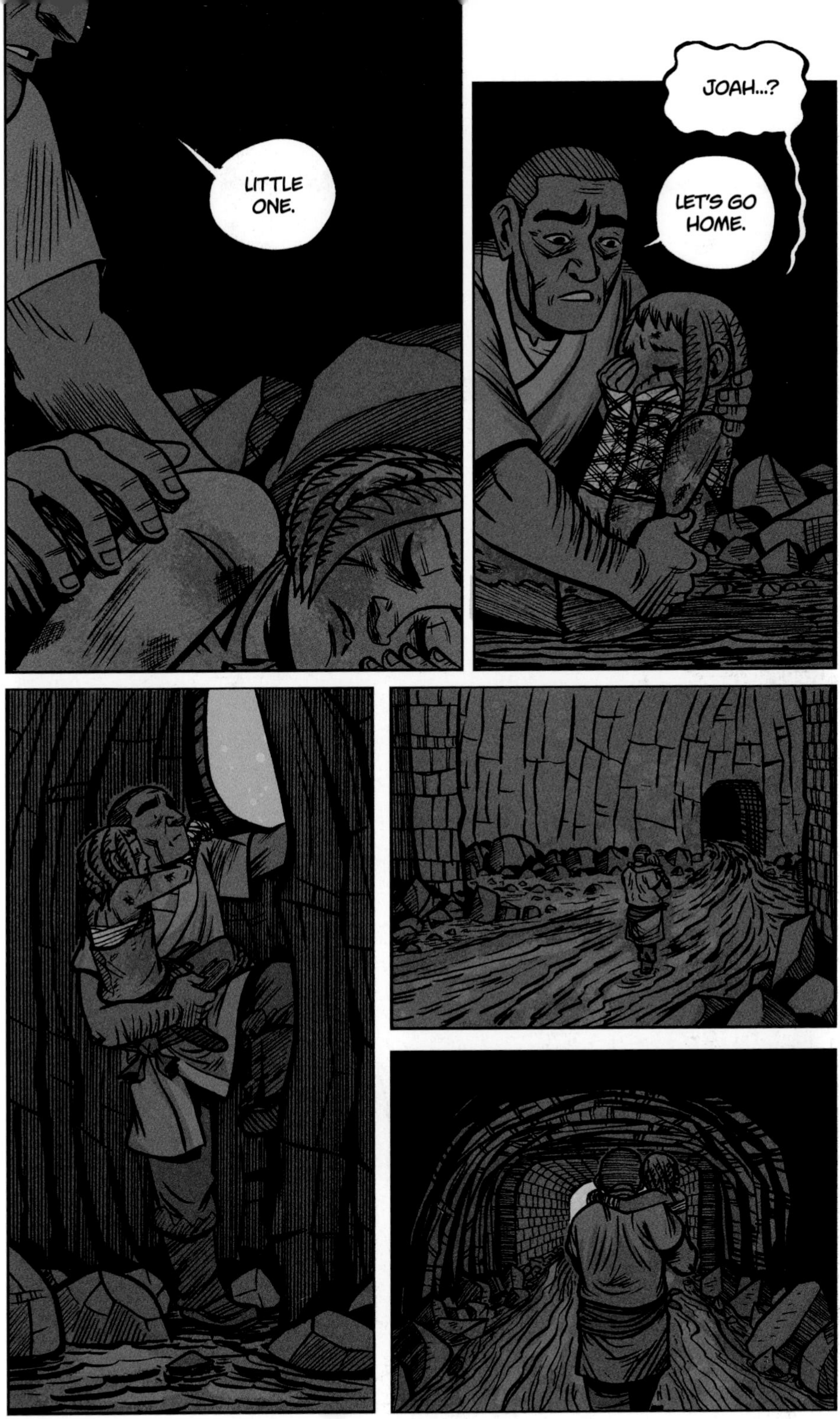
LITTLE ONE.
JOAH...?
LET'S GO HOME.

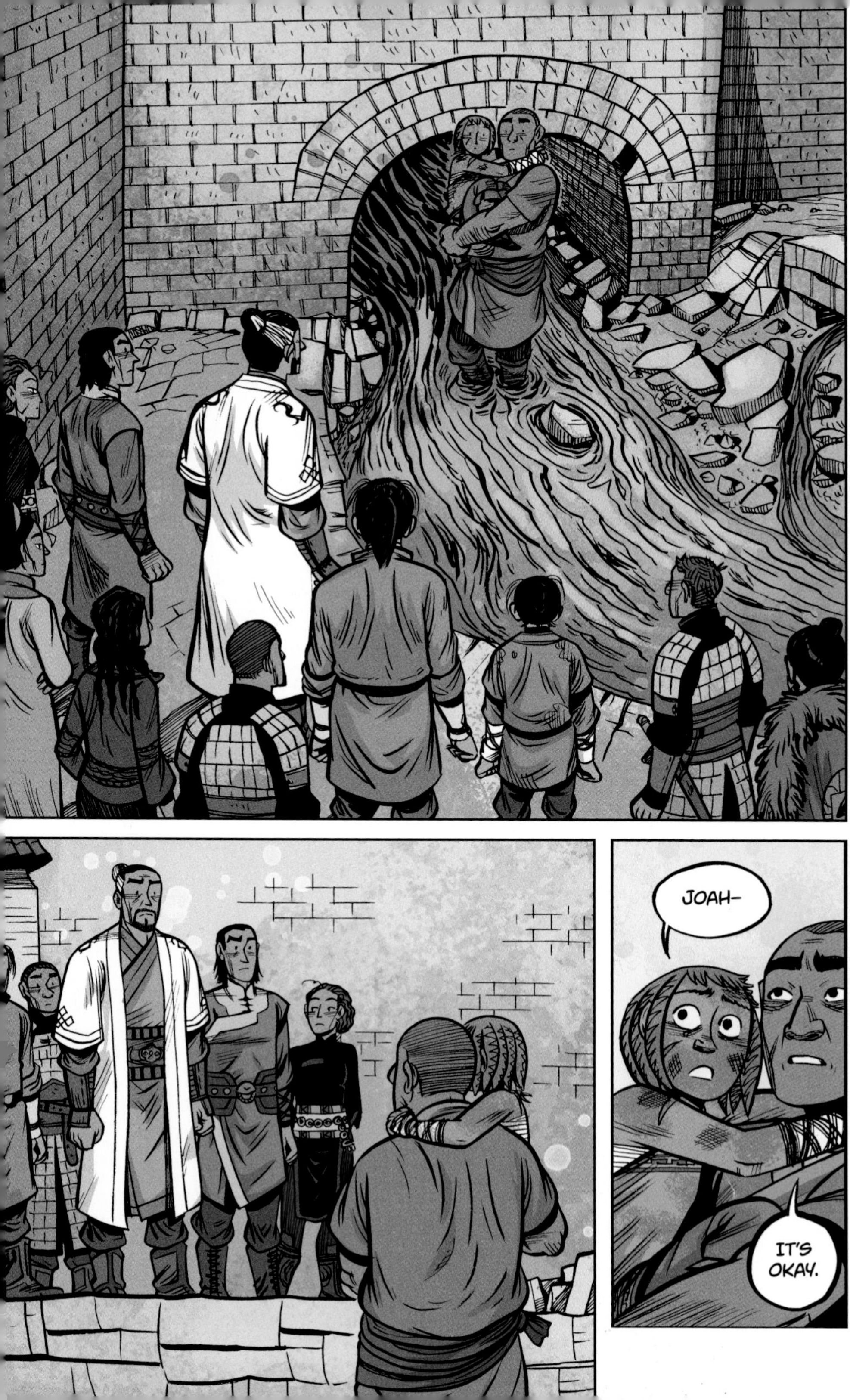
JOAH-
IT'S OKAY.

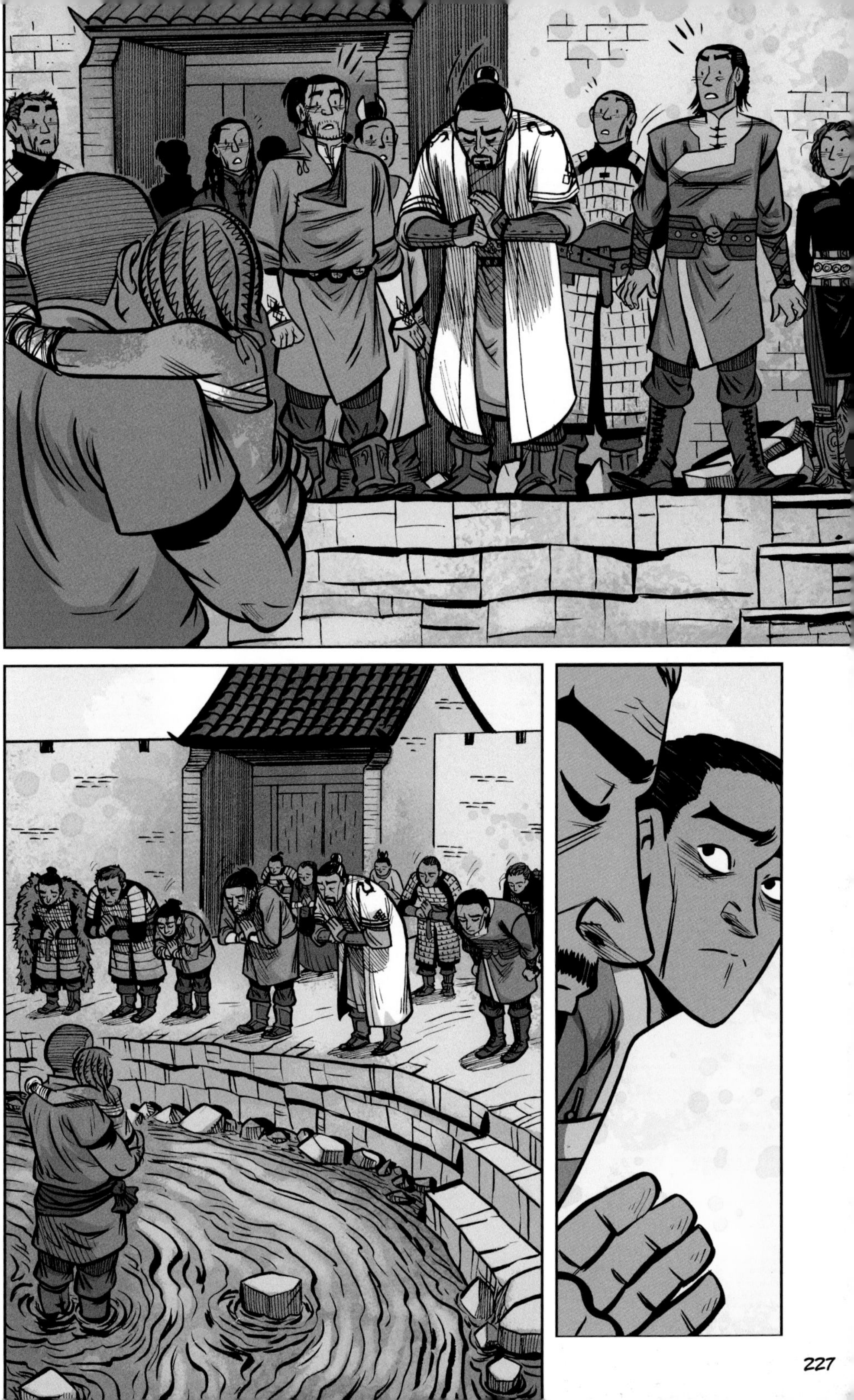

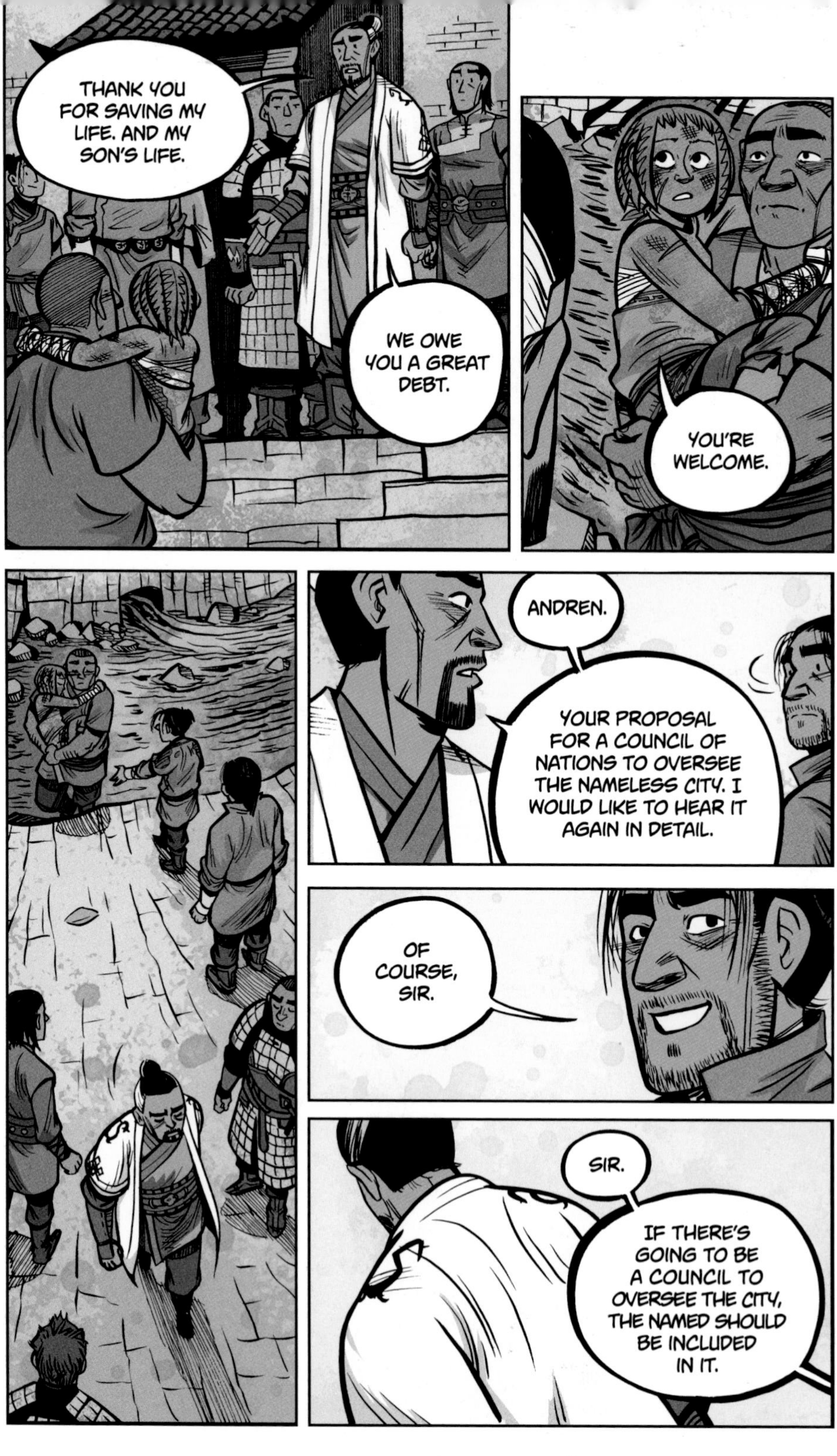
THANK YOU FOR SAVING MY LIFE. AND MY SON'S LIFE.
WE OWE YOU A GREAT DEBT.
YOU'RE WELCOME.
ANDREN.
YOUR PROPOSAL FOR A COUNCIL OF NATIONS TO OVERSEE THE NAMELESS CITY. I WOULD LIKE TO HEAR IT AGAIN IN DETAIL.
OF COURSE, SIR.
SIR.
IF THERE'S GOING TO BE A COUNCIL TO OVERSEE THE CITY, THE NAMED SHOULD BE INCLUDED IN IT.

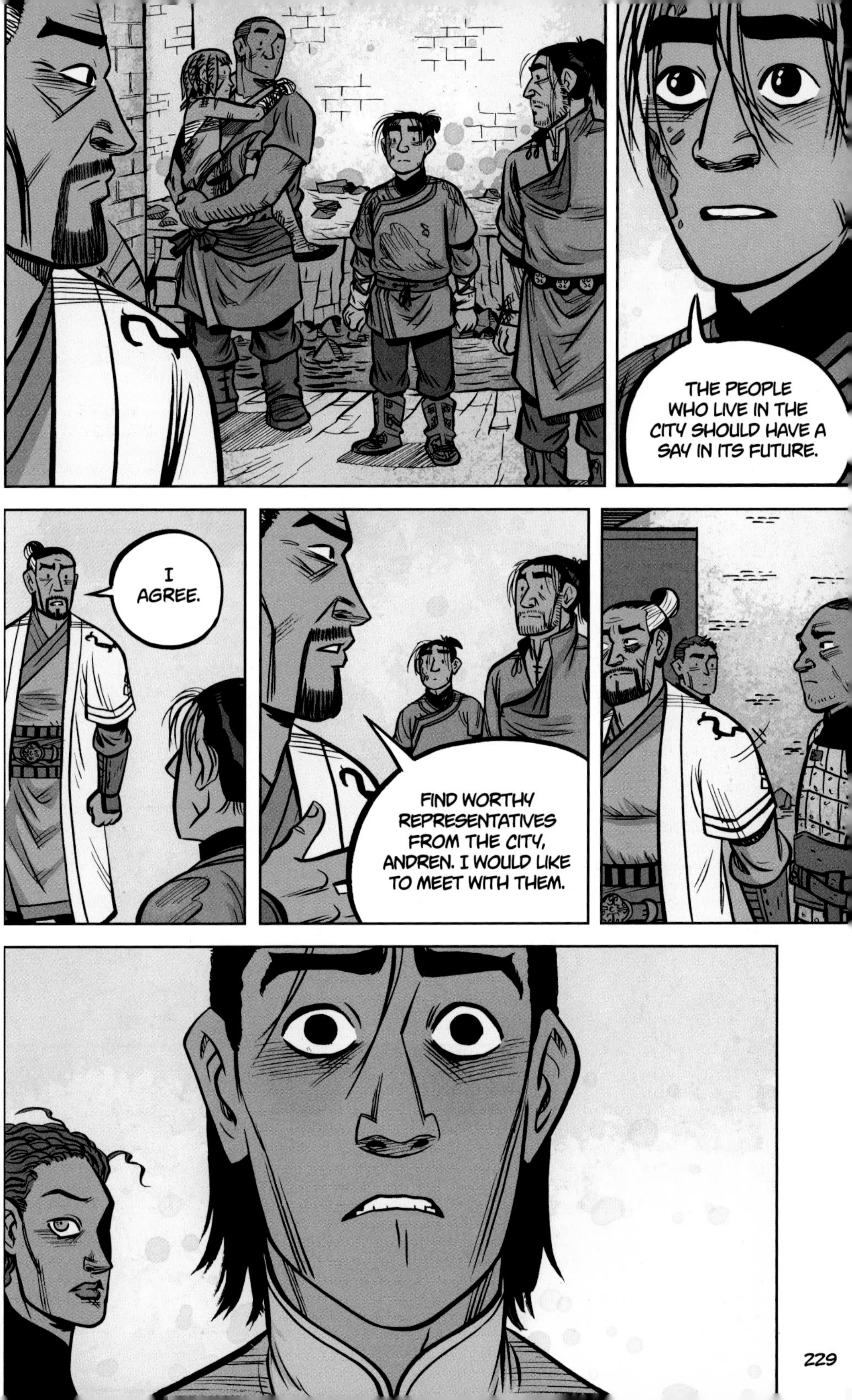
THE PEOPLE WHO LIVE IN THE CITY SHOULD HAVE A SAY IN ITS FUTURE.
I AGREE.
FIND WORTHY REPRESENTATIVES FROM THE CITY, ANDREN. I WOULD LIKE TO MEET WITH THEM.

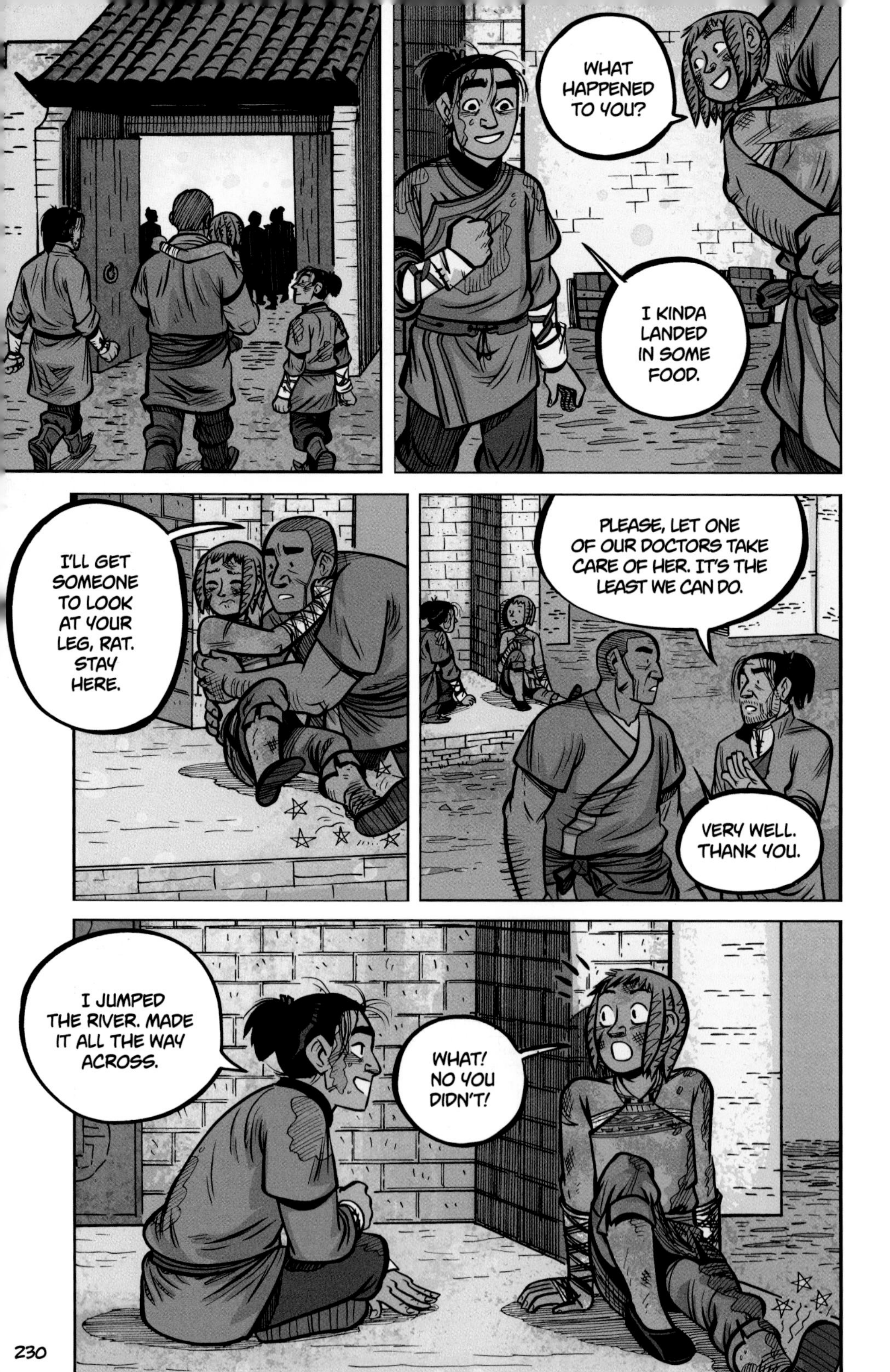
WHAT HAPPENED TO YOU?
I KINDA LANDED IN SOME FOOD.
I'LL GET SOMEONE TO LOOK AT YOUR LEG, RAT. STAY HERE.
PLEASE, LET ONE OF OUR DOCTORS TAKE CARE OF HER. IT'S THE LEAST WE CAN DO.
VERY WELL. THANK YOU.
I JUMPED THE RIVER. MADE IT ALL THE WAY ACROSS.
WHAT! NO YOU DIDN'T!

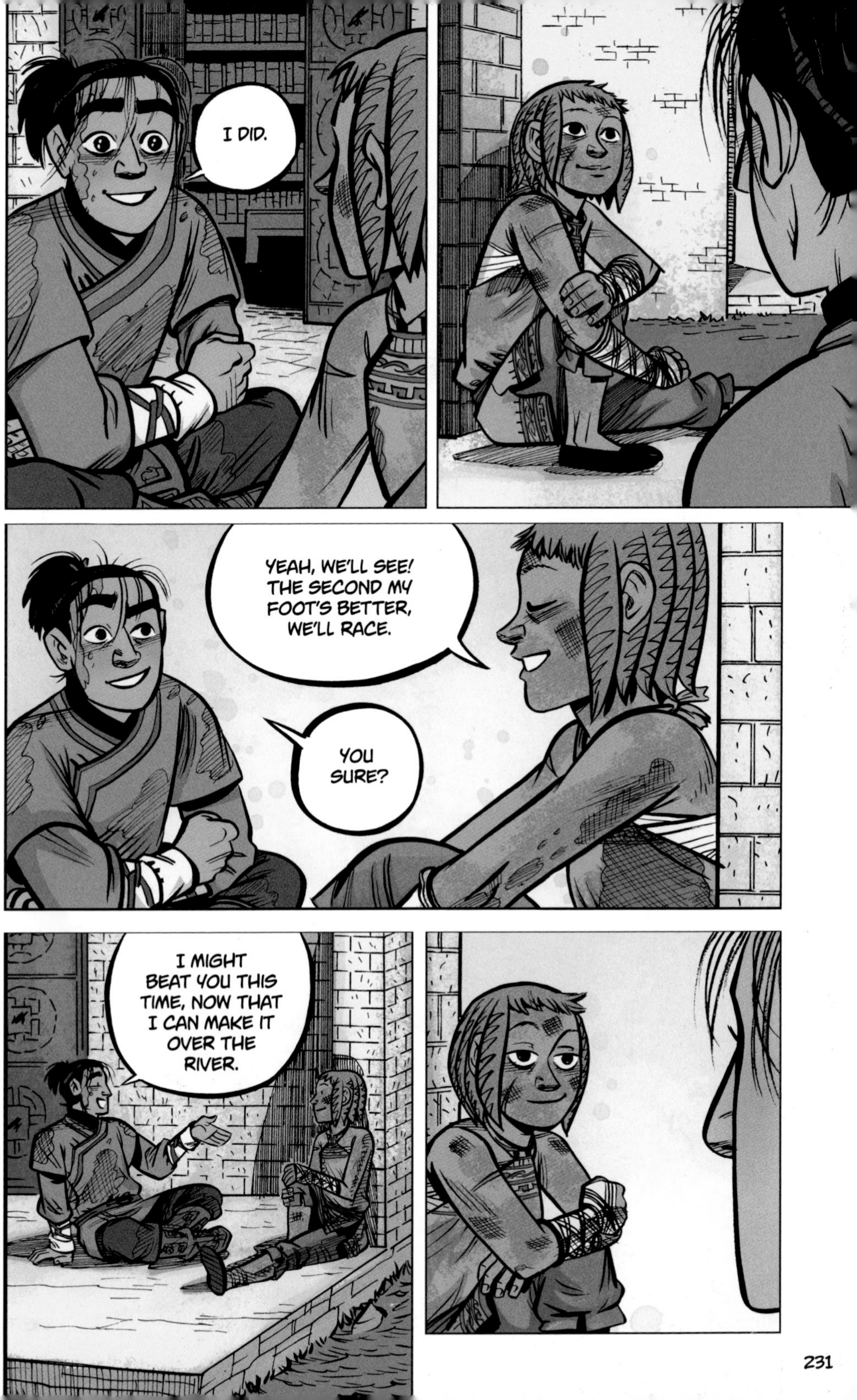
I DID.
YEAH, WE'LL SEE! THE SECOND MY FOOT'S BETTER, WE'LL RACE.
YOU SURE?
I MIGHT BEAT YOU THIS TIME, NOW THAT I CAN MAKE IT OVER THE RIVER.

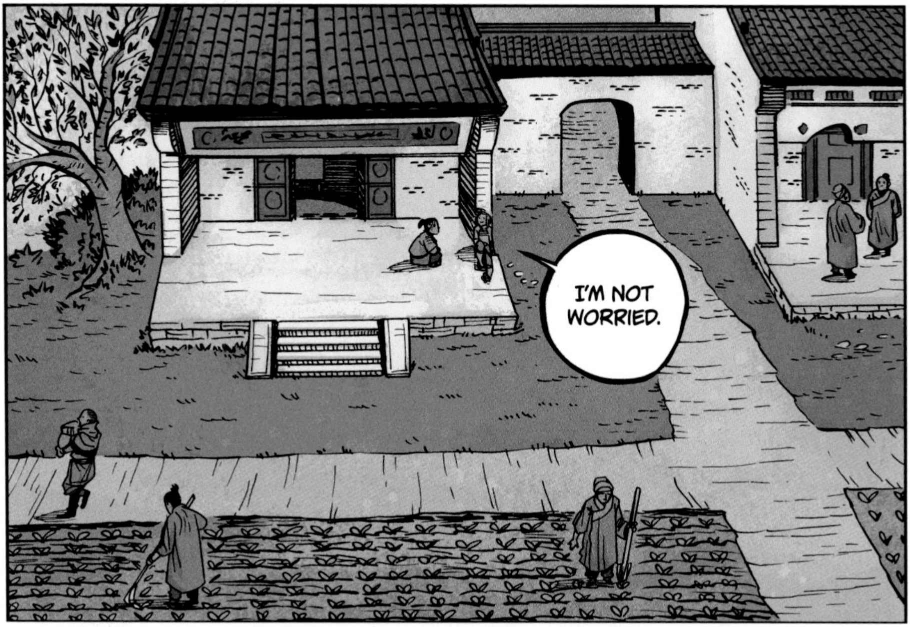
I'M NOT
WORRIED.

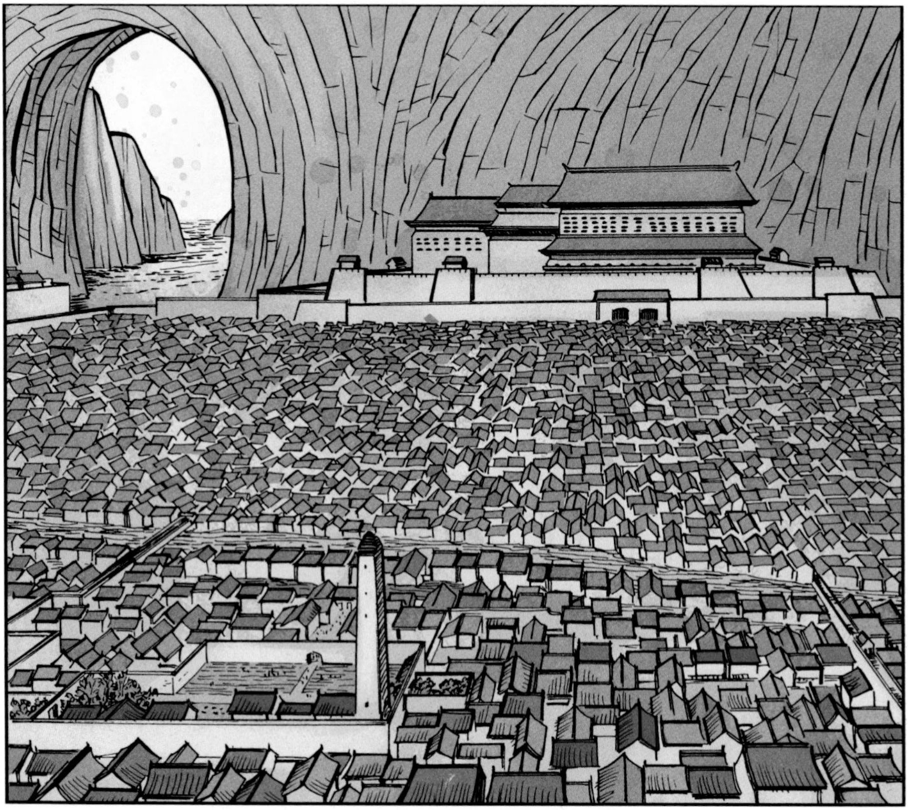

TO BE CONTINUED IN

THE STONE HEART

BOOK 2 OF THE NAMELESS CITY SERIES

CONCEPT ART

I've been working on *The Nameless City* for a long time, and the characters have changed a lot. I hope you enjoy seeing their evolution.
-FAITH ERIN HICKS

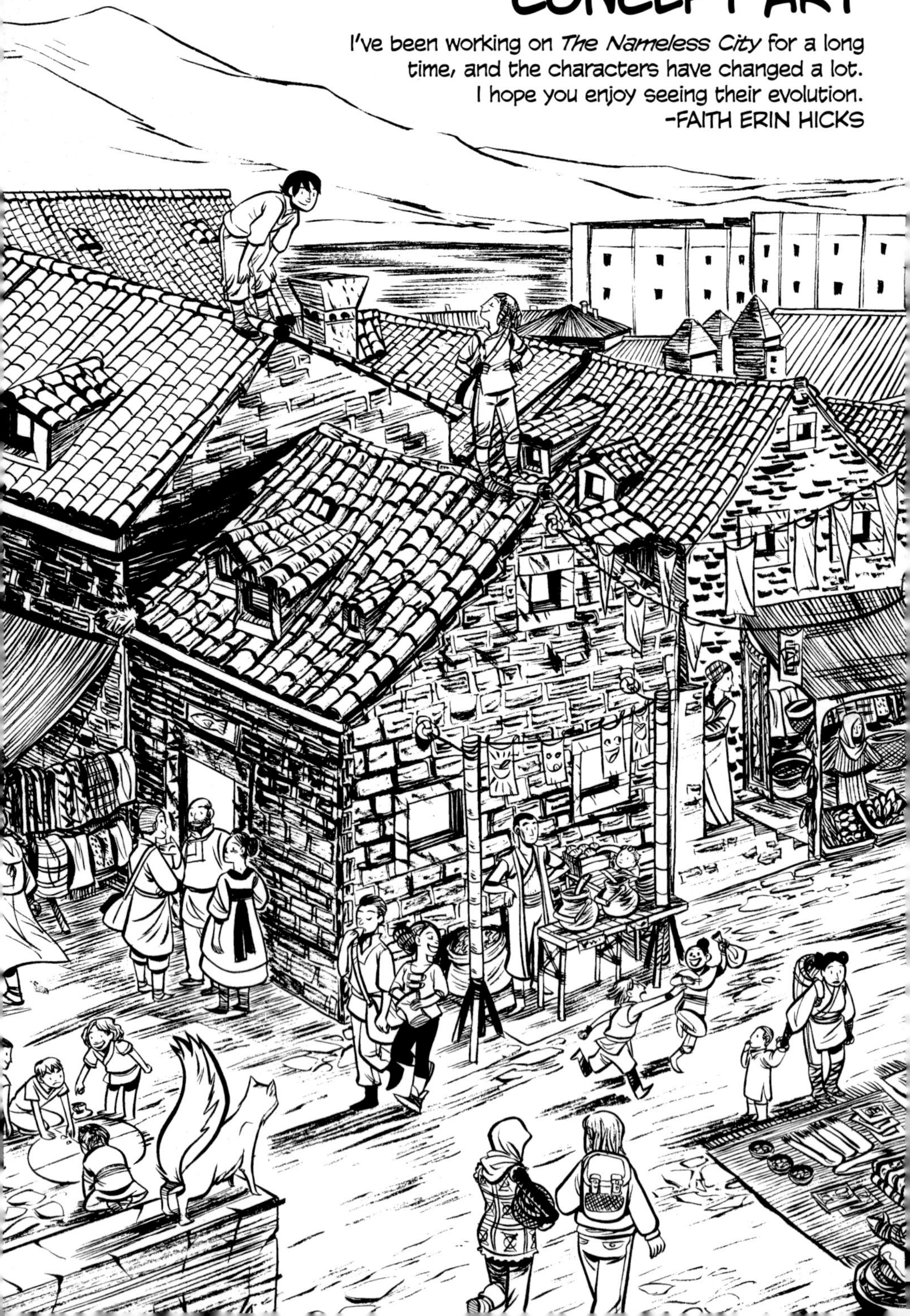

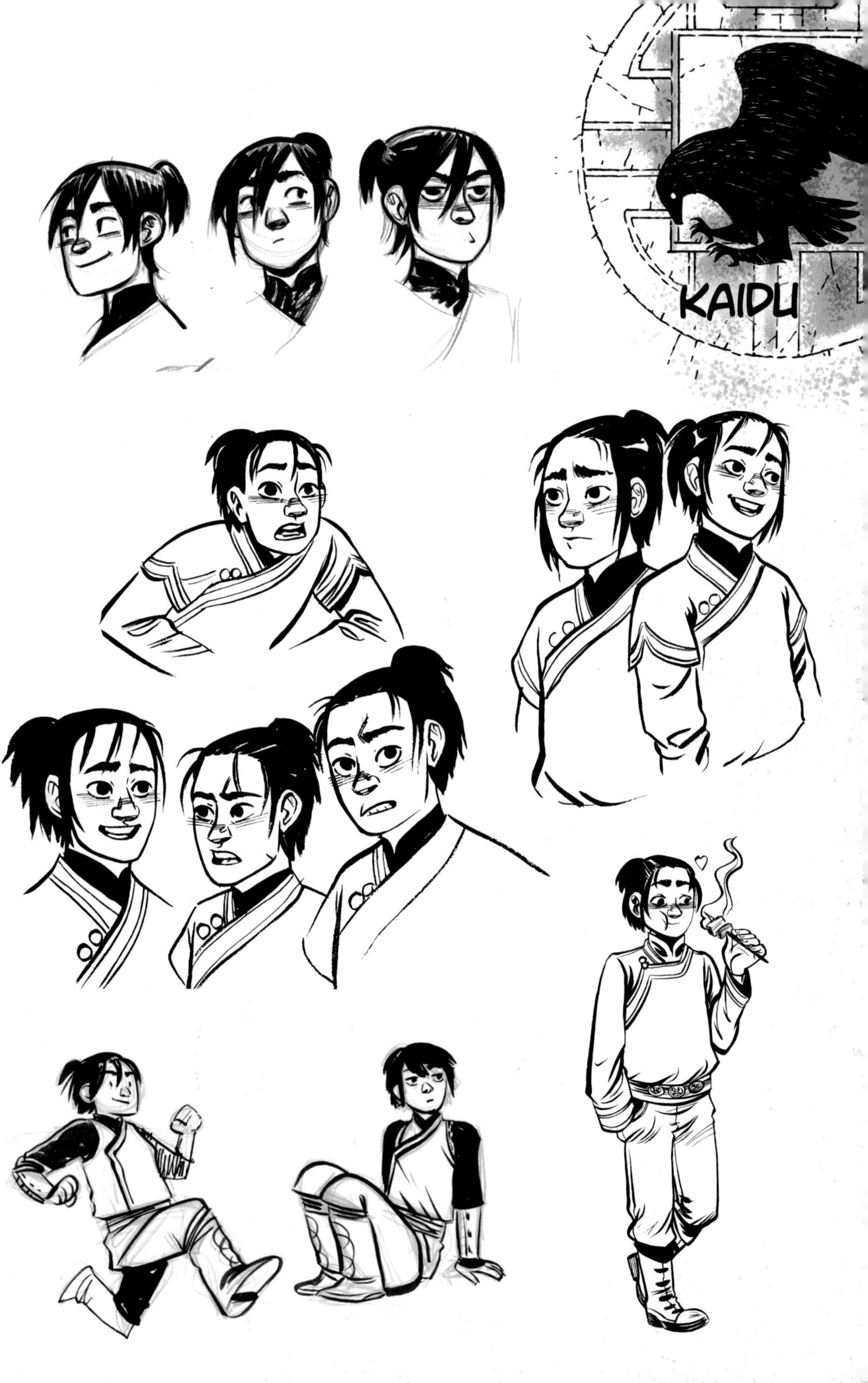
KAIDU

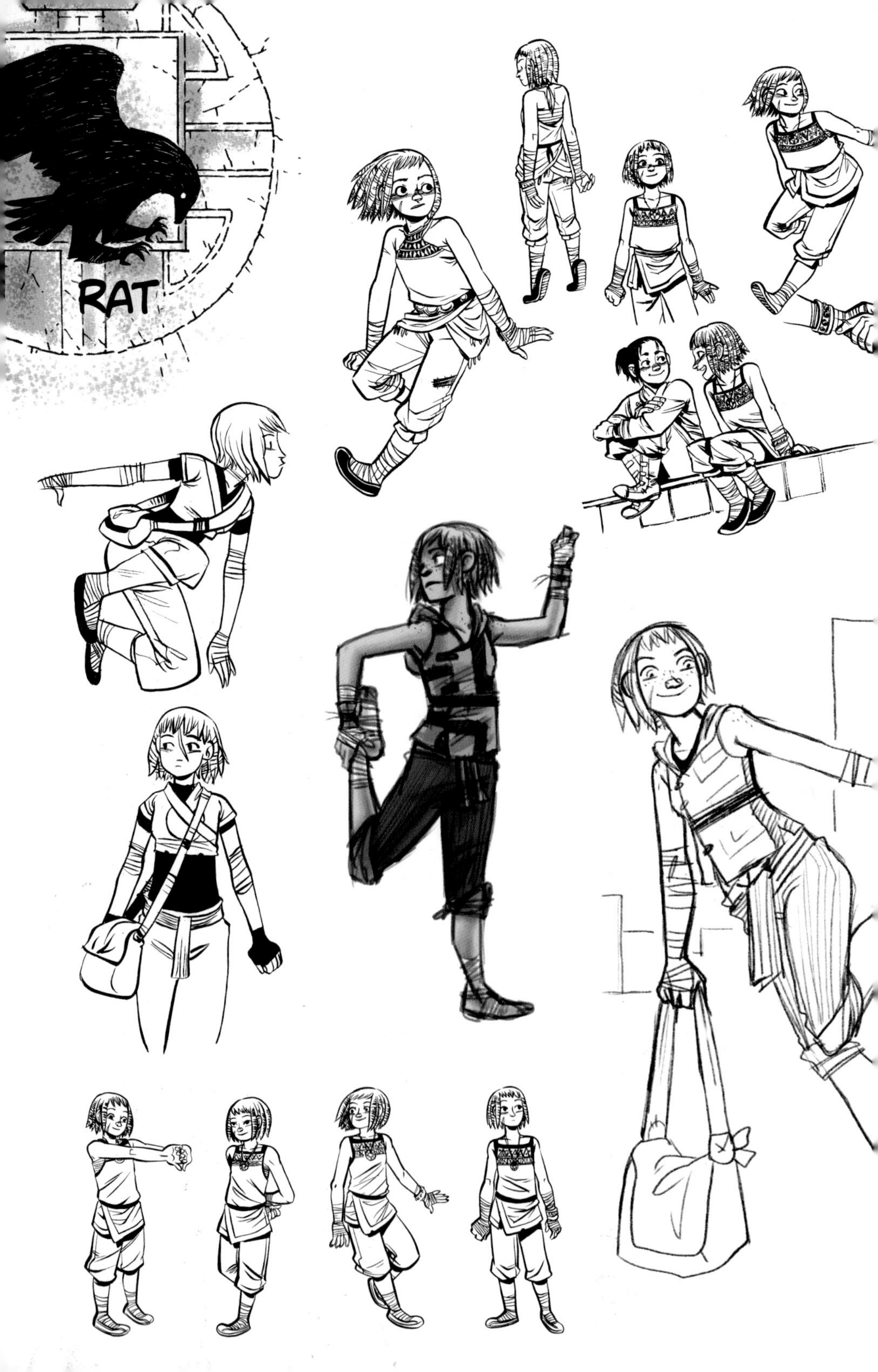
RAT

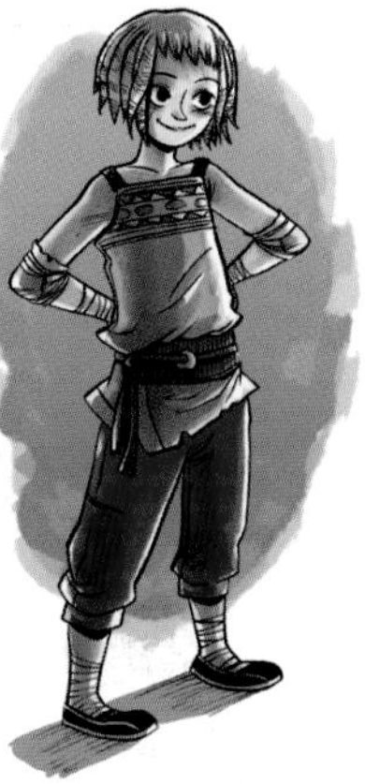

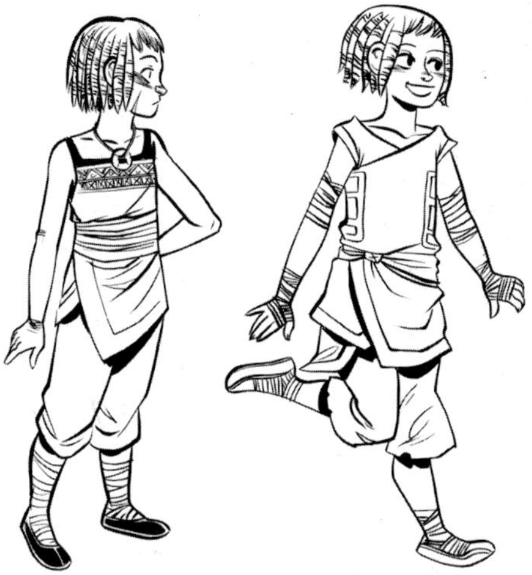

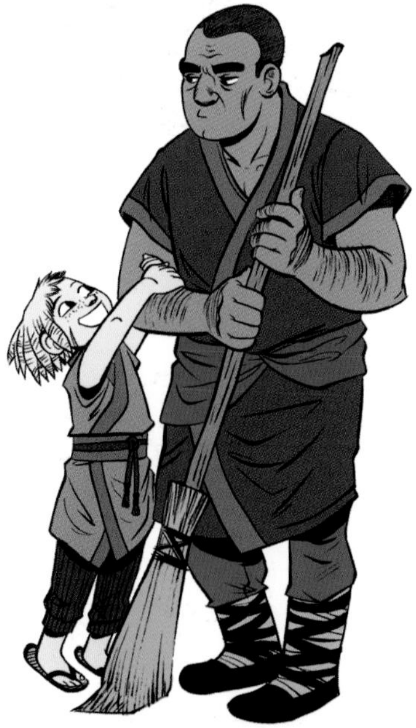

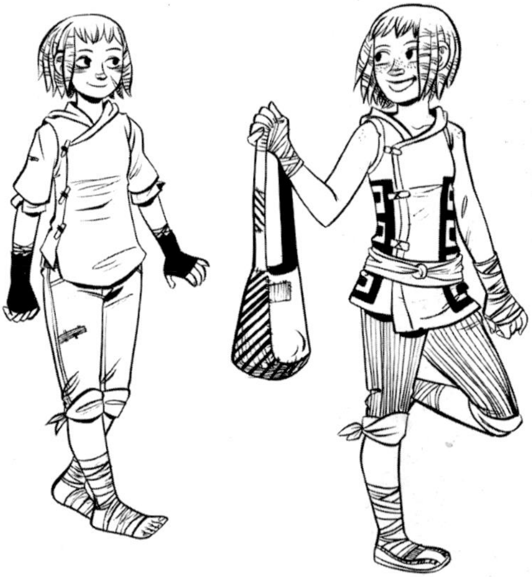

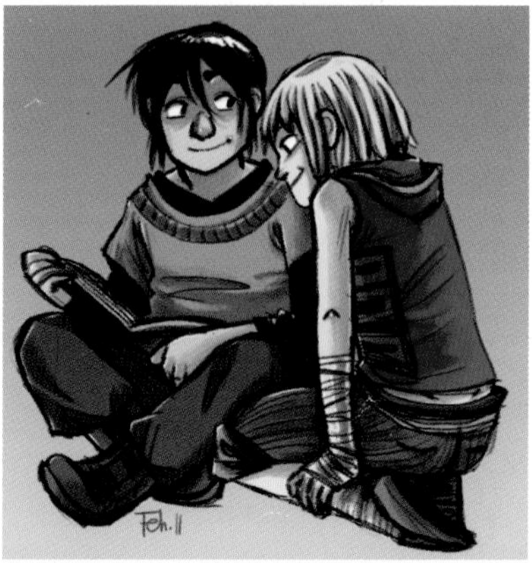

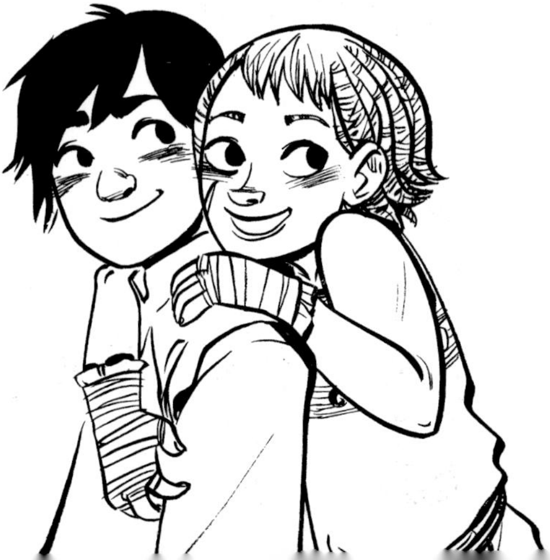

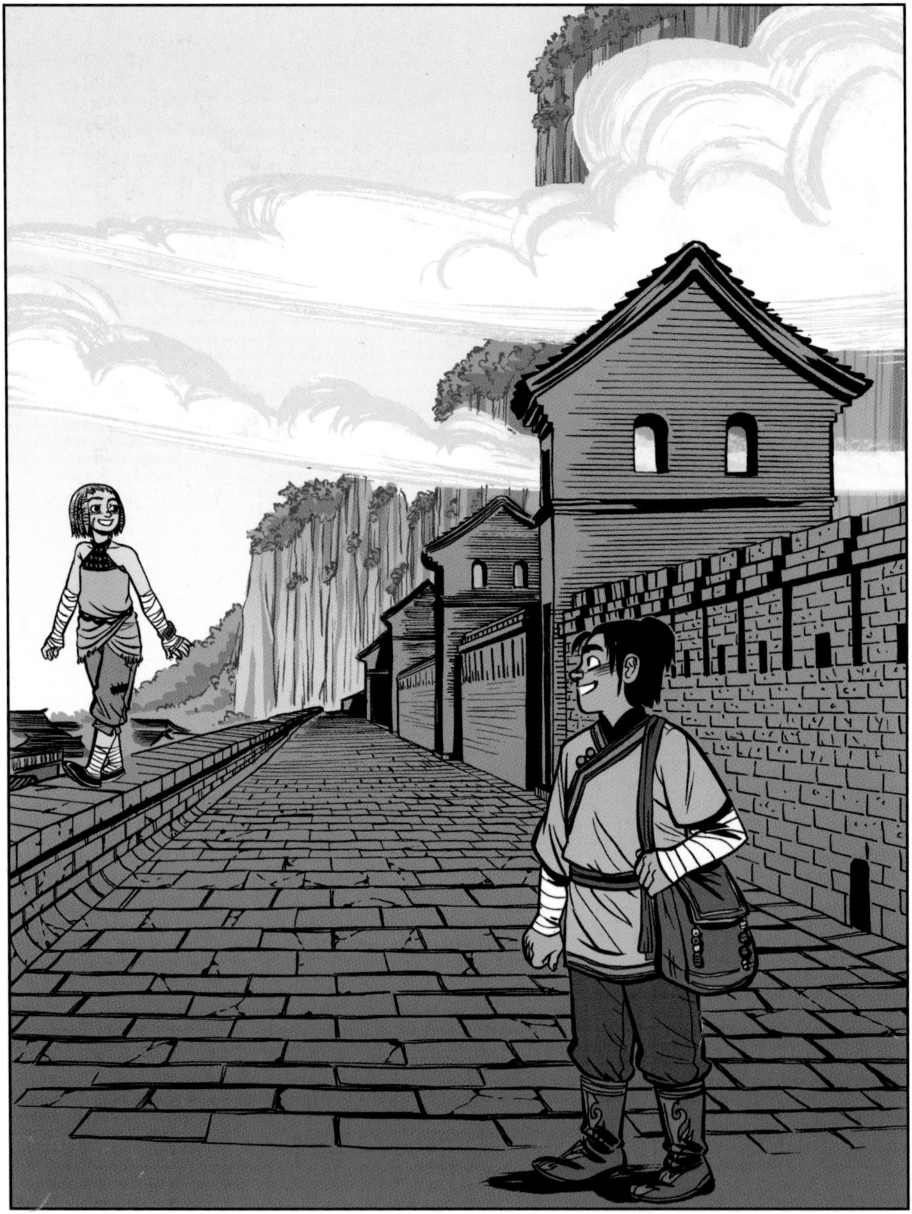

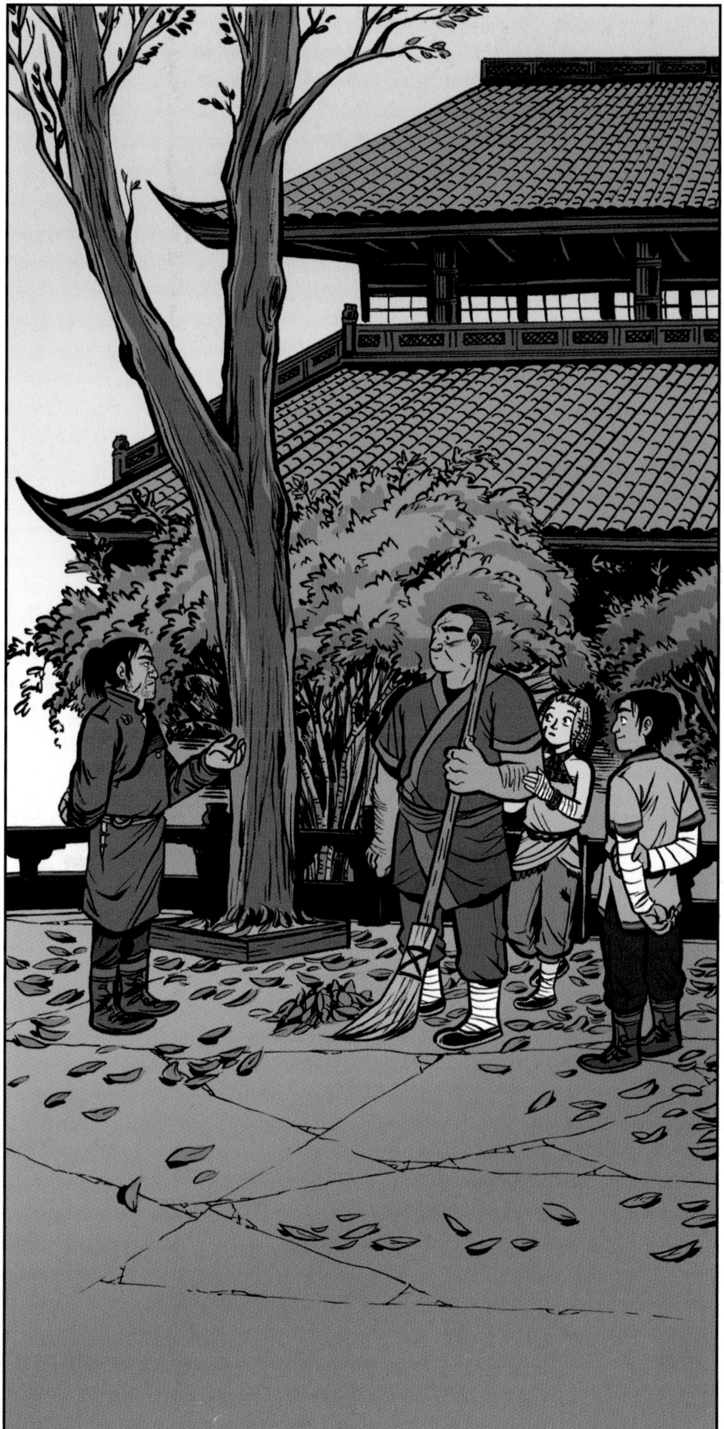

Canada Council Conseil des arts
for the Arts du Canada

Faith Erin Hicks acknowledges the support of the Canada Council for the Arts, which
last year invested $153 million to bring the arts to Canadians throughout the country.

Faith Erin Hicks remercions le Conseil des arts du Canada de son soutien. L'an
dernier, le Conseil a investi 153 millions de dollars pour mettre de l'art dans la vie des
Canadiennes et des Canadiens de tout le pays.

First Second

Published by First Second
First Second is an imprint of Roaring Brook Press, a division of
Holtzbrinck Publishing Holdings Limited Partnership
175 Fifth Avenue, New York, New York 10010
All rights reserved ·

Library of Congress Control Number: 2015020651

Hardcover ISBN: 978-1-62672-157-9
Paperback ISBN: 978-1-62672-156-2

First Second books may be purchased for business or promotional use. For information
on bulk purchases please contact Macmillan Corporate and Premium Sales Department at
(800) 221-7945 x5442 or by email at specialmarkets@macmillan.com.

FIRST
EDITION

First edition 2016

Interior art colored by Jordie Bellaire
Cover art colored by Hilary Sycamore
Book design by Danielle Ceccolini
Printed in the United States of America by Worzalla, Stevens Point, Wisconsin

Hardcover: 10 9 8 7 6 5 4 3 2
Paperback: 10 9 8 7 6 5 4 3

BY ART
WE LIVE